P9-CQC-272
REMINGTON
1894

Look for These Exciting Series from

WILLIAM W. JOHNSTONE

with J. A. Johnstone

The Mountain Man

Preacher: The First Mountain Man

Matt Jensen, the Last Mountain Man

Luke Jensen, Bounty Hunter

Those Jensen Boys!

The Family Jensen

MacCallister

Flintlock

The Brothers O'Brien

The Kerrigans: A Texas Dynasty

Sixkiller, U.S. Marshal

Hell's Half Acre

Texas John Slaughter

Will Tanner, U.S. Deputy Marshal

Eagles

The Frontiersman

AVAILABLE FROM PINNACLE BOOKS

REMINGTON 1894

WILLIAM W. JOHNSTONE
with J.A. Johnstone

PINNACLE BOOKS
Kensington Publishing Corp.
www.kensingtonbooks.com

PINNACLE BOOKS are published by

Kensington Publishing Corp.
119 West 40th Street
New York, NY 10018

PUBLISHER'S NOTE
Following the death of William W. Johnstone, the Johnstone family is working with a carefully selected writer to organize and complete Mr. Johnstone's outlines and many unfinished manuscripts to create additional novels in all of his series like The Last Gunfighter, Mountain Man, and Eagles, among others. This novel was inspired by Mr. Johnstone's superb storytelling.

ISBN-13: 978-0-7860-4040-7
ISBN-10: 0-7860-4040-8

First Kensington hardcover printing: June 2017
First Pinnacle mass market printing: November 2017

10 9 8 7 6 5 4 3 2 1

Printed in the United States of America

First electronic edition: November 2017

ISBN-13: 978-0-7860-4075-9
ISBN-10: 0-7860-4075-0

Chapter 1

"*Hola* . . . hombre?"

Jerking awake, John McMasters opened his eyes and inwardly cursed himself for falling asleep. He wet his cracked lips, and glanced at his right thigh. Blood-soaked . . . even though he'd tied his bandanna over the wound, secured the frayed piece of cotton to the barrel of his Colt .45-caliber Peacemaker and twisted the long barrel to tighten his makeshift tourniquet. How long had he been asleep? He wasn't certain. Sweat stung his eyes and he blinked before he turned the revolver with his left hand, loosening the bandanna, letting blood flow a little more freely.

He remembered that from what the sawbones had told him more than thirty years earlier.

"Blood has to flow, else it destroys the tissue, leads to moist gangrene." The doctor took a long pull from a bottle, shook his head, and laughed. "Problem is, you slow the blood too much, and that can lead to dry gangrene. Your sergeant,

well, he don't have to worry about moist or dry. Hold 'em down, boy, as I saw off his leg."

The Mexican's voice made the image of that Union doctor vanish. "Hombre? Are you alive?"

McMasters almost laughed. Had the Mexican kept quiet, he likely could have climbed right up the ridge, planted a revolver barrel against McMasters's temple, and blown his head off.

"Yeah." His own voice was barely audible. He coughed, wiped away more sweat, tried to swallow, and attempted to speak again. "Still here."

"Bueno," the Mexican said. *"Buenos tardes.* We . . . ah . . . *Negociar.* Parley. Me and you. I speak for Butcher."

The name made McMasters stiffen. He fought down the bile. *Moses Butcher.* Shaking his head to clear his thoughts, McMasters looked down at his leg again and next tried to find the sun, but had no luck. The air turned cooler in those tree-studded hills near Bisbee, not far from the Mexican border. He looked at the blood pouring out of the hole in his woolen trousers, grimaced, and twisted the barrel of the Colt until the blood stopped flowing and his leg resumed an intense throbbing.

Straightening, he gathered his shotgun and found the bandit—more of a blur than an actual target. McMasters had lost his eyeglasses scrambling up the hill.

"Hombre?" the Mexican called once more.

What was the bandit's name? Again, John McMasters shook his head. He studied the rugged terrain, the only way out of the canyon that McMasters now guarded.

The sweat hampered his view . . . which did not help his lousy eyesight to begin with.

"You are alone, hombre," the Mexican said, "and have fought a good fight. But now . . . we think it is best that you quit. Señor, you are foolish to have come here alone. You should have brought a posse with you."

"Yeah," McMasters said with a bitter laugh, though too softly for the bandit to hear him. "I had a posse. A posse straight out of hell." He had hired them to help him track down Moses Butcher and his killers, then, at the last moment, had turned them loose. Sent them away. Well, it wasn't like he could have stopped them anyway. Besides, he wanted to kill Moses Butcher himself. Not with the Colt, though. The .45 had a more important job—keeping McMasters from bleeding to death. And the .45 was empty.

"Hombre?"

McMasters found the strength from somewhere and managed to push himself up against the boulder he leaned against. He had to catch his breath. Blinking away more sweat, he turned his head. His left hand held the handle of the empty revolver. His right hand moved the other weapon, bracing it against the twisted branch of a dead juniper. The shotgun weighed just less than eight pounds. It felt like eight hundred.

"Yeah." He remembered the name of the bandit, or at least, the name on the wanted dodgers. "What do you want, Greaser?" *Greaser. Greaser Gomez.* John McMasters had never cared much for that derogatory name many Arizona whites called Mexicans. *Greasers. Bean-eaters.* Hell, the Mexicans had been in this country long before the white men. So had the Apaches, but most of those were long gone. *Greasers.* The term reviled a Wisconsin-born Yankee like him. But *Greaser Gomez* sickened McMasters even more. Especially now that he saw the outlaw had tied a scarf around the barrel of his Winchester repeater. He could not see the killer so distinctly, but the scarf . . . that came to him clearer than his memories or his dreams. Gomez kept waving that barrel back and forth, the whiteness of the silk showing brilliantly in the sun shining from a clearing. It illuminated the killer. Mostly, it turned the silk scarf into a beacon.

John McMasters could not take his eyes off the waving cloth.

"Listen, hombre, you are tough to kill."

"I'm alive," McMasters whispered, more to himself.

"That is what Butcher says," the bandit went on. "You are tough, hombre. And I agree." The carbine stopped waving, and Gomez's right hand moved away from the holstered revolver on his hip, reached over the big sugarloaf sombrero, and began pointing. "This is what we call"—he grinned—"a Mexican standoff." He laughed at his joke . . . or what he thought was a joke. "You cannot go anywhere. We cannot go anywhere." The hand returned to its perch on the pearl handle of the revolver. "There is no point."

"Isn't there?" McMasters called out. He strained, trying to guess how far away Gomez stood, while silently cursing his vision. *Forty yards? Fifty? Maybe as far away as sixty.* He looked at the shotgun, the barrels still perched on the dead branch, the stock braced against Gomez's right shoulder. Fifty, McMasters finally guessed. A long way for a shotgun, and pushing the accuracy of a revolver, although everyone said Greaser Gomez rarely missed. The outlaw also held that Winchester repeater in his left hand.

"We don't even know who you are . . . or why you chase us."

"Don't you?" McMasters wet his lips and looked beyond Gomez.

The Mexican stepped closer.

Was that a trick? McMasters listened with intent for anything out of the ordinary—the clattering of a stone, the snapping of a branch. Nothing. No animals, not even birds, not even flies made a noise, and the wind no longer blew. The silk scarf hung limp along the barrel of Gomez's carbine.

"No, hombre. You tell us. You want money? *Dinero?* We might be able to work out a deal. Butcher, he has some gold, some greenbacks."

"No deal."

The Mexican shook his head. "But why? For what reason do you chase us? *Digame.* You have trailed us a long time. But even those men who were with you earlier, back in the Superstitions and at that boom town, they realized that there was no point. They left you, hombre." Beneath that ugly beard, Gomez grinned again, a vile, evil, despicable smile that did not require the eyesight of a twenty-year-old to detect. "They left you . . . alone."

"Like you said, you have nowhere to go . . . as long as I'm here."

"You won't be here long, hombre." The humor had left Gomez's voice, and his grips tightened on both the revolver and the Winchester. "We are many. You are one."

"You aren't as many as you were earlier."

Again, Gomez shook his head. "This parley . . . it works on my throat. I have a flask in my back pocket." The right hand left the revolver, and a finger pointed behind him. "Is it all right with you, hombre, if I wet my windpipe?"

Trying to get at me, McMasters thought. *Drink some tequila, or mescal, or whiskey, or even water. Water would be better. Remind me of how they have water, and my canteen is on the saddle of a dead horse out there . . . in the open . . . unreachable without catching lead.*

"*Salud,*" he said.

Laughing, Gomez found the flask, twisted off the cap, and brought the engraved pewter container to his lips. His Adam's apple bobbed, and the laughter returned to the killer's dark eyes.

McMasters glanced at his thigh, loosened the barrel of the Colt, let the blood flow a little more, and then tightened the bandanna again when he heard Gomez sighing with pleasure.

The flask returned to the rear pocket of the killer's denim britches. The right hand found its rest on the butt of the holstered revolver, and he stepped still closer. Closer to being able to kill John McMasters.

Yet also closer to McMasters and his shotgun.

"It is many hours before sunset, amigo," the outlaw said.

So we're friends now, McMasters thought.

"I would like to take my siesta, but I would rather take it with a *puta*"—he grinned once more—"in Bisbee."

"Bisbee?" McMasters said with skepticism.

The Mexican laughed. "Well, no, not Bisbee. There is law in Bisbee. You *norteamericanos* frown upon men of *mi honestidad.* But south of Bisbee. In the country where my father and mother were born. In the country where I was born. My homeland."

McMasters did not reply. He kept listening, but did not want to take his eyes off Greaser Gomez. Do that, make that one mistake, and the killer would try to kill him.

The shotgun, despite braced against the tree and partially by the boulder, felt even heavier. McMasters's leg pounded, and he wished he had not let Gomez drink from that flask, for his throat felt raw, drier than it had. His stomach began to rebel, a bullet was lodged in his thigh, and he had lost a lot of blood. He had no water. No food. Nothing but an empty .45 revolver and a double-barrel shotgun. And resolve.

And . . .

The Winchester began swaying again, making the silk scarf wave.

And . . . memories. McMaster's heart ached. He bit his bottom lip to keep it from quavering.

"There is something you should know, hombre," Greaser Gomez said.

"Yeah." Speaking that one syllable hurt.

"I told you that it was time for my siesta. That is an important thing in my country, with my people. But"—the Winchester stopped waving, and his right hand lifted to point in McMaster's direction—"I . . . Moses Butcher . . . the others . . . well, we can take a little siesta. We can sleep all day. All night. But you, amigo, you must stay awake."

I was sleeping just before you started talking, you damned idiot. McMasters knew Gomez spoke the truth and did not need to explain his veiled threat.

John McMasters was alone, wounded, weak . . . and growing weaker with every passing second.

He counted what he knew of Butcher's men. He had more than just Greaser Gomez. Five more. Total of seven, including Butcher and Gomez.

He shook his head. *No. No, only six.* The seventh lay spread-eagled near his bloating horse.

And maybe not even six. McMasters had emptied his Colt as he ran for shelter in the rocks and trees. He had heard a shot before starting the last gunfight, and knew one of Butcher's men had been wounded earlier. So maybe that man was out of commission, even dead, and maybe McMasters had killed some others.

Maybe . . . If . . . He sighed. Even if he had killed or wounded one or two others, there would still be too many. At some point, he would fall asleep again. His leg throbbed even worse than earlier, and he loosened the tourniquet for only a moment.

Another thought numbed him. *Or I'll just bleed to death.*

"So"—Greaser Gomez waved the scarf briefly—"hombre, here is our . . . how do you call it? Moses, he told me. A truce. Sí. *Tregua.* Truce. Sí. We will ride away. I tell Moses. I say, '*Vámonos, que me muero de hambre.*' " Gomez laughed at his joke. "Moses, he tells me to come up and parley with you. So this is how it *will* be." The smile seemed to disappear in Gomez's thick, matted, black beard. "We ride out down this trail. One at a time. If you break our *tregua* . . . our . . . um . . . truce . . . then we kill you. And you will not enjoy your death for it will be a long time before it comes to you, amigo. Savvy?"

A breeze kicked up, and the scarf began waving again without any help from Greaser Gomez. McMasters watched it, remembering, and did not look at the killer. Clearly, he studied that flag of truce.

"When we are gone—all gone and all alive—we leave you in peace. That is our proposal. Do you find the terms acceptable?"

Just as quickly as it had started, the wind died, and the white fabric fell again, wrapping around the Winchester's barrel.

McMasters's cold blue eyes locked on Greaser Gomez. "No," he answered flatly.

With a sigh, Gomez shook his head. "I am sorry, hombre, for I am truly hungry and wanted to leave here, and leave you alive. A man like you, so tough, so full of valor, I will not enjoy killing you. But . . . now one of us, perhaps it will be me, will have to kill you."

"It won't be you," McMasters said.

Gomez's face went taut. "What—?"

McMasters cut him off. "Butcher was smart, not coming up here by himself. He sent you. You weren't smart, Gomez."

Beneath that black beard, the outlaw's darkened face seemed to pale. He stepped back, waving the carbine frantically, pointing to it with his right hand. "Señor . . . hombre . . . amigo . . . do you not recognize this? What this means? *Por Díos*, it is "

"It *was*," McMasters corrected, not letting the killer answer. "It was a Christmas gift. Last December. I gave it to my oldest daughter, Rosalee." He tightened the shotgun's stock against his shoulder. "Before you,

Butcher, and the rest of you black-hearted sons of bitches cut her down . . . and the rest of my family."

The Winchester dropped. So did Gomez's right hand, and he sang out some curse, or perhaps a prayer, in Spanish. As the carbine clanged against the rocks, soiling that white piece of silk, the revolver jerked out of the Mexican's holster. McMasters did not have time to think why Gomez would go for his short gun when a carbine seemed the wiser choice.

McMasters turned his focus on aiming his shotgun. There were no hammers to cock on that model. It would be a chancy shot, especially for a fifty-year-old man who needed spectacles to see far. Greaser Gomez had been more blur than features. It was why John McMasters carried the Remington Model 1894 twelve-gauge shotgun with him.

It was why he had loaded both barrels with buckshot.

Remembering Rosalee, remembering his wife, his sons, his youngest daughter . . . remembering the life he had once enjoyed . . . and seeing clearly—or so it seemed—Greaser Gomez thumbing back the hammer of his pistol, John McMasters squeezed both triggers.

CHAPTER 2

Nine days earlier

The colt looked up, perked its ears, and snorted.

Snorted? John McMasters figured the stubborn bay was laughing at him. Slowly, he swung down from the dun he rode and easily removed the lariat. It was July, but high up on the Mogollon Rim, the air felt cool and dark clouds threatened rain later in the afternoon. In Arizona, they called that time of year "monsoon season," and McMasters wanted to get home with the runaway colt before there came a soaking, hard, cold rain. maybe some hail. He remembered Old Jake Willis. Caught in a monsoon two summers back, he and his horse had been killed by a lightning strike.

"Easy, boy," McMasters said to the colt. He ground-reined his dun, and his boots clopped on the hard-rock surface as he approached the edge of the rim.

The colt took a step back and McMasters stopped. He had come too far to watch his colt tumble over the edge of the rim. Behind was the vast empty. Only a few pines poked above the rim, growing from the side of the hill or maybe a ridge outcropping. If the colt fell to the ridge, McMasters would have no way of getting it up—not even if he had plenty of help. If the colt missed the ridge, it was a long, long way down to nothing but more pine trees and rocks.

Two ravens flew past, fighting hard against the wind that picked up with fury. McMasters raised his left hand to pull down his hat tighter on his head. He looked back at his saddle, knowing what he would find. Nothing. Not even a bedroll. He should have brought along a slicker, but when he had discovered that James, his son, had left the corral open that morning, he didn't think he would still be looking for the runaway colt far away from his ranch and high up on the Mogollon in the afternoon.

He could smell rain. Worse, he could feel the electricity in the air.

The colt whinnied, but did not move away from the rim's edge.

McMasters took another step. Slowly. Another. He began to sing.

The Union forever! Hurrah, boys, hurrah!
Down with the traitor, up with the star;
While we rally round the flag, boys, rally once again,
Shouting the battle cry of freedom!

The colt stared. The wind turned into a roar. McMasters raised his voice.

We are springing to the call with a million freemen more,
Shouting the battle cry of freedom!

And we'll fill our vacant ranks of our brothers gone before,
Shouting the battle cry of freedom!

He reached the colt, let it smell his scent, and rubbed the bay's neck, widening the loop of the lariat and still singing.

The Union forever! Hurrah, boys, hurrah!
Down with the traitor, up with the star;
While we rally round the flag, boys, rally once again,
Shouting the battle cry of freedom!

Slowly, carefully, he brought the lariat's loop over the colt's head, and let out a sigh of relief. He took a moment to stare at the view. The pines bent to the wind, but beyond that he saw those pine-covered hills, the deep, verdant valley, and beyond that more mountains. It was almost the last thing John McMasters ever saw.

The young colt pulled back, and its rear hooves slipped on the flat rocks. Squealing, the animal started backwards over the cliff. McMasters pulled hard on the rope and leaned back with all his might. The lariat burned through his gloves as the colt kicked and lunged. Somehow, the animal regained its footing on the rock and ran forward. By then, McMasters was on his knees, the leather chaps protecting him. He came up, keeping a tight grip on the lariat, and stopped the colt from running.

Heart racing, sweating profusely, McMasters stepped again toward the horse. He shot a glance at his own horse, relieved to see the dun staring at him with a bemused look.

"That wasn't so damned funny."

He sang again, "Yankee Doodle Dandy" but his voice cracked from the fear. It took awhile for his nerves to calm and his hands to stop shaking. Had the bay gone over the rim, McMasters knew he would have gone over with it. He would have been too damned stubborn to let go of the lariat.

When the colt seemed calm, McMasters turned back to look at the view and shook his head.

Years of experience and memories of Old Jake Willis should have reminded him not to tarry. The Mogollon might be a beautiful place, but it could turn deadly in a heartbeat.

"Come on, boy," he told the colt, "let's go home." He kept singing, though softer as he guided the runaway toward the dun.

We will welcome to our numbers the loyal, true and brave,
Shouting the battle cry of freedom!
And although he may be poor, he shall never be a slave,
Shouting the battle cry of freedom!

Keeping a tight hold on the end of the lariat, McMasters swung into the saddle, gave the dun a kick, and led the bay colt away from the rim's edge. Hooves clapped against the stone until they reached the softer dirt, churned by wagon wheels and shod horses over the years, and took the trail that went down the Mogollon and into Payson. Before he reached Payson, however, he would be home.

Maybe, he thought, *I might even beat the monsoon home.*

Thunder cracked. Both the dun and the bay jumped, but McMasters kept his seat in the creaking saddle. Even more important, he kept his grip on the lead rope. He started to sing the next verse of "The Battle Cry of Freedom" . . . if he could remember it.

Soon it felt as though he were riding through the waterfall at Tonto Bridge . . . and quickly felt more like Niagara Falls.

Numbingly cold rain stung more like hailstones than raindrops, and might indeed turn into hail before he ever reached his horse ranch. Sometimes the summer storms blew out quickly. Other times, they turned roads into mud bogs and could leave a man with a bad case of pneumonia . . . or fried to a crisp by lightning.

John McMasters kept riding down the trail, pulling the colt behind him. He jerked down the brim of his hat, but that did not keep him dry. Hell, the monsoon had already soaked his clothes. The wet saddle rubbed against his wet pants.

"Happy birthday," McMasters said with resigned bitterness, "to me."

"My God, John, get out of those wet clothes—now!" Bea practically jerked him inside their two-story home.

Dripping wet, even though the monsoon had stopped thirty minutes before he reached the ranch, McMasters turned toward the potbelly stove with the coffee pot that looked so inviting, but his wife pushed him away and toward the bedroom.

"After you've dressed," she ordered. "Do you need a hot bath?"

"I never want to feel water on me again," he mumbled and settled into the chair.

"I said—"

"Let me get my boots off," he told Bea. "Don't want me tracking mud to the bedroom."

Although the rain had stopped before he reached home, it had turned the yard from the corrals and barn to the nice home into a quagmire. He had already hung his chaps and his hat, both soaking wet, on a peg on the porch. Bea had to help him with the boots, so wet they felt like they had shrunk and sealed to his socks. The socks he somehow managed to pull off without his wife's help.

At last he stood, shooting a glance at the coffee, but Bea gave him that look of a ranch foreman . . . or an Army major, and he slowly moved toward the door that led to the bedroom.

"I'll get you a towel," she said.

"I might need a quilt."

"You touch Grandmother Albertine's quilt and you'll be sleeping in the barn, young man!"

"I'm not a young man anymore, Bea." He pulled off his eyeglasses, left them on the table by the rocker near the fireplace, and pushed open the door to the bedroom.

"You're only fifty," she told him.

"Today, fifty feels like Methuselah."

"I bet I can change that."

McMasters turned to see that devilish twinkle in her eyes.

"Tonight." She grinned. "Happy birthday, John."

He stood inside the bedroom, staring at her.

She had turned forty years old in January, but—even had he been wearing his spectacles—still looked twenty . . . the age she had been when they had married on July 4, 1876. It was the best Independence Day he could recall since that day at Gettysburg, Pennsylvania, when he and the rest of Company G, and all the rest of General Meade's army, had stared across the mud and blood-soaked fields as the rain poured and they had realized that there would be no battle, that they would live another day, that no more men killed, and that Robert E. Lee would be taking his Rebs out of Pennsylvania.

Come to think on it, McMasters decided, July 4, 1863, hadn't been much of a national holiday after all.

Hell, he thought, *our twentieth anniversary passed two weeks earlier, and I forgot it. Have to make that up.*

Flour coated her hands, and he smelled a cake baking. Usually that time of year, Bea would be using the summer kitchen outside, but the thunderstorm had stopped that. She wore a plain dress of green calico, which accented her emerald eyes, and an apron. A yellow scarf kept her blond hair up. Four kids later, she still looked slim, and maybe even more beautiful than when he had first laid eyes on her in Independence, Missouri. She had been butchering a pig then, and blood—not flour—stained her hands.

Every time he would remind her of that day, how he had walked into the butcher's tent by mistake, he would laugh. Her—frantically trying to push the hair out of her eyes, leaving pig blood streaking her cheeks and forehead. Him—eyes bulging, mouth hanging open, trying to find the words of an apology, but only "You aren't Ted Chambers" coming out of his mouth.

Bea never found his remembrance so funny. But the children always laughed, no matter how many times they had heard that story.

"Get out of those clothes, mister," she said, stepping across the plank floor still wet from his clothes. She grabbed the knob to the door and pulled it shut. "And do not put them on our bed."

The clothes came off, but not without a struggle. He found the towel by the washbasin and dried himself off as best as possible. Beyond the door and in the kitchen, he heard the noise of a spoon whipping something in a bowl, and his wife's boots on the floor.

"You found the colt?" she called out.

"Finally. Where's James?"

"Don't be hard on him. You've left the gate open yourself a time or two."

McMasters had not seen James, but he had not gone to the barn. Wet as he was, tired as he felt, he had unsaddled his horse, and left both the dun and the colt in the round pen. He would see to them once he was dry, and after he had downed at least a gallon of hot coffee.

"I'm not going to whip him." He opened the armoire—burled ash with paneled doors inlaid with tulips of satinwood. Made in France, it had crossed the Atlantic in the 1790s when Bea's great-grandparents had fled Paris during the French Revolution. McMasters never knew how they had managed to get that piece of furniture—the damned thing weighed nigh a ton—out of their home, into a wagon, and onto a ship. Let alone how it had survived New York City; Cincinnati, Ohio; Independence, Missouri; and every stop he and Bea had made before settling a few miles outside of Payson, Arizona Territory.

"Where's Rosalee?" he asked as he opened a drawer to find a pair of cotton underwear.

"She went on a buggy ride with Dan."

That would be Dan Kilpatrick. A deputy U.S. marshal who had found the courage three months earlier to come up to McMasters and ask for Rosalee's hand in marriage.

McMasters had snapped, "That's a bit forward, don't you think! You want to marry a twelve-year-old! Why not, Eugénia? She's only eight!" He smiled as he remembered Bea's calm voice. *"John . . . Rosalee is eighteen. And Eugénia, fourteen."*

He liked Kilpatrick. The young man, twenty-eight or thereabouts, came from good stock. He wasn't sure how he felt about having a lawman for a son-in-law, but Payson was not as lawless as some towns. There had not been a killing in town in five or six years. The 20th Century would be welcomed in just a few more years, and peace seemed to be settling on Arizona Territory. Besides, Dan Kilpatrick did not always plan on wearing a star. He'd told McMasters that he wanted to read the law, hang his shingle in Payson. As a deputy marshal, that boy—twenty-eight was still a boy in McMasters's mind, and Rosalee would never look or seem older than twelve—sure followed the law by the book. He'd make a fine solicitor. Probably even become attorney general for the territory.

"I thought Dan was picking up prisoners at Verde."

"He did," Bea said. "Got back sooner than expected.

Wanted to see his fiancée before he takes that trash to Yuma. You can't blame him for that."

"I hope," McMasters called through the closed door as he found a pair of socks, "that that buggy has a top. That was a regular turd float."

"Watch your language," Bea told him. "And before you ask, Eugénia and Nate are at Lilly's."

Lilly was the daughter of their neighbors, Ned and Jane Lynch. Ned ran a sawmill. He had served in the First Texas, Hood's brigade, but unlike a lot of former Confederates, had never held a grudge that McMasters had, as Lynch liked to say, "worn the blue."

"Actually," McMasters would reply to that with a grin, "my uniform was green."

"And you ain't even Irish," Lynch would say.

"Scotch-Irish," McMasters would say.

"Then that calls for a drink." And Ned Lynch would find a jug or bottle.

"They'll be back, though," Bea said. "I told them all that today's a special day."

Eugénia and Nate were the youngest, fourteen and ten years old, respectively. Eugénia was the spitting image of Bea, but God had cursed Nate with his father's features, the poor kid.

"There's nothing special about this day." McMasters finished dressing—duck trousers with canvas suspenders, a blue pullover cotton shirt with colorful flower prints, battered bandanna, and brown Wellington boots. Nothing special. Just another day in the life of John McMasters.

The front door opened, and McMasters heard someone step inside. Bea lowered her voice, whispering something, while he crossed the bedroom to the dressing table near the four-poster bed. He found the brush and worked on his hair, looking at his bronzed face in the mirror. He guessed that the newcomer would be James, and Bea was reassuring him that his father would hold no grudge, that the colt had been found, but that he must remember to make sure that gate is closed.

James was sixteen, looked more like Bea, thank the Good Lord, except he had thick, dark hair. McMasters frowned. Well, his hair had once been darker than the ace of spades, but it appeared a whole lot grayer. Not completely, but certainly more salt than pepper.

His eyes looked to the left of the mirror, and he smiled at the tintype taken on his wedding day. Bea hadn't changed. He sure had. He looked to the right and frowned. Bea made him keep the medal framed and insisted that it hang on the wall. From bottom to top, a richly engraved five-point star hung from the talons of an American eagle. Above the eagle was a ribbon made of red and white vertical stripes and a wide horizontal blue stripe that was affixed to a highly polished pin. They had compromised, however, when they'd moved to the horse ranch near Payson, and had kept it on display but in the bedroom. Not where any visitor might see it.

Two years ago, he had found Nate staring at the medal. Turning around, flushing when his father entered the room, Nate had mumbled something that McMasters could not catch.

"I'm sorry," his youngest son had finally said.

"No apology needed," McMasters had said.

The scene replayed in McMaster's head.

"Ben Ford says no one in Payson, maybe no one in the whole territory, has one of these." Ned gestured at the medal.

"I wouldn't go that far."

"But Ben Ford says they don't give these out to anyone. That you're a bona fide hero."

McMasters felt his stomach go tight, and he had to block out those memories. At least the nightmares had stopped, for the most part, twelve or thirteen years earlier.

"The bona fide heroes, son," he said gently, "were the ones who didn't come home from that war. Three hundred thousand or more. Maybe four hundred thousand. Maybe even more. Those are the ones who deserve that. Not me."

"You never talk about it," Nate said. "Ben Ford's pa . . . he talks about the war all the time, Ben says. He served in the Second Wisconsin Infantry. So he hails from Wisconsin, same as you. Ben's pa, I mean."

McMasters nodded. "Brave unit. They were in a lot of the same fights we were in."

"But Ben Ford's pa talks about it all the time. You never say nothing about the war."

McMasters put his hand on his son's shoulder, pulled him away from the wall, and led him out of the bedroom. "I've spent thirty years trying to forget about it."

Staring at the medal, McMasters heard the roar of musketry, smelled the stink of gunpowder, felt the Sharps rifle slamming against his shoulder. He wished he had insisted more, that Bea would have listened to him, and that he could have put the medal in a trunk. But, no, Bea was too proud of her husband, and McMasters loved her too much to disappoint her.

He shook his head, hoping the nightmares would not return. With a sigh, he turned away from the Medal of Honor they had pinned on his uniform thirty-one years ago, crossed the room, and opened the bedroom door.

Chapter 3

"*Surprise!*"

The curse died on John McMasters's lips, as his heart started beating again.

Eugénia ran to him and wrapped her arms around his waist. Dan Kilpatrick, still wearing a yellow slicker over his Sunday-go-to-meetings, grinned, and pulled Rosalee closer to him. James beamed with joy. Nate blew on a whistle McMasters had carved for him two winters back. Bea held a cake with five candles burning atop it.

After living near Payson for better than a dozen years, folks knew that John McMasters could be hard to get a drop on—but Bea and the family had caught him by surprise.

"Happy birthday, Pa!" Eugénia pulled away from him, only to jump up, wrapping her arms around his neck, and pulling him close.

He kissed her forehead. She frowned so he rubbed his nose against hers. That brought out a radiant smile, and he kissed her blond hair again and lowered her to the floor.

"I thought you were visiting Lilly," he told her.

"Mama lied," she said and scurried back toward the table. "I was hiding in the barn with James and Nate."

"I see." McMasters found his eyeglasses, wiping the lenses with an end of his bandanna, and after he had set them on his nose, he held out his right hand to the approaching Dan Kilpatrick.

The lawman, his soon-to-be son-in-law, had removed the slicker while McMasters had been preoccupied with Eugénia. The six-point tin star pinned to the lapel of his green coat reflected the flickering light of the candles as Bea set the cake on the center of the table.

"Good evening, sir," Kilpatrick said. He had a strong grip, but not as hard as McMasters'.

Working horses—especially the temperamental ones McMasters seemed to be drawn to—did that to a man's hands . . . and the rest of his body.

"Where were you two hiding?"

"Up the road apiece where we could see you when you turned off the road."

"Hope I didn't keep you waiting," McMasters said, "or wet."

"We did not mind, Pa," Rosalee said.

McMasters frowned and gave Kilpatrick his hardest, most fatherly stare. The deputy's Adam's apple bobbed, and he suddenly looked almost frightened. Those law books, and that tin star, would not help him.

To give Rosalee's betrothed a moment to gather

himself, McMasters turned to face James, who was loading one side of the table with wrapped gifts.

"I suppose you left that gate open on purpose."

James beamed. "It was Ma's idea."

Bea had returned to collect plates and utensils. Rosalee and Eugénia joined to help. Nate kept tooting his whistle.

"You couldn't have sent me to town on some fool's errand?" McMasters said.

"You're too suspicious," Bea said. "We needed a plan that you would not suspect. Though it took much longer than we had anticipated."

Shaking his head, McMasters laughed . . . just to ease any tension. He couldn't be angry at Bea or his family or even Dan Kilpatrick for too long. But some time later, he decided, he might explain to his wife the folly of her plan to get her husband out of the house long enough to bake a cake and plan a birthday surprise.

Let's see, he thought as he moved to watch the bees busy themselves setting the supper table. *What all might have happened? That damned fool colt could have gone over the edge of the Mogollon. I came this close to going over the rim with that wanna-be widow maker. I could have been killed by lightning. Drowned. Caught a fever and died in bed. Got stranded by a flash flood and spent the night in a cave or underneath a bunch of pines while you ate my cake.*

"Where did you finally find that harebrained colt?" Kilpatrick asked.

McMasters shrugged. "Up the road a piece." Maybe he wouldn't let anyone know where he had found the bay after all. No sense in putting worry in Bea's head or frightening his children. Besides, that cake smelled wonderful.

"Have a seat," Bea commanded. "And, Nate, I think you have serenaded us enough with your whistle."

The music—if one might call Nate's renditions *music*—came to a merciful end as James pulled out McMasters's chair.

"You're a mite short on candles." McMasters jutted his chin toward the cake.

"One for each decade," Bea told him.

"No supper?"

"It's your birthday, John. Cake first. Supper later."

"I can't wait till *my* birthday," Nate said, and everyone laughed.

With a belly full of lemon cake, mashed potatoes, stewed carrots, roasted venison, sourdough biscuits, and black coffee, John McMasters forgot all about his adventures on the Mogollon Rim.

Nate had presented him with a pair of socks, likely woven by his sisters, but McMasters went through so many socks in a year that they were always welcomed. James had given him a blue bandanna, silk with white snowflakes, or some design similar to snowflakes. Kilpatrick's present was a gold-plated double watch chain with an ivory fob that had been hand-carved into a Federal eagle. The fob likely set the deputy marshal back a lot more than the chain. From Eugénia, he received a book, *The Minor Poems of John Milton,* published in England in 1889, with gilt on the cover and spine. Bea would have picked that one out for his youngest daughter at Blake's Books, Newspapers, and Candies, and likely had Isaac Blake let Eugénia pick out a special piece of peppermint for herself. Rosalee had made him a shirt, and it looked nice, red and black checks with mother-of-pearl buttons, even two pockets on the front and a collar to boot.

He held a heavy watch—fourteen-karat solid gold, a Waltham repeater with a porcelain dial, Arabic numerals, and straw-colored spade hands—in his hand. His initials were engraved on the shield on the checkered hunter's case. It sang its song as he removed his eyeglasses and wiped his eyes with the bandanna James had given him.

McMasters had been admiring that watch at Brandenberger's shop for two years, always fearing the Swiss merchant would sell it—even though the price on the tag told him nobody in the county could afford it. He wondered how Bea had managed to buy it . . . or what from her family treasures she had traded for it.

He snapped the case shut, ending the mechanical serenade, and put his glasses back on. "Well, if I'd known I'd be getting all this plunder, I would've turned fifty years ago." He cleared the frog out of his throat. Frog? Hell, it felt more like a whale.

"Happy birthday, Pa," James said.

"Yeah," his daughters chimed in. "We love you."

"Can I eat the rest of the cake?" Nate asked.

"No," Bea answered firmly, "you may not." Shaking her head at the youngest child's audacity, she grinned at her husband. "Brandy, dear?"

His head bobbed. He could not find any more words. The brandy helped, although only he and Kilpatrick drank.

"More cake?" she asked her husband.

"Not if I want to get up before daylight," McMasters said.

"That reminds me," Kilpatrick said as he pushed his chair from the table and stood. "I need to be getting back to Payson."

"You'll do no such thing, Dan Kilpatrick," Bea said. "It is too late and far too dark for you to be going anywhere."

"The buggy I let from Dunkirk's livery has headlamps, Missus McMasters," the deputy argued. "I only rented it for one day."

"Dunkirk can wait and so can those prisoners." Bea had assumed command. "Rosalee, make a pallet for James by the fireplace. Dan, you will sleep in the boys' bed upstairs. Eugénia, help your sister. Nate, collect the trash. I'll do the dishes."

"Missus McMasters," Kilpatrick protested, "I can sleep on the pallet. I won't put James out—"

"No," James said. "This will be like camping on the trail."

"We want to do it," Nate said. "It's an adventure."

James whirled. "But . . . Ma . . ."

Everyone stopped, remembering something. McMasters looked around, suspicious.

"Oh, yes. Fetch it, James." Bea beamed at her husband. "There's one more thing, John."

"Not more cake, I hope."

James vanished up the staircase, but came down quickly, holding a long box, wrapped in red, white, and blue bunting. Unable to control his excitement, he shoved the last gift into his father's arms. Whatever the box held, it was heavy.

"Looks like it's for the Fourth of July rather than my birthday," McMasters said.

"Hush. Just open it," Bea ordered.

The bunting came off easily, revealing a long wooden box. Laying that on the tabletop, he opened the lid and stared at the shotgun that rested on red cushioning.

"It's a Remington," James sang out. "Model 1894. Ma said that Evans of yours might blow up in your face and a nine-gauge is too much for you anyhow unless you're hunting buffalo . . . and there ain't no buffalo in Arizona these days."

"Hardly anywhere," Rosalee added.

James couldn't shut up. He was more excited than his father. "Besides, you don't even have that old gun you carried in the war, and you rarely even shoot the Henry anymore."

"That *old gun* your father carried in the war was a Sharps," Kilpatrick said. "Too much for anything around these parts. But that Remington"—he stared at McMasters—"that's the best of its class, sir."

It looked that way. McMasters lifted it out of the box. A side-by-side twelve gauge, double triggers but without hammers. Damascus barrels, graded walnut stock with a leather covered, hard-rubber butt plate. He read the engraving just above and in front of the trigger guard. *REMINGTON ARMS CO.*

And on the other side

TO JOHN MCMASTERS
Happy Birthday, 1896
from your devoted family

He loved the balance of the weapon, and opened the breech. The smell of gun oil and newness, enthralled him. It had been a long time since a weapon had made him feel like that. A long, long time.

Somehow, he managed to swallow down that whale in his throat.

Bea had been ready for him. She had refilled his snifter with brandy.

Setting the shotgun back . . . atop, but not inside, the box, he picked up the glass and sipped.

"I don't know what to say."

"Can I hold the gun, Pa?" James asked.

McMasters bobbed his head, and with excitement, the boy hefted the Remington then looked at his mother.

"Did you get the shells, Ma?"

"James," Kilpatrick began, "it is much too late—"

"Oh, fiddlesticks!" Bea's cry stopped Kilpatrick and made McMasters smile.

"Ma!" James whined.

"I was so excited to find that shotgun, and I'd just bought that Waltham, I just . . . I just . . . I did not think about getting any shells."

"I was hoping I could shoot it," James said, remembering quickly to add, "after Pa shot it once, I mean."

"Why don't you shoot the Evans?" Rosalee asked.

"That cannon!" James's head moved rapidly from side to side. "Not a chance."

"I don't want you to be shooting nothing," Nate said. "My ears will hurt."

"It's too dark to be shooting at anything," Kilpatrick reminded them.

Bea's hands clapped, ending the assaulting voices. "Let your father enjoy his brandy and let's get back to work. A pallet for the boys. Dishes to be washed. Trash to be put in the fireplace. And then"—her hands slapped again—"to bed. To bed. To bed. Your father needs his rest."

"Because I'm ancient," he said.

"Hush. Just sit. Relax. You had a grueling birthday."

McMasters found the snifter and sipped more brandy. French, of course. Bea wouldn't let anything else inside her house, even if she never drank any spirits. The girls busied themselves while Nate, Kilpatrick and James went outside to put away the rented horse and buggy.

Bea settled into a seat beside her husband.

"I am sorry about forgetting that ammunition."

"Don't fret. I'll ride in to Payson in the morning with Dan. I'll buy a box of shells at Johnson's store. Maybe two boxes. Some birdshot so James can shoot a few rounds. We'll go down to the creek, so Nate's eardrums won't burst."

He also thought that maybe, just maybe, before he bought boxes of twelve-gauge loads, he might mosey down the boardwalk from the Johnson's Firearms & Gunsmith to Brandenberger's Clocks and Watches. Perhaps he could talk that old Swiss gentleman into letting him know exactly how much Bea had spent on that Waltham repeater. He hoped it wasn't the price on that tag. McMasters wasn't suffering for money—the horses he bred, raised, and trained had earned him quite the reputation in northern Arizona. He had a nice house, a good half-section with a creek that flowed year-round—even if only a trickle in the dry years—a well, and good pasture for the horses. But he would not consider himself a rich man. He still remembered all those lean years in Missouri . . . Kansas . . . Colorado . . . and New Mexico Territory.

"Don't even think about it," Bea said, interrupting his thoughts.

He drained the brandy and looked into her wonderful eyes. "Think about what?"

"Asking Noah Brandenberger how much I paid for your watch."

He laughed. She knew him too well.

"Now"—she put her hands on the table and pushed herself to her feet—"you need to go to bed. It's been a long day."

"You don't know how long," he said, remembering the Mogollon Rim, the monsoon, and the bay colt. He rose, too, kissed his wife and started for the bedroom.

"John," Bea whispered.

Turning back, he stared into those emerald eyes again.

"Don't go to sleep. Not yet."

Chapter 4

Duke Gold's first shot hit the lead rider plumb center, knocking the white-hatted fool off his paint horse and sending him tumbling down the embankment and into the clear, cold creek that had carved a path between the rugged hills covered by forest.

The second rider quickly snapped a shot at Gold's muzzle flash.

"Ha!" Gold levered another round into his Winchester.

Moses Butcher felt like shooting Duke Gold, but that idiot had started the ball. Butcher knew he had no choice but to finish the dance.

His Winchester already cocked and ready, he drew a bead on the second rider and fired. The .44-40 rifle slammed against his shoulder as the gun roared. He did not bother looking to make sure the man was dead. He knew his aim had been true.

Biting his lip, Butcher watched both horses the posse members had been riding, then swore.

The bay ridden by the man Duke Gold had shot

had tumbled off the road and slid down the embankment, too, causing a minor avalanche of rocks that splashed into the creek. The horse had come up and was swimming across Clear Creek to the far side. Filled with water from all those damned monsoons, it flowed hard and deep, too dangerous to cross at this bend. For all practical purposes, once that bay reached the other bank, it was good as dead. The sorrel, the mount Moses Butcher had just made riderless, was already dead.

Duke Gold had put a bullet in the animal's chest, sending it somersaulting down the dip in the road.

"Damn it!" Gold shouted and fired again.

"Damn you!" Butcher yelled, but no one could hear him. The roar of rifle fire had turned deafening.

It was not supposed to be this way, Butcher thought. But he had not counted on those residents of Winslow being so spirited, and he certainly had not figured on Duke Gold being such an idiot.

Two days earlier, Butcher had led his gang into Winslow for some whiskey to get the boys ready. He'd planned on hitting the westbound Atlantic and Pacific express when it stopped for water down the tracks at Canyon Diablo. His thoughts turned to that day.

The bartender at that rawhide saloon was talking to a cowboy about all the trains that had been held up at Canyon Diablo of late, how the railroad and express offices were getting mighty sick of things, and how the last outlaws who had robbed the A&P had only gotten as far downstream as the Black Falls on the Little Colorado before they had been shot to pieces.

Once he had a glass of rye in his hand, Butcher walked over to the batwing doors and stared across the dusty street at the Winslow Bank. That had not been in town the last time he had ridden through. He looked up and down the street and saw nothing resembling a town marshal's office. Not even a jail.

He did notice telegraph wires, and what he assumed was a telephone wire that would connect the desolate patch of desert with the law in Holbrook to the east and Flagstaff to the west. Those, of course, could be cut down. There was nothing but rough country south. He quickly planned on going in that direction—take a long trip through the rich conifer forests along the Mogollon Rim and into the Sonoran Desert. Cross the border into Mexico. Drink tequila and eat spicy food until the money ran out.

Just like he had been doing for ten years.

Ten men were riding with him, including his kid brother, Ben. Gomez, the big Mexican, and Milt Hanks, who had started with Butcher back in Texas, were veterans. Dirk Mannagan, Miami, and Bitter Page had been with him for five years. The others, the taciturn Indian who called himself Zuni, the two drifters—Cherry and Parks—and the pockmarked kid named Duke Gold were new. Gold was the most recent recruit.

Robbing a bank—especially one in a flea-bitten wind trap like Winslow—would be better than an express car for breaking in the rookies, Butcher figured. Banks usually did not send many Pinkerton or Wells Fargo agents after robbers. Just posses from hayseed desert towns.

He walked back to the bar, drained the worst rye he had tasted in years, and signaled to Greaser Gomez and Milt Hanks to follow him outside. "Change of plans. The bank," he said quickly, then separated from them.

Robbing banks was nothing new. They knew their parts.

Staggering their exits, the others left the saloon in twos the same way they'd entered the town. Eleven men riding into any place attracted too much attention, especially in a desert burg like Winslow. Butcher was nowhere to be seen, but Gomez and Hanks stood on opposite corners. Mannagan, Miami, and Page knew their parts and walked right on by. The newest members stopped and struck up a conversation, receiving their parts in the new plan.

Butcher's plan was simple. Duke Gold and Parks were to hold the horses for the "inside" men—Butcher and his brother along with Gomez and Miami. The others would stay mounted and throw lead at any fool who dared show his face, raise a weapon or even a rock.

Then they'd gallop out of town, tearing down the telephone and telegraph wires before heading west—to throw off any pursuers—and then south.

Simple. But it didn't turn out that way.

Turned out, a lawman happened to be depositing some greenbacks when Butcher walked inside. He recognized the outlaw from all those wanted posters and pulled a pistol. Butcher blew him in half with a .45 Colt, and Miami shot down the teller who tried to palm a derringer. Some idiot clerk ran to the vault, slamming the door shut and spinning the lock before Greaser Gomez blew him apart with his carbine.

"Get what's in the till!" Butcher yelled to his kid brother as way more gunshots than normal sounded outside.

The four robbers ran out of the bank feeling lead whip over their heads like a swarm of bees. Somehow, they found their horses and managed to take a fast lope out of Winslow.

Butcher had to give Duke Gold and Parks some credit. They hadn't shirked their duties or turned yellow. He looked over his gang. They'd taken some hits. Down one man and two horses. Parks hadn't made it, shot out of his saddle while trying to mount. Hanks and Ben's horses got shot out from under them, but Gomez had picked up Hanks and Zuni had picked up Ben.

The Winslow boys had formed a posse mighty quick and had not given up yet. Butcher figured they would soon as two more Winslow boys fell dead, but some boy in overalls surprised him by grabbing the reins of the dead idiots' horses and leading the animals back around the bend.

Gunshots clipped the branches over Moses Butcher's head, and he cursed again. Duke Gold had fired too early, before most of those men from Winslow had rounded the curve in the road. The posse was taking cover on the other side of the road.

"God a'mighty!" Duke Gold slammed against the boulder behind him and slid partway down the rocky bank. The fool groaned, whimpered, and brought both hands to his shoulder as the rifle he had been firing cartwheeled into the creek.

Butcher looked across the creek. The bay horse had reached the other side. Dripping freezing water even in July, it trudged off into the dense forest.

"Hold your fire!"

That shout had come from someone out of view, one of the Winslow boys. Butcher's men had already stopped shooting. There were no targets . . . thanks to Duke Gold. No men to shoot. Worse, no horses. Horses were the main reason Butcher had set up the ambush. Trying to replace the two they'd already lost.

As the echoes of gunfire died away, he began reloading his rifle. Next, he untied his bandanna and wiped sweat off his face, retied it, and called out. "Any man hurt?"

"I-I-I," Duke Gold stuttered. "I . . . g-g-got . . . hit . . . in . . . in . . . in . . . m-m-my . . . sh-shoulder. Oh, Lordy, Lordy, Lordy, I'm h-h-hurtin' s-s-some . . . somethin' awful."

Butcher leaned the Winchester, its barrel burning hot, against the pine.

"I said is there any *man* hurt?"

No answer.

Of course, if one of the outlaws were dead, he wouldn't be able to answer.

"Ben?" Butcher called out.

"I'm all right," his brother replied.

"And the others?"

"None hurt."

"I'm h-h-hurt!" Duke Gold sobbed. "I'm h-hurtin' . . . awful."

"Shut up."

Butcher removed the cavalry hat he had taken off a sergeant he had murdered a few years back down in El Paso. They had been playing poker at the Gem Saloon, and the dumb Yankee had accused Butcher of cheating—which he had been, naturally. When the horse soldier tried for his Remington .44, Butcher had shot him dead. He had needed a new hat and had always admired that cheap tan slouch number, so he had tried it on, and, well, as his Auntie Faye had always told him, *"The Lord works in mysterious ways."* The hat fit him . . . perfectly.

A big man, Butcher took after sweet Auntie Faye, who had raised him and Ben. Six-foot-four before he pulled on his boots, he weighed close to two hundred and twenty pounds . . . probably a bit more considering the lead he had acquired since he had taken to the owlhoot trail—buckshot in his back from a messenger on a stagecoach near Fort Worth; a .41-caliber derringer slug from a bounty hunter in Trinidad; and that .44-40 in his left thigh he had acquired when they had robbed the KATY near Muskogee. He could have weighed even more, but Bitter Page had dug out some slugs in line shacks and caves, and an old sawbones had managed to get the worst bullet—the one under his ribs—after they had taken thirty grand from a bank in Tucson.

He wore striped britches, a red shirt, black vest, and peach-colored bandanna, all covered with dust and grime from traipsing across northern Arizona Territory. Two weeks of beard flecked with gray covered his face, which like his attire, needed a good scrubbing. His guns, however, remained clean—the Winchester .44-40 he placed across his lap as he settled in for a long standoff with the posse from Winslow; the .45 Colt in the well-greased holster on his right hip; and his backup pistol, a .38-caliber Colt Lightning. That's another thing Auntie Faye had always taught him. *"Keep your guns clean, boy. And always loaded."*

Removing his bandanna, he blew out a heavy sigh and began rubbing down the still warm barrel of his rifle.

As the sun sank behind the pine-covered hills, the air turned cooler. Butcher bit off a plug of tobacco and worked it with his molars. Auntie Faye had taught him that chewing tobacco relaxed one's nerves, curbed the appetite, and made a body think better. And Auntie Faye . . . damned how she could spit. Could hit a spittoon twenty feet away and not stain the floor.

He heard the rocks tumbling down the bank of the creek and saw Bitter Page making his way up.

No telling what Page's given name was, but *Bitter* fit him to a *T*. He never smiled, and his long, lean face reminded Butcher of all the undertakers and grave robbers he had known over the years. Almost as tall as Butcher and three times as lean, the gunman reached up to grab a branch and pull himself onto the embankment across from the gang leader, who did nothing to help. Getting that tobacco moist and chewable had become Butcher's primary concern.

"Pulled out," Page said.

Butcher pushed himself up. "Skedaddled? Or up to something?"

"Runnin' fer home. Found some blood droplets. We put a hurt into 'em."

"You certain?"

Page raised one of his uncommonly long arms and pointed one of his thin, white fingers across the road. "Too tough a country. Woods too thick. Would have to leave their horses behind."

The tobacco felt good, so Butcher tested and spit on a beetle. Never able to spit as good as Auntie Faye, he wiped his mouth. "That would've helped us out a mite."

Page shrugged.

"All right." After grabbing his Winchester and butting the rifle on the ground, Moses Butcher pushed himself up. With Page following, the outlaw climbed up onto the road, bellowing for the boys to come on up and get their horses. He walked over to the horse Duke Gold had killed, and spit tobacco into the pool of blood that had dried into a dark stain on the sand.

"God," Gold muttered. "I'm hurt plumb awful."

Turning toward the gang, Butcher pointed the Winchester's barrel at the dead horse.

"The idea was to get us horses. *Live* horses. We're short of mounts."

Gold paled even more. "That horse jumped up. Else I woulda kilt the rider true. Just like I done that first hombre."

"And that horse made it to the far side of the creek. We still need two horses. By now, every law dog in the territory knows we're headin' south."

"We need more than two horses, boss," Dirk Mannagan said. "Ours are already played out. No way they'll get us across that desert once we've cleared the Mogollon."

Butcher's negative-thinking brother said, "*If* we get out. A mighty big *if*."

After spitting again, Butcher blew out a long breath and studied the rough country. "Ain't likely to find even a wild, ornery mustang in these woods."

Silence.

The coming darkness matched Butcher's mood.

"South a mite," Gold mumbled.

Butcher gathered his Winchester into his arms and faced him.

"Huh?"

"There's a feller who raises good stock down around Payson."

"Is your knowledge of good stock better than your aim?"

"Cowboys for the Hashknife Outfit swear by 'em."

Butcher considered.

"Name's McMasters," the wounded Gold said. "His place is east of Payson."

The silent Indian, Zuni, not only grunted, but even spoke. "True. I have heard of this McMasters. But morc of his horscs."

That sealed the deal for Moses Butcher. "All right. We'll pay McMasters a visit."

"And there's a doctor in Payson, too," Gold said. "I'll pay him a visit."

"Nah." Butcher swung the barrel of the Winchester around until it was touching Gold's belly.

Startled, Gold grabbed the barrel with both hands, but instead of jerking the rifle away, he brought it up. The .44-40 roared, sending him backwards, sliding down the embankment, and into the creek. His head disappeared beneath the water, but most of his body would remain dry—at least until the ravens and coyotes came to visit.

Once the ripples had faded, no bubbles came to the surface.

That was a pity, Butcher thought. Had Duke Gold not been an idiot and jerked the barrel up, he would have ended up gut-shot, taking a long time to die. He said what his Auntie Faye always said, "*Que sera sera,*" then turned to his brother.

"Ben, you take Duke's horse. We ride."

"At night?" Cherry asked. "In this country?"

"You can stay with Duke if you want." Butcher jacked a fresh round into the rifle.

Cherry offered a weak smile. "Always wanted to see Payson."

Chapter 5

Royal Andersen had parked his tumbleweed wagon—that rolling jail cell used to haul federal prisoners to the territorial prison in Yuma—exactly where John McMasters figured to find it. So McMasters reined in the buckskin, swung out of the saddle, and wrapped his reins around the hitching rail in front of the Sawmill Saloon.

He had not reached the batwing doors before Mayor Ash Ashby—who always insisted that, yes, that was the handle his ma and pa hand put on him—stopped him on the boardwalk.

"Rodeo's next month."

Grinning but shaking his head at the same time, McMasters turned around, adjusted his eyeglasses, and held out his right hand. The smile faded just a bit when McMasters recognized the man in the unkempt sack suit standing to Ashby's right.

"So I hear." McMasters shook hands with the mayor, and without any hesitation—despite how he felt—and offered his big right hand to the man in the suit. "Tom. How are things in Globe?"

"Quiet," Tom Billings said.

"That's good," McMasters told the Gila County sheriff.

"Now about our rodeo . . ."

The smile returned in earnest when McMasters faced the mayor again and leaned against the rough pine planks of the saloon next to the batwing doors.

"Why don't you supply us with some good horses for those boys to ride in our August Doin's this year?" the mayor continued.

The rodeo had been going on for about as long as the town had been going by the name Payson. Cowboys from across the territory would come into Payson, gathering in the center of town near August Pieper's rawhide saloon to try their hand at roping steers, riding broncs, and racing horses . . . not to mention that bloody game called chicken-pulling.

"You don't want *good* horses," McMasters pointed out.

"Well." The mayor shuffled his Chicago-ordered shoes on the rough pine. "Before you train them horses, I know they are rank animals that even the best twister ever to fork a saddle at the August Doin's would be hard-pressed to ride."

"Yeah." The county sheriff had decided to put in his two cents.

Must be an election year, McMasters decided. He could not think of any other reason Tom Billings would ride eighty miles north to visit Payson. "And you got your start here match-racin', or so I hear."

McMasters did not bother to look at Billings or acknowledge his statement, which was true.

Mayor Ashby was speaking up for McMasters.

"That's a fact, Tom. I saw John here beat a thoroughbred back in '89. Last time you raced, wasn't it?"

McMasters did not bother answering. "You can get some Indian ponies up at San Carlos, Mayor, or send some cowhands into the hills to round up what's left of mustangs like I do."

Ashby shrugged. "You're a bona fide hero, John. Only Medal of Honor winner I've ever met. Made us all proud when you'd compete in the rodeo or match your best horse against any and all comers. Hell, I have to think that cowboys from as far away as New Mexico came here because of you . . . and your reputation. Might not even be any August Doin's if not for you."

"I got old," McMasters told him.

"Well, look at it this way, John." Ashby could be one persistent cuss at that time of year. "Rodeos. Our August Doin's. That's about all of the Wild West that's left in the world . . . unless you're traveling with Buffalo Bill Cody or one of those other—"

"Dog and pony shows," the county sheriff interrupted.

"This is 1896," Ashby continued. "Before long, there won't be any rodeos."

McMasters laughed. "And no chicken heads and blood to clean up after the August Doin's."

"Horse apples!"

Royal Andersen's blue-coated arms leaned across the batwing doors of the Sawmill.

Stepping away from the wall, McMasters smiled even as he smelled the whiskey on the deputy's breath.

"This country is fer from becomin' no paradise, gents. Hell's fires and by golly, it ain't no tamer than it was when I was ridin' with Crook, scoutin' fer the Army, chasin' Nana and Cochise and Juh and Victorio and Geronimo. We never would have taken 'em bucks if it weren't fer Crook. You know what the gen'ral told us?"

" 'It takes an Apache to track an Apache,' " McMasters said. Hell, he had heard it enough from Royal Andersen over the years.

"Takes an Apache to track an Apache," Andersen said as if he were deaf and McMasters had lost his voice.

The mayor and sheriff had heard enough and, as two career politicians, knew better than to stay around a person who would never let them speak, or who had never voted once in his life. Nodding their good-byes, both men hurried down the boardwalk.

Royal Andersen pushed his way through the doors and grinned.

Lean, tall, leathery, and harder than a fencepost, Royal Andersen pushed up the brim of his kepi, the blue wool practically bleached white by thirty-plus years in the elements. A cap like that did little to protect a man's face the way McMasters's equally battered wide-brimmed Stetson did, and Andersen's face seemed darker than an Apache. He might even have been mistaken for an Indian if not for the thick white whiskers and his piercing hazel eyes.

Despite the summer heat, Andersen wore an old Army blouse—although the brass buttons had long since vanished—over a muslin shirt and fringed buckskin britches stuffed inside old cavalry-issue boots that would never pass a by-the-book sergeant's inspection. No spurs, but he did not need spurs when he drove the jailer's wagon parked in the muddy street. Strapped across his waist, securing his Army-issue coat and likely keeping the britches from falling to his ankles, a black gun belt held a Remington in a cross-draw, flapped holster and the longest Bowie knife John McMasters had ever seen.

They shook hands . . . and this time, John McMasters enjoyed the experience.

"Been a long while, John," Andersen said. "Dan said you'd be comin'. Said you was 'posed to come with him this morn, but you and 'em hosses you raise interfered."

McMasters smiled. "Dan wasn't in any particular hurry to leave this morning, either. It's good to see you, old friend."

The old-timer grinned. "I hear you got somethin' fancy fer yer birthday."

Knowing Andersen would not mean the watch, McMasters gestured to the scabbard, and watched the tall ex-Army scout, and before that, a veteran of the 6th Wisconsin Infantry, stride to the buckskin and stare at the gleaming stock of the Remington. He cast a glance at McMasters, who nodded, and then his gnarled hands reached to pull the shotgun from the leather.

"The onliest thing I ever got on my birthday," Andersen said, "was a hair of the dog that bit me."

"No difference than any other day," McMasters said.

"No hammers." Andersen opened the breech. "Smells

sweet." He snapped the barrels into place, turned, and trained both barrels on the backs of the sheriff and mayor.

"Out of range," McMasters said, "and ammunition. Need to get some shells over at Johnson's."

"Yeah." The old man slid the shotgun back into the scabbard. "How old are you?"

"Fifty."

"Hell's fires, son, you ain't old. You ought to be carryin' a long gun."

With exaggeration, McMasters removed his glasses, cleaned the lenses with his bandanna, and returned them. "My eyes beg to differ."

"Son, I'm nigh twenty years older than you now, but my eyes is as good as they ever was." He tilted his head toward the batwing doors. "Buy you a better present than that scattergun?"

McMasters pointed at the empty tumbleweed wagon. "Is that where your prisoners are?"

The old man laughed. "No. I don't drink with owlhoots. Dan's signin' all 'em papers it takes a body to get a man to prison in these dandified days."

"How many are you hauling to Yuma?"

"Six." He walked through the batwing doors and signaled to the beer jerker.

McMasters followed Andersen through the doors, let his eyes adjust to the dim light, and made his way to the bar. Two mugs already waited on the polished bar top when he set his right boot on the brass rail. To his surprise, he found Andersen's mug only half full. Maybe, he thought, Daniel Kilpatrick had ordered the deputy to cut down on the liquor. Then he watched as the bartender topped off the beer with rye.

"Six of the worst scum you ever laid eyes on."

Their mugs clinked. "That what brought the sheriff to town?"

"Nah." Andersen drank about half of his beer-rye mix, and wiped the foam off his beard. "He ain't got nothin' to do with no owlhoot. Likely a-feared they might cut his heart out. And these six . . . they'd do it. One's Bloody Zeke The Younger."

McMasters set down his beer, untouched.

"I thought he was in Yuma already."

"Was." Andersen finished his drink and motioned to the bartender for another. "Not so much beer this time, Joe." He turned around, leaning against the bar, staring at the empty saloon, which would not be empty during the whole run of the August Doin's.

"Flew the coop. Probably come huntin' Moses Butcher."

"Yeah." McMasters sipped the beer.

Bloody Zeke The Younger had left dead men across the country, but none in Arizona Territory. That's why, when he had ridden with Moses Butcher to rob a bank in Tucson, he had not been put on the gallows. Oh, from what McMasters had read in the newspapers and heard in the barbershop and horse corrals, three states, one territory, and even the government of Mexico had asked for extradition so they could have the honor and privilege of hanging the cold-blooded blackheart. But the governor of Arizona and the Yuma warden decided that it would be a much bigger feather to claim Bloody Zeke for their own, and keep him behind the walls of Yuma.

"Bet the governor wishes he had sent Bloody Zeke to Texas or Kansas now," McMasters said.

"Mebe so. His pa was worser, though."

"Before my time."

"Stirred up trouble with the Apaches when Cochise was makin' things hard down south. I was with the soldier-boys who caught up with the original Bloody Zeke back in '71." Andersen drank his new beer-rye blend, still looking through the door, his mind lost in thought. "Tubac. South of Tucson. Caught him. Found a good saguaro cactus. Crucified him."

"Damn." The beer no longer tasted so good.

"Just like he done a ten-year-old girl after he . . . well . . . never you mind 'bout that. No trial. No judge. No extradition. Justice. That's all."

Suddenly, Royal Andersen laughed. Reaching behind him, he found the mug, drained it, set it back on the bar and said, "Takes an Apache to track an Apache. Took a vermin to find a vermin. Wouldn't have found the Original Bloody Zeke—he didn't earn that *Original* handle till his boy started raising hell ten-fifteen years later, long after he was nothin' but whitewashed bones and bad memories. Anyway, we busted one of his compadres out of the Tubac calaboose. Made him track down his pard. Killed him, too. Didn't nail him to no cactus. Just put a bullet between his eyes. But I reckon he thought that was better 'n what we done to Bloody Zeke, the sick bastard."

"And you're taking him to Yuma." McMasters shook his head and turned back to the bar, sliding the beer mug away. "And five other men."

"No." Andersen smiled and stepped back to lean against the bar, facing the tequila bottles, rye bottles, and even a few jugs of wine. "Four men. Bloody Zeke The Younger. And a damned petticoat."

"A woman?" The bartender joined the conversation.

"Well, she ain't one you'd bring home to meet your mother, Joe. But, yeah, she's female. And there's a colored boy. Big cuss. Done some scoutin' for the Army till we run off all the Apaches. Damned good scout, they tell me, but he up and turned killer."

Andersen pointed at the empty glass, but Joe shook his head.

"Marshal Kilpatrick would load me into that wagon if I gave you another, Royal," the bartender said, waving his hands in surrender.

With a snort, Andersen grabbed McMaster's mug and drained his beer. "Yeah. Handsome gal, or so I'm told, but don't turn your back on her. She and her pard robbed a stage outside of Flagstaff."

"A woman robbed a stage?" The bartender sounded curious.

"But that ain't why she's bound for Yuma."

The bartender waited. And waited. John McMasters had to laugh.

In defeat, Joe drew Andersen another beer, but he refused to add any rye, or tequila, or even wine to the drink.

It was enough to placate Andersen.

He sipped, or what he would consider a sip, and nodded at Joe. "Well, it's one reason I reckon. The robbery, I mean. But then she up and kilt her pard, the feller she'd robbed the coach with. Shot 'im down like the dirty dog he was."

"I'll be damned," Joe said.

"So would she . . . had she been a man. Instead, the law just sent her to Yuma."

"That's damnation in its own way," McMasters said.

The batwing doors banged, and two cowboys came in, motioned for the bartender, and found a table by the window.

As Joe drew two more beers and headed to serve the newcomers, Royal Andersen sighed.

"How come you don't do that rodeo no more, John?" He finished the beer in two gulps. "You pret' much bought that place of yourn racin' horses back in the day. And you did bring in a crowd."

McMasters wished he had another beer or even some rye . . . if Royal Andersen had left any at the Sawmill. With a sigh, he shook his head.

"Didn't like all that brag. All that stuff they said about me. Trying to make me out like some hero."

"They don't give that there medal you won to cowards, son."

"Sometimes . . ." He never liked talking about the war. Or what he had done, what he had seen, or even why they had pinned that Medal of Honor on him—and not those others. "I don't know. I was a snake in the grass."

"Horse apples."

"Didn't like thinking that they gave me the medal for killing."

The bartender was back, but staying on the other end of the bar, perhaps understanding that this conversation was not meant for even bartenders to hear.

"That's what we was there for . . . killin' Rebs."

"Well. I did my share. But you"—McMasters tried to smile, but his heart weighed down those corners of his lips—"charging that railway cut north of Chambersburg Pike at Gettysburg? Capturing the flag of the . . . what was it? The Third Mississippi?"

"Second," Andersen corrected.

"Then holding on at Culp's Hill. You boys deserved all the medals there were to give."

Andersen grinned. "Our corporal, Mr. Walker, he got one. Just like you." He set down his beer.

"You should have gotten it," McMasters said.

"Horse apples. Corporal Walker . . . he was the one who got that Reb flag. So he got the medal."

"I captured no flag," McMasters said.

"And I ain't sure I killed nobody. Not at Gettysburg anyhow. Fired a lot of lead, though."

The opening above the batwing doors darkened, and McMasters saw the tall man standing outside. Instinctively, protectively, McMasters reached over and lifted Royal Andersen's beer mug, bringing it to his lips and drinking what little remained, most of that being suds.

Deputy Marshal Daniel Kilpatrick pushed through the doors, stood blocking the entrance, and placed both hands on his hips.

CHAPTER 6

"The Payson place?" The hayseed in overalls and a straw hat stepped around the mule he was leading and pointed up the road. "Two miles on the Rim Road. Pass the crick, and jus' head . . ." The words seemed to stick in his throat, and he looked again at the smiling Ben Butcher. "Ya boys ain't from 'round here, is you?"

"If we were," Ben Butcher said, "we'd know where that old horse trader lived, now, wouldn't we?" He showed the hayseed his pearly whites, which, actually, were more yellow than white.

"I reckon." The hayseed tried to grin, but something warned him. He looked at the men, the horses, and all the guns they carried. Guns that, for the time being, remained holstered, sheathed, or hidden. "But ya do look familiar." He was staring straight at Moses Butcher. "Ya ain't been to Payson before?"

"First time," Ben Butcher said.

"Listen," Bitter Page tried, "we ride for the Hashknife."

That troubled the hayseed even more, and Moses Butcher wished Page, who meant well, would have kept his trap shut. They did not look anything like cowboys.

Butcher decided he had better speak up.

"Been deputized by the law."

That made the hayseed look even more sickly.

"Case you ain't heard it, Moses Butcher's gang robbed a bank up in Winslow."

"Moses . . . Butcher?" The hayseed couldn't take his eyes off Butcher, and his hands kept pulling at the lead rope on his mule.

"Yeah. Shot the town to pieces. Rode south. The sheriff figured they was comin' this way, rode to the outfit, asked us to help. Only, Smith here, his horse went lame. Some hayseed told us about this Mac—" Butcher's tongue tripped. He couldn't remember that horseman's name.

"McMasters," his brother said.

"Yeah. McMasters. We need a fresh horse for Smith."

The hayseed swallowed. "'Pears like ya need more 'n one horse."

For a hayseed pulling a mule packed down with sticks, the hick did not miss much.

"Right. And everybody at the Hashknife knows that McMasters has the best horses in Arizona."

A long silence separated the hayseed from Butcher and his men. The man with the mule wet his lips, swallowed, and wiped his forehead with a filthy shirtsleeve.

"Well"—the curious but taciturn hayseed found his tongue . . . and would not keep quiet—"I'd love to join up with ya boys. Ride with ya. Bring 'em bad men to justice. But"—he nodded at the mule, swallowed, and pointed up the pike—"like I told ya. Four miles up the road. Oncet ya starts the real hard climb, ya will finds a loggin' road off to the left. Foller that one for two-three miles and there you'll find John's place."

"A logging road," Ben Butcher repeated.

"Yeah. Good luck, boys. Tell ol' John and his missus that I said howdy." He tugged on the rope, leading the mule and his sticks through Butcher's boys, not stopping, picking up his pace quickly, and definitely not looking back.

"Four miles and then a logging road," Bitter Page said.

"Sí," Greaser Gomez noted. "But before that, he say two miles and a creek."

"You shouldn't have mentioned your name or Winslow, Moses," Ben said. "He recognized us. Will fetch the law."

Just like Ben Butcher, finding something down.

"I can handle that," Moses said, and began pulling his .45.

"No!" Ben spoke with authority.

Butcher glared at his brother.

"Ben ees right," Greaser Gomez said. "Too close to town. The *pistola* will be heard."

The .45 slammed back into the holster. "Two miles," Butcher said. "A creek. Shouldn't be hard to find after that."

"But what if that old fool wasn't right the first time?" Cherry sounded like Butcher's brother. "What if that place is down that loggin' road?"

"What the hell would he be feeding his horses, you damned fool?" Butcher snapped. "Sawdust? The creek. That's where we'll find this horseman."

"And"—Dirk Mannagan grinned—"that sodbuster said somethin' 'bout a missus."

"Let's pay our respects," Milt Hanks said.

"You know Marshal Meade's rules about wagon drivers," Daniel Kilpatrick said. "And drinking on duty."

Sometimes, John McMasters did not understand what Rosalee saw in her intended. Oh, Dan was a good man, would make a fine provider, but he stood so ramrod straight and followed the law by the letter . . . which wasn't how Arizona or any place west of the Mississippi had been tamed.

"He just had one beer, Dan," McMasters lied, pointing at one of the empty mugs. "Bought a few for my birthday."

Kilpatrick gave McMasters a hard stare. "Paid with what?"

McMasters grinned. "We're Wisconsin boys. His credit's good."

"And there ain't no prisoners in that cast-iron Conestoga," Andersen said, somehow not slurring his words.

"It's not a Conestoga."

That was another thing about Dan Kilpatrick that McMasters did not understand. The boy wouldn't know a joke if it bit him in the nose.

"What would you know?" Andersen snorted. "You

never saw one in your life . . . except maybe in one of 'em illustrated newspapers or storybooks."

McMasters set down the glass he had borrowed from the old scout turned jailer, found some coins, and dropped them on the bar, nodding at Joe. Royal Andersen, in his cups, would start a fight with anyone from preacher to schoolmarm . . . and despite Kilpatrick's low opinion of his wagon driver, anyone hauling Bloody Zeke The Younger and five other hard rocks would have need of a man with Andersen's experience. At best, it would take them fifteen days to reach Yuma from Payson.

"Here, Dan," McMasters said. "I'll help you load the prisoners in the tumbleweed wagon."

"No need, sir." The young lawman spit with disgust into a nearby spittoon. "I already got them in."

That stopped McMasters. "Did—" No, he let that stupid question go unfinished. Tom Billings, twice elected sheriff of Gila County, would not dare come within an arm's length of a bunch of cutthroats.

"I did it by myself." Kilpatrick almost laughed at the look on McMasters's face. "It wasn't that hard, sir. Legs shackled. Wrists in manacles. And you're not the only one in these parts with one of these." He held up the shotgun McMasters had scarcely noticed.

It was a double-barrel like McMasters's birthday present, a twelve-gauge too from the looks of the barrels, only those Damascus barrels had been sawed off to just above the forestock. Unlike the 1894 in McMasters's scabbard, Kilpatrick's had hammers.

"A Greener?" McMasters asked.

"Yep. It talks big."

"Bigger 'n yer law books." Andersen snorted. "Well, let's take those boys—I mean, the boys and that man-killin' petticoat—and get 'em to the prison." He stepped away from the bar.

Dan Kilpatrick placed both barrels of the sawed-off twelve-gauge on the old-timer's stomach just above the buckle on the gun belt.

"You don't go near that wagon, Royal," Dan said in a hushed tone. "Wearin' that rig."

"Boy"—Andersen's right hand rested on the flap over his holster—"you point a gun at me, you damn sure better be willin' to pull 'em two triggers."

"Take off the pistol." Kilpatrick did not waver. "And the knife."

Andersen stepped back, almost falling against the bar. He jerked the ancient kepi off his head, slammed it against the bar, and shook his head. "Boy. Nursemaidin' whiskey runners and forgers and even robbers is one thing. But you expect me to go nigh three hunnert miles with Bloody Zeke—hell, son, I helped kill that cur's daddy!—and five other scum-suckin' swine?"

"It's the way Marshal Meade says things must be done." The Greener had not lowered.

"Royal." McMasters spoke softly, watched the old-timer slowly take his glare off Kilpatrick, then smiled.

Andersen, eventually, shook his head, laughed, and pulled the battered Army cap back over his unruly white mane.

"All right, John. You've become a regular peacekeeper, forgettin' all . . ." The words died, and regret filled Andersen's face, but he unbuckled the rig, and held it out for Kilpatrick to take.

Far from green, he kept the Greener on his driver.

"Sir," Kilpatrick said softly to McMasters. "Would you mind?"

After taking the gun belt, McMasters led the way outside and draped Andersen's rig over the deputy U.S. marshal's saddle horn. Kilpatrick would ride the black horse alongside Andersen's jail-on-wheels for two weeks. The kid had guts. And a lot of patience, putting up with old Andersen. Maybe that's what Rosalee saw in him.

McMasters looked into the wagon. Five men and one woman, all shackled, all staring with malevolent eyes through the iron bars.

He recognized Bloody Zeke The Younger from the wanted posters he had seen tacked up outside the town marshal's office and the woodcut engraving from *Frank Leslie's* and *Harper's Weekly* illustrated periodicals. The dark-eyed man stared right through McMasters.

The others he barely considered. One man, perhaps even older than Royal Andersen, still wore old Confederate trousers, though more patches of various colors than gray wool, with a brown leather patch over his right eye. Next to him sat a younger man with a green Prince Albert coat and a yellow brocade vest. Beside him, a Mexican snored, his battered sombrero serving as a pillow against the iron bars. Those, McMasters could see. The others sat opposite of Bloody Zeke The Younger and the three others. One man was black with a shaved massive head and shoulders that reminded McMasters of an ox. That would be the ex-Army scout Andersen had mentioned. The other, far away from the Negro and the closest to the door in the back, had to be the woman stagecoach robber and murderess. She wore a dress of the same fabric and design as the one Bea had donned yesterday. Green calico. The prisoner's was filthy. And, unlike Bea, she had hair the color of ginger.

Grumbling, Royal Andersen climbed into the driver's box.

McMasters faced Kilpatrick.

"You want some company?"

Kilpatrick looked stunned. "You?"

"That's a long way to go." McMasters tilted his head toward the prisoners. "And a rough lot of customers."

"And it won't be like shooting fish in a barrel . . ."

He watched his future son-in-law's face turn ashen.

The young man wet his lips, stuttered, backed up, and finally managed, "I didn't mean . . . that didn't sound . . . I'm—"

"It's all right, Dan." McMasters made himself smile. "But the offer still stands. Three hundred miles to Yuma—"

"Closer to two hundred and seventy-five."

McMasters laughed genuinely, even if Royal Andersen swore underneath his breath.

"John." Daniel Kilpatrick swallowed, likely wondering if he could get away with addressing Rosalee's father with such familiarity. When McMasters failed to react, one way or the other, the deputy marshal explained, "I don't have the authority to deputize you. Only Marshal Meade could do that, and he's in Phoenix."

"Phoenix is on the way," McMasters tried again.

"Thanks, sir. I appreciate it. But—" Kilpatrick let out a sigh. "Royal and I can handle these men . . . and the woman. Tell Rosalee that I'll see her in a month at the most." He held out his hand.

"Good luck, Dan," McMasters said, and walked to his horse before remembering just what had brought him into town. Johnson's gun shop stood just a block away and across the street. McMasters left his horse in front of the Sawmill Saloon and walked therc, glanc-ing just once to watch the tumbleweed wagon and Daniel Kilpatrick head south on the trail to Phoenix. Then he stepped inside Johnson's store.

"What'll you need?" Johnson called out.

McMasters remembered. If James and Nate wanted to test out that Remington shotgun, he should start them out with something that wouldn't knock them on their buttocks.

"Birdshot."

"From what I heard, I took that horseman to be some old coot," Ben Butcher said. He pointed at the girl hauling the bucket of water from the stream. "She looks mighty ripe."

"I like the littler one." Greaser Gomez, grinning broadly, pointed the barrel of his carbine at another girl, maybe in her teens, who appeared to be gather-ing eggs beside the barn.

Moses Butcher spit tobacco onto an anthill.

"We're here," he reminded the boys, "for horses."

Most of his gang giggled.

"Remember, that square-head with the mule is likely yellin' at the law in Payson. Horses," he insisted, and spurred his horse down the ridge, out of the woods, and onto the path that ran alongside the creek.

The outlaws followed him.

Out of the corner of his eye, he saw the girl with the bucket of water stop what she'd been doing. As he drew nearer, he had to agree with his kid brother that she looked ripe and fine. Likewise, the one hunting eggs stopped to stare. Moses Butcher tried to focus on the horses. He saw one colt and plenty of good horseflesh. Whoever had bragged about this McMasters knew about horses. Any of these animals would do for the journey south to Mexico.

Grinning despite his weariness and hunger, Butcher managed to remove his stolen cavalry hat as he reined in in front of the girl with the water.

"Howdy," he said, but could not take his eyes off the girl's perky breasts. She blushed, lowered the bucket to the ground, and crossed her arms.

A tough cookie, Butcher thought as he returned his hat.

"Saul Gray from Holbrook bragged that McMasters has the best horses for sale in all of the territory." Straightening in the saddle, he pointed at the nearest round pen. "From how I see things, Saul understated things." He had made up the name Saul Gray on the spot. Well, he had thought of it in a hurry. Saul Gray had been a drummer who stopped by the place back home. He had been the first man Auntie Faye had murdered, a long, long time ago.

Looking back at the girl with the firm breasts, Butcher frowned. The girl had not lowered her arms, nor that intense stare.

He cleared his throat. "Your pa around, ma'am? We'd like to do some horse trading."

That's when the door to the two-story home opened, and a woman in a yellow dress and nice apron stepped onto the porch. Hell, she looked better than this prim little bitch. Maybe the boys were right. Maybe there was a little time to kill . . . if McMasters and no other men were around.

The saddle leather squeaked as Moses Butcher dismounted. It was rude, he knew, to get off his horse before being invited, but he did not give a damn.

Chapter 7

He had wasted most of the late morning, chatting with Royal Andersen, sipping a beer at the Sawmill—a rarity for him—and then buying the birdshot at Johnson's gun shop. Bea probably would not believe him, but he had not gone into Brandenberger's Clocks and Watches to see exactly how much that Waltham repeater had set his wife, maybe even himself, back. At least he would have the afternoon to work that colt . . . unless it had escaped again.

John McMasters rode easily up the Rim Road. He didn't feel fifty years old, not today, not after last night, not even after seeing a cutthroat like Bloody Zeke The Younger and hearing about the killer's father. Andersen had been known to tell a windy or few in his time, but that story—hanging a man from a saguaro's arms—struck him as too gory, too real to have been conjured up from a rye- and beer-soaked morning.

Dust caught his eye, and he reined in the buckskin and looked down into the valley that had been cleared of forest not far from his home. A lot of dust. Standing in the stirrups, he studied the scene. More than a half-dozen men were working their horses into a frenzy . . . and the afternoon had turned far too hot to be riding horses that hard. They moved more south than west, probably toward Tonto Creek and the Sierra Ancha range. If John McMasters had to guess, he would have to figure they were making a beeline for the road to Globe. Only it would be a lot easier for anyone to ride into Payson and pick up the southern road there. Nobody would want to cut through that country. Unless—

Even if McMasters saw through the eyes he had thirty years ago, he would not have been able to identify the men or their horses. Not from that distance. Not through that much dust. Not as fast as they rode. He counted them, though, now that they had spread out. Loosely speaking, they formed a column of threes. Nine men.

Riders from the Hashknife Outfit? He shook his head. *No.* The Aztec Land and Cattle Company did not always hire cowhands of savory character, but surely wouldn't pay anyone who treated horses that hard. Besides, Commodore Perry Owens had been elected sheriff up in Navajo County a year ago, and he ran a tight, tight ship. Even the Hashknife boys knew better than to get on Perry's bad side.

You're thinking too much, McMasters told himself. Settling back into the saddle, he shot one final glance at the hard-riding nine just before the last of the riders disappeared behind boulders and trees. Kicking the buckskin back into a walk, he spotted something else . . . and it was far more terrifying than a bunch of galloping horsemen.

Swearing, he reined in again. *Smoke.*

Sure, July was monsoon season, but those thunderstorms brought lightning with it, and no matter how wet the showers wet the ground, it was still Arizona Territory. The ground soaked up moisture like a bartender's towel, often leaving the country dry as a regular tinderbox. Forest fires struck fear into anyone and everyone who called the Mogollon Rim home.

"Oh, God," McMasters said, realizing the smoke wasn't gray or white. Black plumes rose above the tree line, and that meant more than wood burned. It also was coming from where his ranch lay.

"Come on, boy!" Whipping off his eyeglasses and shoving them inside a vest pocket for protection, he raked the spurs across the buckskin's side. The horse exploded beneath him as McMasters leaned in the saddle, giving the animal he had trained as much rein as he dared. Wind blasted his face, and he whipped the buckskin's sides with the ends of his reins.

"Come on!" he cried.

Then he began saying something else.

"No . . . no . . . please, God, no . . ."

He could smell smoke and began to pray.

The smoke stung his eyes, and the smell left him gagging. He dropped to his knees, trying to hold on to the reins and calm the buckskin, but the smoke, the intensity of the flames, and that awful stench prevented it. Even a horse trained by the legendary John McMasters couldn't be calmed. The reins slipped through his gloved fingers, and the buckskin bolted down the pathway, splashed across the creek, and kept running toward the Rim Road.

"Bea!" he screamed, unable to hear his own voice, only the hideous roar of flames, the crackling of timbers, the shattering of glass inside what once had been his home. He moved to the inferno, shielding his face with his arms, already burning.

"Bea! Rosalee!" The heat, the smoke, the fury drove him back. He coughed, tried again, only to retreat toward the well. He tripped over a bucket, which smoked from the heat. McMasters kicked it away. "Nate! James!"

No answer. Flames engulfed the barn, too. And the lean-to. The summer kitchen. Even his toolshed. McMasters shook his head. No lightning strike had done this. "Eugénia!"

The fire mocked him.

"God!" He saw the colt, the one that had come close to pulling him over the edge of the rim a day earlier. The rails to the corral had been knocked to the ground, and the two other horses that McMasters had put in the pen that morning were gone. Only the bay colt remained. In a pool of blood. Its throat had been slit.

McMasters staggered to it. The animal was dead, of course. Closer, he saw the bullet some bastard had put in the colt's head. Behind the animal, however, lay the source of the ungodly amount of blood, and then he understood that the blood did not come from that colt.

He fell on his knees and vomited.

"God." Somehow, he summoned the strength to move closer, to make himself see. He wished to God he hadn't. His voice became weak, hollow. "Ro . . . Rose . . ." Tears and sobs took over, and he fell away. "No. No. Not . . . Rosalee."

A new thought struck terror into him. He shot to his feet. "Bea! Bea!" He dashed to the house. Again, the fire beat him back. He looked to the other pens. Empty. Gates open. Rails knocked aside, strewn this way and that. All the horses gone.

He stumbled back and fell beside the bucket. His fingers clawed the ground, and he noticed something else. Tracks. The tracks of shod horses. Many horses.

McMasters remembered the men he had seen. Riding south toward the road to Globe. Riding hard. Something else caught his eye, and he stared to the hill east of his house . . . or what once had been his home. *A bear? Fleeing the fire. No, not a bear.* He blinked, strained to see. A horse, head down, played out, was making its way up the incline away from the hell that had become McMasters' ranch. He blinked again. *No. Two horses. Make that three.* Not saddled. Played out. Trying to get away from the raging torrent of flame and smoke.

He understood.

Those weren't his horses. Even at that distance, even with his eyeglasses still in his vest pocket, he wouldn't have traded a wooden nickel for any of those mounts.

Suddenly he figured it out. The men he had seen riding across the valley had been there. They had stolen his animals, left theirs behind, killed the colt for no good reason and run the rest of his stock away. *Why?* He shook his head. *You damned fool. They drove the horses they didn't need off so no one could follow them. They had . . .*

He came up, vomited again, fell, and saw something else. Boots. Sticking from the other side of the woodpile. He ran, tripped, and crashed against the cord of pine, leaving splinters in his hand. "God!" Tears blinded him.

McMasters sank to his knees, steeled himself, made his right hand move, and slowly turn the body over. Again, he choked, sobbed, vomited until he had no breakfast, no beer, nothing inside, yet he couldn't stop dry-heaving until he collapsed. When he could breathe, he pushed himself up, but made the mistake of looking at the corpse again.

If not for the boots the figure wore, McMasters never would have recognized the body of what once had been his youngest son. The murderers had shot him in the back of the head with a large-caliber rifle, maybe a Sharps. The exit wound had blown apart the poor kid's face.

"No!" He pushed away, crawled toward the overturned bucket, and stood. Weaving like a drunkard, he made his way to the well and leaned against the stone side. He needed water. Water to think, to survive, but lacked the strength to do anything. He stared at the fire, not seeing it anymore, seeing nothing clearly. His glasses wouldn't help. He smelled the stink again, and wished he were dead.

He remembered.

"War's a hell of a thing."

Colonel Hiram Berdan removed his hat and ran a hand across his hair, curly, but thin and gray on top, then brought it to his sweat-soaked mustache and Dundreary whiskers.

Early September, 1862, it was a few days after the Second Battle of Bull Run. Assigned to detached skirmish duty, Berdan's U.S. Sharpshooters had been pursuing a ragtag group of Rebs.

Cut off from any hope of catching the victorious army that had whipped the Federals at Manassas Junction, the six or seven graycoats had taken shelter in an abandoned boxcar on the Orange & Alexandria Railroad tracks.

Trapped like rats, Berdan called out for the Rebs to surrender. They answered with sporadic musket and revolver fire.

"Show those secesh what a Sharps can do," Berdan ordered.

So McMasters and six others each sent a round through the thin wood of the boxcar.

One of those rounds must have shattered a lantern or something. No one ever knew. But seconds later, they smelled smoke, and saw it—and flame—shooting through the cracks.

"That'll drive those boys out," Berdan said.

But it didn't.

They watched in horror as the flames engulfed the entire car. They heard a few screams, and then nothing but the roar of flames.

But there was a smell of more than pitch wood and scorching iron.

"Damn, McMasters," Corporal Warren Long said as he turned away and hurried to the nearby stream, "I won't ever eat fried beefsteak again."

Pulling himself up, McMasters turned away from the carnage. He found the crank to the well, saw a jug—not his—on the edge. It had to belong to one of the killers, he thought, and must be empty or they would never have left it behind. He reached for it, not to drink, but with hopes that it might offer him some clue, speak to him of its owner, give him someone to tell the law about. But he was clumsy, half-mad with grief, and his hand slammed against the pottery. It went over the edge and fell into the well. He waited for the splash.

Clunk.

He heard that clearly. Confused, he leaned over the stones and peered inside. Wells ran deep in that country, but at that time of day, and with all the flames, he could see the outline, see the reflection of fire in the water. He could see the figure floating in the well.

"Bea?" he called out, wiping away the tears.

No. Not his wife. James. James . . . poor James.

Gagging again, McMasters stumbled away, moving to the fire-ravaged barn. A basket lay near the flames, also smoking, and he saw the dead chickens, the busted eggs. He tried to think. What day was it? Who had egg patrol that morning?

He gasped.

"Eugénia!"

He ran.

The basket burst into flames, almost disintegrating before his eyes. Beside it, however, he saw the shoe, also smoldering. And more tracks—boot prints and the little ditches carved by someone being dragged inside the barn.

"Eugénia." That came out as a whisper.

He knew what burning hay smelled like, and the logs of cedar and pine and other woods. Of burning tack. Burning oats. Burning hell. And he knew the smell that came from the barn, too, for it was the same stench that had sickened him all those years ago after Second Bull Run. It was the same smell that came from what once had been John McMasters's house.

He looked at the carnage. A rafter crashed, sending out a shower of sparks that forced him to cover his face with his arms, driving him backwards.

Last night, on his fiftieth birthday he had made love to his wife in the bedroom. This morning, he had laughed with his two sons and two daughters as they ate hotcakes, bacon, and eggs.

Now . . . all he felt inside was death. He was dead. His family dead. Butchered. Murdered.

Bea, his beloved wife, so radiant, so wonderful, inside that house. As hot as those flames felt, he did not think he would ever find bones. Eugénia? Burned . . . *By God, please, God, please have spared her. Please, tell me that those vermin killed her before . . .*

The screams of the men inside that boxcar in 1862 echoed in his memories.

He moved to the woodpile, but couldn't go there. Not see Nate, not see that face. He wanted to remember that young, loving boy playing the flute. He heard his son's voice, heard him saying *You never talk about it.* He saw him staring at that Medal of Honor, which was now ash . . . now nothing. *Like Bea. Like Eugénia.*

He looked at the dead colt. *Dead.* That would have been a fine animal. He looked at the well, where James lay floating.

He had no rope. No shovels. No pickaxes. He couldn't get James from the well. He couldn't bury Nate or—His eyes found the blood and Rosalee.

John McMasters turned toward the sky. He prayed for God to kill him. Just send one bolt of lightning and end his torment.

The sky showed nothing except eternal blue.

CHAPTER 8

Soot, dirt, and grime blackened his face and hands. He staggered through the middle of the creek, fell to his knees, bent, made himself clean his hands as best as he could. Then made himself drink. He gagged and vomited again, but forced more water down. He had to drink.

With a sigh, he fell onto his buttocks, feeling the coolness of the creek, and looked back through the trees. He saw the ruins, mostly smoke although the flames had not flickered out by any stretch of one's imagination. His hands felt raw, and the water burned.

John McMasters had not burned himself. But he had managed to bury, as best as he could, poor Nate. The boy's young voice had sung out to him clearly. *Can I eat the rest of the cake?* McMasters wanted to smile at that memory, the youthful innocence of his son, but couldn't. All he could see were the mutilated head of his youngest child and the flames and smoke of what had been, for him, paradise.

Until today.

He had buried the brutalized body of Rosalee, too, covering her as best he could with his vest. He had fished the spectacles out of his vest pocket, hooking the wires behind his ears, and finding the most comfortable position on his nose, but avoided looking at his daughter. He had seen enough without the aid of eyeglasses. His wallet he had shoved into one of the deep, mule-ear pockets on his trousers. And his new watch? He slid it into his pants' watch pocket, although he had debated simply tossing it away or burying it with Rosalee. It would just remind him of this day, he briefly thought, but almost immediately understood that no watch, nothing, would he need to remember what had happened, what he had seen.

The vest did not come close to being a shroud, but it was all he had. He had not taken a bedroll on his horse. Riding to Payson and back, he hadn't needed one. Even if he had, McMasters did not know how far the buckskin, fearing the flames and carnage, had run.

No tools. No blankets. Nothing. Not even a funeral, for McMasters could find no words to say. He had just buried two of his children.

Buried? No. Not on that hard earth, not with no tools. He had covered their bodies. Maybe that would protect them from coyotes and wolves.

All the while, he waited for help. Surely someone in Payson or up at one of the sawmills would see the smoke. Black smoke. They had to know that meant someone's home was burning, not pines and shrubs and underbrush. At least from town, they could tell from the distance that it had to be the McMasters place. From one of the sawmills or logging outfits up the Rim Road? Maybe they couldn't see, half-blinded by sawdust or seeing nothing except tall trees. But in Payson? They had to see the smoke. Yet no one came.

Maybe, he thought, they knew it was his place, but also knew how much land he had cleared of timber. He remembered telling Mayor Ash Ashby, Harold Johnson, and a few others at the saloon known as The Dive about how he had cleared that land. Not to sell the timber, although he had, but to protect his place from a raging forest fire. And to clear some good pastureland for his horses, and a hayfield on the other side of the creek. He shook his head. *No.* He hadn't been telling them. Hell, he had been bragging.

"Harold," he remembered saying over a bourbon, "no forest fire, no lightning strike, or some drunk logger who can't crush out his cigarette with his boot heel is going to burn my home down."

Well, it hadn't been a forest fire. It hadn't been caused by lightning or a burning cigarette. But his home . . . his life . . . had been reduced to ash and embers.

Maybe the men in Payson saw the smoke and ignored it. Not that he could blame them. The last thing anyone who lived in those forests wanted to happen was to get caught in a fire. Be . . . burned . . .

He shook his head again, tightened his eyelids closed, and tried to forget those horrible memories of the Orange & Alexandria Railroad. And the stink of burning flesh. Tried to think of September 1862 . . . and of today . . . July—he couldn't place the date, couldn't even recall his birthday—1896.

As if in a trance, McMasters unfastened the knot securing his bandanna. He dipped the new piece of silk—another fiftieth birthday present—in the stream, brought it up to his neck, and felt more cold water running down his back.

Again, he looked through the woods and regretted keeping his spectacles, wishing that he had left them in the vest he had used to cover Rosalee's body. The eye doctor in Globe had done too good a job with the latest pair. John McMasters, even with water dripping down his forehead and running between his eyes and his nose, saw everything.

Look away, he told himself.

But he couldn't.

How long he sat in the cold stream he did not know, but at some point he understood that sitting there would solve nothing. He might even catch pneumonia. Not that he had anything to live for.

Something stepped into the water behind him, and McMasters tensed. His right hand moved down his hip, only to stop. It was 1896. A man no longer needed a six-shooter for protection. The Schofield .45 he carried at times he had left holstered on the elk horn hanging on the wall over his desk.

That thumb-busting revolver had burned in the home. Along with that old nine-gauge shotgun. Along with . . .

His head shook and his eyes tightened again as he waited for the bullet to enter his brain, but no one shot. The foot stepped into the water again. If someone came back to kill him, he was making a hell of a lot of noise. If someone came from Payson to fight the fire, he was a damned sight late.

A snort followed. Then . . . as McMasters understood . . . the sound of an animal slurping water reached his ears. It was not just *any* animal. He knew by the mere sound that it was no bear, no dog, no deer, no wolf.

Slowly, he rose to his feet and turned.

"Easy, fella," he said, and made his way to the buckskin.

The horse lifted its head, water dripping from its nose and mouth, but did not step back or even try to run away. The current carried the reins downstream, toward McMasters. He waded through the water, keeping an eye on the animal's ears—to learn what the animal was thinking. Ears flat against the head and he had a right to be nervous, for that meant the animal was feeling its oats or damned angry. Ear turned back, and the horse might just be bored, but maybe sick. Ears flopping to either side could also mean sick . . . or sleepy.

The buckskin's ears pricked forward. That meant he was alert, but in a good mood—which made sense. He recognized McMasters, probably expected a carrot or a handful of oats. Since the wind blew in the other direction—away from McMasters, the horse, and Payson—and the smoke was dying, the buckskin wouldn't smell anything.

Bending but never taking his eyes off the buckskin, McMasters clutched one rein and then the other, and rose again.

"You drink your fill?" he asked, surprised he could even speak.

The horse nudged him, and McMasters rubbed its neck in a circular motion. He stepped to the side, dropped one rein over the horse's neck, and kept the other rein wrapped twice around his hand. If something spooked the buckskin, he'd be taking John McMasters with him. He opened the saddlebag with one hand, found the sack of grain, and reached inside with his free hand, drawing out enough to satisfy the buckskin.

Happily, it ate.

"You like that, eh, boy?" McMasters had always liked everything about a horse, including a coarse tongue. Maybe that's why he raised them, trained them, and loved them.

Horses were loyal and true. Oh, they were individuals, and you might find a few bad ones, but rarely. Bad horses? Most of those came from bad owners. A good horse did what you asked it to. If it bucked in the morning after you'd just saddled it, he was just feeling his oats a bit and would settle down after a couple jumps. A horse would ride itself to death for its master. A horse did not kill men with telescope-outfitted rifles with double-set triggers from a distance of two hundred, four hundred, even six hundred yards.

"I haven't given you a name, have I, boy?"

The horse dipped its head, drank some more water.

"Berdan." He didn't know why. *Yes, you know exactly why.*

"Come on, Berdan," he said when the buckskin had finished drinking. Leading the horse out of the stream, McMasters knew what he had to do. He had waited too damned long already. Those nine men he had seen crossing the valley toward the Sierra Ancha Range had a damned good head start. But that valley would become rough soon, impassable at some spots, and tough at others for even a mountain goat.

Head to Payson, he told himself. *Find—*

He spit. *Tom Billings, the county sheriff? What the hell would that yellow-backed politician do? The town marshal?*

McMasters shook his head. He had to give them a try. Tom Billings and Tony Jessop were lawmen. And John McMasters had many friends in Payson. They'd help him. They'd form a posse and light out of town, catch those bastards before they got halfway to Globe. Bring them to trial. Hang them.

That's what John McMasters told himself, what he kept telling himself. That's why he did not look at the ruins of his place. He pulled the buckskin, newly christened *Berdan,* out of the creek and looked at the scabbard. He saw the Remington's stock, still gleaming with its newness. The birdshot he had bought from Harold Johnson just a few hours earlier had been shoved inside the saddlebag on the other side of the horse. Birdshot he had planned on letting James and Nate shoot this afternoon.

He liked to keep his long gun—be it the old nine-gauge or that old Henry .44—in the scabbard, butt forward, angled deeply on his near side. Others did not sheath their long guns that way, but it was merely a personal preference. John McMasters liked to swing down from a horse holding his reins in his left hand and pulling rifle or shotgun out with his right. That was one reason. But not the main one.

He didn't like to feel the weapon underneath his leg, and he didn't like the way a long gun might rub against a horse's leg, producing sores. He stared at the Remington's stock. A beautiful shotgun, but he longed for that Henry. He shook his head. No, not with his eyesight. That's why he hadn't left the ranch with that old rimfire long gun in years. That's why Bea had given him a shotgun for his birthday. One didn't have to have great vision to fire a shotgun, especially one that shot as true as everyone said an 1894 Remington did.

As he stepped around to mount the buckskin on the high side, the New York accent of Colonel Hiram Berdan came to him clearly.

"You were born to fire a Sharps, young man. I would hate to compete against you in a contest of marksmanship, soldier. I would hate to come under the sights of your rifle."

"Not anymore, Colonel," McMasters heard himself answering as he swung into the saddle.

The old .44-caliber Henry had been burned with everything in his home. But that .52-caliber Sharps that he had carried during the War to Preserve the Union? That he had sold as soon as he had been mustered out of the Army, no longer with the First U.S. Sharpshooters or even the Second but with the Sixth Wisconsin as both of Berdan's "snakes-in-the-grass" outfits had been disbanded by February of '65. A Sharps, especially one used by a member of the U.S. Sharpshooters, still equipped with a long telescopic scope for added accuracy, had commanded a premium price in 1865.

It had bought John McMasters tickets as far west as he could travel. Not to Wisconsin. He could no longer see himself returning to Manitowoc, building schooners or clippers or fishing all across Lake Michigan. The money had taken him as far away from Virginia as St. Louis, Missouri, where he had drunk almost enough whiskey to forget about the men he had killed in the war. Most of those men had never even seen him taking aim, nor heard the crack of the rifle that had killed them.

He tugged the reins, and Berdan responded. The horse climbed the bank, the little hill, and McMasters leaned forward, ducking underneath the low branches until man and beast had reached the trail that led from the Rim Road to his home—what had been his home, anyway.

John McMasters did not look back.

He could still smell smoke. He did not need to look back. Never, even if he lived longer than Methuselah, would he ever forget what he had seen that afternoon. He came to the Rim Road and turned Berdan toward Payson. The sun, to his surprise, he could still see, but it would be sinking fast. Still he felt suddenly warm from the far-reaching rays, and when he kicked the buckskin into a lope, he knew the wind would dry his clothes by the time he reached Payson.

A lope, then a gallop . . . but not too hard, not too fast. McMasters had to save the buckskin.

Oh, he planned on getting the law behind him. Let Sheriff Billings or Marshal Jessop deputize a posse, do everything legal. But when that posse rode out of Payson in an hour, maybe even less, John McMasters knew that he would be riding with them.

Hell, he would be leading the damned posse.

CHAPTER 9

The first person he saw in Payson was the Swiss clockmaker and watch salesman. Noah Brandenberger was coming out of the little café on the edge of town. Reining in the buckskin, John McMasters called out to the merchant.

Brandenberger turned as he stepped off the boardwalk to cross the street. His mouth opened, and stayed open, no words coming out as his blue eyes widened.

"Have you seen Sheriff Billings?" McMasters asked.

The old Swiss gentleman must have gone into shock. Not that McMasters could blame him.

He thought *I must look like Death himself.*

Even that dip in the creek that ran alongside his house—or what once had been a house—had likely not removed all the grime, the soot, and all that death. Certainly, his hands had not been cleansed . . . and his shirt was ripped and peppered with holes caused by embers from the inferno.

"Billings?" McMasters repeated.

"I . . . I . . . think . . ." The old man glanced toward the center of town.

"Thanks." McMasters guided Berdan away, trying to find his composure, steady his nerves, and control all that boiled in his stomach and chest. His heart felt as though it might explode at any second.

As he rode past Todd's Livery, a timid voice called his name. McMasters wheeled around, hoping to find a friend, or even the fool sheriff, but let out a sigh of disappointment to see Whit Rogers standing in front of his mule.

"My . . . word . . ." Rogers stepped back toward the picket building.

"Have you seen Tom Billings?" McMasters made himself ask.

"Ummmm . . ." Rogers's head shook.

Depending on whom you asked in Payson, Whit Rogers was either a simpleton, a tramp, or just plain lazy. He slept in the woods or inside a lean-to or in an empty stall in the livery, in exchange for mucking out stalls. He might earn a few bits sweeping out a store, but most of his money came from selling kindling, which he gathered in the mountains and led down to town on his mule. Nobody even knew if Whit Rogers actually owned that mule.

Seeing McMasters, Rogers looked about as startled, as frightened, as Noah Brandenberger had.

McMasters had no time for conversation.

"I'll find him." He slapped the reins to go.

"I saw . . . some . . . men."

Turning back in his saddle, McMasters stared through the skeletal bum in the straw hat.

Rogers's Adam's apple bobbed. "Thought," he managed to say, "I ought to warn . . . to . . . ummmm . . . tell you."

McMasters tensed. "Tell me."

The tramp gestured toward the Rim Road. "Comin' down the hills with—" He nodded at the mule. "Had some sticks to sell." He wet his lips, paused, fearing how much he should say.

"Tell me." No trace of friendliness could be detected in McMasters's voice.

"They was lookin' fer horses. Lookin' fer yer place."

Blood rushed to McMasters's head, and his heart thundered against his chest. He made himself swallow. "When?"

"Few hours back."

"How many?"

Rogers's head shook. "Ain't rightly certain." His brow furrowed. "Can't quite recollect. Six. Seven. Maybe a dozen." His head shook. "Maybe not quite that many."

"Nine." McMasters remembered counting the men as they rode across the valley's floor.

"Could be." Rogers looked away, turned back. "I . . . well . . ." He sighed and found some strength to face McMasters's hard eyes again. "I started . . . well, I sorta tol' 'em where yer place is . . ." Quickly, he added. "But then I tol' 'em somethin' dif'rent."

"Why?" The word came out like a pistol shot. McMasters tried to steady himself. "Why? Did . . . something bother you . . . about how they . . . looked?"

Again, the tramp swallowed. "They said they rode fer the Hashknife."

"And?"

"Didn't look like no cowpunchers. Horses all played out. Said they'd been deputized. Was on the trail . . ."

McMasters waited.

"Of Moses Butcher."

Butcher. McMasters thought about Bloody Zeke The Younger, one of the prisoners Dan Kilpatrick and Royal Andersen were hauling to Yuma. Moses Butcher was the worst killer on the frontier.

"They said Butcher'd robbed a bank somewheres . . . ummmm . . . Holbrook, Flagstaff, Winslow . . . some place like that. And they was chasin' him and his men."

No. McMasters knew a posse coming from the north would have stopped in Payson for remounts. Not at Todd's flea-bitten trap, but one of the good livery stables in town.

McMasters swung off his horse, clenching his fists.

"And?" he demanded.

Whit Rogers backed against the picket wall of Todd's Livery, almost falling through it, but he didn't have enough muscle or weight to even break through the flimsy walls.

"Well . . . when this feller said *Butcher* . . . well . . . well, one of 'em just looked like . . . like 'em posters I've seen of Butcher."

"You"—McMasters spaced out the words carefully—"think you sent Moses Butcher and his killers to my place?"

Never a dark-skinned man, Whit Rogers turned into a ghost. "I . . . I tol' 'em somethin' dif'rent . . . but"—he let out a heavy sigh—"thought you oughts to know. 'Cause iffen they's ridin' up the Rim Road, wouldn't be hard to . . . find yer . . . ranch."

McMasters took two steps toward the vagrant before he stopped himself, whirled, quickly grabbed the reins to the buckskin and made himself swing into the saddle. He did not thank Whit Rogers for the information, could not even look at the man. He rode toward the town's center, desperately trying to find the sheriff, the town marshal, or anyone, but mostly to get away from Whit Rogers.

The fool had sent Moses Butcher to McMasters' ranch. The fool had damned his family to death. Had McMasters taken one more step toward Whit Rogers, he knew what he would have done. He would have killed the man. Beaten him to death with his hands, which began turning white from the force with which he gripped the reins.

He urged the buckskin into a lope. Mayor Ash Ashby stood next to Tom Billings on the boardwalk in front of the Hotel Payson—the owner bragged that *Hotel Payson* sounded classier than the *Payson Hotel.* They were talking to the Reverend Rutledge and even Payson's town marshal, Tony Jessop.

Seeing them, McMasters maneuvered around the independently run stagecoach parked in front where tenders were hitching a fresh team of mules onto the mud wagon. He reined up and slid from the saddle before the horse had come to a complete stop.

"Sheriff!" he snapped, stumbling to his knees in the still-muddy street.

"Good Lord!" Ash Ashby staggered against the hotel door, rattling the window.

"John, what's happened?" Tony Jessop cried out.

"My"—McMasters felt one of the liverymen lifting him to his feet—"family." When the young black man let go of his arm, McMasters had to grip the hotel's wooden column for support.

"Dead," he managed to say.

"You're kidding." Seeing McMasters' glare, Sheriff Tom Billings took a few steps back. Likely, he saw the same thing in John McMasters' eyes that Whit Rogers had spotted a few minutes earlier.

The Reverend Wilson Rutledge, in his maple-coated Southern accent, began praying for the souls of the blessed departed.

"John," Jessop pleaded. "Tell us . . . everything."

McMasters told them. Trying to control his emotions and not leave out anything, he described seeing the fire.

"We didn't see any smoke," Ashby said. "Did you, Tony?"

Jessop shook his head.

The preacher began another prayer and asked the others to join him. Most removed their hats, but only Rutledge prayed. The others looked across the street at the mountains.

Stupidly, McMasters looked back toward his place, too. Maybe . . . maybe no one *had* seen the smoke. From there, smoke would've been hard to see, and the wind had been blowing. His head shook. It did not matter. Nothing mattered anymore. Nothing except justice . . . revenge.

"I found Nate. Shot dead. And . . . Rosalee." His voice cracked. "She was . . . killed . . . too."

"Good God," Ashby cried.

"Heavenly Father, please let us all awaken from this nightmare," the preacher said. "Your will be done."

"Eugénia?" Jessop asked timidly. "And . . . Bea?"

"Burned. I suspect. The—" His head shook savagely, and he tried to block away those images, the pungent reminder of burning flesh.

"Oh, God," the preacher wailed, "pray that those are the only flames those poor children and blessed woman will feel. Tell me, sir, that their souls were saved."

McMasters looked away from Rutledge. His eyes locked on Sheriff Billings.

"It was . . . Moses Butcher."

Having finished hitching the mules to the mud wagon, the livery workers quickly retired to the stables across the street . . . likely to spread the gossip. A few other townsmen gathered around, along with the stagecoach's messenger and driver.

"How . . . can you be sure?" Jessop asked.

"Whit Rogers," McMasters said. "He told me."

"Whit Rogers?" Those were about the only words Sheriff Tom Billings said.

It did not occur to McMasters until later that the county sheriff had not asked one question or even uttered more than one or two words.

"John"—Mayor Ashby shook his head—"you can't believe anything that reprobate has to say. Why, Whit Rogers is crazy as—"

"Stop." McMasters cut Ashby off, explaining what the tramp and peddler of kindling had just told him about the strangers on the Rim Road asking for directions to his place, about the Butcher Gang having robbed the bank up north in Flagstaff, Winslow, or Holbrook.

"We haven't heard about any robbery." Ashby looked at Marshal Jessop. "Have we?"

"No telegraph wire runs directly from Winslow, Holbrook, or Flag," the stagecoach's messenger said. "Have to run to Verde. Or up from Phoenix."

"And," Jessop said, "I haven't been to my office since after breakfast."

"That worthless Stevenson at the telegraph office wouldn't know better than to track you down with a wire of that importance." Ashby shook his head.

Why are these fools just standing around? Bantering about a telegraph operator?

McMasters quickly explained about seeing those riders cutting across the valley, heading south toward Globe. Nine riders.

"That," Ashby pointed out, "doesn't mean it was the Butcher Gang."

"I don't give a damn if it was William McKinley or William Jennings Bryant or any of their gangs!" McMasters roared, referring to the recent Republican and Democratic nominees for the upcoming presidential election.

"Easy, John," Jessop pleaded. "What else can you tell us?"

They had stolen his horses, McMasters managed to say, turned loose what they did not find, killed his wife and all four of his children, even butchered a young colt for spite.

"Riding south," he repeated. "Toward Globe."

"Rough terrain," the messenger said, and the stagecoach driver's head nodded in agreement. "I expect they'll cut to the road as quick as possible."

"Maybe not if it's Moses Butcher," said Dixon Stuart, who ran a billiard hall across the street. "From what

I've read about him, he'll do whatever the law won't expect."

"If he robbed a bank, he'll head for Mexico," the stagecoach driver said.

"Yep," the messenger agreed.

"I cannot believe I'm hearing this," Ashby said. "There hasn't been any blood spilled near Payson in years. None of consequence, anyhow."

McMasters roared.

He looked into the faces of civilized men, men of peace, men of 1896. None of those, he thought, had even fired a weapon during the Civil War. None had seen the bodies of brave men in blue and gray littering fields so thick you could walk two hundred yards and never touch the ground. They were too young, and lacked enough guts. Hell, for decades John McMasters hadn't told the truth to anyone who asked about his Medal of Honor. Hadn't told what the War had been actually like. He had always said that he did not know. That he wasn't a real soldier, not on the front lines like Royal Andersen or others who had fought so hard for so long. But he had been there. He had seen Seven Days . . . Mechanicsville . . . Malvern Hill . . . Second Bull Run . . . Antietam . . . Fredericksburg . . . Chancellorsville . . . Gettysburg . . . Wilderness . . . Spotsylvania . . . Cold Harbor . . . Petersburg. And after the First and Second U.S. Sharpshooters disbanded, he had been with the Sixth Wisconsin and Royal Andersen at Weldon Railroad and Five Forks.

The God-fearing men in front of him were peace-loving townsmen. They had not scratched a living for years on failed homesteads across the west before landing in northern Arizona Territory. Hell, they could not even believe what McMasters was telling them.

They might think I have lost all reason, that I've gone crazier than Whit Rogers.

And maybe I have.

Certainly, none had just seen his ranch, his way of life, burned to the ground. None had comc across thc body of his youngest son with the front of his head blown off from a point-blank shot. Seen his daughter . . . his daughter . . . his daughter . . . At that horrible image, his head shook once again.

The men on the boardwalk of Payson babbled about this and that. They pointed this way and that way, at each other, off toward the Rim Road and the rising hills. They had been too busy with their lives to have even noticed smoke from the hills and could not accept everything that John McMasters had told them.

"The Lord is my shepherd," the preacher was saying.

"This can't be true," Ash Ashby said. "This just cannot be happening."

"There must be some mistake," Tony Jessop offered.

The messenger bit off a mouthful of chewing tobacco and passed the quid to his driver.

"What are y'all doing?" McMasters tightened his fists again. "There's no time for talk. Senseless words." He pointed directly at Sheriff Tom Billings. "We need to form a posse."

Chapter 10

"Now, not so fast there, John." Tom Billings had found his voice again. "We need to do this by the book."

McMasters swore. The Reverend Rutledge stopped his prayer and glared.

"Mayor"—doing his best to ignore McMasters, the county sheriff turned to Ash Ashby—"first thing you ought to do is ride out to John's place."

"Me?" The mayor managed to swallow.

"You're the duly appointed deputy sheriff for this region. It's your job."

"What about *your* job?" Marshal Jessop said.

"I have an appointment in Globe. But don't worry, if that is the Butcher Gang, and if those vermin are indeed heading south toward Globe, I'll get up a posse when I'm in the county seat and will meet up with those villains."

McMasters could not believe what he was hearing.

Obviously, the sheriff was coming up with the plan as he spoke. His head bobbed in excitement as he turned to the preacher, the messenger, and the stagecoach driver. "We'll catch those swine in a vise. You boys from the north, and my posse from the south."

Like, McMasters thought savagely, *you'll ever leave your office once you're back in Globe.*

"This talk isn't catching the sons of bitches that butchered my family!" McMasters roared.

"We'll catch them, John," Billings said. "I promise you."

McMasters spit and shook his head, thinking he never should have stopped in town.

"We need to get going," the sheriff told the stagecoach operators. "Get to Globe as quickly as possible. Don't worry. Justice will prevail." He practically sprang into the mud wagon, and the driver and messenger glanced at each other nervously before turning back to stare at the mayor and the town marshal. None dared to look at John McMasters.

When nobody said anything or barely moved, the two men climbed aboard the stagecoach. The messenger picked up the shotgun, opened the breech to check the loads, and the driver released the brake, gathered the lines, and whipped the mules. With one passenger, the wagon crept along the main street, turned, and picked up speed as it moved south.

"I guess—" Ashby hesitated. "Reverend, I think it's best if you accompany me to John's . . . to . . . well . . . I think a man of God . . ."

"Of course." The preacher managed to look at McMasters. His grim smile indicated that the ranch owner was forgiven for his coarse language. "We will see that Bea and your children get Christian burials, son."

"You do that." McMasters waited for more.

"Tony . . ." Ashby began.

The town lawman almost shook himself out of his boots.

"Can you—"

"I have no jurisdiction outside of the Payson town limits," Jessop interrupted the mayor. "You know that, Ash. There's nothing I can do."

Ashby mustered up a modicum of nerve.

"You can gather some men, Tony. That you can do for me. The Reverend Rutledge and I will ride out to John's place. You send some men—anyone who can ride, knows the country, or can pull a trigger. Maybe—" His eyes brightened and he turned to McMasters. Unable to keep his voice from squeaking, he said, "John, have you thought about sending word to Commodore Perry?"

"It's not his jurisdiction, either," McMasters said.

"Well . . . yes . . . I suppose . . . yes . . . silly of me. Do you wish to ride out with us, John? I mean . . . I know . . . well . . . what you've already seen . . . but—"

"You go on," McMasters said. To his surprise, his voice had turned calm. Glancing down, he saw that his fists had unclenched. His arms no longer shook. His heart and breathing had returned to normal. He felt almost calm . . . but his mind raced.

The mayor and preacher hurried around the corner, leaving McMasters alone with the town lawman.

"John," Jessop managed, "you know I really want to help."

"Yeah." McMasters glanced across the street.

"By thunder, I can't believe this is happening. For God's sake, this is 1896. We're civilized. This—"

"It's happening," McMasters said.

"John," Jessop tried again, "I'd go after them. You know I would. But I just don't have the . . . the . . ."

"Jurisdiction."

"Right. And with Ashby gone, and Billings gone, someone has to protect Payson. I mean"—Jessop's face paled—"what if . . . Butcher comes back here?"

I was a fool to think anything else could have happened. I've given Moses Butcher too much of a head start. I need—

"What you need is a U.S. marshal," Jessop said.

"A tracker," McMasters said, their words overlapping.

"Your son . . . Rosalee's . . . um . . . well . . . Dan . . . Dan Kilpatrick. He just left a few hours ago." Jessop looked at the buckskin. "Maybe he could help."

McMasters was already turning away, moving back to Berdan, and removing the saddlebags. "You better get your posse together, Tony," he said without looking back as he slung the saddlebags over his shoulder and began crossing the muddy street. "And make sure my children, my wife, get a proper burial."

He heard Jessop speaking, but did not catch the words. His boots hit the boardwalk and he moved past three buildings, his right hand finding the knob, pushing the door open.

"John McMasters!" Harold Johnson grinned as he lowered the Remington .44-caliber revolver he was cleaning. "You already out of birdshot?"

The smile vanished when he realized the wretchedness of stink on McMasters's clothes. He dropped the .44 on his worktable, removed his apron, and wiped his hands on his trousers as he moved around the counter.

"Good God, John, what has happened?"

McMasters was not about to explain everything again.

"I need a few things, Harold." He pulled out his pocket watch, the solid gold repeater, and dropped it on the counter's hard, glossy top. "Starting with"—he pointed at the boxes shelved behind the cash register—"buckshot."

He figured to trade the watch for ammunition.

But Harold Johnson, once he heard briefly what McMasters told him, refused.

"You pay me when you get back, John."

McMasters thought grimly *If I get back.*

He filled one saddlebag with buckshot shells, keeping the two boxes of birdshot he had bought that morning—a lifetime ago. Birdshot might come in handy for any quails or small game he happened across. He would have to eat. He knew it would take days . . . or longer . . . to catch up with Moses Butcher.

There was the gun belt and Colt—a .45-caliber with a seven-and-a-half-inch barrel and one-piece walnut grips. Johnson guessed that the weapon had been manufactured somewhere around 1877 but swore it shot true.

"I don't know how I can thank you for all this," McMasters said as he shook hands.

"Thank me by killing those bastards." Johnson did not blink as he spoke. "And come back in one piece."

"I'll try."

"I'd go with you, John . . ." He sighed and pointed at his right leg.

It was wooden. He had lost it at Chancellorsville, which always made McMasters feel remorse. Johnson had never said how he had been wounded, and Mc-

Masters knew not to ask. It was bad enough to know that while serving in the Confederate army, Johnson had been maimed in a battle in which McMasters had been firing from afar. He didn't know how he would feel if he learned that Johnson had lost his right leg to a .52-caliber round fired from a Yankee sniper's rifle.

Quickly, McMasters walked out of the shop, buckling on the gun rig and again crossing the street.

He remembered Colonel Berdan's words from early in the war. *"Eat when you can. As a sniper, you never know when you might be able to eat again. If you move for even a bit of hardtack or jerky, you might give away your position. Eat when you can."*

McMasters looked at the café, but ignored it. Eating would take time, and if he walked in looking as he did, he would panic the patrons, or at least spoil their early supper. He entered the neighboring general store.

The merchant, a newcomer to Payson, showed no generosity. In fact, he wasn't sure he wanted the Waltham repeater that Johnson had refused to take, but eventually the general store owner relented. Or maybe it was just how rough and deadly McMasters looked.

He piled supplies on the counter.

An extra canteen. A bedroll. Knife. Beef jerky, chewing tobacco, and peppermint sticks to curb his appetite or at least keep him in the saddle. New clothes. Changing in the back room, he found a washbasin, and scrubbed off most of the dirt and grime. The soap burned his hands and fingers, but those scars would heal, and the water and soap would help. Halfway human—at least in appearance—he reentered the store and gathered a war bag, just a canvas sack to slip over his horn or secure behind the cantle. To the counter, he added coffee, a cup, a spoon, and a fork. A rain slicker. At the last moment, he saw a compass, and tossed it on top of two extra scarves and a spare shirt and two extra pairs of socks. He also found a hat that would work and a pair of binoculars. Behind a glass cabinet was a Remington over-and-under derringer, and got it, as well, with one box of .41-caliber shells. A hideaway gun might come in handy. He would leave it in the saddlebags.

It would have totaled a right large sum, but nowhere near as much as Bea had spent on that sold gold watch at Brandenberger's.

The store owner seemed to have remorse. He opened the hunter's case and heard the music. He felt the heft of the piece.

"This is worth too much. I should give you more."

"I have all I need," McMasters said.

"But—"

"What good does a watch do? It's nothing but a reminder of time."

The clerk shook his head, and McMasters accepted a sack of grain for Berdan and some more jerky and beans. He also took fifty dollars in greenbacks.

Still the store man knew he had not paid McMasters enough.

"Just wait one more minute, sir. I have something else that might make this all a fair trade."

McMasters waited till the man walked into the backroom. Then he gathered all of his plunder, and walked back onto the boardwalk. He wasn't going to wait any longer.

Hurriedly, he stuffed his supplies into the war bag,

wrapped the extra shirt and socks inside the bedroll, and fastened it behind the saddle's cantle. He looked up and down the street. No sign of the mayor. No sign of Marshal Jessop. But he could feel the stares of the men and women of Payson.

Maybe he had too much stuff from the store. If he were a smart man, he would have bartered at Todd's ramshackle livery stables for a pack mule . . . but a mule would slow him down. Hell, he had too much already. The ammunition and hardware he carried would weigh down Berdan. Besides, he might see Whit Rogers at Todd's livery and, fearing his own deadly temper, John McMasters did not want to see that tramp again.

He could hear whispers. See lips moving. See an occasional finger point in his direction.

Word spread fast on the streets. It would soon reach the stores, the homes, and maybe even that damned newspaper editor. McMasters wanted to be out of Payson. He wanted to push the buckskin into a good run. A tumbleweed wagon hauling prisoners would not make good time.

That was his first stop. He had to find Dan Kilpatrick first. Get Kilpatrick and Royal Andersen on his side. Get them to ride with him. The way he had it figured, that was his only chance.

He opened the saddlebags, broke open a box of buckshot, and slid two shells into the twin barrels of the 1894 Remington. The weapon felt different, like it was part of him. He placed his thumb on the flat-ribbed switch and put the twelve-gauge into its SAFE mode indicated by the engraved word above the switch and just below the lever that opened the breech.

He slid the shotgun back inside the scabbard.

The merchant stepped outside the store in a hurry. Ignoring the clerk and the long rifle that he held, McMasters swung into the saddle. He recognized the weapon and knew that it might indeed even out the trade. It was a buffalo rifle, without one of those telescopic sights. With his eyeglasses on, he might have been able to line up a target . . . but he did not know how long he would be able to keep his spectacles.

The .45 Colt revolver and the twelve-gauge Remington shotgun would do. And the .41-caliber derringer, if it came to that.

McMasters turned the buckskin around in a hurry, eased the horse down the street, and turned south. He saw the ruts made by the stagecoach hauling the county sheriff back to the comforts and safety of his office in Globe. McMasters hoped he did not find that mud wagon on his ride south. Hell, he might let Tom Billings have both barrels.

Out of town, he spurred the buckskin into a trot. He would keep Berdan at a trot for a while, then into a lope, and back into a walk. The horse was all he had . . . for now.

Be smart, he told himself. *Find Kilpatrick. Find the tumbleweed wagon.* That had to be first. Maybe it would work out . . . maybe.

The wind blew into his face. Darkness would come shortly. He had to cover as much ground as he could. The fork in the road came directly, and McMasters knew which way to go. Not to Globe, though that was likely the way Moses Butcher and his black-hearted bastards had gone.

John McMasters turned the buckskin on the road to Phoenix and gave the horse more rein.

Again, Colonel Berdan's words reached him. The memory came from later in the war, Mine Run in Orange County, Virginia, if he recalled correctly. A little set-to that no one remembered. That late in 1863, in the early months of winter, and for such a stupid little fight, it wasn't much of a skirmish. He didn't remember much of the fight, but he would never forget Berdan's fire and brimstone sermon, for it did not match the nature of the quiet inventor and engineer.

On that November day, a few months before he resigned his commission, Berdan had quoted from The Book of Revelation.

"*'And I looked, and behold a pale horse: and his name that sat on him was Death, and Hell followed with him. And power was given unto them over the fourth part of the earth, to kill with sword, and with hunger, and with death, and with the beasts of the earth.'*"

The buckskin was pale. John McMasters was Death.

Chapter 11

The damned fool driver hit every hole on the road, and Bloody Zeke The Younger knew that son of a bitch done it a-purpose. But that was all right. Just fine. Those hills and the road were bad enough to make the going mighty slow. Took more time, Bloody Zeke knew . . . and time meant life. Besides, the black hat he wore protected his head just a little bit from slamming against the iron bars of the tumbleweed wagon.

One of the wheels squeaked. In fact, that noisy racket irritated the deputy marshal so much, he kept stopping, having the old coot of a driver get out the grease bucket and slop on more of that junk . . . which quieted things for a short while. Once they got on the road again and had moved on a bit, the noise started up, sounding even louder. At that rate, they'd never make it to the Yuma Territorial Prison.

That was just fine and dandy with Bloody Zeke The Younger.

As the wagon moved along, the squeaking axle had a harmony. The chains rattled. The wind blew. The piss pot in the center of the wagon already stank to high heaven. And they had been on the road only a few hours. Two weeks it would take to get to Yuma. Maybe a little more. Perhaps less. No, not any less. Not as long as that fool of a deputy kept stopping the wagon.

Of course, Bloody Zeke had no plans to return to that hell some folks called a prison.

He looked across the wagon.

Sitting across from him at the rear of the wagon, the redheaded bitch had shown some brains. She had a pillow, probably from some fancy whorehouse, that she used to rest her head against, protecting herself from busting her skull against the bars.

Brains, he thought, *and a good looker.* He imagined what her flesh looked like beneath that green calico. The dress was dirty as all hell, but not full enough for her to be wearing a petticoat. He figured her body was white as a baby's bottom.

Her green eyes locked on him.

Bloody Zeke grinned.

"Ain't you gonna take a piss?"

Beside him, the old Rebel in patched britches laughed.

The woman spit in his direction.

"Feisty." Bloody Zeke laughed. "I like that."

She looked away, but only briefly.

The colored giant chained next to her said, "Shut up."

Bloody Zeke turned toward the big cuss who was chained near the front of the wagon, but on the same side as the redhead. He wore no hat, just a red silk bandanna tied across his forehead like some old Apache. Only this man—Alamo Carter he had heard the law dogs call him—was no Apache. His head was shaved bald, a big head, and he was blacker than Bloody Zeke's soul. He wore old cavalry boots, canvas trousers, and a muslin shirt that had no sleeves.

Torn off, Bloody Zeke figured, to show off those muscles. He had never seen anyone with that much muscle. The Negro was a giant. Six-foot-four, maybe even taller. It was hard to tell sitting in such a cramped, miserable jail on wheels.

"You talkin' to me, boy?" Bloody Zeke asked.

"You show respect for the lady," the black giant said.

Bloody Zeke laughed. He nodded at the redhead. "I'd take off my hat, ma'am, but, well, they chained my hands to the floor. Along with my legs. I sure did not mean to offend you, honey."

He faced the Negro again.

"That suit you, son?"

The giant's eyes narrowed. Bloody Zeke spit at him, and laughed again.

"Hey," called the Reb chained beside Zeke. "Hey, Yank!"

The driver of the wagon, that tall drink of water wearing the bluecoat kepi, said without taking his eyes off the mules, "What do you want?"

"We needs another slop bucket," the Reb said.

"You've filled one already?"

"Nah." The Reb cackled like a coyote. "But that one's for white men and the pret' lil thing. You ain't lettin' him piss or do-do in our bucket."

"Do-do?" Bloody Zeke turned to the Reb.

The old-timer grinned as he looked at Bloody Zeke. "I's watchin' my language in front of the lady."

"Shut the hell up," the driver said.

The old Reb laughed. So did the gambler, who was chained next to the Reb. The Mexican, next to the gambler and at the front of the wagon, said nothing. Hell, he was probably still asleep. Maybe dead.

"I'm serious, Yank," the Reb said.

"If he and Bloody Zeke have to piss or crap, they'll do it in their pants!" the driver yelled back. "Now shut up or I'll shut you up."

All except the woman had been shackled to the wagon's hard bed, but only two of the male prisoners had their wrist manacles also fastened to the bed—Bloody Zeke and Alamo Carter, the big black killer.

Bloody Zeke figured, if they had chained her leg irons to the floor, she couldn't relieve herself.

The driver was right. Chained to the floor, Bloody Zeke and Alamo Carter could barely move.

Bloody Zeke brought up his wrist irons as far as they could go. He grinned across the wagon, first at the woman, and then at the colored giant.

"See . . . they think we're the most dangersome of the whole bunch. And I think, they's right."

The black, one mean, uppity giant, glared again before turning away, leaning his hard head against the hard bars, and closed his eyes.

That satisfied Bloody Zeke real fine. The woman didn't look at him, probably wouldn't look at him. The Reb—his name was Emory something or other—shifted, kicking his legs out, rattling those chains again, trying to find a comfortable spot to catch a little sleep. Bloody Zeke breathed easier. The mean, cadaverous Reb wore a patch over his right eye, so he wouldn't be able to get a good look at what Bloody Zeke was about to do. On the other side of the Reb, those two other prisoners—the gambler in the fancy vest and the burly bean-eater—would not have a clear view, either . . . as long as none of them got up to use the piss bucket.

Zeke looked at the leg chains. He'd never be able to twist his way out of those, securely fastened iron on iron as they were.

The wrist manacles were a different story. The rig Zeke's wrists were fastened to wasn't that strong. The tumbleweed wagon wasn't designed for wrist manacles. The fool deputy marshal had merely asked that old codger driving the wagon to nail a big U-shaped pin to the floor.

"To disillusion Zeke and Carter from trying anything," the law dog had said.

Zeke pulled the bracelets that shackled his wrists as tight as possible, bit his lip, and began pulling at the iron pin that held them to the floor. He was not a big man—especially compared to that bald-headed cuss sitting on the other side of the wagon—but he did not lack strength in that wiry frame of his.

Just a pull here and there, and the pin would come up.

The wagon kept jostling, that wheel kept squeaking, and no one paid any mind to Bloody Zeke The Younger.

Fools did not know how hard it was to disillusion Bloody Zeke The Younger about anything.

He had his own illusions. First, he'd catch one of the law dogs unaware. Easy enough. He figured men who wore badges were stupid. Get him in a headlock and make the other lawman set him loose. Then he'd be on his way. He'd pin the law dogs inside the tumbleweed wagon, and let the big colored boy and the others beat them to death, most likely, as Bloody Zeke took the deputy's horse and rode away.

He'd leave the prisoners inside the wagon. As hot as the weather got, they all might be dead by the time some passer-by came across the wagon. But the redhead? Well, maybe Bloody Zeke would take her along. For a little bit. Then he'd leave her in an arroyo or behind some tree or cactus and go after Moses Butcher.

The mere thought of Butcher made Bloody Zeke work harder on freeing the wrist chains from the big U-shaped pin.

He drifted in from New Mexico Territory and found himself drinking down in the border town of Nogales when Butcher entered the same saloon. Situated on the Mexican side and the Arizona side, the town never minded what crimes anybody had committed in any town other than Nogales, so it was always a safe place to stay if you had a price on your head. No bounty hunter was crazy enough to go to Nogales. Wanted men would protect one another from some low-down cur who'd take a man in for money.

After a few bottles of tequila, Moses Butcher told Bloody Zeke about a little bank up in Tucson. Not much of a haul, except on two Saturdays a year. Then the bank held $50,000 . . . and one of those Saturdays was coming up in about a week.

"A piece of cake to rob," Moses Butcher said. The bankers never wanted to call attention to just how much they had in the vaults on those two Saturdays, so they never hired any extra guards. Just kept business as usual. "A cinch," *he said.*

Just drunk enough to buy that bag of horse apples, Bloody

Zeke left Nogales with Moses Butcher, following him to his hideout in the Superstition Mountains. And then they rode into Tucson.

If the Gadsden American Bank did not hire any extra guards it was because it did not need any more than the dozen that patrolled the building—in front, on the roof, across the street, and in the alleys. Oh, they let Butcher and the boys inside fair enough. Maybe to give them a sporting chance. But when the last of the bank robbers stepped onto the street and headed for their horses, things got noisier than the Fourth of July.

The two kids hired to watch the street and horses got blown out of their saddles. Moses Butcher took one bullet in his chest or belly, and two other gang members fell dead in the street before Butcher, his kid brother, and some of the other veterans made it out alive. Bloody Zeke carried Butcher on the back of his horse.

They didn't stop until they reached an old mission west of the Santa Cruz. The one folks called The White Dove. Mission San Xavier del Bac. Butcher had told his pards that fresh horses would be waiting for the gang there, but when Bloody Zeke dismounted and ran to the corral, he found only burros. When he turned around, he saw Moses Butcher clutching his bleeding belly with one hand and a .44 Remington in the other.

Oh, Butcher swore that some son of a bitch betrayed them, that there were supposed to be horses waiting, but the dust cloud off to the north meant a posse was coming and that they had a better chance of reaching the border if they didn't share a horse.

"Stay here," Butcher told Bloody Zeke. "Ask the padre for asylum. They got to give it to ya. We'll split up the money later. But first . . . hand over your gun belt to Milt Hanks."

Once that last transaction had been handled, Butcher led his boys down the trail to Nogales—the Mexican side of the town.

That story about asking a priest for asylum, that it would have to be granted? That didn't happen. Maybe . . . just maybe . . . a good Mexican padre would have done what he was supposed to do, but Bloody Zeke wasn't given a good Mexican padre. He found only one . . . who had known Bloody Zeke's daddy, and who was old enough to remember the stories of a ten-year-old girl ravaged, murdered, and strung to a saguaro cactus.

The priest gladly turned Bloody Zeke over to the law.

The take was not fifty grand. Only thirty. Or so things had been sworn to in the trial a month later.

Sentenced to twenty years for armed robbery in the territorial prison, he served one of those years, plus two months, then escaped. Instead of heading south to the nearby border, he foolishly made his way north.

In his cups, Butcher had told Bloody Zeke a lot, explaining why he planned on heading north a bit after the Tucson robbery, and where he liked to hide out.

The law captured Bloody Zeke near Apache Junction. Chained him up. Sent him to jail to await the tumbleweed wagon. Rode all the way to Payson, chained in with the black bastard, the woman, the Reb, and the cardsharper before the law dogs had picked up their final prisoner, the bean-eater, in Payson.

The pin came out, rattling on the floor, shaking Zeke from his reverie. No one noticed. Carefully, he slid his hands over, picked up the pin, considered it for a moment, and then slipped it underneath his left boot heel. Maybe the law dogs would not notice the missing pin.

He went to work on the painful part of freeing himself. Folks told him they had heard that Billy the Kid, some punk of a killer who got himself killed a long while ago over in New Mexico, could do what Zeke was planning. He thought maybe he was kin to Billy Bonney or whatever his name was. It had to be better than being the son of Bloody Zeke The Elder, but if his pa was responsible for giving him one particular feature, well, then at least Bloody Zeke The Elder had been good for one thing. He had that going for him.

Large wrists.

Small hands.

Of course, the law dogs had tightened those manacles till the iron practically cut off Bloody Zeke's circulation. Maybe they had heard the stories about how Bloody Zeke could twist and tear his hands free from any cuffs. Tight as the iron was on his skin, they likely figured that would do the job.

But Bloody Zeke The Younger had always been a stubborn bastard, and pain did not deter him.

"Stop that damned wagon!" the deputy law dog called out.

Bloody Zeke grinned. Well, it was about time. The sun had started to sink behind the hills. Night was slow a-coming that time of summer, and he doubted if they had made six or eight miles since leaving Payson. Of course, they had gotten a late start. The deputy had waited a few extra hours so the old driver could sober up, and stopping every few miles to grease the axle had delayed and delayed and delayed things. And given Bloody Zeke The Younger plenty of time.

The tumbleweed wagon, mercifully, came to a stop.

"Do we have any grease left?" the deputy asked.

"Told you afore," said the old man in the driver's box. "Emptied it the last stop."

The deputy swore. "Well . . . maybe we can get more at Fort McDowell."

Once a regular Army post, it currently served as a reservation for mostly Mojave and Apache Indians, and some Pimas.

"Mebe so."

"That's a hell of a long way to listen to that damned noise, though." The deputy swung down from his horse. "I guess we might as well camp here."

"All right."

"I'm going to answer nature's call in the bushes. See to the prisoners."

"Yep. Don't step on no rattler, bub."

The young law dog shook his head, his only response, and hurried to the brush along the side of the hill.

Bloody Zeke The Younger tried to control his breathing. So far, it was working out better than he could have hoped. The lead marshal walking off the road to relieve himself. That old drunken fool—who bragged how he had been part of the gang that had killed Bloody Zeke's pa—moving on the other side of the wagon, past the Negro, then to the woman.

"You need to find a privy, too?" the graybeard asked. He was flirting.

The green-eyed gal turned to him.

"I suppose."

"Well . . ." Turning, the old Army campaigner looked off the road to where the deputy had disappeared.

That was all Bloody Zeke needed. He would get no better chance.

He sprang, avoiding the slop bucket. Everyone jumped, and the driver turned, but too late. Bloody Zeke's aim was true as the manacle he'd freed from his right wrist sliced between the bars, catching the boozing drunk right above his left eye. Before the guard could fall, Bloody Zeke reached through the bars and caught the old-timer's collar, holding him up. Swinging his left hand up, he caught the manacle in his right hand and pulled the iron chain tight against the driver's throat.

"Dan—" the man tried, before iron cut off his throat.

The one-eyed Reb laughed.

"What the—?" the cardsharper cried out.

The greaser mumbled, "*¡Dios Mío!*"

The black giant just looked on.

The guard kicked and jerked, and Bloody Zeke pulled the chain tighter.

It did not take long.

The deputy marshal came running out of the brushes, suspenders hanging at the sides, his fly unbuttoned, jerking a pistol from the holster.

"Let him go!" the law dog wailed.

"No." Bloody Zeke laughed. "You let me go."

"I'll shoot you!"

Bloody Zeke said, "Go ahead."

It would have worked . . . but God played a dirty joke on Bloody Zeke. One even worse than the one Moses Butcher had pulled after the Tucson holdup.

Out of the corner of his eye, he spotted movement along the road. He turned away from the law dog with the pistol, staring past the big black prisoner and up the road. A rider, just one man, just one mean jasper, was trotting toward them on a light-colored horse.

"Let Royal go, damn it!" the deputy said.

Bloody Zeke did not bother looking back at the law dog. He even forgot about the old drunk who was kicking and gagging.

Well, he thought, *looks like I ain't gonna catch up to Moses Butcher after all. What a damned pity. But . . . maybe now they'll just shoot me dead. Beats melting in Yuma. Or getting sent back to Texas or Kansas to swing from a rope.*

CHAPTER 12

Close enough for everything to become clear, John McMasters kicked the buckskin into a gallop, pulling the shotgun free of the scabbard as he raced to the tumbleweed wagon. He saw the revolver wavering in Daniel Kilpatrick's right hand, saw the prisoner—Bloody Zeke The Younger—behind the limp body of Royal Andersen, who was being held up with a chain across his throat.

Hearing the hooves on the hard-packed road, Kilpatrick whirled, bringing up the revolver but quickly recognizing McMasters. He swung back, yelling at Bloody Zeke, but the thundering hooves drowned out whatever Kilpatrick shouted.

McMasters pulled hard on the reins with his left hand, and Berdan slid to a stop. Kicking free of the stirrups, McMasters leaped from the saddle and brought the Remington twelve-gauge's stock to his shoulder. Instinctively, his thumbs reached forward to pull back the hammers only to fall against the Damascus steel. He kept forgetting.

The Remington Model 1894 had no hammers.

That would take some getting used to.

"Let him go!" McMasters shouted.

"With pleasure," he heard the dark-eyed prisoner say.

The chain and iron cuff rattled as they scraped against the wagon. Royal Andersen dropped into a heap.

Kilpatrick clumsily dropped his pistol and ran to the wagon.

McMasters kept the shotgun aimed at Bloody Zeke inside the wagon.

Moving away from the bars, Zeke picked up his hat, placed it on his head, and stepped back to his place in the wagon, chains rattling with every step. The other prisoners stared, first at Bloody Zeke, then at John McMasters. The woman and the black man turned to look at Royal Andersen as Daniel Kilpatrick rolled the old veteran over on his back. On the other side of the wagon, the gambler with the yellow vest and the Mexican stood and tried to see Andersen. The one-eyed ex-Rebel, sitting closest to Bloody Zeke, just looked up at the cold-blooded killer.

Bloody Zeke had dark hair that hung to his shoulders. The hair needed a curry comb and a sharp pair of scissors. Beard stubble covered his face. He wore high-topped stovepipe cowboy boots, but his clothes remained the striped uniform of a prisoner at Yuma. In a real hurry to find Moses Butcher, he had not bothered to find any fresh clothes, something inconspicuous.

McMasters saw that none in the jail on wheels was armed, that the back door to the wagon remained locked, and that most of the prisoners remained in chains. Even Bloody Zeke's ankles were shackled, giving him just enough room to walk around—and catch Royal Andersen . . . somehow.

"How is—?"

McMasters stopped. One glance at the veteran of the Wisconsin Sixth Volunteer Infantry was all it took. The old man stared up at the darkening sky with eyes that saw nothing. At least . . . nothing on this earth.

"You son of a bitch." McMasters brought the barrels of the Remington back up toward Bloody Zeke. Almost instantly he remembered why he was there, remembered what had happened at his ranch. He lowered the shotgun, breathed in, exhaled, and looked down at his old friend.

Sniffling, Deputy U.S. Marshal Daniel Kilpatrick closed the dead man's eyes.

"What happened?" McMasters asked.

"I . . . don't know." Gently, Kilpatrick laid Andersen's head on the grass, covered his face with the kepi that had fallen beneath the wagon, and folded his arms across his chest.

Andersen might have looked peaceful in death, but the chains to the iron bracelets had carved a ditch across his throat, and blood still ran in rivulets down his neck and across his shirt and old Union blouse.

Kilpatrick came to his knees, but when he tried to push himself to his feet, he fell back, catching himself with his hands to keep from falling face-first. He gagged once, twice, and then sprayed the dirt with vomit.

"Get some water," McMasters told him. "I'll keep an eye on these." He looked at the Negro, then at the woman, and across the wagon at the four others.

Kilpatrick did not listen. After wiping spittle and remnants of jerky and breakfast on his sleeve, he made himself stand. He stared at McMasters.

"Thanks for . . . trying to . . . help. But"—the young man cocked his head at an angle—"what the hell are you doing here?"

McMasters put the Remington back on safety and tucked the shotgun underneath the crook of his right arm.

"I'm going to say this once. And don't ever ask me again. Rosalee's dead. Bea's dead." He steeled his voice. "They're all dead. Murdered."

Kilpatrick fell to his knees again.

"It . . . that . . . that can't . . . it can't be."

"Murdered"—McMasters looked up as he finished, wanting to see the reaction in Bloody Zeke The Younger's eyes—"by Moses Butcher and his gang of killers."

He told Kilpatrick most of everything, but spared him—hell, he had spared himself—by not describing what Rosalee must have endured before death had mercifully taken her to God's home.

"The law? Is there—" Kilpatrick might have been in shock. First seeing Royal Andersen strangled to death. Then learning that his bride-to-be had been murdered.

"Tom Billings?" McMasters spit into the dust. "He's a yellow bastard. I told you. I saw nine men riding south across the valley southwest of my place. Probably heading toward the Globe road."

"Butcher. He"—Kilpatrick blinked—"wouldn't go to Globe."

"No. He wouldn't."

"Well . . ." Kilpatrick managed to stand and lean against the wagon's front wheel, away from the reach of Bloody Zeke. Away from any of the scum chained behind the bars. "We need . . . a posse."

"That's what I figured. That's why I'm here."

Kilpatrick blinked again.

McMasters raised the barrel of the shotgun, aiming it at Bloody Zeke The Younger. "I want him. And him." He pointed toward the black man, Alamo Carter.

"What?"

"Bloody Zeke knows enough about Butcher. And Royal"—McMasters shook off any sentiment, any regret, any human emotion he might still have and refused to look down at the lifeless body of his old friend—"told me this black man was a scout, and a good one. I need a tracker."

"John"—Kilpatrick stared at McMasters as if he thought he had become a madman—"you can't be serious."

"I am serious."

"You can't—"

"I will."

"John, I've been a lawman since I was eighteen years old. The law's my life. You're asking me to— Come to your senses, man."

"The law was *your* life. Bea and my children were *mine.*"

"But—" Kilpatrick's head shook violently as if he had to wake himself from some horrible nightmare.

"Those killers butchered Rosalee. They burned Eugénia and Bea. They tossed James into a well. They blew off Nate's face. They—" He stopped himself, remembering his promise to spare Daniel Kilpatrick, to spare himself. "I aim to find them."

"I can't let you do this, John. By God, I'm a deputy United States marshal. I swore an oath."

"I made a vow." McMasters turned the Remington toward Daniel Kilpatrick. A thumb reached up and lowered the safety switch. "I aim to see it through."

Kilpatrick took one step back. Then his right hand reached toward the holster but stopped, not because staring down the giant bores of a twelve-gauge shotgun intimidated him. He just remembered he had dropped his revolver.

"John," he tried again. "Think this through."

"I have." McMasters had thought of something else, too. "Royal Andersen always said it took an Apache to track an Apache. So I figure it would take a butcher to track down the Butchers." Without turning the Remington away from Daniel Kilpatrick, McMasters tilted his head toward the prisoners of the tumbleweed wagon.

"Bloody Zeke . . . and the black man. That's all I want. You take the other four to Yuma."

"And how do I explain what happened to those two?"

"Tell them I stole them from you. I don't care. This is how it has to be done. It's the only way. We wait on Tom Billings or any of that yellow-livered bunch up in Payson to do anything, Butcher will be in Mexico. He gets into that country, and I'll never find the son of a bitch."

"I will go with you, amigo," Bloody Zeke The Younger said.

"I wasn't asking you to volunteer," McMasters said.

"What deal do you make us?" the black giant asked.

"He's making no deal!" Kilpatrick shouted. "All he's doing is getting himself a trip to Yuma, too." The deputy marshal took a quick step toward him, but stopped when the Remington's barrels came closer.

"John." Kilpatrick tried to wet his lips, but could find no moisture on his tongue. "John . . . you have to be reasonable. Think about it. You break these two men out and you'll be sent to Yuma . . . if you're not killed. We have to follow the law."

"I'm following *my* law."

"How many men did you say you're after?"

It was the redhead who spoke.

McMasters shot her a glance. He had not expected her question. Oh, he'd known he would never talk Daniel Kilpatrick into releasing Alamo Carter and Bloody Zeke The Younger, but he had figured Royal Andersen would have gone along with his crazy plan, that Andersen would have assisted him, even to the point of handcuffing Kilpatrick to a wagon spoke. Maybe . . . just *maybe* Kilpatrick *might* have seen things another way . . . but that had been a long shot. He had not expected the lawman—even after learning of Rosalee's murder—to break the law. That boy *was* the law. But McMasters had not expected to find Royal Andersen dead, either.

He did not look at the woman. She might have been trying to distract McMasters and let Kilpatrick get the drop on him . . . which likely would have gotten Kilpatrick's head blown off.

McMasters did not answer her.

The Mexican did.

"Nueve." The burly Mexican raised nine fingers in his shackled hands.

"Three against nine." The cardsharper in the yellow vest laughed without any humor. "I wouldn't find myself betting against those long odds."

"Nor would I," said the redhead.

"From what I've heard about Moses Butcher," the one-eyed Reb said, "he'd make the late, great William Quantrill or even Bloody Bill Anderson look like my great-grandmammie or maybe even that there Pope I keep hearin' 'bout."

"Or Christ hisself," Bloody Zeke said.

"Do not mock the Lord," the Mexican said.

"All I want is Bloody Zeke and the black man," McMasters told Kilpatrick again, trying to ignore the conversation in the jail on wheels.

"My name is Alamo Carter," the black prisoner said. "And if you want me to do something, you ask me, mister. I ain't nobody's slave. Not no more I ain't."

CHAPTER 13

"He's not asking anyone for anything," Kilpatrick said, almost pleading. "He's just asking for a long, long, damned long prison sentence for himself. Or a bullet in the back of his head."

"Nine against three?" the redhead said. "Or nine against seven?"

"Now I'd place a large stack of chips on the latter," the prisoner in the yellow vest said.

McMasters found himself listening. He wet his lips.

Kilpatrick opened his mouth as if to argue more, to try, somehow, to persuade McMasters that his plan was nothing but the thinking of a man overcome by grief.

The redhead cut him off before he could utter one syllable.

"You said it takes a butcher to track down the Butchers. Well, hell, mister, you've got six of the worst killers in the territory right here."

The big black man rattled his chains. "I'm still waitin', mistah, for you to ask me. And ask me . . . real . . . polite."

"Ya don't asks the likes of you to do nothin'," the

one-eyed man said with a malicious grin. "Ya tells 'im. An' ya whips 'im iffen he gets uppity."

The black giant and the rail-thin old Confederate glared at one another. Silence fell with the darkness, and McMasters considered the redhead's suggestion. The Reb, however, had just made a good argument to forget that idea. Those killers would likely kill each other . . . over the woman, over the Remington shotgun, over nothing . . . after they slit McMasters's throat. And yet . . . it made sense. Somehow—maybe he was loco—it made a lot of sense.

"You turn them loose, they'll kill you the first chance they get," Kilpatrick said, "and the law will be after you."

"I can live with that."

"Not for long. Not with that scum."

"We'll see."

Kilpatrick swore. "What you'll see is eternal damnation. Those men—even that woman—will kill you. You'll see—"

"What I saw was Rosalee," McMasters snapped. "And all of my family. You didn't see that. Thank God for that."

The deputy's mouth quivered, but he steeled himself. "You're using my murdered fiancé to get to me. That's not fair, John. I loved her."

"I did, too. All my children. My wife. I'm not using Rosalee for anything. But I am going to use *them*. All of them." He gestured at the prisoners. "To get Moses Butcher and every one of those bastards."

"Hot damn!" the gambler said as his chains rattled.

"I'm still waitin'," the black man said.

The air had turned cool, and the sun had slipped

behind the mountains off to the west. Noticing the lamps on the front of the wagon to make traveling at night a bit safer, McMasters pointed the Remington at the nearest one. "Get those lit."

As Daniel Kilpatrick struck a match and lighted the wick of the left-side lamp, McMasters did the same for the lantern hanging over the rear door. He stepped back, watching Kilpatrick walk around the six mules that pulled the heavy tumbleweed wagon, stop by the right-side lamp, and light it.

Yellow light bathed the killers inside, the mules, and the corpse of Royal Andersen. Dan Kilpatrick walked to the rear of the wagon.

"Unlock the door." McMasters aimed the shotgun at Kilpatrick, and the deputy cursed bitterly underneath his breath, but stepped closer to the door.

McMasters never lowered the shotgun but moved in the other direction, stopping next to the black man. "Your name's Carter, right?"

"That's what I'm called. Alamo Carter."

"All right, *Mister* Carter. I need a scout. You track down Moses Butcher for me, I'll pay you."

"Pay me what?"

"A hundred dollars." McMasters had no idea where he would come up with the money, but even if he had to sell the property, or round up mustangs and break them and sell them to the Indians at Fort McDowell, he would do it.

"That ain't much," Carter said.

"It's better than Yuma."

"We do this for you," the Mex said, "you let us go?"

McMasters had read about the Mexican in the *Payson Enterprise.* The man had murdered some homesteaders along the Verde River near old Fort Verde. He had drifted into Payson, where Tony Jessop had arrested him for drunkenness, only to discover that the drunk he held was an escaped murderer named Emilio Vasquez, wanted on both sides of the border.

"You hang in six weeks," McMasters told him.

The Mexican grinned. "No, señor. I no hang. My lawyer . . . he work on an . . . how you say? Appeal?"

"Then wait here with Marshal Kilpatrick," McMasters said. "And good luck with your appeal."

The Mexican's handcuffs rattled as he placed his big sombrero atop his hat. "No, señor. I think I ride with you. But you let us go . . . when we have done this job?"

"A hundred dollars each," McMasters said. "And then I'll fight to have your sentences commuted, fight to get you pardoned, or at least not to be executed. Nothing more."

"Ain't much of no deal," the Reb said.

"The voice of a respected rancher and Medal of Honor winner should carry some weight at the territorial governor's office. Could possibly lead to a parole, if not an outright pardon."

"I don't think that's a game I'm willing to play," the cardsharper said.

"Then don't."

The gambler grinned. "You'd be one I'd like to play poker with, sir. You read my bluff. Forty years in Yuma . . . I'd rather ride with you."

By then, Kilpatrick had opened the door. He stepped inside the wagon, and moved toward the driver's box, fishing out more keys before bending over to free the Mexican, Emilio Vasquez. McMasters stepped closer, put the Remington's barrel between two vertical iron bars, and told Vasquez, "You try anything, I blow you apart."

The leg manacles came off. Then the cuffs. The Mexican did not take his eyes off McMasters as he gripped the bars and pulled himself to his feet.

"Stay there," McMasters said. "Don't move. None of you move. You stand. You stay still. Or you die. Lay one hand on the marshal, I kill you."

"You shoot that scattergun," the redhead said, "and you'll likely blow that greenhorn of a lawman apart, too."

"Could be. Could be a lot of you'd catch buckshot."

She laughed. The gambler's smile turned into a frown, and his face whitened.

"What's your name?" McMasters asked.

"Marcus Patton." The gambler massaged his wrists.

"Gambler," McMasters said.

"Killer," Kilpatrick said as he moved from Patton to the Reb. "Ten men."

"A forty-year sentence for killing ten men?" McMasters asked.

Rising, the gambler chuckled. "They weren't much in the way of men."

Metal clanged. The thin old Reb's manacles fell to the floor, and the one-eyed vermin stood, grinning. "And, suh, my name is—"

"Emory Logan," McMasters said. "Rode with Quantrill. Rode with Jesse James. Rode with Ike Clanton."

"And now . . . you." He found a plug of tobacco in a pocket, and bit off a sizeable chaw. "And"—he spit in the direction of the black man—"him." The word sounded like a curse.

"Stay if you want, Logan," McMasters said.

"No." The old-timer chuckled. "Got no desire to see Yuma . . . again."

"Because he butchered two guards when he escaped six months ago," Kilpatrick said. "They're going to hang him in Yuma."

"Not now." The old man laughed.

Kilpatrick turned, staring through the bars and over the Remington at McMasters. The one prisoner the deputy did not want to free was Bloody Zeke The Younger, but he was the one McMasters needed the most.

"Go ahead," McMasters said.

The dark-eyed killer also rubbed his wrists where the iron cuffs had chaffed his skin, almost to the point of scarring him for life. That's how tight the bracelets had been. His feet turned to the sides, stretching the muscles, the joints, and Kilpatrick backed away, toward the woman, but not taking his eyes off Bloody Zeke. The killer, on the other hand, never let his gaze leave John McMasters.

"You can find Moses Butcher?" McMasters asked him.

The man wet his lips, tilted his head toward Alamo Carter. "Isn't that why you have him?"

"He knows tracks. You know Butcher."

"Not that well."

"Well enough."

Bloody Zeke grinned as he shook his head. "That isn't why you want me. I rode for him for maybe a week. One miserable, badly planned bank job. You want me because I want to kill him. Just like you do."

"That's right. This is your chance."

"And I'll take it, amigo."

"I'm not your friend."

With another curse, Kilpatrick moved toward the woman, but McMasters stopped him.

"Not her." His head tilted toward Alamo Carter. "Him."

He saw the woman turn to glare at him, but McMasters ignored her. After withdrawing the Remington from within the cage, he stepped back, and trained both barrels on the Negro's broad back, while keeping the other freed killers in his peripheral vision.

"You watch that black bastard," Emory Logan warned, pointing a finger at Carter as Kilpatrick began turning the key in the leg manacles. "He kilt six men . . . with his bare hands."

"You might be Number Seven," Carter said.

The one-eyed Reb backed against the bars, and shifted the tobacco to another cheek, his teeth and jaws working furiously on the tobacco, trying, McMasters understood, to steady his nerves. Emory Logan was an old man. A hardened killer, but he would be no match for Alamo Carter. He'd be no match for any of this crew, except, maybe the woman.

Kilpatrick backed away against the front of the wagon, glancing at the Mexican to his right and Alamo Carter to his left. To get out of the wagon, he would have to run the gauntlet. Understanding this, McMasters brought up the shotgun again, training the barrels on the most dangerous of the lot. Bloody Zeke The Younger.

"Come on, Dan," McMasters said. He reminded the criminals that if they did anything McMasters did not like or understand, they would die where they stood.

Kilpatrick swallowed and moved toward the open

door, stopping when he came to the woman. He turned to stare at McMasters.

"She stays," McMasters said.

"The hell I do," the redhead snapped.

"I'm not taking a woman with me. Not across the desert. Not chasing after Moses Butcher."

"She's no woman." The gambler tossed his head back and laughed. "That's Mary Lovelace."

"She stays . . . with Kilpatrick."

"I'm coming with you," the woman said.

"I'd bring her along, mister," the gambler, Marcus Patton, said. "She killed her pard after they robbed a stagecoach near Flagstaff."

"I heared it was her papa," Emory Logan said with a snort.

"It was my husband," Mary Lovelace said. "And he was a bastard." She turned and stared through the bars at McMasters. He never thought green eyes could look so hard. "And I've got more right to find Moses Butcher than any of you sons of bitches."

"Son of a gun." The Reb's one eye twinkled. "That Butcher sure got around, didn't he!"

"Shut up, you old codger." The woman did not look away from McMasters. "I'm coming with you."

"Why? Yuma won't be that hard on you."

"For starters, it was my idea. You were just going to take Carter and Bloody Zeke."

"Why?" McMasters asked again.

"That's my business. But I know Butcher, too. Better than him." With just a little twitch of her head, but without looking away from McMasters or even blinking, she indicated Bloody Zeke The Younger. "So you need me."

McMasters shook his head. "No. You're staying. With Kilpatrick."

To his surprise, McMasters watched Daniel Kilpatrick kneel in front of Mary Lovelace and search for the key to her leg irons. When the key slipped inside the lock, McMasters blurted out, "What the hell are you doing? I said—"

"She can't stay here . . . alone." One iron opened, and Kilpatrick moved to the other.

"She won't be alone. You're staying with her."

"No."

"Yes. You can't come with me." McMasters had given up any hope of having Dan Kilpatrick along with him, not the way he was so *by-the-law,* refusing to bend. Hell, he had not even shed a tear over Rosalee's murder. And, deep down, John McMasters did not want the boy with him. Not on that dirty, hellish task.

"You need to take care of—" He stopped. He'd started to look down at Royal Andersen's body, but his stomach soured and he could not look at his old friend. He forced down the bile rising in this throat, and stepped closer to Kilpatrick, who was freeing the redhead's wrist manacles.

"Stop it." McMasters raised the Remington.

"No." Kilpatrick stood as the iron handcuffs fell onto the floor. Staring over the twin barrels of the twelve-gauge and into McMasters's eyes, he said, "These are my prisoners. I'm responsible for them. So I'll be coming with you." He turned, studying each of the six killers, then stepped out of the wagon, leaving the door open.

He walked until he stood only a few feet in front of McMasters. "I won't try to stop you . . . or them"—he motioned at the vermin in the jail on wheels—"even if they try to kill you. This is your doing. Your idea. But I'm coming with you."

"Shoot that bastard, mister!" the Reb cried out. "He'll just bring us all trouble."

"Kill him," the Mexican said.

"Blow his head off," the gambler said.

"We needs to get movin'," the Reb said. "Gettin' darker each minute. Somebody's bound to come along. And, hell, these lyin' curs 'll likely say that I strangled that old goat."

"Shut up!" McMasters snapped. "You don't say anything about him. He was a top soldier. A good man. He was my friend."

Bloody Zeke The Younger merely laughed. The woman and the black man remained silent.

McMasters felt a sudden chill. Maybe it was the night. Beyond the glow of the lanterns, the country had disappeared into a black void. It amazed him how quickly daylight could turn to midnight in those hills. He had not noticed how dark the night had become, but that was all right with him. They'd move better in the darkness. Yet Dan Kilpatrick was muddying up the waters.

"I said I'm coming with you, John. The only way you can stop me is with that." He pointed at the giant bores of the double-barrel.

"Shoot him!" the Reb begged.

McMasters just stared into Kilpatrick's eyes.

"But you need to know this. I am a deputy U.S. marshal. If you somehow manage to live through this, I'll be taking you to Yuma, Mr. McMasters."

Chapter 14

"Hell," Carter said, "we ain't going nowhere."

McMasters lowered the shotgun. "All right, Dan." Only then, did he turn toward the big black killer.

"How you plan on tracking down Butcher, Mister . . . Hell, I don't even know your name."

"John McMasters," the Mexican said.

McMasters looked at Emilio Vasquez.

"You hear of me, señor. Well, I hear of you." Realizing that he knew something the other prisoners did not know, he grinned, and stepped into the center of the jail wagon. "Sí. He raises horses. I hear many men speak of John McMasters." He faked a shiver as he said the name. "Big soldier in your war between your states many years ago. Win big medal. Big honor. Big hero. This man"—he whipped off his hat and bowed in the direction of where Royal Andersen lay—"he speak much of the great John McMasters. So we have nothing to fear, amigos. We are being lead by a hero."

"Well," Alamo Carter said. "Mister John McMasters, it's full dark now. How you expect me to pick up

Butcher's trail? Go back to your place? Ain't it likely somebody'll be going to your place . . . or what's left of it? Ain't it also true that your place be in the opposite direction of where Butcher's goin'?"

"We don't need to go back to Payson," Bloody Zeke The Younger said. "But I don't think we want to be traveling in this." The killer stepped to the door, put his hands on the bars, and looked at McMasters as the shotgun came up. He stepped down, and the others followed, stopping in a semicircle that faced McMasters and Kilpatrick.

"Dan," McMasters said in a steady voice. "You think you can find your revolver in the dark?"

"Yes."

"Then find it. And cock it."

Kilpatrick moved toward the revolver, and McMasters waited, wondering if the deputy marshal might just shoot him—to maim, wound or kill—once he held that Colt. He heard the metallic click of the hammer coming to full cock, but did not look at the young deputy. He kept his attention on the five men and the woman.

"I can't track from the back of a tumbleweed wagon," Alamo Carter said.

Ignoring the black man, McMasters trained his eyes and the Remington's barrels, at Bloody Zeke. "Why wouldn't we need to go back to Payson?"

"We'll pick up his trail south of here," Bloody Zeke answered.

"All we have to do," Mary Lovelace said, "is make a beeline for the Superstition Mountains."

Bloody Zeke turned and gave the redhead a curious but respectful look. He laughed and shook his head. "You do know Moses Butcher, don't you?"

"Enough," she said, "to know that I wish I didn't."

"Well," the gambler said, "there is one problem that Zeke has already pointed out. As did the colored boy."

"I'm no *boy*, gambler. You best lose that word from your vocabulary."

"No offense, Carter."

"I took offense."

"My apology, sir."

"Accepted," Carter shook his head and smiled. "Don't you think traveling in a prison wagon will arouse suspicion, Mr. McMasters?"

"Logan," McMasters called out to the Reb.

"Yeah?"

"You and Patton unhitch the team. Six mules. Six riders."

"Why us?" the Reb asked.

"Because you don't move too good," McMasters said. "And I can see Patton's yellow vest well enough in the dark."

The gambler laughed and started toward the front of the wagon.

"One mule at a time," McMasters instructed. "Tie the first two to that shrub yonder." He gestured with a tilt of his head before turning his attention to the black man and Bloody Zeke. "You two. Pick up Royal Andersen . . . gently . . . respectfully . . . and put him in the back of the wagon. I don't want any wolves or ravens getting to him."

"There's a bedroll in the driver's box," Kilpatrick said.

"You." McMasters jutted his jaw at the Mexican. "Get the bedroll. You'll cover his body."

"Sí." Emilio Vasquez crossed himself.

McMasters breathed just a hair easier. He could see the Reb and the gambler with the mules, and the jail on wheels was lighted well enough to watch Bloody Zeke and Alamo Carter serve as pallbearers of a sort as they laid poor, brave Royal Andersen on the floor of the tumbleweed wagon. The Mexican made a lot of racket but eventually came away with the old coarse blue woolen bedroll.

He came away with something else, too.

"Vasquez." McMaster's voice carried a threat as he pointed the barrels of the twelve-gauge at the killer's head.

"Andersen's pistol—the one he wasn't allowed to carry. The one you found in the box. Why don't you just drop it at your feet?"

"Señor." Emilio Vasquez shook his head and laughed. "You are sadly mistaken."

"Then I'll sadly apologize over your body after I've blown it in half."

McMasters' right forefinger tightened on the front trigger.

The Mexican stiffened, smiled, and shifted the bedroll over his right shoulder. As his left had moved carefully behind his back, the first finger on his right hand pointed at his eyes.

"For a man wearin' . . . *los anteojos* . . . you must have eyes in the back of your head, no?"

McMasters tightened his middle finger on the rear trigger as Royal Andersen's revolver appeared. Vasquez held it between his thumb and forefinger, then dropped it onto the dirt in front of his boots.

"My hearing's even better," McMasters said. Relaxing the pressure against the triggers, he pointed the shotgun at the tumbleweed wagon, indicating for Vasquez to do his chore. Bloody Zeke and Alamo Carter stepped out of the wagon, moved to the side, and found a place to stand between the two wheels. Bloody Zeke cast a quick glance at Andersen's revolver. Alamo Carter ignored it. The Mexican knelt over Andersen's covered body, removed his hat, and began to pray in Spanish.

McMasters kept the shotgun trained on Carter and Bloody Zeke, who stood a little too close to the revolver in the dirt for McMasters' comfort. He thought about asking Kilpatrick to get it, but dismissed that idea. Either Carter or Zeke could grab him, use him as a shield. He could go for the pistol himself, but then he wouldn't be able to keep an eye on Patton and Logan. He could order or ask Kilpatrick to watch over those two as they unharnessed the remaining mules, but Daniel Kilpatrick would always be a green kid in McMasters's eyes. That left—

"You."

Mary Lovelace studied him.

He could feel her gaze, but did not dare look at her. Keeping the Remington pointed at the two men, he said, "Ma'am, I want you to go over there, pick up the revolver, and bring it to me."

Inside the wagon, the Mexican finished his prayer, crossed himself, put on his hat and stood.

"You," McMasters said to him. "You stay where you are. For a minute."

"*¿Con este hombre muerto?*" Fear shown in Vasquez's voice and eyes as he looked down at the covered corpse.

"For one moment. *Por favor.*" He nodded, still focused on Carter and Bloody Zeke. "Ma'am? If you'd be so kind."

"Well," Mary Lovelace said, "since you're asking politely."

He saw her move carefully, considering each step, until she stopped between Bloody Zeke and Alamo Carter. Slowly, turning toward McMasters—just so he could see that she didn't plan on using Andersen's pistol on him—she knelt. She swallowed, and slowly gripped the butt of the revolver, and then she started to stand.

A flash of movement caught McMasters's attention. Alamo Carter had shot down his left hand—damned fast for a man that big. McMasters swung the shotgun directly at the former slave, saw the big man's massive arms and both hands fly back up, high over his head, high even above the top of the jail on wheels.

"Just swattin' away a damned horsefly!" Carter shouted.

That was a lie. A way to distract McMasters. And it worked.

"Son of a bitch."

While McMasters had trained the 1894 Remington and all of his attention on the big black killer, Bloody Zeke The Younger made his move.

He shot down, wrapping his left arm around Mary Lovelace's waist, his right arm coming across her throat. Like a cat, he jerked her up, stepping back toward the tumbleweed wagon.

McMasters moved quickly, turning the shotgun's cavernous barrels at Bloody Zeke. Behind McMasters, off in the darkness, Daniel Kilpatrick swore. Likely he aimed his pistol, too, but McMasters did not look behind him. And it did not matter. Bloody Zeke had moved too quickly, like a rattlesnake, and he had Mary Lovelace as a shield.

Or would have.

Mary Lovelace moved like a mountain lion, twisting despite Bloody Zeke's strong grip until she turned toward him, facing him with her back to McMasters's shotgun. She also still held Andersen's revolver, and this she brought up with lightning-like reflexes, ramming the barrel into the soft flesh beneath the dark-eyed killer's chin.

In the darkness of night, the cocking of that iron hammer sounded like thunder.

"That's the last mistake my late husband ever made, Zeke," she said, shoving the pistol tighter against his throat, forcing him to bend his head back until it slapped against the iron bars. "Let go of me now. Or I blow your damned head off."

Bloody Zeke released her instantly, did not breathe, and did not blink. His hat fell to the dirt. Mary Lovelace backed away, keeping the barrel aimed at the killer.

Inside the wagon, Emilio Vasquez began to pray again.

Outside the wagon, Alamo Carter laughed until he almost doubled over.

Dan Kilpatrick ran until he stood on the edge of the light. He kept his pistol aimed at Bloody Zeke.

Straightening, the dark-eyed killer rubbed the spot between his chin and throat where a circular bruise would soon be forming. His other hand rubbed the back of his head. Eventually, he picked up his hat, and in an effort to regain some of his dignity, his manhood, his authority . . . or just to keep from shaking . . . he looked at Alamo Carter, shrugged, and tried to laugh, too.

"It was a good idea. It just did not work."

Later, McMasters would wonder if the two had planned that together. Had they come up with the idea in whispers while inside the wagon? Had they read each other's minds? Had there been a signal? Or was it just plain luck? He'd never ask. And he would always wonder how things would have turned out . . . had it all worked.

"Hurry up with those mules." McMasters felt the shotgun shaking in his arms, so he lowered it and watched Mary Lovelace walk toward him, no longer considering Bloody Zeke or Alamo Carter. McMasters glanced at the revolver she still carried. It remained cocked, yet he did not, could not, raise the shotgun. Damn her green eyes. They reminded him so much of Bea. Besides that, John McMasters had never pointed a weapon at a woman.

Stopping suddenly, Mary Lovelace looked at the pistol in her right hand. The thumb came up, resting against the hammer. She squeezed the trigger gently, just to loosen the mechanism, and safely lowered the hammer. The pistol spun in her slender hand, and she offered it, butt forward, to McMasters.

"Ya stupid bitch!" Emory Logan roared from the wagon tongue. "Ya shoulda blowed his head off whilst ya had the chance!"

"Shut up!" Dan Kilpatrick roared.

Mary Lovelace's eyes locked with McMasters'. He could not look away from her, but shifted the shotgun to his right hand, and took the pistol in his left. She released her hold as soon as he held the heavy iron. Without another word, she turned to walk back to the wagon.

"Stupid bitch!" Emory Logan yelled again.

"I told you to shut up!" Kilpatrick roared.

Marcus Patton, the gambler, led two mules away from the wagon tongue.

McMasters shoved Andersen's revolver into his waistband. His heart pounded against his ribs. His temples throbbed. He did not know if his lungs were working or if he still held his breath. He just watched Mary Lovelace go and stand between the black giant and the dark-eyed killer.

As if nothing had happened.

"You can get out of the wagon now, Vasquez." McMasters wondered how his voice sounded.

The Mexican did not hesitate, but skedaddled out of the makeshift hearse, slammed the door behind him, and slid in front of the rear wheel near Bloody Zeke.

"Just hitch those two mules over yonder," McMasters told Patton, offering some vague direction with the tilt of his head. He kept his eyes on Emory Logan, who struggled with the harness on a dark mule.

Dan Kilpatrick moved to stand beside McMasters. "Now do you understand what pure folly this is?" The hammer clicked as he lowered the pistol, but did not holster it. "Now can you see what'll happen if you continue with this insanity? You won't last two days. You might not even be alive by the time the sun rises. Give it up, John. Stop now. I'll . . . I'll forget everything that has happened."

McMasters swallowed. Forgetting the law had to be hard for a man—a boy—like Dan Kilpatrick. The fool lived by the book, and his own stubborn code. John McMasters lived by his own code, too. Just different from Kilpatrick's.

"There ain't no saddles for these damned mules," Emory Logan yelled from the darkness. "You expect us to go chasin' after Moses Butcher bareback?"

"Yes," McMasters answered.

"John . . ." Kilpatrick whispered his plea.

"That will make it harder for us to catch him, señor," Emilio Vasquez said.

"And harder for you to get away." McMasters was again breathing in regular breaths, and his heart did not run out of control. He did not feel sweat running down his spine, and the pounding in his head had ceased.

"John, in the name of God, for you own sake, for your soul, don't do this," Kilpatrick said.

"I have to, Dan. You stay here. You can send the law after me. I don't care. You stay here. See"—he felt that pain again—"I'd like for you to at least see Rosalee, Bea, my boys, Eugénia buried. Be at . . . the funeral."

The pistol slammed into Kilpatrick's holster.

"I meant what I said, John. I'm riding with you. And when it's over, if by some miracle you and I aren't dead, I'll be taking you to jail. Or maybe even up the thirteen steps to a hangman's noose."

By then, Emory Logan was leading the last of the mules into the light.

"All right," McMasters said evenly. "Let's ride."

Chapter 15

They could smell the coffee when the door to the adobe hut opened. Candles and a fire in the kiva-style fireplace cast light into the darkness. No one stood in the doorway, however. A squaw stepped briefly into the light, but a muffled voice commanded her to move, and she did, quickly stepping out of view. Whoever had opened the door wasn't stupid.

The squaw, Moses Butcher thought, looked mighty inviting.

"What do you want?" a man's voice called from behind the door.

Butcher knew the thick solid door was sturdy enough to stop a .45 bullet . . . and those adobe walls had to be at least two feet thick.

"Fresh horses," he called. "Supper. Coffee smells good."

"Late to be horse trading," the voice said.

"Late for supper, too. But we can pay."

"Script or gold?"

Lead, Butcher thought, but answered, "Greenbacks. Plus you can keep the horses."

A long silence filled the night.

"We were told," Butcher said, "that Bear Aztec will trade with anybody . . . at any time."

"Who the hell told you that?" Bear Aztec called from behind the door.

"A runt named Duke Gold." That much was true. Duke Gold had mentioned the trader named Bear Aztec.

He'd told Butcher the old reprobate ran a post in the Mazatzal Mountains between Payson and Fort McDowell and usually kept plenty of horses in the barn and corral, and had scores of saddles, blankets, and anything else those Indians had to offer, pinned up as they were on what had become the Fort McDowell Reservation. They trusted Bear Aztec on account he had married a Pima wench.

For the brief glance Butcher had caught of the dark-haired girl in the doorway, he doubted she had been an old peddler's squaw.

"He ought to know," the voice said. "He stole two horses of mine last September."

"He won't steal any more," Butcher said. "I shot him dead."

Another thing Duke Gold had said about the trader—if he knew a fellow was on the run from the law, he'd be glad to do business. He'd jack up the price a real pretty penny on whatever that man needs.

Butcher tried to guess when he had strung two sentences together that were completely factual. He gave up quickly. Behind the door, Bear Aztec laughed. A shadow moved, and Butcher grinned. The door had moved. He saw another shadow on the hut's sod floor, and watched Bear Aztec step into the light.

Oh, that man remained cautious. He held a rifle—a repeater by Butcher's best guess—at his hip, keeping the barrel trained on Moses Butcher who had ridden close enough to the place so the trader could see him.

"You alone?" Bear Aztec said.

"Yeah." Hell, there was no way Butcher could make it three sentences in a row without a lie.

The rifle came up to the old man's shoulder. "I'm no fool. I heard more than one pony when you rode up."

Butcher chuckled and turned in his saddle, looking back down the dusty trail that led from the Phoenix Road to Aztec's trading post. "Gomez, Dirk, Ben, Page. Come ahead. Slow. Careful."

"And hands where I can see them," Bear Aztec said.

"And hands," Butcher repeated, "where he can see them."

The rifle looked like a sapling twig in the hands of Bear Aztec. The trader lived up to his name. He was a big man, and looked as strong as any bear you'd find in the wilderness off to the north, six-foot-two, probably two hundred pounds, dressed in Apache moccasins, buckskin britches, and a yellow shirt. Beads and silver chains hung around his neck, silver bracelets covered both wrists, and his hair was long, dark like an Indian's but streaked with gray, silver and white. Scars covered his face, and one ear was missing. For a one-eared man, Bear Aztec heard pretty good. But not good enough.

Greaser Gomez and Dirk Mannagan led their horses from the corner of the corral. Bitter Page and Butcher's kid brother, still in their saddles, eased their mounts slowly, keeping their hands on the reins in front of them. Mannagan's piebald gelding limped badly. Gomez limped, too, and his bay mare dragged its rear left leg. The five men stared at Bear Aztec, saying nothing.

Five men at the front of the cabin. Milt Hanks and Miami would be behind the hut, creeping along the sides, Zuni would be behind the water trough at the round pen with a Sharps rifle aimed at Aztec's chest, and Cherry would be in the barn.

Aztec frowned at sight of the two horses without riders.

"Man ought to treat a horse better 'n that."

"The greaser's horse threw a shoe, split a hoof on the rocks."

"But the Mex kept riding it," Aztec said.

"Well . . . it seemed prudent at the time."

"Don't know what happened to Dirk's pinto. Just played out."

"What do you want for trade?"

"The best horses you've got," Butcher answered.

"You won't get far," Bear Aztec said. "Not if you treat your horses the way you treated them you rode in on."

"Hell, Aztec." Moses Butcher chuckled. "These ain't nothin' but nags."

"Like hell they are." Aztec brought the rifle to his shoulder, aimed the big Henry right at Moses Butcher's chest. "Those are John McMasters horses."

"No," Ben Butcher lied quickly. "No . . . we got these up in Holbrook."

"Mister." The Henry's sights did not budge. "I was with John way over on Cherry Creek when he trapped that paint horse and the two you ugly boys are riding.

If you've run horses almost to death from just up in Payson, then I'm betting you've killed or waylaid John. So I'm going to have to kill you. All of you."

And he might have done it. He sure didn't lack in temperament or will. But Zuni cut loose with the .50-caliber Sharps from the water trough, and blood erupted from Bear Aztec's stomach and back. His rifle bounced off the thatch awning, toppled to the ground, and Bear Aztec was flung inside his hut, sliding across the dirt until he stopped underneath the table, leaving a trail of crimson to mark his route.

That should have been easy, ending it, but suddenly gun barrels jutted out from the slots in the closed shutters—and hell followed.

Butcher's horse screamed and toppled, two bullets cutting it down, and another round tore off Butcher's hat. Would have blown his head off if he hadn't leaped out of the saddle. He landed on the ground, rolling over out of fear the horse might crush him or kick him, but the horse was dead. Another shot grazed Butcher's neck as he scrambled out of the light, his ears ringing from the bullets.

He recognized the report of Zuni's Sharps, but that was a single-shot rifle—not that handy for offering a covering fire. From the barn, Cherry finally opened up with the Winchester. Mannagan's horse dropped to the dirt, rolling over, riddled by bullets, while Mannagan somehow scrambled away. A bullet spun him around, but he pulled the trigger on his double-action revolver and leaped behind Butcher's dead horse for protection.

Ben Butcher had spurred his horse before he

leaped out of the saddle. The horse kept running. So did Ben until the darkness swallowed him. Greaser Gomez had let loose of the reins to his mount, which took off toward the barn while Gomez bolted to the other side of the hut.

"Over here, Moses!"

Butcher recognized Milt Hank's voice then blinked. The muzzle flashes, the lantern light, the darkness were disturbing his eyesight. He saw the movement as the gunman waved at him from the corner of the post. Butcher leaped, ran, and dived the last few feet, landing with a thud, the breath leaving his lungs in a violent explosion. He tried to get up, fell to his face, and felt Hanks jerking him over, rolling him to the building's corner.

"That trader ain't alone," Hanks said in a dry voice.

Butcher spit, swore, and sat up. "You got any other news you think I ain't figured out yet?"

The gunfire and its violent echoes faded in the night. Horses galloped nervously around the corrals, and one was kicking its stall repeatedly in the barn.

Even though he knew it would be hopeless, Butcher cleared his throat and called out, "You in the house. Toss out your guns and come on out. Do it now, we let you live. Otherwise, we'll burn you out."

"Light your fire, asshole!" came the reply.

"Place ain't gonna burn, Moses," Hanks said as he reloaded his two revolvers. "Dirt on the roof's two feet thick. That Bear Aztec knew what he was doing when he built this damned place."

"Any back window? Door?"

"No." Hanks shoved one pistol into his shoulder

holster, and thumbed back the hammer on the long-barreled Colt he kept in his right hand. "Just the two windows and the door out front."

"Tunnel?" Butcher asked, fearing that whoever was inside might be escaping or even sneaking up behind them.

"Ground's too hard for any fool to dig a tunnel. That's solid rock we're standing on."

Butcher managed a laugh. "Don't I know it."

"I don't know how the hell we're gonna get those bastards out of there," Hanks said. "The way this place is laid out, they'll be able to shoot any of us who tries to steal a horse from any of those pens or barn."

"They can't see that far," Butcher said.

Hanks pointed the Colt's barrel toward the east. "Moon's rising. And it's full or nigh full."

With a sigh, Moses Butcher holstered his revolver.

"You want to skedaddle?" Hanks asked. "Find some other less ornery folks who'll let us steal their horses?"

"No." The outlaw leader was already fishing bullets from his shell belt, and shoving the cartridges into his pocket. "Let me have some bullets. Ten or so. Then help boost me up atop that roof."

"They'll shoot your arse off it."

"Not as thick as that dirt is." Butcher grinned.

Hanks chuckled and pulled cartridges from the bandoleers that crisscrossed his chest. When Butcher had enough rounds, Milt Hanks locked his fingers together to form a stirrup with his two hands. Bracing his right hand, still holding his Colt, against the adobe wall, Moses Butcher put his left foot in Hanks's hands, and the man grunted as he straightened and lifted.

Butcher's right hand shot up, took hold of the roof. His left followed, and he felt Hanks shoving him skyward.

Butcher pulled himself onto the hard-packed roof and rolled over, catching his breath, listening. He could smell the dust and rat droppings. He spit out the taste, came to his knees, and crept along toward the chimney. Remembering the kiva fireplace, he laughed.

I can't burn 'em out. But they'll soon wish I had.

He fished out the shells in one pocket, grinned, and called out into the night, "Cut loose, boys!"

Gunfire erupted again, and Butcher hoped those fools knew better than to shoot high. He heard the thud of lead against adobe and wood, and that would provide enough noise and command the attention from those inside the miserable hut. The chimney was hot, and the smoke irritated his eyes, but Butcher did not mind. He dropped the bullets into the chimney, brought out another handful, and let them fall, too. Again. And again. Then he moved away from the chimney just in case one of those bullets happened to fire up through the chimney and not across the inside of the post.

"Hold your fire!" he yelled, and waited till his men stopped shooting. Then, after creeping a bit toward the front of the trading post, he laid down flat on the roof, and waited.

The first slug exploded and whined off a rock or something. Butcher heard a curse, followed by the shattering of a plate, a glass, a bowl . . . something.

"What the—" someone began, but then the fireplace turned into a Gatling gun.

Butcher laughed, hearing the roar from the fireplace and muffled echoes escaping from the chimney behind him. Someone inside screamed. He glanced to the east, saw the white top of the moon clearing the trees. Wetting his lips, he waited.

"Bastards!" A man stepped out, levering a Winchester rifle, shooting into the darkness.

Dirk Mannagan's Colt Thunderer barked, and the man spun around, giving Moses Butcher a clear aim at the Indian as he fell onto his knees in the dirt beside the outlaw's dead horse.

Butcher squeezed the trigger.

The cannon fire inside the building slowly stopped. Another bullet popped a few seconds later. Then one more. Silence followed, but soon a new noise came from the inside. The moaning of someone maimed, likely riddled with lead. Butcher had not counted just how many rounds he had dropped into the chimney, but his plan had worked.

"Mannagan," he called out.

The gunman rose from behind the dead horse, his left hand hanging limp at its side, blood dripping from his fingers.

"Check it out."

Dirk Mannagan looked up as Butcher stood on the roof. He wet his lips, and started toward the doorway when an ear-splitting shriek cut through the night again.

Mannagan brought the .41-caliber pistol up, but tripped over one of the dead horse's legs and fell to the ground as the figure raced from the building, wielding a hatchet.

Butcher shot the woman in her back. She crumpled, rolled over, and glared at him as he leaped off the roof.

By then, Greaser Gomez and Milt Hanks had rounded the building, along with Miami and Bitter Page. Gomez, Miami, and Page went through the doorway. Gomez's pistol barked. The moaning ceased.

The woman coughed, turned her head, and saw the hatchet she had dropped. She reached for it, but Butcher's boot stepped on her hand, and she grimaced, but did not scream.

"Feisty, ain't you?" Butcher pressed down harder and holstered his Colt. "But I like that in a woman, especially an injun squaw." The moon climbed higher, bathing the compound in white light. He could see his brother coming toward him and Zuni standing up behind the water trough. He could see the dead horses, the lame ones, the played out ones, and those wonderful horses, fresh and full of life in the corrals. He saw Cherry running out of the barn and sprinting across the yard.

Sliding to a stop in front of Butcher, Cherry said,

"I found some Indian ponies in the barn, boss." The gunman gasped to catch his breath.

"And now you tell us," Butcher said.

Cherry took several steps back, horror and fear registering on his face.

Butcher laughed.

"Just don't let nothin' like that happen again, Cherry." He stared at the squaw and unbuckled his gun belt.

Chapter 16

Just past full, the moon had risen . . . but the light found only a few paths through the thick forest. For the fifth time, Emory Logan fell over the mule's side, landing hard on the trail that ran west of the Phoenix road. He rolled out of the way as Dan Kilpatrick and John McMasters reined in their horses.

"Hold up!" McMasters called. He could see the woman, Mary Lovelace, leading the way.

She stopped her mule and turned it around, waiting. The other killers also stopped theirs. Swearing underneath his breath, Alamo Carter even swung down off the animal he rode, and grabbed the hackamore on Logan's, stopping it from running up the trail a bit.

Logan sat up, rubbing his shoulder, his long legs and worn boots sticking out on the road.

"I hate mules. They ain't good for nothin'!" He spit in the general direction of McMasters and Kilpatrick.

"Get up," McMasters said. "And back on."

"Hell, man . . . how you expect us to catch up to 'em bad men . . . with us on mules?"

"Stay on and we won't have to stop so much to pick up your worthless hide," McMasters said.

The big slave dropped the end of the hackamore to Logan's left. "Thought you hailed from Missouri."

"What's it to you?" the one-time Confederate bushwhacker snapped.

"Ain't Missouri knowed for mules?" Carter walked back to his own mule. He was so big, it would have looked downright comical how his legs practically dragged across the dirt, but nothing struck John McMasters as even halfway funny anymore.

"Get up," McMasters said again.

"We need—"

McMasters brought up the Remington. "We need you to stay on the back of your mule for longer than fifteen minutes."

"Then get me a damned saddle."

"You'll get a saddle—maybe even some hot grub—when we get to Aztec's post." He lowered the shotgun as the Reb got to his knees, rose gently, and took the hackamore in his left hand.

"How about weapons?" the Mexican asked.

"In time." McMasters watched Logan move to the high ground, and use that to help him leap onto the mule. He almost slid off immediately, but grabbed the mane tightly. The mule let out an angry *hee-haw*, kicked with its back legs, and snorted. Somehow, Emory Logan managed to stay on its back, and the mule stopped its bucking almost as fast as it had started.

"You see," McMasters said. "It's not that hard."

"Easy fer ya to say. Ya's sittin' in a slick-fork saddle."

"Move."

Grumbling and cursing, Emory Logan kicked the

mule. The redhead turned her animal around and began climbing the hills. The others followed in single file, moving slowly, letting the mules pick their own way up the rocky slope.

McMasters had ordered them off the trail when they'd come to a stream. Any posse following, he had figured, would think they would have turned downstream, which would take them to Tonto Creek. Easier country than moving into the hell that was the Mazatzals.

The name came from some Indians down in Mexico, and meant "Land of the Deer." But so far, all McMasters had seen had been two tarantulas, one greater short-horned lizard, and a Gila monster that had almost spooked his own horse. Farther to the west, the mountains turned into short hills, covered by brush and rocks that became the Sonoran Desert and left the Verde River as a sandy wash. Where they were, the mountains could see snow in the winter. Pines rustled in the wind, and McMasters knew they would be entering a high-walled canyon soon. His posse would have no choice but to ride single file through it.

That was one reason he had made them take it.

He thought back to what Bloody Zeke The Younger had said before they had ridden away from the tumbleweed wagon and the covered body of poor Royal Andersen. He, too, had quoted from Revelation, as if he had read McMasters's mind or had been hiding in the brush when McMasters had ridden away from the embers and smoke and that smell of death at his ranch off the Rim Road—an impossibility, McMasters knew. Bloody Zeke had been in Andersen's wagon by then, shackled to the floor with chains.

" 'And I looked,' " Bloody Zeke had said, " 'and behold a pale horse: and his name that sat on him was Death, and Hell followed with him.' " Laughing, he had swept off his hat, and called out to McMasters. "Lead the way, Death, and we shall follow you."

McMasters had shaken his head slowly.

"I'm no fool. You don't ever get behind me."

As further precaution, he didn't even let Daniel Kilpatrick get behind him. The young deputy marshal rode at McMasters's right.

An hour later, with the moon rising high over their heads, they came to the canyon. The woman had stopped, waiting, and the gambler had dismounted, handing his mule's rope to Emilio Vasquez. Patton walked to a bush, unbuttoned his trousers, and began urinating. McMasters and Kilpatrick stopped their horses, McMasters keeping the shotgun leveled just ahead of him, Kilpatrick stretching, kicking his boots from the stirrups, and twisting his feet this way and that.

"Are we going through that?" Bloody Zeke nodded at the entrance to the canyon.

"Yeah."

"At night?"

"We're not waiting till daybreak."

"That moon won't be shining on us for long," Bloody Zeke said. "Be blacker than the ace of spades."

"Then be glad you're riding a mule. Better footing. Better eyesight."

The gambler returned, stuffing his shirtfront into his britches, and took the rope from the Mexican killer. "Be a right handy place for an ambush," he said before he leaped onto his mule's back.

Four of his companions laughed. The redheaded woman said nothing.

"Ever seen what buckshot can do to a man when it ricochets off granite?" McMasters said. "Tears through a man like grapeshot. Get moving."

The laughter died, and Mary Lovelace guided her mule into the dark, narrow opening.

The walls stood high and rocky, but thin. In some ways, it was like a slot canyon, prone to flash floods during thunderstorms, but the animals found just enough water to soak fetlocks, nothing higher. And the canyon was too narrow for Emory Logan to slide off the mule. If he slipped, he would just bounce against a rock wall.

"What happens—" The gambler stopped. Spooked by his echo in the darkness, he lowered his voice. "If we come to a rockslide?"

McMasters did not reply for he had no answer. There wouldn't be enough room to turn the horses around, and backing up horses and mules out of that hell would slam the door on his chances. He simply rode through the doorway, seeing nothing, just hearing the hooves, the echoes, and labored breathing.

He didn't know if the canyon had a name, but he had always called it The Doorway . . . which is what it was. For years, he had used it as a shortcut. Not for chasing mustangs. Horses would not go through a canyon like it unless forced to by a man like John McMasters. Men did not like traveling through it, either.

A gray light appeared almost as suddenly as the blackness had covered them, and a star twinkled overhead. McMasters breathed easier, seeing the outlines of the riders ahead of him as the trail widened.

"Ride ahead when you're through The Doorway," he called out, his words bouncing off the rocks, but without much of an echo. "If I don't see six of you spread out on the hilltop when I come out, I shoot to kill."

Ahead of him, he saw Daniel Kilpatrick slip his revolver out of its holster. McMasters wet his lips. The gray light was merely the sky, shining brighter because of the moon. Kilpatrick eased his horse through the wide slot, moving to the left.

McMasters rode through on the right, keeping the twelve-gauge aimed across his body and the saddle.

"Whoa." He tugged on the reins, and the buckskin stopped.

Five men. One woman. All on their mules, awash in the rays of the moon.

The Doorway opened, if you were entering it from the north, in the Mogollon Rim country. When you came out on the other side, the coolness of the Rim, the scent of pine and rosin and sometimes turpentine, vanished, and you smelled dust and desert and, every now and then, a sweet scent of desert blooms. But it was too late in the year to smell spring. Behind Mary Lovelace he saw the first saguaro desert.

This, he always told himself, was the beginning of the Sonoran Desert.

It was where hell really began.

"Well?" Bloody Zeke asked.

"Slide off." Using the buckskin to cover his dismount, McMasters slipped to the ground and braced the shotgun across the saddle, watching his hired men climb off the backs of the mules. Off to his left, Daniel

Kilpatrick holstered the revolver and dropped to his feet.

"Give the mules a breather," McMasters said.

"Water?" Patton asked.

"No water for the animals. We'll water them when we reach Bear's place."

"I'm not talking about the damned mules," the gambler said. "I meant for us."

"Carter," McMasters said.

"Yeah."

McMasters unhooked one of the canteens with his left hand, and moved around the buckskin, staying close, practically touching the animal so he wouldn't frighten it, cause it to kick, maybe crush his skull. Once he cleared any potential danger, he held up the canteen. The slave understood and took a few steps.

"Close enough," McMasters told him and tossed the canteen, which the big man caught easily.

McMasters watched, curious. The giant Negro turned and went to the woman, uncorking the canteen and handing it to her.

He started to bark an order, but to McMasters's surprise, Alamo Carter beat him to it. "One sip, ma'am. But make it a good swallow. No more than one swallow."

She tilted her head up, staring at him.

"We're in the desert now, ma'am. Water's precious."

"Hell!" Marcus Patton said. "You said we'd be at that trading post before long. They'll have water."

"Maybe," McMasters said. "Maybe not. Carter's right. One swallow. We save our water from here on out."

The woman drank. Then Bloody Zeke. The ex-slave

turned Army scout turned man-killer let the gambler drink, and then Emilio Vasquez. At length, Alamo Carter walked to Emory Logan.

John McMasters grinned without mirth. He knew what was coming. It wasn't funny, but it was justice. As the fiend who rode with Quantrill reached for the canteen, Alamo Carter lifted the canteen and drank. He swallowed only once, but he held that canteen up and on his lips for the longest while. With an exaggerated sigh of pleasure, he wiped his lips with one massive arm and used the other to extend the canteen toward Emory Logan.

"I ain't drinkin' after him," Logan said. The lean, one-eyed killer whirled toward McMasters. "You fetch me another canteen!"

"No," McMasters said.

The killer folded his bony arms across his chest.

"Then I ain't thirsty." His voice, however, revealed just how much of a lie he had spoken.

"Suit yourself." McMasters drank from his own canteen, saw Kilpatrick doing the same, then he moved back to the front of the horse. "Keep the canteen, Carter," McMasters called out, "in case Logan changes his mind." He could trust the old scout . . . at least when it came to one canteen. He glanced at the moon, frowning. How much time had he given Moses Butcher? He should get his "hired hands" moving, covering as much ground as possible, but he knew better. The animals had not been pushed hard, but that canyon tested the nerves of men and beast. *Five minutes,* he told himself. *Ten.*

"Rest," he said. "But you"—he waved the Remington at Mary Lovelace—"come over here."

The Reb laughed. "Want some horizontal refreshments, mister? Then do we all gets a turn? I don't mind seconds."

"One more word, Logan, and you'll get both barrels."

The man cursed. The woman led her mule through cactus and killers, and stopped a few feet in front of McMasters.

He lowered the shotgun, butt to the ground, and leaned it against a boulder. It had grown so heavy he found it impossible to hold for another minute. He flexed his fingers, trying to get the blood flowing again. He did not realize how tightly he had been gripping the Remington. "Back at the wagon, you said something about Butcher making a beeline for the Superstitions."

"I did." She wasn't going to offer anything. Close-lipped. Like all of the others . . . except the bushwhacking killer from Missouri.

"Why?"

She shrugged.

"Why?" he demanded.

"Why would anyone ride into that country?"

"The Lost Dutchman's Mine?" McMasters shook his head. "He's not that loco."

"Isn't he?"

"With a posse on his trail?"

She grinned. "Posse wouldn't look for him there. And it's country that only fools enter."

"Or hopeless causes trying to find a mine that never existed," McMasters pointed out.

"That's Moses Butcher," Bloody Zeke said from where he sat on a rock several yards away.

McMasters thought about that, shook his head,

and stared directly into Mary Lovelace's eyes. He could not see their greenness at that time of night and with the moon behind her back.

"The Superstitions," McMasters said to himself.

"That all you want from me?" the woman said.

McMasters shot a glance at Dan Kilpatrick.

"Where did you pick up Bloody Zeke?"

"Miami," Kilpatrick answered.

South of here. Closer to Globe than the Superstition Mountains, but close enough, McMasters figured. It had been a big mining town in the 1870s, silver and gold, and once those played out, the miners had started to find some interest in digging for copper. It wasn't as big as Globe, and a man could cut up across the desert from there and get to the Superstitions without being seen by many folks.

Ten minutes had not passed, but McMasters changed his mind about how much rest the animals needed. "Get your mules. We're moving out. You'll walk the animals till I tell you to mount. Now, move. South. Single file. Watch for cactus. The spines hurt like a bastard. Watch for rattlesnakes. Fangs hurt even worse."

Chapter 17

The Dutchman, if John McMasters remembered right, had been called Waltz. Jacob Waltz. He had arrived in Arizona Territory when McMasters had been shooting Sharps rifles at unsuspecting Confederates at Gettysburg, Pennsylvania. Some folks said he had been a farmer, others a merchant, and most called him a rake. But he definitely had money. At least, that's what folks said around Payson and across much of the territory. Gold. Typically, he dealt in gold, and those riches, those nuggets and dust, had not come from his homestead on the Salt River.

From the stories McMasters had heard—he had never met or even seen Jacob Waltz—the Dutchman would leave his farm every winter from a few years after the Civil War to maybe a decade or so ago. He'd come back with gold. Some folks tried to follow him, but he was like a mountain goat and an Apache. Nobody could track him. Nobody could find him or his mine.

About five years back, Jacob Waltz died, and with

him . . . almost . . . died the whereabouts of his mine. The woman taking care of the old-timer had asked him, while the miner was on his deathbed, for the location of the mine. He had drawn her a map.

To John McMasters' way of thinking, that map had been her gold mine. He had been offered—three times—a map to the Lost Dutchman's Mine. The prices had varied, from as high as $500 to as low as $3. A few people had gone off looking for the mine since Waltz's death in 1891. At least two had died looking for the mine. No one had ever found it, or if they had, they hadn't let anyone know.

Would a killer and thief like Moses Butcher go after a mine that might not even exist? Hide out in the harsh Sonoran Mountains with a price on his head and a date with a hangman? Maybe it made sense. No posse would go looking in the Superstitions for a murdering bandit on the run from the law. And a man could find many a place to hide out in that country.

The more McMasters thought, the more sense it made. If Butcher had robbed a bank in Holbrook or Winslow . . . or even Flagstaff or Diablo Canyon, the easiest escape from Arizona justice would have taken him east into New Mexico or north to disappear among the Navajos and that godforsaken Navajo country. Even into Utah. But he had turned south. Across the Mogollon Rim and into the Sonoran Desert. Any posse would figure he was bound for the border. No one would head into the Superstitions.

Gold had never interested John McMasters. He found his gold in horses. And in his family. At least he had.

Dawn broke, and McMasters had the prisoners stop

and dismount. They had been riding for a while, and Emory Logan had not fallen off the mule since before they had traversed The Doorway. The wind blew, and with it came a warmth that would turn into burning heat before long.

McMasters waited until the six killers had slid off their mules before he dismounted.

"You can have water now." He brought up his own canteen, removed the cork, and drank. "One swallow."

"We wait here?" Alamo Carter asked.

"No."

"But not much longer, right?"

"We've a ways to go yet."

Carter shook his head, handed the canteen to the woman, then turned back to McMasters. "You strike me as a smart man. Smart enough, at least, to know you don't travel when the sun gets up too high. That'll play hell on these mules. On us, too. Ride another hour, maybe, then find shade. Rest. Wait till dark. Then ride again."

"We'll rest at Bear Aztec's," McMasters said.

"We know where we're going," Bloody Zeke said. "To the Superstition Mountains."

"We're going . . ." The words died in McMasters's throat. He stepped up, frowned, and quickly swung back into the saddle. "Watch them," he ordered Daniel Kilpatrick. "If they breathe too loud, kill them. Even the woman."

He spurred the buckskin and loped up the ridge, slid off the saddle, found his binoculars, and looked off into the distance.

Buzzards. Circling. Somewhere, the morning . . . or most likely the night . . . had brought Death.

"Damn," he said bitterly, the sickness returning to his stomach, his hands turning clammy. He knew what he would find at Bear Aztec's trading post.

The Remington roared, belching smoke and leaden shot into the morning haze.

Behind him, John McMasters heard Emory Logan scream and his mule snort. He did not hear the crash that sounded as the mule bucked Logan into the dirt. He did hear the flapping of the giant wings of the buzzards as they lifted off the already bloating body of what once had been one of his horses.

That one and another of his horses lay in front of the trading post.

Buckshot began falling like raindrops on the roof. The gunshot faded. McMasters dismounted and wrapped the buckskin's reins around the top rail of the round pen. The pen was empty, but other horses roamed about. A few had bolted up the ridge, frightened by the shotgun blast.

McMasters opened the shotgun's breech, withdrew the spent shell, discarding it and replacing another into the bore. He snapped the breech shut and kept moving toward the human body that lay between the two horses.

When he got close enough to see that it was not Bear Aztec, he stopped.

Maybe . . . he thought, but the prayer, the hope, died immediately. The door to the post had been ripped off its hinges, and he saw the body . . . *bodies* . . . and the blood, already dried to brown and black, that covered the floor.

A Pima Indian leaned against the eastern wall, eyes open, one leg bent, the other stiff and straight, blood covering the front of his shirt. Flies buzzed around the room. He saw the woman, too, and had to turn away. The glasses came off, and he realized he was pouring sweat. He understood that he had not seen an Indian woman on the floor. He had seen Rosalee. He shoved the glasses into a pocket, made himself turn, and cursed.

He ripped off a Navajo blanket that covered the tabletop, and started for the dead woman but stopped suddenly when a groan sounded underneath the table. Spinning around, he stared in disbelief as a hand, stained black with blood, lifted then fell back onto the floor.

"God." McMasters dropped the blanket and flipped over the table, which crashed and landed near the kiva fireplace. He dropped to his knees and gently lifted the head of Bear Aztec.

"Get me some water!" he bellowed to those outside. "Now!"

He knelt closer, trying to find enough moisture in his mouth and throat to swallow.

"Bear," he whispered.

How Bear Aztec had remained alive all this time, McMasters could only marvel. That much blood. Ten butchered hogs would not have bled so much.

The old trader's eyes fluttered open. His mouth opened. He had no strength to utter a noise, but his lips moved.

Juhki? Bear Aztec mouthed.

McMasters did not look at the woman, naked, dead and worse, on the floor.

"She's all right, Bear," he lied.

The big man sighed, but it sounded more like death's rattle in his throat. Alamo Carter entered the room. He swore.

Mary Lovelace followed.

"Dearest God in heaven."

"Get her out of here," McMasters barked to no one in particular. "And give me that water. Now."

Footsteps sounded behind him, and McMasters turned to find the redhead kneeling beside him, removing the cork to the canteen, and gently bringing it to Bear Aztec's cracked lips.

"I said—" McMasters started.

"Shut up," Mary Lovelace told him.

More footsteps sounded then the popping of knee joints as the giant black man bent to lift the blanket McMasters had dropped on the floor. Alamo Carter was covering the body of Juhki, Bear Aztec's young wife.

The trader's eyes locked on Mary as she dabbed his mouth with water from the canteen. He did not seem to notice. Most of the water ran down his cheeks, leaving a trail in the blood that stained his face. He did not appear able to swallow.

"Had your . . . horses," Bear Aztec managed to speak aloud.

"I know," McMasters said.

"I . . . got . . . greedy," Aztec whispered. "And . . . stupid."

"Don't talk." McMasters knew he didn't mean it. He wanted the dying old trader to tell him everything he could. He wanted to hear that Bear Aztec had at least put a hurt on Moses Butcher's bunch, but the sight of the interior, the horses outside, the stench of death . . . The fight had been one-sided.

He looked up, saw the ashes and charred wood that had been blown out of the fireplace, bullet holes in the adobe walls, in the shutters, even splintering the table top. How many shots had been fired? How had all of this happened? How could anyone have gotten the better of Bear Aztec?

"Your family?" Aztec had found enough strength to get one last question.

"Fine." McMasters sounded hollow.

Aztec's eyes hardened. The man found a will to clench his fists into tight, hard balls.

"Juhki!" he cried out, shuddered, and let out one final sigh.

McMasters watched the light leave the big man's eyes, and he cursed again. Bear Aztec had heard the lie in McMasters's voice when he had told his friend that his family was fine. The man knew he had lied, and had realized that he had lied about the Pima woman, too—that Juhki had been killed, murdered, raped, butchered.

McMasters could not move. He just stared into the man's hard, dead eyes, and then they closed. Slowly, he understood that Mary Lovelace had reached over and fingered Bear Aztec's eyelids shut. When he turned to face her, her green eyes registered sympathy, then nothing. She stood and walked out of his view.

Eventually, McMasters heard Alamo Carter's big but soft-touching feet leave the cabin, too.

He made himself stand, glanced again at the carnage, and walked out of the adobe death house.

"They didn't burn this place," Daniel Kilpatrick said. "Like they did yours. Why?"

Bloody Zeke The Younger answered. "Butcher would have needed to draw attention to our boss's place. Give him a better chance at escaping. At least getting a good start. Way I figure things, he rode up here at night. Got the big cuss out in the open, started shooting. But something"—the killer's head shook—"something didn't work out like he planned." The young murderer laughed. "Hell, nothing ever works out like he plans. He's a fool."

"A damned lucky fool," the gambler said.

"Luck runs out," McMasters said.

"Fer ya, too," Emory Logan said.

Ignoring the talk, the big black scout had squatted, his fingers gently brushing some tracks, and he moved over to another set of prints.

McMasters knew to let the scout work. "Vasquez. Logan. Get the bodies out of the house. Behind the barn, you'll find a small cemetery. Bury them."

"Bury 'em!" The Reb's head shook. "Ground's harder than my heart. I ain't—"

"Then we can bury you."

The Reb spit, then turned away, cursing as he followed the Mexican to the barn. They would find the tools first, dig the graves—probably not six feet deep, for Logan had not lied about had hard the earth was—and return to take the bodies in a poor excuse for a funeral procession.

"Horses they rode in on were played out," Alamo Carter said, standing.

"They got fresh mounts." Mary Lovelace was coming from one of the corrals. "Turned the rest loose."

"Patton," McMasters said. "You and Zeke drag these horse carcasses away. Use the mules. Put them in the round pen." He indicated which corral with the Remington's barrels.

"That's nasty work," Bloody Zeke said. "Get the black bastard to do that."

"He's doing his job," McMasters said. "You do yours."

"You need me," Bloody Zeke reminded him.

McMasters looked up. "I know where Butcher's going now. And I have her." He indicated Mary Lovelace.

"She might up and die. Like everyone else has been doin' of late."

"Do it."

McMasters turned, nodding at Kilpatrick.

The deputy marshal understood. Taking the Greener shotgun out of the saddle scabbard, he eared back both hammers. He would watch over the prisoners while McMasters disappeared inside the trading post.

He sucked in a lungful of foul air, exhaled, and pushed his way through the slaughterhouse, using the barrel to push back another blanket that served as a separator, a wall. The blankets had been thrown this way and that, and blood stained the linens and the floor. It sickened him. He knelt at the end of the bed, trying not to look at the reminders of whatever ugly crime had taken place and opened the trunk.

Maybe Butcher and his men had been in too big a hurry that they had not been thorough. They'd come for horses. Horses and bloodlust. They had looked for gold or greenbacks, and those had been easy to find.

McMasters had seen the strongbox in the living area, opened, its contents strewn across the room. They had found the money.

But had they found everything?

McMasters walked out of the cabin and laid one blanket on the ground, then tossed another on top of it. Looking around, he saw that the dead horses were in the corral. Bloody Zeke and the gambler were bringing back two horses, followed closely—but not too closely—by Daniel Kilpatrick. The woman and the big former slave led horses, as well. The redhead brought one and Alamo Carter two. The sound of a spade and a pick hammering through the rock-hard dirt told McMasters that Emory Logan and Emilio Vasquez were still at work with the graves.

"Trail leads west," Alamo Carter said as he tied up his two horses on a hitching post out front.

"Butcher will turn back." McMasters tilted his head. "For the Superstitions."

"If Bloody Zeke and this woman ain't lying."

McMasters nodded then called out to Dan Kilpatrick. "Fetch our grave diggers." The graves, he knew, would be shallow, but Bear Aztec would understand.

Later, when the bodies were covered, the fresh horses saddled, and two mules rigged for packs, John McMasters leaned the Remington against the wall to the adobe house, and unrolled the blanket.

"Here's a gift, payment in advance, from Bear Aztec."

Chapter 18

Bloody Zeke The Younger licked his lips.

Marcus Patton, hooking his thumbs in the pockets of his brocade vest, shook his head. "I'm betting my life on those . . . antiques."

Ignoring both men, McMasters picked up the closest revolver. Originally, back around 1860 or a few years after, the Colt single-action Army model had fired .44-caliber balls with gunpowder ignited by copper percussion caps. Cap-and-ball, it had been called. Antique was right. Metallic cartridges had made 1860 Army Colts in .44 caliber and 1851 Navy Colts in .36 caliber obsolete. But in 1871, Charles B. Richards, who worked for Samuel Colt's company, had managed to acquire a patent that converted those front-loading revolvers into breech-loading revolvers that used metallic cartridges. In the early years, a Richards conversion was considered quite the bargain, selling for roughly half the price of a new Colt.

The one McMasters held had to be close to twenty years old, but it was clean. Bear Aztec did not trade for horses that only a glue factory would want or a weapon that needed to be melted down or tossed away.

McMasters felt the Colt's balance, and tossed the .44 to Marcus Patton. The gambler caught it, grinned, pulled back the trigger and squeezed—while pointing the pistol at the back of Mary Lovelace's head. It clicked.

"Nice." He shoved the Colt into his waistband.

Next McMasters grabbed an old Winchester, commonly called the Yellow Boy. Originally produced in 1866—this one looked old and beaten-up enough to be from that year—the carbine chambered .44 Henry rimfire cartridges, as it was designed as an improvement to the old .44-caliber Henry rifles. The name came from the shiny gunmetal receiver. The weapon would hold fifteen rounds. He handed it to the Mexican.

"I suspect," Vasquez said, "that if I pointed it at your head and pulled the trigger it would go *click*, too."

"Try it if you want," McMasters told him, patting the Colt on his hip. "But click or not, mine will blow your head off."

Laughing, the Mexican slowly worked the lever, and saw that, as he'd suspected, the rifle had not been loaded. "I have no scabbard on my saddle to carry this, señor."

McMasters said, "That means you'll have to carry it in one hand. Keep you occupied."

Vasquez laughed again.

Emory Logan got an 1856 double-action .44 caliber cap and ball pistol from Starr Arms Company of New York. When the bushwhacker saw the stamp on the right side of the pistol, he cursed. "Ya give me this gun!" He spit.

"Figured you knew all about cap-and-balls," McMasters said. "That's what you used with Quantrill, isn't it?"

"We didn't carry no damn Yankee guns."

"Then go unarmed."

The man swore, turned, and shoved the pistol into one of his mule-ear pockets.

The other long gun McMasters tossed to Alamo Carter, who nodded at it with approval. It was a Colt, the company's only effort to produce a lever-action rifle. Colt's New Magazine Rifle—more commonly called a Burgess—fired fifteen rounds in .44 caliber. Somewhere between six thousand and seven thousand had been produced between 1883 and 1885 before Colt decided to focus on short guns and leave the fast-shooting rifles to Winchester.

"Two Remingtons left," the gambler said.

McMasters picked up the first gun, the newest of the bunch, a nickel-plated Remington Model 1890, which fired .44-40 bullets and looked more like a Colt—most folks said Remington Arms had been copying Colt with that one—than any of the earlier Remington revolvers. He spun it and handed it to Mary Lovelace.

She took the pistol, pointed it down, and stared hard at McMasters. Finally, as Bloody Zeke The Younger burst out laughing, she took a few steps back.

"So"—Bloody Zeke stopped laughing and stepped up—"you do not trust me, eh?" He extended his right hand, palm up, for the last pistol.

McMasters handed it to him. The gun looked small, even in Bloody Zeke's small hands. Nowhere near as powerful as the revolver Mary Lovelace still held, the Remington over-and-under derringer was nickel-plated, in .41 caliber, with three-inch barrels and two-piece pearl grips. It seemed to be better suited for the gambler than Bloody Zeke, but he understood why he got the pop gun. He opened the weapon, and looked down the two barrels, seeing the dirt.

"And no bullets for me, either." The weapon snapped shut, and he slipped the derringer into his pants pocket. "And just two shots."

"My shotgun holds only two shots as well, Zeke," McMasters said, referring to the intimidating 1894 shotgun leaning against the adobe wall.

"So you had better make them count."

"As should you."

Stepping back, McMasters grabbed the twelve-gauge. "Pack the mules. Water. Blankets." He motioned at the one on the porch. "Food." He pointed again, but this time at the horses. "You'll find saddles, bridles, horse blankets in the barn. And curry combs, brushes, and hoof picks. Groom your mounts first, and do it right. Do it not to my satisfaction, and you'll walk. It's already a furnace here. Walking's not fun."

"Well," the Reb said. "I'll tell ya somethin' else that ain't no fun. An' that's goin' up again' a bunch of black-hearted killers with guns—but no powder and lead. So, ya avengin' bastard, when do we get bullets?"

"In good time. Get to work." McMasters stepped off the porch, cut through the prisoners, and went to the buckskin. His horse remained strong enough, sturdy enough, game enough to ride into the Superstition Mountains. He would groom it himself, like he always did.

When he led Berdan away from the corral and tied it to a hitching post, he walked to the gambler.

"That pick won't hurt you, and it won't hurt that bay's hoof. Do it right."

A glance told him he need not inspect Alamo Carter's sorrel. The man had served in the U.S. Army. He knew how to care for a horse. McMasters stopped, studied the brown gelding Emory Logan had picked, and frowned. The old Reb had picked a fast one—a good horse with plenty of heart and legs that could carry a killer a long, long way.

Another mistake on my part, McMasters thought. *I should have picked the horses for each of these killers.* Then he remembered all he had heard about William Quantrill and his raiders. They rode only the best mounts and could ride them a long, long way. Almost like Comanches or the Sioux. *Keep an eye on him,* McMasters told himself. Then he laughed.

Hell, I need six pairs of eyes.

He glanced at Daniel Kilpatrick, who had picked a fresh horse, too, a blood bay stallion, then grinned, remembering when he and Bear Aztec had caught that mustang way over near Willow Mountain. The grin turned to a frown. Dan would need watching, too.

"No," McMasters said aloud, "seven pairs."

"Seven what?" Lovelace asked.

McMasters stopped, startled, and stared at her. "Nothing." He took a few steps away, stopped, and walked back to check on her horse.

She had picked a paint horse, more white than black, a rangy mustang that would fit her perfectly. It was a mare with a gentle disposition, but good bottom.

Better suited for climbing mountains than running, but a good desert horse.

He shifted the shotgun to his left hand, reached and lifted the right rear leg, studying the shoe.

The hoof returned to the earth. The mustang snorted and shook its head as the woman stared.

"You know horses," McMasters told her.

"I know a lot of things."

"Including how to kill men," he said.

Her green eyes darkened, and she looked through him.

"One man," she corrected. "Just one."

"That's enough."

She spit and put the brush back on the horse's back, moving it with purpose, but also with a caress, so not to hurt or bother the mare. "And how many have you killed, John McMasters?"

She continued a steady job on the horse.

He shrugged, brought the shotgun back to his right hand, and turned to walk away.

She stopped him. "You didn't answer my question."

He started to walk away, but couldn't. Turning slowly, he looked back into those hard eyes. Damn, she did remind him of Bea . . . only harder, much harder, much more worldly . . . and much more alive than his wife. He felt a mist cover his eyes and his mind flashed back. As much as he tried to stop the memory, he couldn't.

He was grooming the horse, a roan, using the brush too hard. Bea stopped him, scolding him as he might James or Nate.

He snapped, "What the hell do you know about horses?"

"On this Saturday morning," she snapped back, sounding more Irish than French, "a lot more than you, my husband. You'll rub his hide off if you don't stop. So stop it. Right now."

Her green eyes hardened.

He tensed, feeling the anger, that hatred, and then he felt remorse and a sickness. He looked at the brush, the roan, dropped the brush, and turned, staggering away, tripping, catching himself against the stall. His lungs heaved. He heard the noises, the cannon fire, deafening musketry, and the whistling of grapeshot . . . and those horrible screams of men. Even worse, he felt the Sharps kick against his shoulder.

"John!" She was at his side.

He felt the flour on her hands as she reached for him.

"John"—her voice cracked—"what is it?"

"Nothing." He pulled away from her.

But she did not retreat . . . like he so often did. She pressed forward, like some damned Union infantry, marching into battle. Even up the slopes at Cold Harbor, where they would be shot to pieces.

"Tell me," Bea said.

"No." He breathed in deeply, let the air out, and felt better. Well, better than he had. The noise was gone. No more shells exploding. Yet he saw himself rubbing his right shoulder.

"Are you hurt?" she asked.

"No." He dropped his left hand to his side. "I'm fine."

"No, you're not. You're hurting."

He laughed without any humor and raised his right arm over his head. "This does not hurt."

"I am not talking about your shoulder." Her flour-coated fingers rose and tapped on both his temples. "But here. I wish you would tell me why . . . what happened."

"That," he said, "you don't need to know."

"I'm your wife."

"It was before I met you. Before we were married."

She sighed. "I did not marry the John McMasters I met five years ago. I married the John McMasters who was born in 1844."

"Forty-six," he corrected and laughed.

"I married all of you."

"And I'm glad you did."

Her head shook. Her eyes lost their hardness, turning softer, less emerald, more grass, and so damned sad. She could break his heart when she looked at him that way.

And on that one day, that one time, in . . . Missouri? Kansas? Someplace long before Arizona Territory and the Mogollon Rim, he almost granted Bea her wish. He almost told her . . . everything.

"It was during the war," he said with a sigh.

"That much I figured."

"I'm no hero."

"You are to me. Medal of Honor or no Medal of Honor. You're my hero. You'll always be. You can always protect me."

And that almost killed him.

He laughed, pulled her into his arms, and kissed her in that barn on that homestead where the guns did not roar so loudly in his head.

He shook his head as the memory faded, but he continued pondering. He'd taken her to Arizona, but hadn't protected her. He hadn't been able to save her . . . or Rosalee . . . or James . . . or Eugénia . . . or even young Nate.

There were days when he wished he had been killed, laid to rot by a Rebel musket ball on some forgotten or remembered field of battle. Sometimes he cursed God for letting him live. Letting him live with that stupid medal that he did not deserve.

For maybe a year, he had almost forgotten Colonel Berdan, Sharps rifles and telescopic sights. Had blocked out the nightmares, the horrors, and some general pinning a Medal of Honor on his chest.

Then Moses Butcher had turned McMasters' life asunder, murdering his family . . . butchering them. And killed one of his dearest friends. Bear Aztec had helped him forget those horrors, and find peace in horses, in rounding up mustangs, breaking them, training them or other horses. Horses were kind. Horses were forgiving.

But Moses Butcher had picked on the wrong family. By murdering the wrong people, he had resurrected the demons that had controlled John McMasters. He welcomed those demons and would use them to keep him going.

He would kill men he truly hated, not men merely because they wore a uniform of a different color, or because they owned slaves, or wanted to form their own country. He would kill those he hated and he would kill them all.

Suddenly, he remembered something else, something Daniel Kilpatrick had told them as they rode toward The Doorway. "*That shotgun doesn't kill far. That means you'll have to look into the eyes of the man you aim to kill. You will have to see him. And that's different from anything you did in the late unpleasantness.*"

The late unpleasantness. That's what people who had not fought in the Civil War called the damned thing. Unpleasant? Hell, they didn't know anything about the war.

McMasters spit. He almost laughed as he remembered turning to Kilpatrick. So real was the memory, he repeated what he'd said then. "I won't see him. I'll see my wife, my kids. And that's different, too."

"What is?"

McMasters stopped. The image of Daniel Kilpatrick vanished. So did the one of Bea, lovely Bea. He looked up, no longer in that barn, no longer rubbing down a roan colt, and, regretfully, no longer looking at his young, radiant, headstrong wife.

The glasses came off, and he wiped the lenses with the frayed ends of his bandanna.

Mary Lovelace kept her eyes locked on him. She wet her lips, forgot what she had just asked—out of concern—and asked what she had thrown to him earlier with no concern, and not even what she would consider curiosity.

"I asked you how many men you've killed. You're leading us into a gunfight. I figure that's a fair question, McMasters. How many?"

"Too many," he answered, returning the spectacles.

"And you plan on killing more."

"That's right." He stuck the stock of the Remington under his arm and turned to find Emilio Vasquez and inspect the palomino gelding he was grooming.

"Me, too," she told him.

He stopped, turned, and looked back at her. He made himself grin. "Me?" he asked.

"No . . . unless you get in my way."

Chapter 19

The pines disappeared, replaced by saguaro. The hills remained just as rugged, though, and the heat intensified. Still they rode, turning east to skirt around the Fort McDowell reservation, moving southeast toward the Superstition Mountains.

John McMasters loped the buckskin ahead of the others, climbing up the loose rocks, avoiding the arms of the giant cacti. Coming up to the boulder-strewn top, he turned the horse around, and reined up on the hilltop. From the saddlebag, he withdrew the binoculars and looked at the back trail.

It had been a hunch. An itch he could not scratch. He focused the lenses until he could see clearly. A hunch. Now he knew.

Riding the sorrel, Alamo Carter topped the hill first, and moved his horse off to McMasters's right. "I was wonderin' when you'd figure it out." He kicked free of the stirrups as his horse began to urinate.

"When did you?" McMasters did not lower the binoculars, but he did move his right hand to the butt of the holstered revolver. The Remington remained sheathed in the saddle scabbard.

The ex-Scout just chuckled for an answer.

Next up the hill came Mary Lovelace, her face shining with sweat, and the pinto working hard to breathe.

"Best climb down, ma'am," Carter told her. "Take a few sips of water your ownself. Then let that hoss have a little, too."

McMasters did not argue the point.

He lowered the binoculars, and watched the others climb the hill. Marcus Patton on the bay, fanning his face with his hat . . . Vasquez, grinning, mopping his face with his bandanna . . . Emory Logan, pulling the pack mule that McMasters had handed off to him before he rode up the hill . . . and Bloody Zeke, who turned his horse to come around McMasters on his left side. McMasters drew the Colt from the holster, and thumbed back the hammer.

"Not too close, Zeke," he warned.

The killer laughed, pulled the reins and he and his black horse gave McMasters plenty of room.

Last up the hill, pulling the other pack mule, was Daniel Kilpatrick. He stopped his horse and asked McMasters,

"Trouble?"

"You shouldn't be pulling one of the mules. Make Zeke do it. Keep him occupied." McMasters lowered the hammer, holstered the revolver, and nodded toward the hills behind them . . . those they had already descended.

Kilpatrick turned in the saddle, stood in the stirrups, and felt the heat of the sun on the back of his neck. "I don't see anything," he said as he settled back into his seat.

"Because," Alamo Carter said, "they don't want you to."

"Butcher?" Kilpatrick asked.

McMasters slid the Remington out and cradled the shotgun across his thighs.

"No."

A few seconds later, the riders topped the hill, stopping their rangy mustangs. None pointed. None raised a weapon. They just waited. Four men.

"Apaches?" Kilpatrick blurted out.

"Pima," McMasters said, and kicked Berdan into a walk, wetting his cracked lips with his tongue as he rode down, bracing the twelve-gauge's stock on his thigh. "Wait here. Don't let anyone get behind you. And watch our mules."

"They're after our mules?" Kilpatrick said in disbelief.

"They're after us," McMasters said.

The buckskin kicked dirt and stones down the hill but remained surefooted.

Emilio Vasquez twisted the bandanna, soaking wet with his sweat, and tied it around his neck again. He waited. The way he figured things, he knew they were being followed long before either the gringo with the shotgun or the Negro who had scouted for the Army. He knew they were Indians, too. Back in the days when Apaches raided both sides of the border, Emilio Vasquez had made a right tidy sum selling Apache scalps for bounties to the alcaldes in various villages in Chihuahua and Sonora. A hundred pesos for each warrior—or at least a boy fourteen years or older—fifty pesos for each woman, and twenty-five pesos for any kid. And when there were no Apaches to be found, well, Emilio Vasquez learned quickly that the scalp of a Mexican man, woman or even a *chico* or *chica* could pass for that of an Apache.

He watched the tall gringo ride the magnificent horse down the slope toward the Indians and studied the terrain above the far hill. He waited and watched. No, there were no others. Just those four foolish Pima Indians. Pimas were no Apaches. No Yaquis. Too damned tame. Too trusting.

He wet his lips, dried his hands on his pants, and found the foolish gringo with the one eye and told him in an urgent whisper. "Do not let your mule go, amigo. Hold him tight."

Then he moved.

Across the desert, the four Pima Indians kicked their mustangs down the other hill, and spread out once they reached the flats. Keeping the shotgun's barrels pointed skyward, McMasters eased his horse toward them, his throat dry, and sweat dripping down his forehead, but he dared not move a hand to wipe his face.

"Whoa, boy." He tugged back on the reins, and let them drop over the horse's neck.

Three of the riders looked young, but not green. All were thin. The leanest—and probably the youngest—held a bow. He sat on a dun mustang the farthest to McMasters's right. The Indian to the left held an old Springfield musket, stock and forestock decorated with brass tacks, across his lap. Next to him, separated by a saguaro that had not yet sprouted any arms, the meanest of the group sat on the back of a skewbald mare. The man's face had been deeply scarred by some pox, and his left eye showed the brightness that told McMasters he had been blinded in that eye. McMasters saw no weapon, but the man's left hand had disappeared inside a cut-off Army dark wool. McMasters bet it held a revolver.

The last man, the oldest, with silver hair and a yellow headband, kicked his brown horse forward. He did not come too close, however, and he kept his weapon—a Spencer carbine—across his thighs, thumb on the hammer, a finger inside the trigger guard.

McMasters lifted his left hand. His right remained part of the 1894 Remington.

The Indian offered no greeting, just a fierce scowl.

"*Buenos tardes,*" McMasters tried in Spanish. "*¿Tú hablas Inglés?*" He decided to speak informally, as if they were friends, rather than use formal Spanish. It did not work. Or the old Pima did not speak Spanish, either.

"You know why we are here," the old man said, in guttural but easy to understand English.

McMasters nodded. "I have an idea. But you are wrong. We chase the same men."

The Pima did not blink.

"Bear Aztec," McMasters said, "was my friend. His woman was my friend."

The Pima had come across the carnage at Aztec's trading post, and had followed the tracks left by McMasters, Kilpatrick and the six convicted killers. That was something that McMasters had not anticipated, but should have. Other Pima Indians would come to the post, and seeing what had happened, they would not go to Fort McDowell to ask the damned agent for justice. They were Pima Indians. They would seek retribution their way—much as McMasters sought it *his* way.

"You know Bear Aztec," McMasters said. "You have heard him mention The Man Who Is One With Horses." It was not a question. Hoping to see a horse he had traded or helped round up with old Bear Aztec, he looked at the other Indians. But things didn't work out that easily.

The leader did not take his eyes off McMasters, but called out to the pockmarked Indian in the Pima tongue. The grizzled, part-blind Indian answered in a few syllables, studied McMasters with his one good eye, shrugged, but then pointed with his chin up the hill at the others. He said something else, but it took more than his first response.

"The men you ride with," the old one said, "know death."

McMasters understood. "That is why they ride with me."

"You avenge Bear Aztec?" the old man asked.

McMasters nodded. "And my own family."

"And," the Indian said, "Juhki?"

"We buried Bear's wife, too. And the others. If we'd murdered them," McMasters added, hoping it might persuade the old Pima and his companions that he spoke truthfully, "we would not have buried them."

The man frowned. "I would not call that . . . buried."

McMasters sighed. "As best as we could. As I said, I also avenge my family." He waited. "Murdered by the same ones who butchered Bear and Juhki."

"And my nephews," the old one said.

"They all fought bravely," McMasters said. "There were just too many for them to fight."

"How many?"

"Nine."

The man looked past McMasters and up the far hill. "You number seven."

"Eight," McMasters corrected.

The old man's head shook. "One is a woman."

McMasters decided not to argue. He nodded toward the men riding with the old Pima.

"Join us, and there will be eleven." No matter how good they were, he didn't want the Pima Indians with him, but saw no other way out of the fix except by extending them the invitation. If they came along, even if they helped catch or kill a gang of cutthroats like those in the Butcher Gang, White Man's Law would go down hard on any Indians who committed violence against any white men.

A smile, the thinnest as possible, briefly appeared on the man's copper face. He called out to his fellow warriors and kicked his pony toward McMasters, raising the old Spencer up, not in a threatening way, but lifting it over his head in a signal of an alliance.

Most people underestimated just how quick Emilio Vasquez could move. It had left many a *Rurale*, at least one Texas Ranger, two deputy sheriffs in Cochise County, and even a few more jealous husbands, dead or dying.

He moved quickly, and when the deputy lawman

turned, gripping his shotgun, Vasquez slowed down, smiling.

"I keep an eye on the hills, señor," he told him, and tossed his Winchester to the ground, showing the gringo his empty palms. A sign of peace. Of friendliness. "In case more wait over the rise. They are Pimas. Pimas are wise. Cunning."

The idiot of a lawman turned back to look at the big brute on the buckskin horse.

Emilio Vasquez found the knife he had been hiding on his body for three weeks. He pressed the button to open the blade, and shoved the blade in the marshal's back, clamping the man's mouth with his thick right hand to stop any scream.

The man stiffened, groaned, and wet his britches as the shotgun dropped to the earth. Vasquez hated shotguns and hated McMasters, for he carried a shotgun. Besides, Vasquez did not need the Greener as he had already drawn the deputy's revolver and was spinning around to face the others even before the deputy, who Vasquez shoved forward, crashed into the dirt.

Bloody Zeke The Younger and the gambler in the fancy vest started toward him, but the metallic sound of the deputy's revolver coming to full cock stopped them in their tracks.

"Back to your horses. Keep them still."

Both hesitated. Emilio Vasquez aimed the pistol. "Pronto. Or you will travel the journey of the dead." He unloaded the shotgun, smashed it against a rock, and grabbed the Winchester he had dropped. Next he went to the mule the deputy had been leading. He glanced behind him, saw McMasters stopping his horse and saw the Indians. He flung aside the canvas, looked, checked one pack, then the other, and finally opened the saddle bag. His left hand went in, dropped one box, saw the other, and it too fell into the dirt. The third box made him laugh.

HENRY
.44 Caliber
Rimfire

Kissing the box, he ran back and slid to a stop in front of a dead bush that might be sturdy enough to serve as a tripod. He dropped to his knees, spilling several brass cartridges with those big, beautiful lead bullets on the top. Vasquez could not hold back the laughter as he picked up a cartridge and shoved it into the rifle.

He spun, jacking the lever, aiming the Yellow Boy at Bloody Zeke The Younger and the one-eyed man in patchwork britches.

"You stay back! Stay back or die."

Those gringo outlaws stopped, raising their hands.

"Let us help," the one-eyed idiot said.

"I told you to hold that damned mule." Vasquez waved the rifle barrel. "Back. Get back." He lowered his left hand and pulled out the deputy's revolver. "I can shoot with both hands, you bastards."

They backed up. He shot a glance at the others. The big Negro stood closest to him, but kept his eyes trained on what was happening below. The gambler just held the reins to his bay horse, and he too focused on what was playing out on the flats. The woman knelt beside the deputy, who, damn it all to hell, had not died already.

"Don't none of you try to stop me. I'm going to fix the flint on that *hijo de la puta.*" He hated shotguns.

Dropping the Colt onto the dirt by his knee, he swung the Winchester Yellow Boy around. One shot. That's all he had in the rifle. For now. But the man chasing Moses Butcher had made a major mistake. He should have given Emilio Vasquez the derringer . . . because with a long gun, Emilio Vasquez had no equal.

The stock pressed tightly against his right shoulder. He felt the wind blowing in from the storm clouds, and moved the barrel to allow for that.

"You gonna shoot that bastard?" the one-eyed coot called out. "Or not."

Emilio Vasquez grinned. "No. The Indians will kill him." He let out his breath slowly, relaxing, and squeezed the Winchester's trigger.

And just as quickly, the old Pima Indian was somersaulting backwards over the horse, the heavy carbine dropping into the dirt and cactus, blood spurting in the air.

The pony let out a terrifying cry, spun, and galloped back up the hill. About that time, the gunshot from the hill reached McMasters's ears.

"No!" McMasters screamed as he turned in the saddle. He saw the puff from a rifle, heard the report, and felt the bullet buzz past his ear. At the same time, an arrow tore off his hat from behind him. Then McMasters felt himself leaping from the saddle.

The buckskin bolted a few feet. McMasters rolled over on his back, brought up the shotgun, and found the young Indian charging him, nocking another arrow, charging in for the kill.

There was no chance, no other way. He swung the Remington over, and let one barrel of buckshot blow apart the boy's face and chest.

He came up to his knees. A bullet from the Indian tore the sand between his legs. He saw the one-eyed Indian, who had jumped off his pinto mare and charged at him, thumbing back the hammer on a .36-caliber Navy Colt. He had McMasters dead, but the old relic had not had a Richards conversion. It still fired percussion caps, and the cap only fizzled. The Indian cocked again, and McMasters sent the second barrel of buckshot into the man's chest.

Watching the menacing figure fly backwards and slam into a boulder, McMasters pitched the empty shotgun at the remaining Indian, the one with the old Springfield. He had hoped the shotgun would trip him, but no luck. The Indian leaped over, stopped, and did not bother to bring the old rifle to his shoulder. He was about to fire from his hip.

Although he reached for his holstered Colt, McMasters knew he had no chance. He was about to die.

Chapter 20

The mules had not been trained by the man known as John McMasters. That much was obvious to Mary Lovelace. As soon as the Mexican had pulled the trigger, both mules had taken off, kicking, squealing, and heading down the slope. He had let out a string of curses in Spanish and English at the one-eyed Rebel and whoever else was supposed to be holding the other mule.

His first shot had sent the warrior nearest to McMasters over the back of the horse.

Mary Lovelace knew the remaining Indians would kill McMasters. Then they would charge up this hill. Oh, they would not kill them. But the Mexican, once he had done away with the Indians would kill them all. She heard the shotgun blast below then turned toward the groaning deputy marshal. The sneaky bastard had pulled out a revolver from his back waistband.

That surprised her. She hadn't thought a by-the-book prude of a star-packer would carry anything concealed. His hand shook as he tried to thumb back the hammer on the nickel-plated pocket pistol, a Merwin Hulbert with a three-and-a-quarter-inch barrel. Six-shots that fired the Winchester .44-40 caliber cartridge. Fancy for a by-the-book lawman. But he did have the right idea.

Quickly, she reached over and took the pistol from the deputy, too weak to offer any resistance. She pointed the gun at the Mexican, remembering the words of her late bastard of a husband.

"Firing a pistol is more instinct than talent or eyesight. You just aim. Point your finger. And pull the damned trigger."

That's what she did . . . after cocking the hammer. The gun bucked in her hand, and down went the Mexican. Down went his rifle, too, sliding about six yards before catching on rocks. Everyone dashed for Emilio Vasquez.

Mary turned and snapped a shot at Bloody Zeke The Younger with the .44-40 Merwin Hulbert. That dark man had a dark heart, and he frightened her a lot more than the black man, who slid, grabbing the Winchester as he went about ten yards farther down the rise. By then, she had reached the Mexican, who kept rolling this way and that, clutching his side, begging in Spanish, praying in English, swearing in a mixture of languages that some puta had murdered him.

She grabbed the deputy's pistol with her left hand and sent a round kicking up rocks between the one-eyed Reb's legs. That stopped all of them.

A split second later, the black man fired the Yellow Boy, aiming down the slope . . . at the Pima Indians or, she feared, at the old man with the glasses and a bitterness, a hatred that matched if not topped her own.

* * *

The Indian spun to his side, dropping the Springfield unfired in the dirt. McMasters did not hear the gunshot from the hill, but he knew that's what had happened. The man dropped to his knees, and began singing his death song. He never finished. Another bullet hit him in his temple, and he dropped into a heap in the desert sand.

Leaving his Colt in the holster, McMasters dived into the dirt, crawled on his elbows and knees, and picked up the unfired Springfield. Then he rolled, expecting to feel the burning lead of a bullet entering his body at any moment. Rolling, he kept looking up the eastern hill. He saw the dust, heard the mules braying, then saw both mules bolting down the incline. One tripped, stumbled, and cartwheeled down, disappearing in an avalanche of dust and debris. The other? McMasters couldn't tell.

He rolled over until he came to a saguaro. It was not much in the way of cover, but it would have to do.

He tried to breathe normally . . . an impossibility. Looking up into the sun, he stared at the hilltop. He could only see blurs, and he reached up to adjust his eyeglasses.

Swearing, he looked over toward the dead old Indian and where his horse had been before the gunfight started. The glasses had come off when he had leaped off Berdan, and likely lay in the dust and rocks. Maybe busted. Maybe not. But he could not get them without the risk of getting his head blown off.

He glanced at the scene around him. The four Pimas lay dead, two from the Remington, two from whoever had used a gun—a long gun—from the hilltop. All of the ponies ridden by the Indians were raising dust up the western hill. Would they run back to Fort McDowell? Maybe. But it would take them a long time to reach the reservation, and he did not think even the best of trackers would be able to find his group.

He felt a sudden coolness, and a blackness fell over him. Clouds obscured the sun. Thunder boomed. Lightning streaked across the sky.

A monsoon would strike before long.

Sensing the approaching storm, Berdan stared at him and pawed the earth.

McMasters looked over at his horse.

"Stay where you are," he told the buckskin, hoping the horse would listen. He did not want that horse to attract the gunman's attention.

He had to think. *Daniel Kilpatrick? No.* Dan had to be lying up on that hill, dead or wounded.

McMasters wiped away sweat and dirt and cursed again, savagely, vilely, cursing himself and his damned fool idea. He never should have left Kilpatrick up there alone with six hardened killers. And he was trapped beneath the gun sights of six killers. He studied the old Springfield weapon with careful consideration.

A rifled musket from the Civil War, most likely. It fired a .58-caliber minié ball. Better than nothing, but he had only one shot. Maybe there were more powder, caps, and lead in the dead man's pockets. Maybe not. He couldn't risk crawling back to the dead Indian anyway.

He flipped up the leaf sight—300 yards, if he remembered correctly. Just about the distance he had covered. He would be shooting uphill—difficult for even the best marksman—and looking into the sun. The Springfield could be effective at 400 yards, maybe even 500, but McMasters couldn't even find a target at that distance—not without his eyeglasses. And his spectacles lay even farther away.

The Colt in his holster? Not at three hundred yards uphill. Not against six killers, even if one of them was a woman. He thought about the old Pima. That Indian did not think much of the woman, but suddenly, McMasters wondered if maybe the woman had him pinned down.

Writhing in the dust, feeling the coming of a thunderstorm, Emilio Vasquez knew how his brother must have felt that summer evening fifteen years ago.

His kid brother, the one his mother and father had always loved, the one they swore they would give their last piece of bread to, the one they did not work like a donkey or an Indian slave. Miguel Ángel. Oh, didn't that *bastardo* live up to his name? He had become the most holy of all priests at Saint Anthony of Padua in the puissant of a village on the lower Rio Yaqui called Cocori. Oh, how he had kissed his brother's cheeks, let him eat beans and drink wine, and cried about how his mother and father had died. He had prayed for Emilio Vasquez, had asked to hear his confessions, but Emilio, ever the fine brother, had said he had nothing worthy of confession.

As he writhed, Vasquez remembered why he despised shotguns and the men who used them.

* * *

One of the nuns, a fat witch with a nose long enough to stick into anyone's business, sprinted into the rectory and cried out that Emilio Vasquez had been packing an unholy cargo on those mules.

"Scalps!" she cried.

Padre Miguel Ángel felt no remorse about scalps of Apache Indians. The church helped the alcalde pay for such bounties offered in Cocori. But Emilio Vasquez's men had not paid attention to his orders. They had left some ribbons in the hair of some of the younger victims' scalps.

That fat nun wailed that she knew—she would always know—the hair of María Fernanda de la Rosa and her mother, Danna Paola. She pointed at Emilio Vasquez and said that he was no brother, but el Diablo.

His brother gave him a look of pity, of shame, of hatred.

Emilio Vasquez felt he had no choice. He took the cut-down double-barreled shotgun and put a ton of buckshot into his brother's stomach, and then shot the nun in the back of her head as she ran toward the door.

Mary slammed the Merwin Hulbert's checkered hard rubber grips against the Mexican's forehead. That shut him up.

"Shoot that bastard!" Bloody Zeke The Younger bellowed. "Then let's all get our horses and get the hell out of here!"

The woman was shouting at the men. Bloody Zeke and that bigoted old Rebel yelled back. Like some married couple arguing with the husband's daddy joining in to help out his worthless son. The redhead yelled back at Bloody Zeke.

"You stupid fool!" the gambler yelled. "You shot the redskin."

Carter levered another .44 slug into the Winchester, breathed in, exhaled, and fired down the hill again. He hated to do it, but the way he saw things, it was his best chance out of there. Cut loose with Bloody Zeke and the others, he'd be a dead man in three or four days, maybe even just three or four hours. Sticking with the white man with the shotgun didn't bode that well for survival, either, but at least he'd be doing something right.

Slowly, after the man named McMasters had rolled until he was sheltered, partly, by a thin saguaro, Alamo Carter looked off at the threatening sky, then looked at the even more treacherous-looking men. And the woman, who had one of her two pistols aimed at him.

"I heard what you told those boys," Carter said to her as he angled his head toward the other killers.

"But you're still holding that repeater," she said.

"You think you can hold off that bunch?" he asked.

"Don't worry. I won't save the last bullet for myself."

He grinned, lowered but did not drop the Winchester rifle, and gave a slight nod down the slope. Most of the packs had been busted apart when both mules tumbled down the slopes. One had slammed against a pile of boulders, and lay on its side, kicking and bellowing. The other had limped a few paces away. Carter could see boxes of cartridges broken apart, and even though the clouds had started to obscure most of the sun's rays, the brass casings reflected sunlight. *Like diamonds in the rough,* he thought. Food and coffee beans had also been scattered, the sugar mixing with sand to give the ants a mighty tasty dessert.

"You sure this is how you want to play out this hand, ma'am?" Carter asked the redhead.

"No," she answered. "But it's the bet I'm making . . . for the time being."

"Ya stupid whore!" the one-eyed jackal snapped.

"Bitch!" Bloody Zeke said in an icy voice.

Alamo Carter stood. "Well, I'll ride along with you . . . for a while . . . maybe." He rose, glanced at the deputy marshal, saw that somehow that ornery cuss kept right on breathing, turned toward the Mexican, and realized he hadn't died yet, either.

Out of the corner of his eye, McMasters glimpsed five or six fast lightning strikes. He counted. One-thousand-one. One-thousand-two . . . one-thousand-fourteen. Then heard the distant thunder.

"McMasters!" a voice called out after the thunder and wind had died. Even at the distance, he recognized the voice.

"Best get up here pronto. The deputy needs you!"

Chapter 21

McMasters never lowered the Remington twelve-gauge as he rode up the hill, his eyes moving, his mind anticipating anything. But all of the prisoners remained in view, even the Mexican, Vasquez. Unconscious, he was lying on the ground and bleeding from his abdomen. The woman, Mary Lovelace, knelt beside Daniel Kilpatrick, who managed to push himself up, but collapsed against the redhead.

"How bad is he?" McMasters asked, not looking at her or Kilpatrick, but watching the four prisoners standing.

"I'll live," Kilpatrick managed to say. His voice sounded weak, and his face had turned ashen. "Sorry, John. I let the Mex sneak up behind me."

"Don't talk. And lay back down, damn it."

"With . . . pleasure."

Mary Lovelace eased him back onto the ground, his hat serving as a pillow.

"I don't know how deep that knife got him," the redhead said. "Or what it nicked. I've got the bleeding stopped on the outside. Don't know about the inside. But he needs a doctor."

McMasters shot her a look. His eyes touched the two six-shooters—Daniel's revolver and a nickel-plated hideaway gun.

Lovelace saw that. "They're his." She indicated Kilpatrick.

"Both?"

"The small one's empty."

"Then—" He stopped, deciding to wait before taking the big one. He might regret that in a minute, maybe just a second. Swinging down off the buckskin, he asked the black scout,

"What happened?"

Alamo Carter told him concisely, like an Army man would. McMasters studied the unconscious Vasquez, and then looked down the hill. The sight of the mules sickened him. So did the dark clouds and the flashes of lightning.

"I guess," Carter said, "he figured to shoot the buck you was talkin' to, so's it would rile up them others. They'd kill you. I reckon he'd kill the rest."

"He didn't kill them all," McMasters said. "I had to get two." He waited.

Carter shifted the Winchester Yellow Boy. "Couldn't let an Indian kill you like that."

"I'm obliged."

"Don't be," Carter said. "Likely, I'll kill you later."

"Why not now?"

He let the Winchester drop onto the dirt. "Because it's empty."

Turning, McMasters looked at the others, Bloody Zeke,

Emory Logan, and Marcus Patton. "And you three? You could've mounted up, ridden out for parts unknown."

"Without ammunition?" The gambler pointed down the hill at the mules. "Fool animals took off once the shooting started."

"That's a government trained animal for you," McMasters said. "But you could've found ammo at Apache Junction . . . or anywhere on the way to Mexico."

"Bitch wouldn't let us leave," the Reb said.

McMasters glanced at Mary Lovelace, who refused to look at him and kept bathing Daniel Kilpatrick's face with a handkerchief. Lifting his head, McMasters found Bloody Zeke.

He shrugged.

"She had the gun. Well, the colored cuss had the rifle, but he was too busy saving your hide. She said she'd shoot any one of us who tried to leave here."

"And you believed her?"

Bloody Zeke pointed a wiry finger at the Mexican. "After she shot him, yeah, I believed her."

"All right." McMasters pointed down the hill. "Leave the hardware I loaned you here. Pick up what you can." He walked over to Lovelace and Kilpatrick, bent and picked up Kilpatrick's Colt, and shoved it into his waistband. He saw the busted Greener, and, taking the Merwin Hulbert, he checked the cylinder and saw that, indeed, she had fired every round. He started to hand it to her, but stopped.

"The Remington revolver I gave you . . ."

"You want it back?"

He nodded. She pulled it from her waistband, spun

it on her finger, and handed it, butt forward, toward him.

"Lay it down on Dan's stomach."

She grinned without humor. "Think I'd pull a border shift on you, McMasters? With an empty pistol."

"The Remington fires the same cartridges as this." He jostled the Merwin Hulbert, and stuck it behind his back.

She placed the 1890 Remington on Kilpatrick's stomach, and McMasters picked it up, stuck it in the front of his waistband, and followed the others down the hill.

"I'm sorry, fellow." Standing up, McMasters put the barrel of his Colt against the fallen mule's head, and squeezed the trigger. He never could look at a horse or mule or even a donkey after he had put the suffering beast out of its misery. Turning away abruptly, he moved along the precarious slope and came to the other mule.

He checked the animal's legs and hooves, and after a glance behind him, lowered the Remington on the ground, and removed the packsaddle. He patted the mule's rump, grabbed the canteens, and a sack of jerky and corn dodgers, and dumped most of the grain from another sack for the mule to eat. Once he had the Remington in his hands again, he walked back to where the prisoners sat or squatted, picking up spilled cartridges and depositing them in sacks. He did not look at the mule he had just killed.

Alamo Carter looked up. "No good?"

"He'll live if the wolves or a mountain lion doesn't

get him," McMasters said, and shot a glance back at the mule, which grazed on the grain. He studied the skies.

"All right. That's all we're getting. Leave the rest, and head back up the hill. We need to find some shelter before that storm hits." He walked up ahead of the others, and when he got to the pile where they had all placed their weapons, he turned around and waited.

"The bags with the ammo," he said once the men had stopped, "will go on Dan's horse. Put the food on the palomino."

"It ain't much food," the Reb said.

"Ain't much ammo, either," said the gambler.

"You can blame that on Vasquez. Go ahead. Get those sacks tied on those horses." McMasters walked over to Mary Lovelace while the prisoners performed their tasks.

"Can he ride?"

"I'll ride," Daniel Kilpatrick answered.

"Not far," the redhead told him.

"He'll catch his death if he stays here," McMasters said. "We'll find shelter for the night. Tomorrow we'll be at Apache Junction. Should be a doctor there."

She nodded and pointed toward the Mexican. "What about him?"

"He'll ride or I'll tie him on," McMasters said before returning to the weapons. There, he waited until the four men had returned.

"We get our guns back now?" the Reb asked.

"Sort of." McMasters pointed the Remington's barrels at the gambler. "Why don't you take the Starr?"

"But I had the Army conversion," Marcus Patton protested.

"I know. But change is a good thing, don't you think?" He grinned. They had been picking up ammunition. There was no way he was going to let them have their own guns back. Hell, every one of them had to have pocketed a few extra rounds for themselves, to load when he wasn't looking, and to use on him the first chance they got.

Bloody Zeke laughed. "In that case, I would like to have the redhead's Remington .44-40. It is a fine gun."

"You get the Army," McMasters said.

The Burgess went to the Reb. McMasters tossed Carter Kilpatrick's hideaway pistol.

"What about the Mex?" Bloody Zeke asked. "Does he get my derringer?"

"He gets to live." Picking up the Winchester Yellow Boy and the derringer, he walked over to Emilio Vasquez and toed him with his boot.

The bandit's eyes fluttered and he turned his head away.

"I know you're awake," McMasters said. "And if those eyes don't open in two seconds, they'll never open again." He pressed the Remington's barrels on the outlaw's neck.

"Do not shoot, amigo." Vasquez rolled over and managed a weak smile. "I am shot in the belly. I am dying. I would like to find a priest . . ."

"That bullet went through and, unfortunately, I doubt if it took out anything but some fat," McMasters said. "So you better stand up and get to your palomino."

Slowly, the man sat up, looked at his bloody-stained shirt, and grinned. "Who bandaged my belly? The puta who shot me?"

"Patton," McMasters answered.

"*Muy bueno.* He should be a doctor, not a gambler."

"Get up. Get on your horse. And keep your hands out of the bags of food strapped to the horn and your bedroll."

Emilio Vasquez managed to stand, and he beat the dust off his hat on his legs before settling the big sombrero on his head. "And what gun do I get now?"

The killer's ears were not hurting, McMasters determined. "Well you proved how good you are with the Yellow Boy, so I guess you can have this." He swung the weapon around and slammed the stock against Vasquez's head. The man dropped to the ground, screaming and rolling over. He cursed, came to his feet like a cat, and stopped. The Winchester lay on the ground. The Remington twelve-gauge was pointed inches from Vasquez's face.

"You pull a stunt like that again and I'll kill you," McMasters said. "You even think about it and I'll kill you. You look at me and make me think that you're even considering it, and I blow your damned head off."

"I am bleeding again." The killer pointed at his bloody side. "And I cannot see so well."

"I can," McMasters said. "I found my glasses before I came up this ridge. I can see well enough to blow your head off right now."

"*Por favor.*" The killer scrambled to his feet. "I go. I do harm to no one. I go to my horse. I be a good posse from this moment until we have caught and scalped the last member of the Butcher Gang."

"You'll need this." McMasters lowered the shotgun, pulled the derringer out of his vest pocket, and tossed it at Vasquez's feet.

The man grunted and groaned as he bent to pick it up, and, clutching his bleeding side, he hurried toward the palomino.

McMasters waited until his heart stopped racing and his breathing returned to normal then he picked up the Yellow Boy and walked to Mary Lovelace and Daniel Kilpatrick. He withdrew the 1890 Remington and offered it, butt forward, to Mary.

"That's the same gun I had before," she told him.

"I figure you can use it."

"I shot the Mexican with your friend's pistol."

"I figure you can use any gun you happen to pick up."

She smiled. "Not that one." Her jaw jutted toward the Remington shotgun.

"Let's ride," he said, and moved to gather the reins to Berdan.

It did not rain that afternoon, at least, it did not rain on John McMasters and his cobbled-together posse. The storm skirted off to the northwest, and underneath an overhang, he spent a dry evening with a wounded deputy marshal and six hardened killers.

The men kept their distance from one another. That had been one of McMasters's orders. "You get close and I send a load of buckshot your way," he had told them. "Probably one of you'll be killed outright. The other'll just be maimed. So if you've been thinking about trading with each other for ammunition you stole that no longer works in your new weapon, think about double-ought buckshot in your belly and arms."

"What I'd rather think about," Marcus Patton said,

"is bacon that isn't covered with sand. That damned Vasquez."

"I am the one with a hole in my belly," the Mexican whined. "You should have stopped that puta from shooting me. We could all be down in the Mescal Mountains, sipping tequila, eating enchiladas. But no . . ."

"Shut up," Patton said, spitting out part of his supper. Sand-coated bacon and sand-coated coffee. Hardtack, which tasted like dirt and was harder than granite, even after it was soaked in coffee for ten minutes. That was supper.

McMasters refilled his cup and settled next to Daniel Kilpatrick, who was still being tended to by Mary Lovelace. "You all right?" he asked the deputy marshal.

Kilpatrick shrugged.

"You might consider making a travois," Mary Lovelace told McMasters. "I don't like the way that wound looks."

"You're not hauling me behind some horse," Kilpatrick said.

"You don't watch it," Lovelace told him, "and we'll be hauling your corpse strapped over your saddle."

McMasters sipped coffee, staring at the green-eyed redhead and not at the lawman who had planned to marry Rosalee. "We'll rig something up in the morning." He felt Kilpatrick's eyes blazing through him. "It's a short ride, Dan, to Apache Junction. Leave you with a doctor."

"You know what I'll do once I'm there," the deputy said.

McMasters nodded. "I got a good hunch."

"Well, let me spell it out for you, old man." He tried to sit up, but fell back and kept his eyes closed for a while until the pain subsided enough for him to breathe again . . . and to stare into McMasters's cold, hard eyes. "I won't ask the sawbones you leave me with to send that telegraph. Couldn't trust him. So I'll do it myself. I'll put every lawman in the southern part of the territory on your trail. The Superstitions will be filled with federal marshals, county sheriffs, posses from as far away as Tucson and Verde. And I have to think maybe a dozen or so bounty hunters. But they won't be chasing after Moses Butcher. They'll be after you . . . and your posse of killers."

"A man needs to do what he thinks best." McMasters waited until the redhead looked up at him. "Same for a woman."

Her green eyes did not look away.

"You must really hate Moses Butcher," he told her.

She just stared.

"That's why you didn't let those others skedaddle. You want Butcher as bad as I do. I'd like to know why."

"I don't see how that's any of your business," she said.

He finished the coffee and stood. "I'll be sleeping out there." He pointed away from the overhang, glad it had not rained.

"Not with us?" Bloody Zeke called out.

"You want me. Try to find me. But guess wrong and you'll find buckshot instead."

Bloody Zeke and the Rebel laughed.

"If you need to relieve yourselves," McMasters said, "do it now. One at a time. At separate bushes. Anyone goes to the same bush, I blow him apart. I'll be watching from the dark. Any of you get close to each other,

I blow you both apart. Pleasant dreams." He walked away from the fire and let the night swallow him.

"You, too, gringo," Vasquez called out and chuckled.

John McMasters knew he would not sleep. He could not afford to. The problem, he understood, was how could he ever go to sleep . . . with those six, seven if he counted Daniel Kilpatrick . . . waiting for their chance.

Chapter 22

McMasters woke to the grayness before dawn and cursed himself for falling asleep at all. At least he had not dozed for too long. He didn't ache. And he felt as though he had not even slept more than a minute. He stood, stifled a yawn, and moved around the boulder and through the brush, keeping an eye and an ear wide open for movement or the whirl of a rattlesnake. He heard only snores and one of the horses stamping its feet.

Stopping, he studied the bedrolls until he felt confident that someone slept underneath all of those covers. Then he moved to the fire, stoking the embers and feeding a few twigs and grass to get it going. A bedroll moved, and the woman raised her head. He studied her a moment, before turning to the coffeepot.

"What's for breakfast?" Bloody Zeke asked from a bedroll a few yards away.

"One cup of coffee," McMasters said. "Then we ride."

Grumbles and curses followed as the convicts slowly

wakened. The redhead was the first to actually climb out of her bedroll, which she rolled up, tied up, and tossed near her saddle. She moved over to Daniel Kilpatrick, and once McMasters had the fire going and the coffeepot hanging from a tripod over the blaze, he followed her. First he kicked the boots of Emilio Vasquez.

The outlaw cursed in Spanish.

"Get up," McMasters ordered. "Saddle the horses."

"I will saddle my own," Vasquez mumbled beneath the canvas. "And only after I have had my coffee."

"You will saddle them all," McMasters told him. "Then you can have some coffee."

The man sighed and slowly rose, rubbing his eyes and beating some shape back into the sombrero that he had used as a pillow. Slowly, still muttering his curses, he tossed aside his blankets and moved to the horses. McMasters watched him, and then moved over toward Mary Lovelace and Daniel Kilpatrick.

"I'm not being pulled anywhere," the deputy marshal said firmly. "I ride that horse."

"Till you fall off," McMasters told him.

Kilpatrick nodded and repeated, "Till I fall off."

When McMasters glanced at the redhead, she shrugged and stood. "I'll get him some coffee."

He watched her go and was about to check on the Mexican when Kilpatrick cleared his throat. McMasters looked at him.

"I meant what I said yesterday."

"I never doubted you," McMasters said.

"You think . . . I'm wrong," Kilpatrick said. "That I . . . didn't . . . love her . . . enough. Otherwise . . . I'd . . ."

McMasters held up his coffee cup and shook his

head. "We're different generations. That's all. You think one way. I think another. You do what you think right. I'm doing what I know is right."

"Right for you, maybe. But not right in my eyes. Or in the eyes of the law."

He sipped coffee. "We'll see what a judge and jury say when it's all said and done."

Kilpatrick shook his head. "You ride into the Superstitions or down into Mexico with this bunch, you won't live to see a judge or a jury."

"Maybe so." McMasters had the Winchester Yellow Boy with him.

"You trade that shotgun in for a long gun?" Kilpatrick said.

"No." McMasters tilted his head toward the rocks and brush. "Remington's over there." He laid the rifle by Kilpatrick's side. "Vasquez broke your Greener. I know you've got your Colt, but you might have need of this, too. I loaded it. Vasquez and Carter proved it shoots true yesterday."

Kilpatrick studied the rifle. His lips moved, but no words were spoken, and at length he looked back at McMasters. "After I practically got us both killed yesterday, you trust me with a gun."

"Man's got to trust somebody. Now, I better get that Remington. Feel kind of naked without it."

"I won't change my mind, John," Kilpatrick said. "You get me near a telegraph, near a sheriff or town marshal, I'm doing what I know is right. You can't bribe me."

Distaste filled McMasters's mouth. He sucked in a deep breath, let it out, and drank some more coffee. "Wasn't meant for a bribe. It's meant to maybe keep us alive between here and Apache Junction. You work far with that rifle. I work close with the Remington. If need be. Maybe there won't be any trouble today."

Maybe. That had to be odds even Marcus Patton would not bet against.

The redhead was bringing Kilpatrick his coffee, and McMasters stood. He did not want to find his cinch loose or his stirrups compromised. He had better check and double-check Vasquez's work. As he walked toward the nearest horse, Kilpatrick called out his name. McMasters stopped, but only half-turned, keeping most of his attention on Vasquez and the sorrel he was saddling.

"I did love her," Kilpatrick said.

McMasters did not answer. He went to fetch his shotgun, and then he walked over to the Mexican as he finished with Carter's horse.

They made lousy time, and McMasters could only blame Daniel Kilpatrick for that. No. He couldn't blame the young lawman. He had only John Christopher McMasters to blame. It was a fool idea, and the clopping of the hooves on the hard rock as they climbed the rugged hills just made him even sleepier.

At noon, they stopped at an abandoned adobe hut along some creek bed that rarely saw water. They dismounted, for the incline became steeper, rockier, and much more narrow on the trail that led into the Superstitions, and to the village of Apache Junction.

"You'd think a body would know better than to try to homestead here." The gambler, Marcus Patton, picked up a piece of a China plate, shook his head, laughed, and tossed it into a clump of cactus. "Farmers. Damned fools. This is a damned desert. Didn't anyone tell them?"

McMasters knelt by what once had been a garden. Or at least, the homesteaders had tried to make a garden. He wondered how long they had lasted. Not five years. Not long enough to prove up their claim and get their own land. Maybe not five months. Perhaps not even five weeks. He found a thin strand of barbed wire.

Seeing that, Marcus Patton laughed again. "And I guess they got some of that devil's rope to keep cattle out of their garden. Damn, damn those fools. This ain't even fit for cattle. It's a country only fit for—" His head shook.

"Death," Emory Logan said.

The gambler's eyes appeared to tear over. His voice even cracked as he turned away. "Yeah," he said, and hurried to his bay horse. "Yeah. Death."

McMasters carefully studied the wire then took it with him to the buckskin. Unfastening one of the saddlebags, he laid the wire with its sharp barbs, more razors than hooks, atop the boxes of buckshot.

"What ya want that rusty wire fer?" Emory Logan asked.

"To wrap it around your manhood if you get cross with me, Reb," McMasters said.

With his mouth open, Emory Logan just stared with his one good eye. Once McMasters refastened the saddlebag, he grabbed the horn, and pulled himself into the saddle, pulling the Remington from the scabbard even before his right foot found the stirrup.

"All right. Mount up. Quit burning daylight."

Single file they rode, McMasters pulling up the rear.

In the afternoon, he saw storm clouds beginning to form to the south, dark and menacing, but so far, offering only a threat of moisture. And so far, no lessening of hellfire's heat. At the point, climbing the ridge, rode the woman. Behind her, Alamo Carter had dismounted and was leading the sorrel. That made sense to McMasters. No sense in making the beast carry Carter's bulk up the hill. They had a long way to go.

McMasters had thought they would make it in to Apache Junction by early evening. At the rate they were moving, they'd be lucky to get there by midnight. There was nowhere else to go. Junction was the nearest town.

He found Kilpatrick maybe twenty or thirty yards behind Alamo Carter. The boy gripped the horn with both hands and slumped forward. He was stubborn. He should have let them make a travois, and if things did not improve in a hurry, McMasters would make him dismount and be pulled behind. Even if he had to handcuff the kid to the travois posts with his own manacles.

Behind Kilpatrick came the Mexican, who was singing some song in Spanish. McMasters focused on the bags of food strapped to Vasquez's palomino. Next, he looked ahead at Kilpatrick's horse and the sacks of ammunition. Nothing seemed out of the ordinary.

After Vasquez rode the gambler, who was fanning himself with his hat, and ten yards farther down the hill was Bloody Zeke. Just ahead of McMasters rode the one-eyed bigot.

McMasters's horse began to urinate, so McMasters shifted in the saddle, shoved the Remington into the scabbard, and fetched his canteen. He rubbed his raw lips across the spout, letting the moisture ease the pain, and took one small sip. After he returned the canteen's strap to the horn, he removed his eyeglasses and began cleaning the lenses with his bandanna.

"Vamonos muchachos. Viva Padre Miguel Ángel."

McMasters' head shot up, and he quickly slid the eyeglasses back on, reaching for the Remington as he did. He caught a glimpse of the palomino bolting out of the line, loping up toward Kilpatrick. Near the crest of the hill, Mary Lovelace had turned the pinto around.

"Look out!" she screamed. Her words echoed across the desert.

"Dan!" McMasters spurred the buckskin. He thundered past the Reb, so close that the brown horse began to buck.

Emory Logan squealed as he tried to keep his seat, tried not to be bucked off and over the ridge into the rocks and hell below. By the time McMasters reached Bloody Zeke, who had reined his black to a stop, Emilio Vasquez had pulled up alongside Daniel Kilpatrick.

"No!" McMasters screamed, and watched, horrified, as the Mexican killer shoved the deputy marshal as he lifted his head and turned around, one hand reaching for the Winchester in the scabbard. Then Daniel Kilpatrick was gone, and McMasters saw only an empty saddle.

But he heard, briefly, the scream.

Not from Dan.

Mary Lovelace had dismounted and left her horse as she ran down the slope. The Negro whirled, straightened, and reached instinctively for a belted gun, only to realize once he pulled the Merwin Hulbert that all he held was a bunch of metal—worthless without bullets.

McMasters saw in horror as Vasquez jerked the Winchester from the scabbard, wheeled the palomino around, and worked the lever.

"Son of a bitch!" the gambler cried, and Marcus Patton slid off the bay horse, and quickly went around the horse as Vasquez thundered past.

The first shot whined off a boulder ahead of McMasters. Vasquez galloped toward Bloody Zeke, who stopped the black, holding the reins firmly, and watched the rider, leaning low in the saddle, working the lever, and firing, one-handed again.

McMasters swore and pulled hard on the reins, bringing Berdan to a hard, sliding stop. He leaped from the saddle, tried to keep his feet, but tripped and slid forward on both knees. A roar reached his ears, coming simultaneously with a searing pain across his left cheek as a bullet tore a gash. He tasted blood. He blinked away sweat. Somehow, his glasses remained seated on his nose and ears, and Emilio Vasquez and the thundering palomino came clearly into view. The Mexican levered the gun, dropped the reins, and brought the Yellow Boy to his shoulder. He aimed and he smiled.

And McMasters pulled both triggers of the Remington.

He did not even remember bringing the twelve-gauge to his shoulder. Hell, maybe he hadn't. Maybe he had just braced the shotgun against his stomach, tilted it upward, and fired. He was up and seeing through the dust. Suddenly realizing what was coming right for him, he dived toward the rocks on his left. The horse, that beautiful palomino, tumbled mane over tail, barely missing McMasters and knocking the shotgun from his hands. The Remington fell onto the trail and McMasters slammed into the rocks. Cactus spines speared his fingers. At least, he seemed to grasp, that he was on the hill side of the path, in no danger of falling over the ledge. But Emilio Vasquez, his brain told him, could still shoot him dead.

McMasters pushed away and looked up the hill, saw more dust. A body that did not move seemed to be sitting on the road, legs stretched out, the back leaning against the rocky wall. But no head. McMasters could not see a head.

Suddenly, Berdan snorted and let out a fearful cry.

Vasquez, McMasters told himself, *is dead.* He spun around. The palomino, dead like its rider, had rolled into the rocks, coming to a stop, but McMasters's buckskin was rearing, backing up, getting close to the edge. McMasters ran. He had no time to try to soothe his horse, no lullabies to sing, no calming words to call out. He jumped, grabbed the reins in both hands, and pulled hard. He remembered the colt, and that day a lifetime ago on his birthday. The colt had almost pulled him over the Mogollon Rim. The buckskin weighed a damned sight more than a colt, and was five times as strong.

Fear shined brightly in the buckskin's eyes, and the horse backed up, losing its footing. One leg went over the edge, pawing desperately to locate solid ground.

Somewhere, McMasters found the strength, and Berdan regained his footing. Probably realizing he was about to fall into a vast emptiness, that terrifying void, the buckskin jumped forward. His shoulder caught McMasters and sent him reeling, gasping, and bleeding from his cheeks. His palms scarred by the pull of leather reins across flesh, he landed on his knees again. Through the dust, he saw something else. Gritting his teeth, he reached for his .45-caliber Colt, which cleared the leather and pointed at the figure holding the Remington shotgun.

Chapter 23

"It ain't loaded," Alamo Carter told him. "And I ain't got no shells."

"Keep it that way." McMasters looked past the black killer and felt the hurt . . . and guilt . . . as he saw the others peering over the ridge. He bit his lip.

"Rope's on your horse," Carter said. "We'll need it."

That gave McMasters hope. "Is he alive?"

The ex-Army scout gave a slight shrug. "If he is, it'll be a miracle."

McMasters walked ahead of Alamo Carter, pulling Berdan behind him. He thought about mounting the buckskin, but wasn't certain he'd have enough strength to even get one foot into a stirrup. He had taken the Remington from Carter and shoved the weapon into the scabbard. He did not look at the mangled, bloody thing that had once been Emilio Vasquez, and did not bother to pick up the Winchester repeater that the killer had dropped. He just walked up that hill.

By then, most of the others had turned to watch his

approach. Only the redhead kept looking into the abyss.

McMasters heard her shout, "Kil-pat-rick?", spacing out the syllables.

Her echo answered and nothing else.

When he reached them, he wrapped the buckskin's reins around a clump of creosote and moved to the rim's edge. Below, he found a garden of stone boulders that led to the Salt River four hundred feet below. Saguaros dotted the hills, even an Arizona walnut, and paloverde trees covered the riverbanks. Less than halfway down the slope, pinned between two jagged dark rocks, lay Daniel Kilpatrick.

"Kil-pat-rick?" Mary Lovelace called out again.

His left leg was bent at a hideous angle, both arms drooped over the sandstone edges, and his head hung facedown as if he stared at something in the shade. Twenty-five or thirty yards below, a green bush had snagged his hat. His left boot lay in a bare spot between the rugged boulders.

McMasters could see the blood on the stone ten feet below that marked where Kilpatrick had first hit after Vasquez had shoved him off his horse and over the edge. He did not need Alamo Carter to read the sign for him. McMasters could tell. Kilpatrick had bounced off that rock, landed on another natural cairn, slammed hard and rolled down the clear spot and dropped off the next ledge, rolling and smashing his way to his final resting place.

It could very well be just that.

"Leave him," Bloody Zeke The Younger said. "Ain't nothing we can do for him now."

McMasters pushed himself up and took the coiled lariat from his saddle.

Alamo Carter stepped in front of him and held out his hands.

"I'll go down there. Fetch him."

McMasters shook his head. "My job. I got him killed. No sense in risking your neck."

"You didn't get him killed, McMasters," the former slave said. "That Mex had that knife for a long time. Like as not, he would've slit that deputy's throat long before we ever got to Yuma. And killed that old driver, too."

"In which case," Emory Logan said with a snort before he sprayed dirt with tobacco juice, "we'd be free and not on some fool's errand bein' led by a crazed ol' hoss-lover."

McMasters secured the end of the lariat to a giant boulder, pulled it tight, and tossed the rest of the hemp down the canyon.

"That ain't nowhere near long enough," Mary Lovelace said.

"Shut up," the gambler told her. He smiled and nodded at McMasters. "If he wants to go, let him go. That's his friend down there." He cleared his throat. "But you just tell us what we can do to help, McMasters."

McMasters shook his head and fished gloves out of the back pocket of his britches. He pulled them on and again tested the firmness of the rope.

"You're seventy-five feet short of Kilpatrick," Mary Lovelace told him.

"Close enough," McMasters said. "I can make my way down to his . . . body. Get him up to the rope." No wind, no threatening clouds anywhere to be found, just the relentless late July sun, yet he felt a coldness despite the heat.

"And then what?" Alamo Carter asked.

"Just wait for me"—McMasters started down then looked up—"unless I get killed."

His boots found a hold below, and he began lowering himself.

"Fat chance," the gambler said.

Then they were out of view, except for Mary Lovelace and Alamo Carter. "Fat chance," McMasters said softly and chuckled. *Fat chance,* he thought, *that they'll be there when I've gotten Dan's body? Or fat chance that I'll get killed?*

He stopped thinking and concentrated on what he was doing. He came to the clear spot, felt his boots sliding on the loose gravel, and had to dig his heels into the dirt to stop from going over the drop-off. He looked down, sucked in a deep breath, and glanced back up. Mary Lovelace had disappeared, but Alamo Carter kept staring at him. The big man was sitting, his legs dangling over the edge, holding the rope with both hands and bracing his back against the boulder.

If McMasters had been betting, he would have wagered that one of them—including Alamo Carter—would be cutting that rope to send John McMasters to join Daniel Kilpatrick in the deathtrap below. He looked down again, picking out the best path.

He figured the others had already gathered their horses, filled their weapons with bullets, and were loping up or down the trail. There was nothing he could do to stop them, just as he could do nothing if Alamo Carter had decided to loosen the rope and let McMasters drop to his death.

Maybe they'd let him live, figuring—McMasters chuckled without humor—that he'd die trying to get Kilpatrick off those rocks anyway. They would not stay, and that, if McMasters somehow survived, would not be a bad thing. Emilio Vasquez had taught him that much. It had been an insane idea to persuade six hardened killers facing execution, life imprisonment, or long sentences in the dungeon called Yuma Territorial Prison to join him on a suicide mission. Trust them?

He leaped down, feeling his feet send loose stones tumbling. He bounced off the rock wall, came back, bounced off again, and knew he had come to the end of the line. He let go of the rope and dropped the rest of the way.

His boots hit rocks and dirt, and he fell over, twisting to land on his buttocks and sliding ten feet to the forest of boulders. Breathing heavily, sweating like a pig, he looked up. The rope dangled there. He waited for it to start creeping up to the ridge above, leaving him trapped below, more than three hundred feet of treacherous terrain to the Salt River below, about fifty or so feet of an even harder climb up.

The rope, however, just dangled, still within his grasp. He had time, maybe, to change his mind. Save his hide. Although, once he got back to the trail, if those five killers remained waiting for him, he figured they would have loaded their guns and would not hesitate to use them on him.

He turned back and slid down to the rocky edge.

McMasters jumped the next two-foot drop, bending when he hit and stumbling into the hot sandstone. He caught his breath, reached above him until he had a good hold of a boulder, and struggled to pull himself up. Once he had reached the boulder's top, he sat, feeling the sharp points of jagged rocks leaving indentations in his buttocks and thighs. He saw Daniel Kilpatrick's body. He did not bother to look up at Alamo Carter or anyone else who might be staring down at him. He doubted if the black man remained up there. *Even God isn't watching anymore.*

McMasters removed his glasses, stuck them in his pocket, and wiped his face and eyes . . . and some tears . . . with the bandanna. He had known it in his heart, but so close to Kilpatrick, no more than twenty-five feet below him, he could tell that the young deputy marshal was dead.

Still, McMasters moved carefully, stopping once when he caught the rattling of a snake. He wet his lips, waiting, until he decided that the rattler's warning came from several yards to his right. Not near Kilpatrick's body. He bent his knees, using his arms for balance, and took one precarious step after another, until some long while later, he was touching the hair of what had once been the young man who was to become his son-in-law.

John McMasters reached down and fingered the boy's eyelids shut.

"I'm sorry, Dan," he whispered. "But I'm still going after Butcher."

His words lacked confidence. To keep his date with vengeance, he had to get back to the road. And that would take a bloody miracle.

He tugged the body free from the rocks, ignoring the blood, the bones protruding from Kilpatrick's clothes and flesh, and the gray, grotesque matter that seeped from the splits in the boy's skull and natural orifices.

Daniel Kilpatrick felt light. McMasters dragged him across the rocks, avoiding the rattlesnake hidden in some hole or underneath a slab of sandstone. Grunting, sweating, shoving, and swearing, he managed to get the corpse up on the ledge above him. The legs dangled in his face, and McMasters noticed the other boot had been pulled off, along with the sock from the foot already missing a boot.

He looked away, fought down the gall in his throat and gut, and moved down a few feet, trying to find the easiest path to get himself up that five feet without knocking the corpse back down, possibly sending it to the banks of the Salt River below.

Five minutes later, he was on the ledge, breathing heavily, chest aching, heart pounding. He came to his knees and looked, first at the body of Daniel Kilpatrick—still there—and then at the rocks above where the rope might still be waiting for him.

Again, he wiped sweat from his eyes. Not wanting to use his glasses out of fear he would drop them or lose them for he had a long way to go yet, he squinted.

The rope remained.

And Alamo Carter's big, bald, black head reappeared.

"You need help?"

"I will," McMasters said, realizing he could barely hear himself. He tried to clear his throat, but lacked enough moisture or strength. Even shaking his head took more energy than he had.

He turned, slid back to the body of the deputy marshal, and reached down to grasp the corpse's arms.

Grunting and sliding, he backed his way up, dragging Kilpatrick's legs to solid ground.

Then he rose and dragged the body toward the dangling end of the lariat.

Not enough rope hung down to tie to Kilpatrick's body, and the overhang was too far for McMasters to push the corpse atop. He looked around, thinking, and saw an avalanche of boulders on the far side of the rocks. *Maybe.*

Slinging the body over his left shoulder, McMasters stumbled in that direction, pausing frequently to catch his breath and wipe away more sweat. Reaching the boulders, he swallowed what he could and crept and crawled up that makeshift staircase. The rocks only went so high, but that was close enough. With a grunt and heave, McMasters managed to get Kilpatrick's body on to the top of the ledge. Then, somehow, he managed to get himself up above. Lying in the dirt and rocks, he breathed heavily, sand and dried twigs sticking to his clothes and his flesh.

His body and mind craved for water and for rest, but he knew better than to stop while he had momentum.

Somehow, he managed to push himself up, came to his knees, and looked up. Alamo Carter was standing, but he saw no one else. Likely, they were all raising dust for Mexico. Perhaps Carter had drawn the short straw and had been ordered behind to wait. To kill McMasters. *No.* McMasters shook his head. The black man had had plenty of chances to make sure McMasters was dead.

He turned back and reached for the corpse.

He dragged and pulled and positioned Kilpatrick

over his shoulder again, and staggered toward the final wall. Once, he tripped, falling to his knees, but by some miracle he did not drop the dead man. With a groan and giant effort, he made himself stand, lifting the dead weight on his shoulder. He zigged and zagged until he dropped to his knees again, falling on purpose, and slowly, gently, lowered the body onto the ground.

Turning back, leaning against the rocks, he began pulling the rope until it lay in a loose, rough coil near him. Next he brought the rope underneath Kilpatrick's body and wrapped it underneath the dead man's armpits and chest, making a good tight knot. He lifted the body, let it fall again over his left shoulder, and with his gloved hands, he reached out and gripped the rope firmly. At least, as tight as his cramped, aching hands and fingers could manage.

Above him, Alamo Carter nodded.

McMasters did the same, and the big killer disappeared with the rope braced against his shoulders and back.

McMasters felt himself lifted as stones tumbled onto the clearing, bouncing and pounding their way toward the river below. He reached the next ridge and kept his momentum going forward, feeling the rope in his hands and shifting the body closer. He slipped, the body tearing away from him, moving toward the road while McMasters slid down. He stopped himself from dropping over the next ridge and saw Daniel Kilpatrick's legs and feet—both without boots or socks—disappear onto the ridge . . . the safety . . . above.

McMasters sat up, chest heaving, still aching. He waited. He listened. Then he heard a curse, a pistol shot, and saw the rope . . . his precious lifeline . . . flinging over the top. He lunged for it, but it was nowhere near him, and he fell onto his face. Coming up, he looked down, and saw the rope falling, spinning, silently making its way toward the Salt River. It hit the rocks, and the sandstone swallowed it.

He looked up. Six feet. That's all he needed. Six feet and he would be on the road. He could drink water. He could eat corn dodgers or jerky. He could rest. Sleep. Six feet. That's all. It looked like six miles.

Suddenly, startlingly, Alamo Carter leaned over the edge, holding the Winchester Yellow Boy. His giant right hand shoved into the lever, the barrel pointing straight down at McMasters's chest.

Chapter 24

"Grab hold," the black killer said.

McMasters lacked strength to move. If that giant planned on killing him, he might as well just do it from where he lay. McMasters wasn't getting any closer to that .44-caliber rifle.

"Damn it," the big man barked. "Take hold of the barrel. I'll pull you up."

McMasters blinked.

"Now. The rifle's all I got."

Hell, McMasters thought, *I don't even have strength enough to pull the Colt. If he wants to kill me . . .*

He stood, somehow, and staggered to the dangling rifle. It hurt to lift both arms over his head. It hurt to tighten his grip around the rifle's barrel. His lips pressed hard against one another. He focused on holding onto the Winchester as hard as he could. He did not even bother trying to steel himself for the bullet that surely would come tearing through his body.

"On three," Carter said. "One . . . two . . ." His head

vanished as he turned away from the edge and his bulging right arm began pulling and lifting.

McMasters did not hear the final number and braced his feet against the rocky terrain, trying to assist the massive Negro. His hands felt sweaty, but the gloves, still dry on the outside, did not slip. A moment later, he saw the road, the blue skies, white clouds, and Mary Lovelace holding the 1890 Remington in her right hand. She wasn't aiming the .44-40 at McMasters. That was all he saw.

Rolling over away from the cliff, Alamo Carter gave a giant groan, and the Winchester slipped and toppled to the dust. So did John McMasters, who lay there, his right cheek on pebbles and ancient horse dung. His vision blurred briefly. His chest heaved. All the pain he had endured, all the muscles he had used, began attacking his body for such abuse. Yet he had to stand. No, not stand. He did, however, make himself sit up.

Ahead of him, in the center of the road, holding the reins to their horses, Emory Logan and Marcus Patton stood. They did not look happy. A few yards away from McMasters, Bloody Zeke The Younger sat on a boulder, right arm folded across his chest. The left elbow was braced on his thigh, and his hand pressed hard against his ear. Blood seeped between his fingers and dribbled down his shirtsleeve. Hatred filled his eyes, but he wasn't looking at John McMasters.

Turning, McMasters saw Mary Lovelace again. The pistol moved from Bloody Zeke to the other two. Finally, once Alamo Carter managed to sit up, she lowered the revolver, but not the hammer.

She gave McMasters a brief look.

"You all right?" Immediately, she put all her attention on Logan, Patton, and Bloody Zeke.

"I'll live." McMasters wasn't quite sure, though.

He thought he knew what had happened. Once Daniel Kilpatrick's body had reached the road and after Carter had removed the rope, Bloody Zeke had rolled up the lariat. Carter and Mary Lovelace must have thought he was doing that to help, but Bloody Zeke The Younger only helped himself. Throwing the rope over the side was a good way to help himself, he must have figured. That got his left earlobe shot off by Mary Lovelace.

The gambler and the bushwhacker might not have thrown in on Mary's or Zeke's side, but standing with their horses in the middle of the trail was a safe place for them to be. Safe for themselves. Safe for Mary Lovelace and Alamo Carter.

McMasters rose, stumbled to the buckskin, and found his canteen. One sip, he told himself, but his brain, muscles, and body did not listen. He drank greedily until he coughed, spitting out dust and water and phlegm. He wanted more, but made himself cork the container and push it back against the buckskin and the saddle. Then he staggered over, picked up the Winchester, and leaned against the boulder to which Alamo Carter had tied the rope earlier. He looked at Mary.

"Must've been . . . some party . . ." His breathing still came deeply, quickly. He did not know how long it would be until he could inhale and exhale normally, and without so much damned pain in his ribs, side, and chest.

"You did all the dancing," she told him. "Was it worth it?"

He looked at the body, then down the road where the dead palomino and what remained of Emilio Vasquez lay. McMasters looked at the sky and saw more than the bright blue and the white clouds. He saw the buzzards circling overhead.

"You brought him up all this way," Bloody Zeke said. "For what? Ain't a thing up here to bury him with."

"We'll take him . . . to . . . Apache Junction. Bury him there. A cemetery. A real funeral." *Another I won't be able to attend.*

Resting the Winchester across his thighs, he turned toward the Rebel and the gambler. "Get the food off that horse. The saddlebags. Bedroll. And get the saddle blanket."

"Saddle?" Marcus Patton asked. "Bridle?"

"Just the blanket, bags, and food."

The blanket and bedroll he could use to cover Daniel Kilpatrick's body.

"What about the Mex?" Emory Logan asked. "You gonna see that he gets planted, too. Gets hisself a real funeral."

McMasters looked at the dead body of Emilio Vasquez. Then he looked at that pretty palomino that had taken some of the buckshot that had not found the Mexican bandit's body.

"Bring him in," Marcus Patton suggested, "and maybe we . . . er, I mean . . . ahem, ummm, you . . . you could claim any reward there might be posted on that bandito. Law's sure to have learned that we ain't goin' to Yuma. Posses likely swarmin' all over the country.

Got to be papers on all our heads by now." He grinned at McMasters. "Including yours."

"Did you see what that Remington done to that bean-eater?" Logan asked. "Did you get a good look at his face. There ain't no face. Hell, there ain't even no head."

"It's worth a try," Patton said. "Got to be some money on him."

"On us." Alamo Carter's strength had returned. He sat up and mopped his own sweat-covered face with a rag.

"Law wouldn't expect one of us to bring in the Mex for a reward," Patton said.

Logan spit, wiped his mouth, and cursed before he turned toward McMasters. "Well? What do you think?"

McMasters kept looking at the buzzards.

"Leave him."

They would not make it into Apache Junction. Not after all the time and strength it had taken to bring Daniel Kilpatrick's body out of the rocks. McMasters wasn't even certain they would make it up the hill, but, somehow, they did.

Up that hill and down it, and then they entered a canyon, cleared it, and saw the clouds again. By then, dusk was not far away, and McMasters could smell rain in the air. "Should be what passes for a cave a mile up this road!" He had to shout to be heard above the wind as it roared through the canyon. "We'll camp there for the night! Make Apache Junction in the morning."

Bloody Zeke had slid his hat off his head and left it

dangling on his back by a stampede string. A scarf wrapped tightly around his head was stained with blood over his left ear. He pulled Daniel Kilpatrick's horse behind him. It carried quite the load—the ammunition sacks, the food sacks, and Daniel Kilpatrick's loosely wrapped but tightly tied body. McMasters rode behind them, the Remington, cleaned and reloaded, in his hands. Ahead rode the gambler and the bushwhacker, and at the point the black man and the redheaded woman.

When they reached the cave, they busied themselves—all except Bloody Zeke, who just found a rock and sat on it—picketing the horses, getting coffee started over a fire, and spreading out their bedrolls. McMasters had them all drop their weapons on a blanket, and he checked them to see how many were loaded. To his surprise, he found only Mary's Remington revolver held any shells. To an even bigger surprise, he did not unload it. The Winchester Yellow Boy had bullets, too, but it remained in the scabbard on Kilpatrick's horse. The derringer they had left in the possession of the late Emilio Vasquez.

The rain came as it usually did at that time of day and that time of year—powerfully in a savage torrent. It pounded the earth like buckshot, and mixed with small hailstones. Two of the horses took a bit of a beating, but there was nothing to be done about that. The cave only had so much room. The men and the woman stayed dry, but the storm turned the burning hell into a bitter cold, and the fire and coffee did little to warm them.

Bloody Zeke, brooding from his wounded ear, sat closest to the cave's entrance and covered himself with his bedroll while gnawing on rough, hard jerky. Deepest in the cave sat the gambler and the bushwhacker, playing blackjack while sipping coffee.

The black man squatted over the fire, stirring beans in a pot.

"How is 'em beans comin'?" Emory Logan called out from his card game.

Alamo Carter snorted. "They might be fit to eat . . . for breakfast."

"That's all right." The Missouri killer giggled. "Man, Carter, you's somethin' else. I mean, cookin' and all, you'll make some fine white folks a real good house—"

"Shut up." Mary Lovelace sat across the fire, but she was not looking at the black man or the one-eyed bushwhacker. She wasn't even looking at McMasters. She stared at the wrapped body of Daniel Kilpatrick.

Logan did not notice that. He pointed at Marcus Patton and shook his head. "Now we know why she done what she done after that Mex made his play. She loves the big black turd." He spit. "Lady, don't ya know they's a law ag'in that kind of thing. They'll send 'im and ya both to Yuma fer that. That is, if we don't hang ya two."

"Shut up," McMasters told him.

The bushwhacker obeyed and returned to his blackjack game.

Shaking his head, Alamo Carter set the spoon on a rock near the blackened kettle of beans. He turned on his heels and looked at Mary, then at McMasters. "If it's all right with you, I'm turnin' in. All that work today . . . I'm kinda tuckered out."

McMasters nodded. He sipped coffee and watched

the Negro move toward the far wall, where he had rolled out his bedroll.

"Carter."

The black man turned.

"Thank you," McMasters told him.

"Don't need to thank me, McMasters." Alamo Carter jutted his jaw toward Mary Lovelace. "She had that big pistol in her little ol' hands. I was like Zeke and them other two boys. All set to light a shuck for ol' Mexico. But she had the gun. And she barked the orders. And after she up and shot off Zeke's ear, well, I figured I'd just better do like she told me to do." He chortled, shook his head, and turned around.

McMasters watched him until he reached the bedroll, then looked across the fire at Mary Lovelace.

She did not look up at him.

"You could've been shuck of me and this lot," he told her.

She did not reply.

"You're a damned fool." He set the cup of coffee down. It had lost its flavor, whatever flavor it had earlier. "Did Moses Butcher hurt you that much? What the hell did he do to cause you to hate him so much?"

She stared at him, and those green eyes reflected the flames of the fire.

McMasters felt as though he stared into the fires of Hades.

"What did he do to you, McMasters?" she asked.

"He didn't kill your husband. You did that."

Her head shook, and she made some sort of noise that McMasters couldn't quite grasp. Her gaze returned to the campfire.

McMasters tried to read her, but he couldn't. The dress, once pretty, was soiled . . . maybe like her soul. A thin body, rawhide tough. Maybe she was taller than Bea had been, but not by much, yet Mary was the woman who had managed to hold off those other men, some of the worst killers in the entire Territory of Arizona. No, not *some* of the worst. With the exception of Moses Butcher, they *were* the worst.

McMasters shook his head. He had tried to enlist six hardened criminals, men with no remorse, to join him on a mission of revenge. And if it had not been for Mary Lovelace, he would be dead . . . or dying . . . down on that treacherous slope between the road to Apache Junction and the Salt River.

"So that's it," he said at last, almost a whisper, but the redhead looked up over the fire and the smoke. She did not say anything, just looked.

He listened. He heard the flames eating the dried wood. He heard the wind and the rain, which was starting to slacken a bit, no longer pounding the desert with hail, just hard, cold drops. One of the horses snorted. Another kept tapping the cave floor with a hoof. He heard his own breaths. He felt the soreness from today's events. He felt the pain that had refused to leave him, that had driven him to that cave, with those people, on his mission.

"Butcher hurt you that much," McMasters said. "You could be in Mexico or New Mexico or on a train east or west, north or south, a long way from the reach of Arizona law. But that's not what you want. You're here, with me, because of Moses Butcher. He hurt you so much that the only thing you want is to see him dead. And you're hoping that he'll somehow manage to kill you, too. Revenge. Followed by suicide. That's your plan." His head shook. "Isn't it?"

She stared at him, but did not answer and did not even blink. He waited, but then he looked away, knowing that she would not respond. She did not have to. He knew. He looked at the fire. The coffee cup felt cold in his hand and he had never cared much for cold coffee. He did not even care to drink. Or eat. Or anything.

"Well, you're one to talk."

It took a while before her words registered. She had spoken. To him. He looked up, surprised, and then he understood what she had just said.

Mary Lovelace emptied the cup, dipped it into a bucket of hot water, turned it over, and laid it on a flat rock to dry.

"We're seeking the same damned thing, John McMasters," she said before she turned around and walked to her own bedroll. "Aren't we?"

Saying nothing, he watched her go. He was too tired to argue . . . or even agree. He sat there a long while. Exhaustion worried him, and he poured another cup of coffee but could not stifle a yawn.

Over the rain, only a drizzle that would soon be nothing more than the dripping from rocks, limbs, brush and cacti, a dry laugh bounced across the cavern's walls. McMasters looked over the fire at Bloody Zeke The Younger.

"Old man," the dark-skinned man said, "what you think's gonna happen when you fall asleep. I mean, it's been a long time since you slept, old feller, and, well, you had a right grueling day." He laughed again.

"I won't sleep."

"No?" Bloody Zeke shook his head.

McMasters set the cup on the rock and stood. He moved stiffly to his saddle and saddlebags, and brought out the twist of barbed wire he had found at the abandoned homestead. Once he returned to the campfire, he settled into a comfortable position—but so everyone in the cave could see him—and removed his hat. He brought the strand of wire around his neck and secured it. The barbs pricked just enough, not so deep that they would cause him to bleed. At least, not now. But later, in the depths of night, when he could not stay awake any longer, his head would drop and the barbs would cut deep and painfully, enough to snap his head up and come full awake.

Seeing that and understanding everything, Bloody Zeke shook his head and laughed a bitter laugh of resentment. "I hope that gives you gangrene." He squirmed into his bedroll, positioning himself into a comfortable spot, pulled the hat over his eyes, and soon began snoring.

Chapter 25

A man would be hard-pressed to find the little adobe hut Moses Butcher had picked. It blended in with the yellowish-brownish rocks of the Superstition Mountains. That's why he had picked it. The hut could not be seen until you came right up to it.

To get there, you had to climb up the hill, first through the brittlebush, snakeweed, and creosote, watching for rattlesnakes and scorpions. If those didn't bite you, then the cactus—barrel and cholla and hedgehog and prickly pear—would stick you good. And that didn't even include the saguaro. The rocks—granite and basalt and other types some fellow had told him about—would trip you, too.

The man had called himself a geologist . . . and he'd told Butcher that those mountains had been formed by a volcano millions and millions of years ago, that he was standing in a calderas. But he did say that, most likely, a fellow might happen upon a deposit of gold—which seemed much better than ash, lava, and *welded tuff*.

Butcher shook his head has he rode up the hill. *What the hell is a geologist? And a calderas? What the hell is that?*

He still wouldn't know welded tuff if he stepped on it.

The saguaro's arm pointed the way, but he would have found it anyway. He saw the lone column shooting up off to the west, the garden of boulders leading to the twin flat rocks that stood as guardians to the big, rugged mountain just behind them.

"Come on." He eased his horse up the steep incline and around the creosote. Picking a path through the rocky garden, he felt as though the damned pit remained a volcano in full eruption. Once he maneuvered around the flat rocks at least thirty feet high and a dozen feet thick, the sun disappeared and the air cooled off. He swung out of the saddle and tied the reins to the ironwood rails he had hauled in years ago.

He always rode in from the back. He never lit a fire. There was no fireplace. Besides, smoke gave away hideouts, even in a place as remote as the Superstitions.

No corral. No need. He always left his horses saddled at that camp.

He pushed open the door of the hut, and the air inside told him that no one had been there since he had last hid out. One porthole peered at the desert to the south and west. Anyone traveling across that country and looking in that direction would see only rocks and more rocks. The shack blended in, and the horses, especially at that time of day, would be hidden in shadows.

He stepped through the doorway and saw the straw-stuffed mattress. One bed. One water bucket, which would be empty after all that time. A woman's camisole, a reminder of the last woman he had taken there. It made him smile.

"How long we staying here, Brother?" asked Ben from the doorway.

Butcher's smile disappeared, and he moved toward the porthole, watching the last of the riders—his men—as they rounded the corner. He looked beyond them into the distance and saw nothing but desert.

"Not long."

A rat moved about in the roof, a mix of paloverde and mesquite, cholla and saguaro skeletons, topped with dried brush. The only part of the cabin, other than the door, that would burn. Well, the mattress would, too, if the blood had all dried.

Ben moved to the bed and began bouncing.

Cherry went in next, removed his hat, and began fanning himself . . . or trying to get some fresh air into the stifling shack.

"From appearances, you never found that Dutchman's mine."

Behind him, loosening the girth on his saddle, Greaser Gomez laughed.

The bed had little bounce to it. Dust rose from the blanket, causing Cherry to curse and fan his hands.

Butcher turned from the porthole and motioned Ben and Cherry back outside then followed them out.

"I don't come here for gold," Butcher informed his men. "I just let folks think that."

"There ain't no gold here," Bitter Page said.

"Well, that town on the other side of those hills yonder," Milt Hanks said, "didn't just spring up because of the view."

A few others chuckled.

"Speaking of that town, I think we should ride in for a drink or two, a woman or three, and a card game or twenty."

"That boomtown," Cherry said, "has to have a bank."

Folks said that Moses Butcher could give a look that frightened even the hardest of men. Part Lucifer, part rattlesnake, part Death himself, it was the look he gave Cherry, Ben, and the rest.

"We don't rob banks around here. This is where we rest." *Rest.* Butcher never said *hide.* Hell, he didn't even care for the word *hideout.* Made a body feel like he was a yellow coward. "Go to Junction. Go to Goldfield. Go to some miner's camp for coffee, and even then you offer him for what you drunk or ate. Rob a bank? That gets the law. The law comes lookin' for us. We rest here for a day, two, maybe even a week. All the posses looking for us between Holbrook and Payson and clear down to Tombstone or Nogales don't expect to find us here. That's why we're here. You get that? You understand that? You break that rule . . . I break your neck."

"We get it, Brother," Ben said. "Cherry wasn't meaning nothing."

"Right," Cherry agreed.

"Good."

"It's just that there ain't nothin' to do 'round here," Cherry said.

"Hell. Go look for that lost mine if you want." Butcher turned back toward the door.

Greaser Gomez chuckled.

Milt Hanks, however, was all business. "We left Holbrook at a high lope, Moses. And we didn't get much from either that family of horse breakers or that tired ol' mountain man and his Apache squaw and bucks. Need oats for the horses. Coffee. Bacon."

"A fresh deck of cards," Dirk Mannagan said.

"That ain't marked," Bitter Page added with a snort.

Grinning, Ben Butcher looked at his brother. "Ain't there something you need from town, Brother?"

Butcher gave his brother The Look again. The kid lacked all the good sense Moses and his mother had tried to get through that thick skull. On the other hand, Milt Hanks had a point. As usual.

"All right," Butcher said. "Half of you ride into town tomorrow. Get supplies. Not too much. And not at one place. You go to different stores. And you drink in different saloons."

"Ain't but one place to drink in the Junction," Dirk Mannagan said.

"Don't go there. Go to Goldfield. And don't none of you do nothing stupid." Butcher stepped inside and stared out the porthole once again.

"Good Lord." Mary Lovelace pulled a handkerchief out of nowhere and crossed the cave toward McMasters.

"I'm all right," he said as he removed the barbed-wire necklace.

"Like hell."

He nicked his left thumb as he put the strand in his saddlebag, cursed, and stuck his thumb in his mouth.

"Tell me he'll bleed to death, senorita," Bloody Zeke said, laughing as he threw a saddle onto the blanket covering the black horse's back.

She dipped the piece of silk in the bucket they had used to rinse their dishes, and dabbed the puckered scabs across McMasters's throat.

He flinched from the pain as the water touched the first cut.

"You're a stubborn son of a bitch," she told him then moved on to the next wound.

"I'm alive," he said.

"How many times did you jerk yourself awake?" She softened her touch. When he did not answer, she moved to the final wound, and slowly, carefully, did her best to cleanse it. "You could use some whiskey or something to clean this up better than dishwater."

"I could use whiskey somewhere else," he said.

She pulled away and looked up. He smiled. She shook her head, trying not to grin, but could not stop it. They stared for a second, and then she moved to the bucket to rinse her handkerchief and bathe the cuts once more.

"Deep as you cut yourself," she whispered, "this won't work much longer. You're going to fall asleep, no matter how hard your head drops. Or you'll just cut your jugular and bleed out like a hog in November." She went over the wounds again, and then removed the silk rag she had been using to keep dust out of her mouth, nose, and eyes. This she also rinsed—not in the bucket, but from her canteen—and tied it over his neck, close to the cuts made by the barbed wire.

"You need help," she said in a soft whisper that only

he could hear then stood up. The smile and the tenderness out of her eyes gone, she went back to saddle her own horse.

"That wire hurts, don't it?" Emory Logan said with a snicker. "Ya gonna have so many holes in ya, McMasters, I won't need to find no lead for that big rifle to put through ya. Ya ain't gonna be no target at all afore long. That bob wire it—"

"Shut up about the damned wire," Marcus Patton said. "Just don't even mention the damned thing."

No one mentioned barbed wire after that. But he could not get it out of his mind as they rode out that morning, through the canyon, and up and down the rocky, winding road until they finally cut away from the river and headed into the Superstition Mountains.

Wire. Not just the wire, but that stupid homestead they had passed. Farmers. Sodbusters. Idiots.

He never could figure out why a man like his father, who'd had a good farm in Alabama, would shuck everything and move west. Oh, he knew what his pa had always said . . . about Alabama and all of the South, and how hard things were after the War for Southern Independence for a man who'd worn the gray. But it could not have been as hard as things had been for the Patton family in Nebraska after the war. One homestead, one miserable one hundred and sixty acres, had failed. His father found a job, but just long enough to feed the family and come back and file on another worthless quarter-section of dirt . . . in Nebraska and Minnesota and the Dakota Territory and Kansas and even into Colorado. Marcus Patton had grown up moving from one farm to another. Nothing could please that stupid father of his.

His thoughts returned to the barbed wire . . . and the summer of 1878 when he was twelve years old.

The family landed on a patch of ground in Kansas somewhere between nothing and Dodge City on something called the Great Western Cattle Trail. The first cattle herds came through, marching right over their crops, and the ramrods herding those mangy, raggedy-ass Texas steers refused to pay any damages.

Pa up and bought some barbed wire. "I'll show those fool Texans."

He made Marcus and his brothers help him string it up. "I will laugh in those cowboys' faces when they come up next time."

They came up. Cut the wire. Stampeded the herd through the fields and over the sod hut his father and older brothers had cut into the little bluff, causing the hole in the ground to collapse. It buried Marcus's baby sister. And his mother. And then the cowboys shot Pa in the stomach and shoved the wire into his throat. One brother, Andy, turned to run, and they roped him and dragged him through the vandalized field to the wire. Elmer, Marcus's big brother was a fighter and came at two of the cowboys with an axe. Two bullets from Colt revolvers stopped Elmer dead—really dead—in his tracks.

A lanky man with a walrus mustache and about two months' growth of whiskers on his cheeks and chin spotted Marcus. "We gonna let you live, boy . . . unless you want to try your hand. With this." He reached into his war bag and pulled out a relic of a pistol, an old Navy Colt in .36 caliber, and dropped it onto the stomach of Marcus's dead father.

Marcus just stood there, heard them laugh, and watched them ride away.

A day later, he found Andy wrapped in the damned strands. They had made him eat some wire, too. He buried his family—except for his mother and kid sister. The cowboys had done that job for him. He picked up that Colt. And he walked to Dodge City.

Marcus met Lucas Alabaster, who drove a medicine wagon from town to town, hawking Doctor Alabaster's Cure-What-Ails-You from Ponce de Leon's Fountain of Youth. The bottles sold for a dollar each, but he made more playing card games with the sporting element among the hayseeds. He hired Marcus to do the cooking, refill the bottles, and maybe stitch up a few knife cuts when the local hayseeds didn't appreciate how Patton played various games of chance. Before he was shot dead by a jealous husband in Elizabethtown, New Mexico Territory, Alabaster taught Marcus about cards. And how to shoot that Navy .36.

He decided to avenge the murders of his family . . . and would do it his own way.

Patton's horse jerked suddenly as it climbed upward, shaking him out of his reverie. He looked around. Seeing nothing but rocks, his thoughts returned to avenging the murders and the ten men he'd killed since 1880.

In a saloon in Trinidad, Colorado, a cowboy called him a cheat . . . which he was. So good, though, he rarely got caught. He didn't think the waddie—a terrible loser—actually saw anything, but he shot him anyway.

In Julesburg, he killed another dealer, the saloon owner, and a beer jerker who pulled a shotgun from underneath the bar. He spent almost two years in the prison in Cañon City, Colorado for those killings. Since the victims weren't considered much men, his lawyer won an appeal that called for a retrial, but he had already moved on and did not return for that second trial.

A cowboy in Jacksboro, Texas, reminded him of those who had wiped out his family . . . and he shot him in the back. That was about the only real murder he had ever committed.

A few others he mostly forgot.

The most recent . . . the last two in Phoenix . . . he claimed self-defense. And it might have been, once they started shooting at him.

In the hot Phoenix courtroom, the judge asked,

"Do you have anything to say for yourself before I pass sentence?"

Patton winked. "Judge, I never lose."

And he meant it.

He was sentenced to forty years.

Chapter 26

They heard the bustle, the whistles, even a gunshot long before they ever saw the town atop a hill that jutted above the desert floor between the Superstition Mountains and another mountain range in the Sonoran Desert.

"Hold up there," John McMasters called out then waited until the riders ahead of him stopped. He looked up from the dusty trail, feeling confused. It was not Apache Junction—unless that little speck on a map had up and moved . . . and grown substantially. The Junction should be a bit farther down the road . . . and it had never been on top of a brown hill. It was nothing more than a few houses, a trading post to get tequila and sometimes, a warm beer, with a barber who also patched up bullet wounds.

The gambler in the yellow vest turned in the saddle and grinned. "What's the matter, old man?"

McMasters ignored Patton.

"You ain't never heard of Goldfield." Patton chuckled.

So that was it. Another gold strike. If McMasters kept going up the road, he would likely come to Apache Junction—if anything remained of that small village. When gold was discovered, nearby claims or trading posts or towns or even cities could disappear overnight. Folks would pull out what they could, be it walls or rafters or windows or just canvas and tent poles and head to the latest boom town. Goldfield certainly was booming.

"I ain't heard of no Goldfield," Emory Logan said.

"They discovered gold," Patton said, "three or four years back."

The ore had to be high grade, McMasters understood, to support a town of that size.

He caught a few phrases as the gambler kept talking. He thought about Colonel Berdan and all those campaigns they had fought during the late war. He heard Berdan's in his memories.

"They call us snakes in the grass. Say we're not regular soldiers. Some even say we're cowards. Cold-blooded killers. They don't know anything. We're like any soldiers in blue or in gray—before we go into battle, we study the country. You'll be alone, most likely, in unfamiliar country. Find a way out. An escape route. Don't get boxed in. Don't be where you have to shoot uphill. That's a challenge, even if you have a scope on your Sharps. If we are in a pitched fight in a town, move from building to building till you find the perfect spot. But don't pick something that's obvious. And make sure you have a way out. And, for God's sake, try not to get killed. Sharps rifles with telescopic sights are damned expensive. And I'd

hate to be shot with one that was found by a fool wearing gray."

Following Berdan's directions, McMasters looked around. He saw only one way in and the same way out of town. That was good. It could also turn out bad if he had to leave in a hurry.

He could not see much about the town, but the noise coming from above told him that there would be plenty of people up on that hilltop. The law? He pressed his lips down and studied what he could see.

"Got herself a post office," the gambler went on.

McMasters only half-listened. He studied the road that led up the hill to the town called Goldfield.

A post office, yes . . . but no telegraph. That might mean no one in town had heard about him and Bloody Zeke The Younger and all the others with him. Risky. But McMasters had gotten used to taking risks.

"And a cemetery for that law dog," Patton was saying. "He's getting ripe, McMasters. This is the place to bury him."

McMasters ran various scenarios through his mind then kicked the horse into a walk. He stopped when he came alongside Bloody Zeke The Younger, and kept the shotgun's barrels trained at the killer's side.

"Take out that Army Colt," McMasters ordered.

"It's still empty," the cold-blooded murderer said.

"I know that. Take it out and shove it in your saddlebag."

The dark-eyed man sighed, but his left hand reached down and withdrew the converted pistol. He unfastened the leather covering to his saddle bag, dropped the revolver in it, buckled the covering shut, and looked back at McMasters. Those dark eyes hardened when he saw what McMasters held in his left hand. The right remained on the twelve-gauge, two fingers touching lightly the pair of triggers inside the guard.

"Put these on," McMasters said. Without waiting for a reply or an argument, he tossed the pair of handcuffs to Bloody Zeke.

The man caught them, cursed, but said nothing more as he clicked one cuff on his left wrist, then the other on his right. He did not make them tight.

That was fine with McMasters.

"All right. We ride into Goldfield. You're my posse." He shot Bloody Zeke a glance. "He's our prisoner."

"Why do I have to be the damned prisoner?" Bloody Zeke complained.

"Look at yer clothes, idiot," the Reb said, and shoved the last of his tobacco into his cheek.

Bloody Zeke glanced at the filthy striped shirt and pants he still wore. He sighed, and shook his head. "Shoulda changed these duds a long time ago."

"They'll fix ya up with a new pair when ya's back to Yuma," the Reb said.

"Shut up," Zeke sang out.

"Or maybe even a real suit when they bury ya."

"That's enough," McMasters said. "We ride in. We find an undertaker. We ride out."

"Well . . ." The big Negro, Alamo Carter spoke.

McMasters turned around the buckskin, and studied the old scout. He waited.

"The deputy marshal needs buryin' that's for certain," Carter said. "But we won't likely come across a town this size again. And there's no tellin' how long it'll take us to find Butcher in those mountains, that desert. Hunted for Apaches in those hills long time back, whilst I was scoutin' with Tom Horn and Al Seiber for Gen'ral Crook. Man can hide a long time in that country."

McMasters waited.

"We lost most of our food, what little we had, during that set-to with the Pimas," Carter continued. "Lost some shells for our guns, as well. And . . . we could use fresh horses."

"So could Moses Butcher," McMasters pointed out.

"You know as well as I do that he likely already has his," Carter said. "We catch him and he takes off a-runnin', you ain't gonna catch up to him no time soon. Unless we have fresh horses."

"Food," McMasters said, "and horses cost money. I don't have much, and I know you don't have any."

The Negro shrugged. "I was just sayin'. You're the boss man. Two shavetail lieutenants didn't listen to my advice a time or two whilst I rode with Crook." He grinned. "One regretted it. The other likely did, too, but never said so on account he was dead. Led us straight into an ambush. But he was green. You ain't."

"I am broke," McMasters said.

"But that can be rectified, my friend."

McMasters turned to face the man in the yellow vest, who grinned as he pulled off his hat and began fanning himself again. "Many a wise businessman has staked me for a percentage of my winnings. Usually ten percent. But for you, good man, I'll give you twenty-five. The math is somewhat easier to figure than fifteen and I never cared much for the number twenty."

"And if you lose?" the redhead asked.

"I never lose," Marcus Patton said. "At anything."

"Forty years in Yuma?" McMasters countered.

The gambler smiled and placed his hat on his head. "I'm not in Yuma . . . yet."

"You can't guarantee you'll win at cards," Carter told him.

The gambler laughed again. "Like I said, I never lose." He paused. "I cheat."

McMasters thought on that, but not for long. He found himself easing Berdan toward the gambler on the bay horse and pulled his wallet from a pocket. He removed a few bills and a gold piece and stuck those in the pocket of his vest, but handed the rest to Marcus Patton, who counted the greenbacks and coins.

"Thirteen dollars and seventy-nine cents." He rolled his eyes. "This could take a while."

"How 'bout that stiff deputy?" Emory Logan called out. "Like as not, he's got some money he ain't never gonna spend in hell."

"No." McMasters's word sounded like a gunshot.

"But—"

"We're not robbing the dead, damn you. I'm not Quantrill. And this isn't Lawrence."

Logan spit, but said nothing else.

"You surprise me, McMasters," Patton said.

"Don't lose," McMasters said. "You swing into a saloon. I'll find the undertaker. You try running out on me, you try some double cross, you come out of that saloon and I think that Starr looks loaded, I blow you in half."

The gambler shrugged. "Now why would I want to run out on my friends?"

"You'll find it mighty hard to do. I'll be taking your horse with us when we leave you."

The gambler frowned.

"To trade at the livery," McMasters said.

"Well, if ya's makin' out a grocery list, I need some tobaccy," the one-eyed bushwhacker said. "Plug rather than twist, but I ain't that particular."

"No list. We might not even get into a store." McMasters looked up the road. No point in putting things off anymore. Staying on the road, jabbering, wasn't a good idea. Anyone who happened to look out a hotel window or decided to ride into the desert in search of the Lost Dutchman's Mine might wonder what the posse was all about. "All right. We ride into town."

"Can we eat?" Bloody Zeke asked. "What we've been eating ain't righty fit for hogs."

"I suppose you want us to find some fine café," McMasters said.

"Well, there is . . . er . . . was . . . a fairly reputable place when I was last here," Patton said.

McMasters spun around in the saddle. "You were here before?"

The gambler nodded. "How do you think I know so much about Goldfield?" When McMasters kept staring, Patton laughed. "Don't worry. I did not kill anyone here."

Doubts crept into McMasters's mind, but the horse carrying Daniel Kilpatrick's body snorted, and McMasters knew he had to find a grave for that poor deputy marshal. He wanted a real cemetery for him. And this would be the only chance he had.

Besides, he thought, *if it doesn't work out, if everything goes to hell, well, it won't be the first time.*

What had gone right, or even according to plan, since he'd started out on Butcher's trail?

He pointed at Patton. "When we leave you in the saloon, you have as long as it takes me to find an undertaker and a livery with horses for sale or trade. That's it. You see us waiting out on the street, you politely collect your winnings—if there are any—"

"There will be," Patton said, "but maybe not much seeing I won't be there long and this time of day doesn't bring out the fools who can't play cards."

"You just come outside, get on the horse."

"What about food, powder, and lead?" Carter asked.

"Let's see how much money we have." McMasters pointed.

Nodding, Alamo Carter kicked the sorrel into a walk. That started those riding behind to follow. Those ahead of him also kicked their horses and began climbing the road up the hill to Goldfield.

"If we have any money at all," McMasters whispered to himself. He brought up the Remington twelve-gauge, resting the stock on his right hip and keeping the barrels pointed at the blue sky. He kept his fingers out of the trigger guard, but close . . . just in case. The reins he held in his left hand. Sweat stung the cuts on his neck. Hunger made his stomach tighten. So did the fear of what might wait for them in the booming gold town.

"Or," he said in an even hoarser whisper, "if we're even alive."

CHAPTER 27

From the bottom of the hill, Goldfield looked big but not sprawling. Once they reached the top, however, the town resembled Tucson. The hill wasn't that big, so as many buildings as possible were crammed within a few streets and alleys. It stank of congestion and confusion.

The major mines lay on the far edge of town, and the cemetery was on the only way in—or out—of Goldfield. They passed the cemetery first.

"It's filled up a mite since my last visit," Marcus Patton said.

One wooden cross had toppled over a recent mound. Most of the other graves had been covered with rocks. Two black men were busy slamming pick-axes into the earth, digging a new one.

"Musta knowed we was comin'," said the Reb, who pulled Daniel Kilpatrick's horse—and the deputy marshal's body—behind him.

"Shut up." McMasters studied the street and the people. The men—he counted only a handful of women—

ignored the procession until they saw Kilpatrick's horse. They also stared at the living riders. They did not speak. They did not point. They just looked, lips flat, eyes hard.

Mary Lovelace led the way, followed by Emory Logan and the hallowed cargo. Next rode Marcus Patton. Then Bloody Zeke The Younger, his handcuffs reflecting the noon sun, and Alamo Carter. McMasters brought up the rear.

They passed the first saloon, named, naturally, The First Saloon. Then the second, which was next to a brewery. That made sense. Brewing beer in a place like that had to be cheaper and more practical than trying to get kegs sent up from Phoenix or Tucson. They had a ways to go before they reached the blacksmith shop down the street and off to the right. A few more people came out of saloons and businesses. They watched.

McMasters and the others rode on.

Past a butcher shop. A boarding house, called Mother Ida's. A competing hotel called the Goldfield Hotel with a stagecoach out in front, pulled by a team of six mules.

He looked to the other side of the street. An assayer. The post office. And another saloon.

"That's the one." Marcus Patton wheeled his bay from the line and rode toward it. Only a few horses were tethered to the hitching rail.

"Why this one?" McMasters asked.

The gambler grinned. "I didn't play poker in this one on my last visit." He dismounted and pointed to the building across the alley. "And I figured it's convenient. For you."

McMasters looked at the building and frowned at the sign hanging out front.

JOSIAH AMBROSE
Undertaker
Licensed Gambler
Notary Public

"In case you need anything notarized." The gambler's face changed, hardened, turned serious. He drew in a deep breath and put his hands on the top of the batwing doors. Then, keeping his hold on the doors, he turned his head toward McMasters.

"I'm betting that you would not be so inclined to allow me a few rounds for this Starr."

"I told you what would happen if you walked out of that saloon with a loaded gun," McMasters said.

"There's always the chance," the yellow-vested man said, "that I won't be walking but running, and that the Starr will be empty by then."

He laughed, and without waiting for a response from McMasters, pushed his way into the Dismal Saloon.

Dismal. McMasters shook his head. It certainly looked dismal. He turned Berdan and headed to the next building, motioning for the others to follow.

McMasters dismounted in front of Josiah Ambrose's business.

"You"—he pointed at Logan and Carter—"bring Dan. Be careful."

"Why do you need me?" Bloody Zeke asked.

"I'm not leaving you out here alone," McMasters said.

With a shrug, Bloody Zeke slid from the saddle and handed his reins to Mary Lovelace. "I can't tie up with my hands tied up, lady," he explained then stepped onto the boardwalk and pushed back his hat.

"This is much more pleasant, out of the sun." He watched the black man and the bushwhacker carry the corpse off the street and onto the boardwalk.

Mary Lovelace finished hitching her horse and Bloody Zeke's black to the rail, and stepped into the shade. McMasters fished out the bills he had taken from his own wallet before he had handed it to the gambler and held out the money to Mary.

"What's this for?" she asked.

He signed and pointed to the next building. The sign read BATHS. HOT. 50¢. Painted underneath in bleeding red letters in a scrawl that had been applied with more sloppiness than even those over Josiah Ambrose's door were the words *No damd kredet*

Her eyes narrowed. She did not take the money, but when McMasters put the bills in her hand, she closed her fingers around the cash.

"This is more than fifty cents."

"There's a millinery next door. Your hat's trashed. You can meet us at the general store across the street."

Without waiting for her protest, he moved away and entered the undertaker's shop, carrying his shotgun with him.

Josiah Ambrose looked like he was ready to be embalmed himself, but that wasn't a possibility in Goldfield.

"We don't embalm. We bury. The way I see things, worms don't like those damned embalming juices. Gets 'em drunk."

"I just want a burial," McMasters said. "And a real funeral."

Ambrose was thin, pale, a man of maybe thirty-six years who looked sixty-three. His brown hair was thinning, he had not shaved in two or three days, and he wore black broadcloth pants, scuffed boots, a white shirt with ribbon tie. His coat hung on a peg behind his desk. He rose, picked up a pad and pencil, and motioned with a long, crooked finger at a table off to the side.

"Lay the gent on the table, men."

He stared at Bloody Zeke, then back at McMasters.

"I'll have to examine the body. We don't have a coroner in Goldfield. I do the best I can."

"Would you like us to leave?" McMasters asked.

"I'd like you to tell me what I will find." He suddenly broke into a rough coughing fit, doubling over, and turning around to brace himself by planting his left hand flat on the desk. His right dropped the pencil and pad back on the pine top and found a handkerchief, which he pressed to his mouth. After the fit passed, the cotton was flecked with blood. He returned it to his pants pocket and retrieved the pencil and paper.

The undertaker suffered from consumption.

"It's fitting," Ambrose said when he realized McMasters had seen blood on the handkerchief. "The dying deals with the dead." He coughed slightly again, turning his head out of politeness, and smiled when he looked back at McMasters. "If you tell me what I'll find, it'll save me the trouble."

"He fell off his horse, over a cliff, and onto rocks."

"Fell?" The undertaker trained his eyes on Bloody Zeke.

"He was pushed," McMasters said.

Ambrose wrote on the pad. "By him?" Without looking, he pointed the pencil at Bloody Zeke.

"No."

Ambrose shot glances at Carter and Logan.

"The man who did it is dead." McMasters put the Remington across his left shoulder.

"Well . . ."

McMasters withdrew Daniel Kilpatrick's badge from his pocket and showed it to the undertaker.

"You're a lawman?" he asked.

Without lying, McMasters returned the badge and nodded at Bloody Zeke. "You know who that is." It was not a question.

"I've seen his likeness in the Phoenix and Tucson papers we get up here when the stage comes through," Ambrose said.

"Lately?" McMasters said, trying to keep his voice from betraying him.

"Not since his escape from Yuma. You're taking him back?"

McMasters nodded at the corpse on the table. "That's what Dan wanted." Again, he did not lie. "He was a fine marshal. A good man." Also, not lies.

"Very well." Ambrose flipped a page. "Is there any next of kin to be notified?"

McMasters shook his head.

"No wife?"

"He was engaged." The words came out slowly, and McMasters felt pain in his chest, deep and more agonizing than the wounds on his neck.

"That'll be tough on his intended, I suspect."

"Yes."

"You'll tell her."

His head nodded once.

"So, you desire a preacher and a few mourners. Will you be in attendance?"

McMasters shook his head and gestured at Bloody Zeke. "We have business elsewhere."

"Yes, it is a long, hard journey to Yuma." Ambrose wet the lead tip of the pencil with his tongue and wrote. "Mourners are not a problem in Goldfield, if we have a preacher. I am ordained, by the way, and miners do like to hear me give a hoot and howl and fine Episcopal burial."

"That's not on your sign."

"I can't spell *Episcopal*."

McMasters felt hot, and he wanted to get away, out of Goldfield, or at least away from Ambrose.

"Coffin?"

"Your choice. A woolen blanket or a pine box. The pine's harder to come by, but we happen to have a coffin already made. I can let you have it for ten dollars."

"That's a lot for a pine box," McMasters said.

"Digging the grave is ten also." He smiled and shrugged. "It is hard country with hard ground."

"I see." Oh, McMasters saw everything. "I see two colored men digging a grave in the cemetery and expect that's for the man who is in that pine box you happen to have right now."

Again, the pale undertaker shrugged. "His widow left. She won't be back. She won't know that her late husband is buried in a woolen blanket."

"A blanket will do for Dan," McMasters said.

"Indeed, sir. It is not *how* you are buried or *where* you are buried, but it is how you are remembered. The blanket is five dollars."

McMasters shifted the shotgun.

"It is a clean blanket, sir."

McMasters said nothing, and the undertaker flipped to another page. "How is it you would like the deceased marshal remembered?"

"What do you mean?"

"A wooden cross is two dollars. No name. There's no room to pencil in a name on what wood we have for crosses. Or to carve one. We do offer a flat rock. We can paint the name on it for ten dollars."

"I've seen your painting job," McMasters said.

"Carving a name on the rock is fifteen dollars."

McMasters pulled the tin star out of his pocket. "A wooden cross. Just pin this to it. It's how Dan would like to be remembered."

"That badge will rust," Ambrose said.

McMasters handed him the badge along with a twenty-dollar gold piece. "Like you said, Ambrose, it's not how you're buried or where you're buried." He brought the shotgun down and turned to Bloody Zeke. "It's how you're remembered. Let's go."

Across from the livery, McMasters looked at the schoolhouse. Apparently, Goldfield had more women in town that he thought. From inside the school, he heard the voices of children as they sang.

He remembered the one-room schoolhouse in Nebraska. And the subscription school in Colorado. And he remembered the school in Payson, where all of his children had gone, and he heard their voices at the recital two years back.

The livery man interrupted.

"These ain't bad horses. They ain't bad at all."

Turning around, McMasters put his right foot on the lowest rail of the corral. "Trained by a man I used to know—John McMasters. Helped him with a couple myself."

"Been ridden hard, though." The burly man with the thick black beard stopped looking at the sorrel's mouth. "But"—he pointed at Bloody Zeke—"I guess tracking down an owlhoot like that one wears on a horse."

"And a man," McMasters said.

The man walked to the pinto, ran his hand across the back, and then to the black, and checked its rear hooves. "Well, I can let you have some for your pick of these." He made a vague gesture to some mustangs, mules, and a few quarter horses in the corral. "You throw in all the gear, that shotgun you're holding, and say, fifty dollars cash money. Or gold."

"I've already been robbed by an undertaker. I don't think I'll be robbed again."

"You don't like being robbed, file a complaint with the marshal," the livery man said.

"Where is the marshal?"

"Ain't got one."

"Big town for no law," McMasters said.

"Fifteen hundred folks, minus the one that got cut up at the Dismal Saloon yesterday. We use the miner's court."

McMasters shook his head. "Little late in the century for a miner's court to be the only law in a town."

"Late in the century for a man like Bloody Zeke to be riding loose, too," the livery man said.

"He's not loose."

"He's alive."

McMasters nodded at the horses. "We take our pick of the six horses. We keep the saddles. We keep the tack. You get an extra horse out of the deal. And you can keep that saddle and bridle."

"And that shotgun?" The livery man's eyes gleamed with envy.

"No." McMasters lowered the shotgun and stared hard. "I keep the shotgun."

The livery man, whose name was Wilkinson, looked again at the horses and turned around. "I don't think I can do no trade like that. Horses for horses is what it amounts to. I got my overhead to think about."

McMasters pointed at Berdan. "That buckskin is worth more than your whole damned livery, mister."

"In most places. But this is Goldfield."

"Then we've wasted your time . . . and ours." McMasters gathered the reins to Berdan and headed back toward the main street.

"Now, don't rush off, mister. You said that buckskin was trained by John McMasters?"

"That's what I said." McMasters looked back.

Johnson was wiping his mouth and tugging on his beard. "I've heard of McMasters. Most folks have in this territory. Up from . . . ?"

"Payson."

"You got any proof?"

"His brand on the hip."

"What about a bill of sale? I mean, I can't be buying

no horses on just your word. I need proof that you come by these horses clear and honest."

"This is Goldfield," McMasters said. "There's nothing clear and honest between here and Tucson."

"Well . . ." Johnson straightened. He looked at his horses, at those up for trade, and again at the Remington double-barrel. At length, his head shook. "No, sir. No, I just can't do it. Not without no cash. Or that scattergun. I guess we're done haggling."

"I guess so." McMasters shoved the shotgun into the scabbard. "Let's go. We're burning daylight."

"Wait!" the man called out.

CHAPTER 28

"You drive a damned hard bargain, mister," Johnson said as he opened the money box and counted out ten bills. "Twenty-five dollars. I can't believe I'm doing this."

McMasters stepped to the desk, took the greenbacks, and pocketed the money.

The men, except the handcuffed Bloody Zeke busied themselves with the horses while McMasters and Johnson sealed the deal, signing bills of sale to make everything as legal as things got in a town that had no marshal but still settled cases through a miner's court.

"It was cheaper before you walked away, you know," Johnson said.

"Prices go up."

"And my profits go down." He reached for a bottle behind the cash box, pulled out the cork, drank two or three healthy swallows, and returned the cork. He did not offer McMasters any refreshment.

"We'll saddle our horses and be out of your hair."

"All right." Johnson did not follow McMasters out of the barn and into the corral.

McMasters heard the cork being pulled again from the bottle of whiskey.

He saw Berdan, his saddle forked over the top rail of the fence, and bridle lying across the saddle. Slowly, he moved to the buckskin and rubbed his hand over the horse's neck.

"If that old coot or whoever winds up with you doesn't treat you right, boy," he whispered, "you know what to do."

The horse snorted, and McMasters grinned. "Yeah." He turned away abruptly, gathered his saddle and bridle, and carried it across the corral toward the other horses.

The men had all picked bay horses for themselves and a small mustang for Mary Lovelace. McMasters found a chestnut for himself. He did not look back at Berdan as he moved toward the new horse, which stood better than fifteen hands high. He tried not to think about the buckskin. It was his last tie to the old life, the life Moses Butcher had destroyed. Well, he still had the Remington twelve-gauge. But that was it.

Muscles bulged from the chestnut's neck, and it had strong hindquarters. It was broad, solid, with excellent legs. It would carry a man a long way, even if it were just a quarter horse.

That's what the livery man had tried to tell McMasters anyway. "Just a good for nothing quarter horse. Good for cowboying. Not much else."

But McMasters could see some thoroughbred in the animal.

The sloping shoulders and deep chest. And fifteen hands was tall for a quarter horse. The chestnut would be able to run farther and faster than any cow pony. And that's what he needed.

"Hey, mister," the livery man called out. "Whatever happened to that John McMasters horse trader up in Payson? Is he still breaking mustangs and training them?"

"He's dead." McMasters slid a saddle blanket on the chestnut.

Mary Lovelace stood up from the bench outside Hayley's General Store, walked to the edge of the boardwalk, and leaned against the wooden column when McMasters and the others rode up. He did not recognize her until she removed the new, clean, flat-brimmed tan hat, and her long, red hair fell onto her shoulders.

"Hell." Deep down, he wished she would have run off, stolen a horse or taken the stagecoach that had been parked in front of the hotel when they had arrived.

He could not, however, stop staring at her.

She wore new boots made for riding and outfitted with spurs, and a split skirt of dark purple. A riding skirt. It might have been frowned upon for a woman to wear in a place like Phoenix, but not in Goldfield. Her six-buttoned vest was green and hugged her body—her curves—tightly, leaving no doubt that she was a woman, especially with her face scrubbed clean and her ginger hair freshly washed. It had already dried, since in the desert, drying came fast and easy. A long red silk bandanna was tied around her neck, but for the moment, most of it hung down her back. The long-sleeved cotton shirt was light, white and tan checked, and she had bought a pair of fringed deerskin gloves, too. The Remington revolver was in a russet holster, positioned butt forward on her left hip. He could see that the cartridge loops in the belt, the same color as the holster, remained empty. That didn't, he believed, mean that the cylinders in the .44-40 were empty, too.

The Reb blew out a catcall of a whistle.

She ignored him and pointed at the bay mustang that had no rider.

"I take it that's the one for me."

"What makes ya think the bigger one ain't yourn?" Emory Logan said.

"The big one's for Patton. It's not as much horse as that mustang."

Alamo Carter laughed and turned in his saddle to face McMasters. "We're at the only store I've seen in town. You got some cash money on you. We could buy some grub now."

"Give Patton more time to make his pile," Logan agreed.

"We might need more money," Bloody Zeke said. "Butcher won't stay in the Superstitions for long."

"What makes you think that?" McMasters asked.

"He never does," Mary Lovelace answered.

McMasters swung off the chestnut, wrapped the reins around the post, and stepped onto the wooden planks. "Wait here." He entered the general store, still carrying his shotgun.

Two minutes later, five men rode up the hill from

the desert and came down Goldfield's main road. They rode carefully—like McMasters and the killers had ridden in—studying the town and the people. They rode with their right hands near their guns.

They did not pay much attention to Bloody Zeke, whose back was turned to the bunch, or Alamo Carter or Emory Logan or even the redhead on the boardwalk in front of the general store.

By then, the chippies had come out of the saloons or stood on the balcony at Delilah's House of Wonders and whistled at them as they rode past.

"Later," one of them said.

They dismounted, tethered their horses to the rail in front of the bathhouse—a hitching rail that, unlike the others on that side of the street had been empty before their arrival.

Marcus Patton looked at the whiskey drummer's full house, tens over jacks. "Well now I know why you raised. That's about as good a hand as I've seen today."

The fat drummer's mustache jiggled as he laughed, and the man reached for the money in the center of the table.

"But"—Patton laid his five paste cards on the table—"this is why I happened to call." In front of him was a fairly substantial stack of money. Cash money and coin. The Dismal Saloon was truly dismal. The house did not hand out chips. He would have raised, but that would have aroused suspicion. After all, he had drawn three cards and the drummer had stayed pat all along.

The mustache stopped dancing, and the fat drummer quit laughing. His face paled as he looked at four twos with an ace kicker.

"You drew three?" he finally asked.

"Yeah." Patton could not help himself. "Foolish I know, me holding an ace and two of clubs. You know what I was thinking? Straight flush. And then I pick up three more deuces. But that's poker."

"That's cheating," a voice called from behind him.

Patton slowly gathered the money as the whiskey drummer sank back in his chair. Only then did Patton turn around to see the straw boss from the second-largest mine in Goldfield. The man held a nightstick in his thick right arm and smacked it against his thick left palm.

"Last year," Patton said cheerfully. "Man." He shook his head. "A man with a temper like yours, I figured you'd be dead by now." He drew the Starr revolver, thumbing back the trigger even though it was a double-action pistol, and shoved the barrel into the straw boss's solid gut.

"Drop the billy club, buster," he said, his voice icy, "or I blow a hole in you that's bigger than even the entrance to your sorry mine."

The stick rattled on the floor.

Behind him, Patton heard chair legs scraping against the wooden floor, and pistols being drawn and cocked.

"Easy boys. This miner's a horse's ass. And if you don't want his blood staining your floor, just keep your seats and your guns unfired. Walt?"

Walt was the drummer.

"Sir?"

He was polite, but then he'd said he hailed from Birmingham, Alabama. They were fellow Southerners. Sort of.

Patton gave orders. "Put my money in that grain sack, sir. And that derringer Mr. Dawson left."

Patton had kindly asked Mr. Dawson to leave his derringer behind—as collateral—when he'd left the rest of his month's pay on the table. He'd said he would be back . . . after he got some more cash from his brother-in-law. He'd said he would have enough money to cover what he had bet and owed the gambler.

Suddenly, Patton wished he held that four-shot pistol instead of the .44-caliber Starr. At least the derringer was loaded. If someone called his bluff or noticed there were no caps on the nipples of the revolver's cylinder, his luck would play out. And it would be his blood on the floor of the Dismal Saloon.

"Yes, sir," Walt said.

Patton grinned into the face of the straw boss, who did not grin, and who barely breathed. The man's face turned redder than a beet.

That gave Patton a little more confidence.

"An apoplexy is a terrible way to die, mister, but not as fast or as painful as being gut-shot." He raised his voice to the miners and drunks behind him. "Remember that, boys."

He heard the drummer's gaiters on the floor then saw the man beside him.

"Here you go," the drummer said.

Patton held out his left hand.

"I'll take the derringer then tie the sack to my belt," he ordered.

The drummer obeyed.

"Go back to your seat, Walt. And pray no one foolishly discharges a weapon till I'm out of town. You might get hit by a stray bullet. You've already lost enough for one day." He shoved the derringer against the straw boss's temple.

"Turn around."

The man did.

"We're walking out. My back's broad, boys. If you shoot me, I can't stop you. But I'll kill this big slob . . . and as many of you sons of bitches as I can take to hell with me." He shoved the empty Starr against the angry man's spine.

"Start walking."

He thought he just might make it out of there alive. And then the batwing doorway to the Dismal Saloon filled with five menacing figures wearing guns on their hips.

"That all the buckshot you have?" McMasters asked.

The clerk harrumphed. "In a town like this, folks trade many things." He pulled out a cigar box from beneath the counter and laid it on the top. "See anything that you like?"

McMasters's eyes narrowed. "Actually," he said in surprise, "I do."

A few minutes later, the clerk handed McMasters a yellow slip of paper.

McMasters stared at the final tally and rolled his eyes. "You mind carrying them to my saddlebags. Or do you charge for that, too?"

* * *

Ben Butcher grinned at the scene in front of him. A big cur in a denim jacket and miner's wool hat had a derringer placed against his temple and, undoubtedly, another pistol aimed at the dog's back. The man using the big dude as a shield looked over the dude's shoulder. A professional gambler, Ben figured, from the cut of his clothes. Maybe in his thirties or so, and used to that sort of thing. The sight of Ben and Cherry and Miami and Milt Hanks and Bitter Page did not seem to unsettle him. A guy like that could fit in with his brother's gang.

"Gentlemen," the gambler said in a pleasant enough voice, "if you would step out for a little bit, just long enough for me to get outside, well, then, I'd be obliged and will leave this cheerful establishment to you boys."

"Sure friend." Ben Butcher moved his left hand from the top of the door and gently placed it on Cherry's shoulder. Cherry, still the novice at such things, had been about to draw his revolver. Brother Moses would not care for any violence in Goldfield that brought a posse after the boys.

Ben grinned. "Boys, let the gents leave. We don't want any trouble, just some whiskey and some other kinds of refreshment." He tugged on Cherry and let go of his hold on the door. As he backed down the boardwalk to the end of the large plate glass window he told Milt Hanks, "I told you we should've gone to The First Saloon."

All five men positioned themselves against the large window, so the gambler could see them and know that they posed no threat . . . which was Ben's intention all along. They would let the man in the yellow vest and his hostage alone. After all, it wasn't their fight.

The man in the denim jacket and miner's cap stepped through the doors. The boardwalk creaked underneath his then he stepped to the ground. Quickly, the gent with the two guns, spun the bigger man around and got behind him. He shoved a double-action revolver into his holster, but kept the derringer against the man's head.

"First man who pokes his nose through the doorway gets this idiot killed," he called to the Dismal Saloon's occupants. "Back up," he whispered to the idiot.

They backed up.

Ben Butcher glanced through the window, but no one seemed to have any inclination to call the gambler's bluff. Pretty soon, Ben figured, the stranger would be riding out of Goldfield and then Ben and the boys could finally get a whiskey to cut the dust. He watched the gambler backing his way across the street where other fellows were watching him. An ugly lot. A big black man. A man with only one eye, wearing patched pants. Some decent horses. A dark dude who sat in the saddle on a bay horse with his hands close together. Handcuffed.

"Son of a bitch!" Ben Butcher said.

"Jimmy," the clerk called, "help this gentleman with his supplies."

A pockmarked teen, more bones than meat and with a mane of yellow hair, dropped his dust mop and hurried to the counter. He picked up the supplies and walked ahead of McMasters, whose arms were filled with more sacks and a double-barreled shotgun.

As they stepped outside, a voice on the streets called out, "McMasters, ya might want to get yer ass out here *now!*"

McMasters. That name sounded familiar, but Ben Butcher could not place it. Suddenly he saw the woman in the sharp-looking riding outfit as she stepped away from the store and toward the horses.

He recognized her. Lady Luck or Fate or God, but mostly Mary Elizabeth Carmen ruined everything.

CHAPTER 29

Mary Lovelace moved toward her bay mustang. Thanks to the gambler's foolishness—had he been caught cheating?—they would be riding out of town at a high lope.

She froze when she got a look at the riders who stood on the boardwalk in front of the bucket of blood's large window, watching Patton and his hostage. One of them stepped closer, studying the scene with a mix of amusement and resentment. He looked toward the general store, and eventually his eyes landed on her. She recognized him. And the chill left her paralyzed. But only for a second.

"Son of a bitch!" she roared, cursing herself for not loading the 1890 Remington in her holster, for being such a damned fool, for listening to that hard-rock McMasters's orders, or maybe even trusting him. She knew where she could find bullets and hurried to the chestnut gelding, jerking open the saddlebag.

She caught a glimpse of a gangling teen in front of the store doorway, and then saw high and mighty John

McMasters. Her hands came up with a handful of cartridges.

The Remington twelve-gauge swung toward the gambler and next at Mary.

"That's Butcher!" she bellowed. She no longer saw the kid, just merchandise scattered by the store's door. "His kid brother!"

Even before she'd shouted, McMasters understood something violent was about to happen. He grabbed the teenage clerk and shoved him backwards, hard and furious, sending him into the store, leaving bacon and flour and coffee sacks by the doorway.

"Toss me some!" the Negro commanded. His Merwin Hulbert fired the same .44-40s as her pistol.

She threw a handful in the black giant's direction, seeing them bounce across the rough plank boards, thumbed open the chamber gate, and began feeding brass shells into the empty cylinders.

McMasters' face hardened and the shotgun came up as bullets splintered the column above Mary's head and another slammed into the wooden sign announcing ABSOLUTELY LOWEST PRICES IN GOLDFIELD!

The streets of Goldfield were about to turn into bloody chaos.

The Remington roared, slamming savagely against McMasters's shoulder. He stepped away from the smoke, opening the breech, discarding the remnants of the two shells he had fired simultaneously, and reloading both barrels with more buckshot. A bullet sliced through the crown of his hat, shattering a windowpane behind him. Inside the store, women screamed, and the store owner yelled for everyone to find cover on the floor.

Gunfire on the streets of Goldfield, like most boom

towns, was not what you would call common. But nor was it rare.

The sudden roar of shots sent Bloody Zeke The Younger's bay horse into a fit of bucking. Despite the handcuffs on his wrist and death singing all around him, Zeke kept his seat in the saddle.

Emory Logan leaped off his horse, leaving the Burgess in the scabbard, and wisely grabbed the reins of three other mounts—his own, the one they'd picked for Patton, and Mary Lovelace's mustang—that pulled, reared, and snorted. All those years riding with Quantrill and other murderous gangs had prepared the one-eyed killer for such events. Few people would have been able to keep three horses from charging away. Mary held the reins to McMasters's gelding, and Carter kept the reins to his horse wrapped tightly around his thick left hand. His right hand held the Merwin Hulbert.

Patton dropped to the street, rolling over and over as bullets tore up the ground around him. Bullets and buckshot shattered the big window of the saloon, and McMasters could see men inside diving behind the bar or turning over tables. He swung the barrel toward the man across the street who had leaped onto a horse and gripped the reins with his teeth. He turned the horse around and worked pistols with both hands.

McMasters started to squeeze both triggers, but stopped. The large man in denim—the one Patton had been using as a piece of human armor—was in the way. McMasters found another target, aimed, fired . . . and cursed. His man had leaped on another horse, but the horse had reared. Instead of blowing the outlaw in half, the buckshot tore into the horse's neck and underbelly. It toppled over, crushing the hitching rail and slamming into a water trough. Its rider fell behind the trough and disappeared in gun smoke.

Down went McMasters as more bullets tore over his head. He kept his calm and his resolve, and reloaded the Remington.

Rushing her shots, Mary Lovelace emptied her pistol but didn't hit anyone. Unable to reload with both hands, she cursed McMasters as she struggled to keep his chestnut from pulling free from her grip and leaving him afoot.

Alamo Carter held his pistol cocked, but kept waiting calmly for the right target and a sure shot, or as sure as one could have with a left arm being jerked this way and that by a screaming horse.

McMasters stood up beside the far wooden column at the end of the boardwalk. Two of the five riders had already raised dust out of town. A third ripped shot after shot with a Marlin rifle while kicking free of one stirrup and allowing the killer whose horse had been shot dead to swing up behind him.

McMasters brought them into his sights, but something caught his eye and he dropped down face-first, slamming hard against the boardwalk as a shotgun blew chunks of wood from the column.

Alamo Carter saw it, too, and turned around, leaving his broad back open for any of the gunmen across the street. "Get back in your shop, you damned fool!" the former slave shouted. He snapped a shot—his first—at the citizen next door. The man dropped the single-shot scattergun, yelped, and dived through the open door.

Carter turned around, aimed, and the .44-40 belched

flame and smoke. Rolling onto his back, McMasters glanced at the two riders on the one horse and thought he saw dust pop off the vest of the one in the back. He tilted the barrels of the shotgun up, thinking about trying a desperate shot—shooting from a supine position, through dust—at the riders galloping away, but reason took hold. Colonel Berdan had always stressed *Make sure of your target before you fire. Don't rush your shot. And never take a damned fool shot.*

The two riders on the one horse disappeared in the dust. Only one of the bandits remained. McMasters rolled back onto his stomach, came to his knees, and aimed the 1894 Remington across the street.

Bastards. Gutless wonders. Ben Butcher watched Miami carry Cherry out of Goldfield, leaving him alone as he tried to control his horse enough to get his foot in the stirrup. That was a problem. Stealing horses when on the run meant you didn't have horses trained to stand still when lead was flying and Hell's doors were opening right before your eyes. Cherry's horse lay dead over what had been a hitching rail, and the stink of blood and the roaring gunfire frightened Butcher's horse.

Milt Hanks and Bitter Page had been the first to get out of town, but, well, that's the main reason Milt Hanks and Bitter Page had lived so long.

Bastards. Gutless wonders, he thought again.

Ben fired, aiming in the general direction of the man with the shotgun. For some reason, he was doing most, if not all of the shooting. The gambler in the yellow vest had come up to his knees, but he didn't seem to know what to do, and the gun he held was just a four-shot derringer that would not be so reliable at that distance. One of the dudes was on a bucking horse. It was like that damned rodeo he had seen in Prescott a few years back . . . only nobody had been shooting up the town back in '89.

He raked the spurs across the blue roan's ribs. The horse squealed and turned, and he sent another shot toward the woman. It smashed a pane of glass behind her, about the last piece of glass in the general store's window that had not been shattered.

That was all he had time to do. The damned fool in the denim jacket was still at his stirrups, reaching up, screaming something. It made not one lick of sense, but Ben Butcher had learned after all his years of riding around the Western states and territories with his big, mean, crud of a brother that when the shooting starts and a town turns into hell, people will do the damnedest things.

Not about to lose a stirrup, Ben turned the short-barreled pistol at the miner and shot him in the chest. The man staggered back, still standing, and Ben Butcher cocked the hammer and pulled the trigger again. That one took the dude in his cheek, blew out the eyeball above the wound from some sort of pressure, and sprayed the ground with blood and brains—what the dead dude hit when he dropped to the ground.

Ben Butcher wasn't certain how many shots he had left, but he gave the roan its head, felt the wind rushing past his face as lead tore through his suspenders strap on his back. Another scratched his left shoulder. He cocked, fired, and felt the pistol buck in his hand. Cocked and fired again but felt nothing and knew it was empty. He looked ahead, saw dust, and cursed his brother a blue streak.

He'd told Moses all those years ago that he should have killed that petticoat they had taken off the stagecoach to Florence. But Moses hadn't listened. The son of a bitch never listened. And now Mary Elizabeth Carmen had almost gotten Ben Butcher killed.

Another bulled buzzed past his head and he realized that he still might wind up dead.

"What the hell!" Patton was not sure how he had not been shot to pieces. He wasn't sure what was going on.

In front of the general store, the redheaded killer fired at the last of the bunch leaving town, cursed, holstered the shiny pistol, and tried to leap onto her mustang being held by Logan. McMasters came up, too, aimed at the last rider, then turned back, saw something behind Patton, and the twin barrels of the Remington roared.

"Stay down!" McMasters yelled. "Stay down! That's the Butcher Gang. And we're going after them."

Patton swung back, saw people diving out of view from the shattered remnants of the Dismal's window, and then saw the bloody carcass of what had been the straw boss. "Hell." He started toward Logan and his horse.

A figure appeared in the doorway of a business, gun in hand. The derringer came up and Patton snapped off a shot. He saw the single-shot scattergun drop onto the boardwalk, and heard a man scream out like a school kid.

"Don't shoot at civilians!" McMasters roared. He

grabbed the reins of his chestnut and leaped into the saddle.

"I ain't letting them shoot at me!" Patton took the reins of the gelding and put one foot in the stirrup before it was running down the street, away from the Dismal Saloon and the dead straw boss. But his hands were on the horn, even while his left gripped the derringer. *Don't let me slip,* he prayed. *Let me somehow get into this damned saddle.*

Out of the corner of his eye, he saw that Bloody Zeke The Younger's horse had stopped bucking. Finally under control, Zeke leaned low in the saddle and let his horse carry him into the dust.

Behind him came the redhead's cursing. "After them, damn you! After them! Don't let those damned butchers get away!"

Chapter 30

Reaching the bottom of the hill where the road from Goldfield met with the trail, Alamo Carter and Emory Logan stopped their horses alongside Marcus Patton, who had reined in and stood in his stirrups, looking at the trail of dust that led into the desert and toward the Superstition Mountains. They waited for John McMasters.

McMasters brought his chestnut to a hard stop and glanced behind him and up the hill toward Goldfield. Swinging back, he glared at Patton. "You'll answer to me later, Patton, but first, let's get going."

"I don't think so," Alamo Carter said.

McMaster brought the shotgun up to his thigh, but did not aim at the giant.

"We just got caught with our pants down, capt'n," the black scout said. "Like to have gotten us all shot to hell and gone. That ain't happenin' again, suh." With his left hand, he slowly pulled out the Merwin Hulbert, spun it around, and offered it, butt-forward, to

McMasters. "You ask us to ride with you, to fight with you. But you ask us to do that with empty weapons. Pants down. That ain't no way to fight a war, mister. Load it."

McMasters looked past him at the dust.

"It didn't stop Zeke and Mary."

"They got a stake in this fight," Carter said. "Personal. We don't."

"And 'em two is damned fools," said the one-eyed Reb.

McMasters watched the dust.

"They'll be easy enough to follow and catch, capt'n," Carter said. "But we don't skedaddle here right quick, we'll be answerin' to the citizens in Goldfield."

"Posse'll be down directly," the Reb said.

Carter waved the gun. "Load it, capt'n."

McMasters sank into his saddle. "Load it yourself," he said in a weary voice. "All of you. But be quick." He broke open the Remington to reload its double barrels. "And I'm no captain, Carter. I was a private."

"You're capt'n of our bunch." Carter handed the reins to Logan then shucked out the spent casings from the .44-40, and filled in all six chambers on his revolver. Extra shells he shoved into the pockets of his trousers.

The gambler took a tin of percussion caps and box of paper cartridges for his Starr.

The slave took the reins back and asked Logan,

"That Burgess shoots a .44-40 caliber, right?"

"That's right."

Carter brought out a box, about half-filled, and handed it to the bushwhacker. "Here you go, Mr. Logan," he said with no sarcasm in his voice. "Thanks for holding my horse just now and up yonder during that set-to."

"My pleasure," the bushwhacker said and began feeding shells into the rifle.

"We're still short on ammunition," the gambler said, "since our captain dropped most of his supplies in front of the door of the store. What the hell was that about? I thought you'd be waitin' for me to bring you what I won in cards. Didn't you have no faith in me?"

"What was that all about on the streets? Using a man in front of you as a shield?" McMasters snapped the Remington's breech shut.

"A sore loser from my last visit to Goldfield." Patton grinned.

"You said you didn't shoot anybody when you were here last," McMasters said.

The gambler swung back onto his horse. "I said I didn't *kill* anyone."

The lever cranked a round into the Burgess, and the old Rebel brought the rifle up to his shoulder, aimed up the hill, and squeezed the trigger. The rifle roared, and Logan cocked and fired twice more. McMasters's chestnut spun around, and Patton's kicked once before the gambler regained control and urged the horse into a lope. He rode after the dust.

"That won't keep 'em hidin' up yonder forever." Logan took off right behind the gambler, tapping his bay's rump with the hot barrel of the Burgess repeater.

"He's right, capt'n." Carter urged his gelding into the desert.

McMasters shot one quick glance toward Goldfield then followed his prisoners—his posse.

* * *

Bloody Zeke The Younger slowed down his mount—the bay had so much heart it would run till its heart burst—but Zeke had let some sense creep back into his mind and his heart. He wasn't about to ride into Moses Butcher's camp with his hands in chains and without any bullets in his Army Colt.

The woman, apparently, did not think about such details.

He looked back and saw the others loping along. Swearing, he kicked the bay into a full gallop. Cactus and rocks zipped past as he gained on the woman. Hooves kicking up sand and pebbles in a winding wash, his horse was larger, stronger, older than the mustang the girl rode.

And Zeke had been on horses a lot longer than she had. He came up alongside her.

"Stop!" he barked.

She did not listen.

"Idiot." He wasn't sure he meant the redhead or himself, but he brought the reins to his mouth, let his teeth clamp on them, and leaned toward her. Holding his breath, he reached out with his manacled hands. She saw him then, and leaned up in the saddle, trying to pull the reins away from his grasp. She did, but that turned the mustang sharply, and she felt herself falling, and heard herself cursing Bloody Zeke The Younger, Ben Butcher, and herself.

Stars blazed orange and red and purple behind her closed eyes. She felt her lungs sucking in air and blocked the pain in her head and back. She wiggled her fingers. Then her toes. At least, she thought she did. She heard hooves clop as she bent her left leg up, then her right. She lowered her legs back to the ground, rolled over, pushed herself up, spit blood and sand onto the dirt, and came up to her knees.

Only then did Mary Lovelace open her eyes.

She was alive. She had broken neither neck nor spine, only split her lip and banged up her head a bit. Her vision cleared, and she came to her feet, reaching for the Remington in the holster and praying.

Her fingers touched the hot grips.

It's still there!

She drew it and turned toward the sound of the hooves. The .44-40 pistol came up and the hammer clicked loudly as she pulled it back.

"Lot of good it'll do you, you stupid girl," Bloody Zeke The Younger told her. He had caught her mustang and led it back. "You're empty."

She did not argue. Did not bluff. It did not matter.

"You were going after him with an empty gun."

"And then I let reason take hold." He gestured down the wash. "The rest are coming."

She turned, spit out more blood, and sighed. Sure enough, there rode McMasters and the others. She started to holster the Remington, but Bloody Zeke stopped her.

"Check it for sand. Make sure the cylinder will spin. And make sure the barrel's not clogged with dirt or anything. You don't want that blowing up in your face."

She did as he had instructed her and watched as the riders neared. When the others stopped, McMasters came ahead of them, stopping a few feet in front of Mary, who'd holstered the Remington .44-40 and wiped her busted lip with the back of her hand.

"You'll want bullets for that," McMasters told her and then nodded at Bloody Zeke. "You, too, I suspect." He pulled back the unfastened leather covering of one of his saddle bags, straightened in the saddle, and stood in the stirrups, letting the reins drop over the chestnut's neck but keeping a firm grip on the twelve-gauge.

Mary did not have to turn around. She knew what he was seeing and studying—the dust from Ben Butcher and the others.

"Let's not tarry," the gambler said. "This close, I'd hate to lose them."

"We won't lose them, " Mary said as she walked toward McMasters then reached inside the saddlebag and withdrew a handful of cartridges. The rimfires she let slide back inside, rattling like rain on a roof as they dropped onto others. She found a Winchester round and slipped it into the cylinder. "I know where they're going. So does Zeke."

"That's a fact," Bloody Zeke said. "But they won't be there for long."

Mary stepped away from McMasters and finished loading the revolver, and backed away as Bloody Zeke came to the bag to find bullets for his Richards conversion .44. She noticed that McMasters swung the shotgun into an easier-to-handle position while Zeke loaded his pistol.

"You got a plan?" Bloody Zeke asked McMasters.

* * *

Sound carries a great distance in the desert. Especially gunshots.

"Trouble?" Dirk Mannagan shot a glance at Moses Butcher, who had stepped out of the adobe hut and stared off in the direction of Goldfield.

"That ain't nobody huntin' quail." Butcher cursed bitterly. "Make sure all the cinches are tight," he told Greaser Gomez. "Zuni"—he found the half-breed—"take that Sharps and a couple bandoleers." He pointed. "Make your way up. You know the spot. If that dumb ass brother of mine leads a posse here, you'll have to keep them occupied. Then we'll meet you at the canyon north of Bisbee."

The half-breed drew the big buffalo rifle from the scabbard, nodded without speaking, and grabbed the bandoleers before he turned and began jogging silently up the incline. Butcher watched him until the shadows swallowed him.

"It could be something else," Mannagan said, then corrected himself. "*Somebody* else."

"That's why we ain't runnin'." Butcher drew his revolver, opened the gate, set the hammer to half cock and spun the cylinder on his forearm, checking the cartridges. He always kept six loads. Most folks kept only five, leaving the chamber underneath the hammer empty for safety. Safety, to Moses Butcher, was a fully loaded six-shooter. He swore again and leaned against the doorway, staring at the bed. "If that brother of mine started a ruckus over some petticoat to bring back here, I'll skin the bastard alive."

There was nothing to do, but wait.

* * *

A long while later, Butcher saw the dust, and jacked a round into the Winchester he carried. "What do you make?"

Standing to his side, Greaser Gomez shrugged. "Four."

"Ben better hope he's the one dead on the floor of some brothel in Goldfield."

"Five men." Dirk Mannagan slid off a rock and offered Butcher the spyglass. "Four horses."

"Son of a bitch!"

"They're riding for us," the Mexican said.

Butcher swore again.

Mannagan brought the telescope back to his eyes and scanned the desert floor before him. "Boss, as far as I can tell . . . nobody's following them."

That grabbed Butcher's attention. He stepped away from the shack, shifted the Winchester to his left hand, and held out his right for the telescope. He let Mannagan take the Winchester and peered through the brass spyglass. He could not make out the two riders on the one horse, but he could see his brother whipping his already lathered horse into a deadly run. But that was not what Butcher wanted to see. He looked past them, following the dust on a straight line toward the faraway hill on which Goldfield lay. No dust. No posse.

"They'll still be able to follow their trail," Mannagan said.

"No." Gomez pointed, and Mannagan and Butcher followed his finger.

At first, Butcher thought the Mexican was pointing at the thunderclouds, expecting another monsoon to wipe out any trail. But rain could not be predicted, even during the wet months. He saw more dust in front of the dark clouds. He lowered the spyglass and handed it back to Mannagan.

"Dust storm."

Then Moses Butcher laughed. Shaking his head, he looked up toward the heavens and laughed again. "This is how you reward my idiot kid brother? You spare his hide with a merciful dust storm?" He took the Winchester and eared back the hammer. "I might," he said in a deadly whisper, "kill that fool anyway."

Hanks and Page rode in first, neither bothering to dismount but busying themselves by reloading their weapons. Their horses blew heavily, but despite the lope across the Sonoran range, they weren't finished. Milt Hanks and Bitter Page knew how to keep an animal game enough to give them twenty more miles.

"Wasn't our fault," Milt Hanks said.

When Butcher spit and began to speak, Hanks snapped the chamber gate shut on his Colt. "Wasn't his, either."

Bitter Page did the explaining, saying how they were walking into the saloon when some tinhorn came out with a hostage. "Once we backed out of the saloon to let whatever was about to happen play out between the cardsharper, his patsy, and the good folks of the boomtown, some stupid hussy across the street started screaming and shooting . . . at Ben. The rough lot with her took up the fight, too."

"Some wench?" Moses Butcher asked.

"Redhead. That's about all I saw," Hanks said.

"If she was shootin' at Ben, then it was Ben's—" He didn't finish as Miami and Cherry rode in next.

Cherry slipped off the back of the horse and rolled over on the ground.

"Gawd a'mighty, Gawd a'mighty, Gawd a'mighty." He brought his hand away from his side. Blood stained his fingers and his vest.

"Hell," Butcher said, and motioned for Mannagan to help the wounded outlaw.

A half-minute later, Ben Butcher galloped up the slope and behind the rocks. Moses Butcher raised a finger and started to swear, but his kid brother got in the first shots.

"Don't start that with me. This is your damned fault. You want to know who it was that started that ball? Not me. None of us. It was that damned bitch you brought here all those years back. Remember? The redhead? That little witch?"

Moses Butcher spit. "I've brought a lot of hussies here. And gave them to you after I'd tired of 'em. And all of 'em is buried in the rocks—" He stopped. He remembered.

Ben Butcher spit and began reloading his pistol. "I mean Mary Elizabeth Carmen. The one you sold to that gambler." He shoved his pistol into the holster. "You thought it was funny. Well she wasn't laughin' when she spotted me."

"Hell." Butcher stepped around the corner, picking up the telescope Mannagan had laid on a rock. He looked carefully yet still saw no dust. He swung to the north, found the clouds and the thick churning dust moving southwest, and back toward the path his men had traveled.

He snapped the brass spyglass shut and shoved it into his pants pocket. "We can't chance it. That dust storm could play out. It might not. We ride out. I don't give a damn if that fiery witch happened to spot you or not, Ben. If you've led the law to the best resting place I've had in ten years, I'll stake you out in front of an ant bed."

"We're short one horse," Hanks said.

"Zuni's better on foot than on a horse." Butcher gestured up the rocky mountain. "He'll keep them pinned. If they come. If they don't, he'll steal a horse and meet us in the canyon."

Mannagan helped Cherry to his feet. He had stuffed a handkerchief in the hole in the fool's back, and wrapped it tightly with strips made from the sleeves of the wounded outlaw's shirt.

Moses Butcher looked across the desert, and, seeing no sign of a pursuing posse, he and his men went to work to break camp. They would hide their trail, brushing away the tracks with leafy branches, but careful enough so that most eyes would not notice the signs made by the leafy branches. They would not run. "*Never run,*" sweet Auntie Faye used to say, "*lessen you didn't have no other damned choice. The last way you oughts to die is with a bullet in your back.*"

They broke camp, mounted their horses, and prepared to leave.

Cherry, leaning over in his saddle from the pain of the bullet in his back, straightened, coughed, and flew down from his horse, landing in the cactus with a thump. His groan, as he rolled over, was drowned by the report of a rifle shot that echoed and died in the wind.

CHAPTER 31

At first, Butcher thought Zuni had double-crossed them, had blown Cherry out of the saddle. Then he understood that the shot had come from the opposite direction. Another bullet kicked up sand in front of him, almost causing his horse to bolt. It would have, but his kid brother snatched up the reins and held the horse tightly.

"That shot came from the other direction!" Milt Hanks spurred his horse and took off to the east. Miami followed him.

Beside Cherry, Mannagan cursed as another bullet blew spines off the arms of the pointing cactus. Yet another tore off Ben Butcher's hat.

Grabbing the reins to his horse, Moses Butcher drew his pistol and fired in the general direction of the second gunman.

"Get out of here!" he yelled to his brother, who needed no more encouragement.

"Why ain't that damned breed doin' nothin'?" Mannagan shouted as he snagged the reins to his own horse.

Too many answers to that question, Butcher thought as he dismounted and squatted by Cherry. Another bullet kicked up dust about ten yards in front of him. A shot from behind whined off a rock. But Moses Butcher, remembering his favorite aunt, remained calm. He drew Cherry's pistol from the holster, pried both of Cherry's hands from the ugly wound in the kid's gut, and put the big Schofield in his right hand. Then Butcher drew his own Colt and placed it in Cherry's left hand.

"Son," Butcher told him as two shots ricocheted near him. "They've killed you. You know that. Just take as many of those bastards with you as you can."

Then, Moses Butcher swung into the saddle, leaned low, and let the horse take him through the desert, following the rest of his gang. Bullets buzzed past him and his horse. He just prayed that none hit him in the back. If that happened, Auntie Faye would be disgusted with him when she greeted him at the gates of hell.

Emory Logan lowered the Colt Burgess rifle, and slid down the sloping rock, dropping into the saddle and gathering the reins. "They's runnin'. Looks like Carter got one of 'em. They left him behind."

Standing in the stirrups, McMasters could see the dust caused by the fleeing outlaws. Lowering the binoculars, he let them hang from his neck by the strap and drew the Remington from the saddle scabbard. "Let's ride."

That was all the encouragement Mary Lovelace

needed. She spurred her mustang and took off across the rocks and desert toward Butcher's camp. McMasters and the one-eyed killer from Missouri followed.

They had split up, McMasters, Logan, and Lovelace circling around south and east; Alamo Carter, Bloody Zeke The Younger, and Marcus Patton coming around from the north and west. Zeke and the redheaded woman knew the location of Moses Butcher's hideout. McMasters—from his experience catching wild horses and mustangs—and Carter—as a scout for the U.S. cavalry—knew how to cross the desert without raising dust or being seen. It helped that a dust storm was blowing in behind them. That, they'd guessed, would make Butcher relax . . . or keep his attention there.

Besides, the outlaws would expect a posse to come barreling across the Sonoran like a cavalry charge led by George Custer, following the trail and the dust Butcher's kid brother and his cohorts were leaving. They would not expect anyone to sneak up on them like Apaches.

From what Bloody Zeke and Mary Lovelace had said, McMasters knew that sneaking up on Moses Butcher and his bunch in camp would be practically impossible. They would not stick around anyway. McMasters' plan had been to drive the killers into running. Then his posse would pursue, catch them, and kill them. Every mother's son of them.

Guns in hand, Mary, Logan, and McMasters galloped toward the camp. He saw the dust coming from the far base of the mountain and knew that would be Alamo Carter, the gambler, and Bloody Zeke also making for Butcher's hideout. One rider loped off toward the east, hugging close to the edge of the mountains.

That would be Alamo Carter, making sure he did not lose sight of the running outlaws. Or at least keep on a warm trail.

"Toward the hideout!" McMasters yelled above the thundering hooves.

Mary Lovelace turned in the saddle and glared.

"I'm not leaving a man behind us!" he snapped.

"He's dead!" she called back.

"What if he's not?" McMasters yelled, and thought of something else. "What if he's Moses Butcher?"

She frowned, but tugged the reins and veered toward the cactus, the hill, and the twin rocks.

Reaching the cactus, McMasters brought the chestnut to a stop, swung out of the saddle, and quickly wrapped the reins around a rock. He came up quickly, shotgun ready, and scanned the long way up toward the hidden fortress. "Stay with the horses."

"Like hell," she replied.

"Stay," he snapped. "If it's Butcher, I'll bring you up."

She did not argue.

McMasters nodded at the one-eyed Reb and they took off running, keeping low, and pointing their long arms toward the rocks. McMasters could see the gambler and Bloody Zeke swinging off their horses, too, but those two had a lot more ground to cover.

McMasters pointed off in the distance as he ran. At the rock, he braced his back against it. He could see the brown dust storm as it moved across the desert basin, heading toward Goldfield. That might keep the town posse out of his hair . . . for a little while, at least. Logan was already creeping toward the north and east, so McMasters, checking to make sure the twelve-gauge was not in its SAFE mode, went the other way. He wet his lips, dried his hands on his pants, and moved carefully but quickly. He did not want to give Moses Butcher too much of a head start.

He reached the edge of the rock, held his breath, and looked across the desert toward the slowly approaching Zeke and Patton. He listened, then removed his hat, and held it out with his fingertips. No one shot it out of his hand, but only a greenhorn would have done that. The hat returned to his head, and he dropped to his knees, and then dived away from the rock, landing on the ground, aiming the shotgun at the figure sitting up against a rock. Something told him not to squeeze the trigger.

McMasters was up then, on his knees, keeping the barrels of the 1894 Remington aimed at the man before him. Two pistols lay at his side, but both hands clutched his stomach, blood spilling between the fingers and flowing down his body into a lake between his legs.

The man opened his mouth, trying to say something, but only managed short gasps for breath.

Gut shot. Alamo Carter's Winchester Yellow Boy had aimed true. The man before him would die in agony.

Or not. A gunshot deafened McMasters and he saw the man slam to his side, the top of his head blown off by a shot from close range. A second later, Emory Logan stepped around the rock, smoke still seeping from the barrel of his repeating rifle as he eased the lever down and up, ejecting the spent cartridge and replacing it with another. The one-eyed killer turned toward McMasters and grinned.

McMasters lowered the shotgun. "You didn't have to do that."

The one-eyed killer spit. "It's what we come fer, ain't it?" He shifted the tobacco in his cheek, walked over to the dead man, toed him with his boot, then stepped thorough the doorway of the hidden shack. He came back out, looked at the empty corral, and then stared off toward Bloody Zeke and Patton. "C'mon! Ain't nobody to kill here. Mount up and let's catch 'em other vermin. Afore the law comes."

McMasters looked away from the bloody corpse and saw Bloody Zeke and the gambler coming up, holstering their weapons, and climbing into the stirrups.

Emory Logan was walking back around the rocky wall. "Best hurry, McMasters. That bitch ain't likely to wait fer us." Before he got around the corner, he slammed against the tan rock. The Burgess repeater dropped from his hands, clattering on the ground and bounding toward McMasters.

Only then did McMasters hear the gunshot as it echoed across the Superstition range. He turned, trying to find smoke, anything. Emory Logan staggered forward, spitting up blood, and McMasters saw the red stain against the rock face.

Another bullet whined off the rock, spitting gravel and dirt into McMasters's eyes. He sank quickly and moved into the shadows between the two massive boulders in front of the closed door to Moses Butcher's cabin.

Logan dropped to his knees, and a second later, fell forward, somehow stopping his fall with both arms.

The gun roared again, but that shot had not been aimed at McMasters or the one-eyed bushwhacker.

McMasters cursed as his eyes went up the mountain. Moses Butcher had left a lookout, a man with a high-powered rifle somewhere in those rocks above. That man had a clear shot at anyone crossing the desert.

He was trapped. Pinned down. Like a rat.

Logan spit out more blood. It wasn't fair, he thought, and coughed savagely, but somehow managed not to fall onto the prickly pear near his face. He saw the blood, his blood, clinging to the cactus spines.

He was in the Superstition Mountains with a bullet hole in his chest and back, bleeding like a stuck pig, dying . . . damn it all to hell, he was mortal wounded . . . and all he could think of was Lawrence, Kansas, and the great William Clark Quantrill.

Valiant folks who'd supported the South, or at least Missouri, in that great war always swore up and down that Quantrill and his four hundred patriots never harmed no woman. No kids, neither. They just defended themselves against the abolitionists and slave-freein' red legs who happened to be in Lawrence on that fine August morning back in 18 and 63.

That wasn't exactly how things had gone. Emory Logan knew that. Hell, he had always known that. He had killed five of Kansas's finest that day. One he had shot down as he looked up while milking his cow. Three he had lined up front to back against the front door of a café, and then stepped off fifteen paces, turned around, and brought up his LeMatt revolver. Bevin Kent, a good ol' boy from Clay County, had bet him that the .41-caliber pistol would not go through two bodies, but Emory Logan had said his would kill three.

Hell, they were both wrong. The massive LeMatt had killed four.

All those years later, Emory Logan could still feel the kick of that big pistol in his hand. As he closed his eyes, he remembered. He could picture the three gents.

One still in his nightshirt, slammed against the door to the café and collapsed on the boardwalk. The glass window in the door shattered from the last guy's head as the force of the LeMatt's bullet drove him forward before he fell into a heap at the doorway atop of the other two dead Kansans Jayhawking scum.

He laughed and stepped toward Bevin Kent, waving the heavy gun in his hand. "How's that, Kent?" He pointed at the bullet hole in the door. "Coulda kilt me even one more Yank. Maybe even two. You owe me 'em silver candlesticks you taken from that home we just burnt."

Kent shook his head, and he had stepped away from the three dead men lying atop of one another in front of the café door. "Yeah. I'll go fetch 'em fer you. Then maybe we can eat in that place. I'm hungry."

"Sure, sure," Logan said, stepping to the door. He saw a spot between the dead men where he could plant his left foot, and once he had, he lifted his leg and kicked at the café's door. It crashed, shattering more glass shards, but only opened a few inches. So he kicked it again. It budged, but came back, and he realized something was blocking it on the floor inside.

He leaned forward and looked over the busted glass. He saw the colored woman, probably a cook assigned to clean up the restaurant before they opened that morn. She must've been hiding behind the doorway, and the bullet, having gone through three Kansas Jayhawkers and the door itself, had gone through her back.

He knew he had shot her. He saw the blood flowing across the fancy wood and knew the LeMatt would not have killed five men . . . or women . . . just four. There was no exit wound in her chest, but, well, she was a fat old hen.

Her eyes stared up, not seeing, but haunting him. It sickened him, although he did not understand why. She just wouldn't stop looking at him, even though she was deader than a turnip.

He burned that café. Had seen the lantern on the counter, and aimed the LeMatt through the busted glass and squeezed off a shot. He saw two other lanterns on the wall, and blasted those apart, too, spraying the café with burning kerosene.

"What in tarnation did you do that fer?" Bevin Kent complained as he stopped in the street with his hands full of stolen candlesticks. "I thought we was gonna eat."

"Let's go to the hotel," Logan said. "Where the rest of us is congregatin'. Ain't nothin' hot in this place anyhow."

Bevin Kent laughed. "Is now. It's gonna burn like hell. Like your soul."

"Shut up, Kent."

Blown all to hell and bleeding through mouth, nose, back, and chest, Logan looked down at the prickly pear waiting for his face to drop into those spines. It changed, and he wasn't looking at cactus anymore but at that black colored woman's eyes. Staring at him.

Because of her, he had always told himself, he could never settle down. Couldn't go back to farming up around St. Joseph no more, not after the war, even though some of Quantrill's raiders had managed to go back and live peacefully. Like Logan, others had taken to the owlhoot trail. Whenever he thought he might do something honest, he'd always remember that dead colored woman on the floor of that café.

He tried to raise his head, to look up at the mountain and into the rocks, to at least see the man who had killed him. But he couldn't do it. That man had been a coward. Shooting him like that. Giving him no chance. Emory Logan wasn't no snake in the grass. The folks he had killed, during the war and for all those years after, had at least been looking at him. Except for those three red legs he had back-shot with the LeMatt back in Lawrence that day. And that fat black gal.

"Damned"—he coughed—"damned snake in the grass."

That black cleaning gal's big eyes raced up to meet Emory Logan's face as he fell.

CHAPTER 32

Snake in the grass.

McMasters sucked in a breath, let it out, and peered just long enough to see Emory Logan lying facedown in the dirt. Dead.

The rifle boomed again, echoing. McMasters heard the whine of a ricochet behind him and knew that one had been aimed at Mary Lovelace. He brought the shotgun up, cursed, and set it aside. What good was a scattergun on a man high up in those rocks? As useless as the Colt .45 in his holster.

McMasters thought about Alamo Carter. Would the big man hear the report of the rifle? And if he did, what would he do? Double-back and try to sneak up on and kill the man in the rocks, or keep following the rest of the bunch? Or, more than likely, figure he was finally free of John McMasters and just keep riding straight for old Mexico?

The rifle boomed again. Hearing no ricochet, McMasters figured that shot had been aimed at Bloody Zeke and Patton.

How long will he wait us out?

From where McMasters squatted against the rocks, he could no longer see the cloud of dust whipped into a frenzy by the wind off in the desert.

Eventually, that storm would blow itself out, and the town posse would come from Goldfield. Or some fool and his burro and supplies would make his way toward the mountains in search of the Lost Dutchman's Mine. Either way, the sniper would not risk staying up there forever. He'd have to go.

But when?

McMasters swore again. Noticing the barrel of the Colt Burgess repeating rifle, he knew it was his best chance. He drew in a deep breath, and slowly brought his legs up, pressing himself against the hot, hard rock. Success or death would depend on where the man in the rocks was looking. At Mary Lovelace? At Bloody Zeke and the gambler? Or down at the rocks and the hideout's shack . . . where McMasters was? The latter might get him killed, but he had to take the gamble.

He jumped into the opening, his right hand shooting out and gripping the barrel of the rifle, and then he flung himself toward the far wall of rocks and brush. A bullet smacked into the sand where he had been, flinging dust and dirt and carving a small, narrow ditch in the earth. But it had not been close to McMasters, who brought the Burgess up and held it tightly in his arms.

He looked at where the bullet had struck.

Fifty caliber, he thought. Maybe a .45-70 Remington Rolling Block, but McMasters thought he'd recognized the sound of a Sharps .50 caliber. Hell, he had heard that gun enough thirty years ago.

Hefting the Burgess in his arms, he felt its weight.

Andrew Burgess had known what he was doing when he'd designed the weapon for Colt. It was a fine gun, on par with the Winchester. Why had Colt discontinued producing those weapons? The company could have rivaled Winchester, or at least made it an interesting race. McMaster knew the answer was holstered on his hip. Colt had become synonymous with short guns. Winchester, at least on the American frontier, had become the rifle and carbine of choice.

He guessed the Burgess weighed eight or nine pounds, noticed the barrel was octagonal, not round, and judged it to be about two feet long, which meant the rifle would hold fourteen rounds. Slowly, he began working the lever, but just enough to see that Logan had chambered a fresh .44-40 cartridge.

The unanswered question was how many shots had Logan fired before he had been killed.

It didn't matter. McMasters had what he had. He braced the barrel against the rock, found the sight, and aimed at the rocks high above him.

He stopped, brought the Burgess back toward him, and leaned it against the rock. He removed his eyeglasses and began wiping the lenses with his bandanna. The spectacles went back on his head, he blinked, and picked up the rifle.

"You're a fifty-year-old man . . . with fifty-year-old eyes. What the hell do you think you're doing?"

He had not meant to speak the words aloud, but he had, and his own voice startled him. He steadied his arms, tightened the stock against his shoulder, and looked above the sight.

"McMasters?"

Mary Lovelace's voice echoed.

He wet his lips.

"Logan?"

"Stay put," McMasters yelled, and the Sharps in the rocks roared again.

Still looking at the rocks, he saw the puff of white smoke.

"There you are," he whispered, and leaned closer, trying to focus on the sight. The smoke erupted again, and he heard the shot moments later. He heard something else.

"Son of a bitch. That was close!" the gambler shouted.

McMasters aimed, and his finger curled around the trigger, but he stopped, releasing the tension and letting out a heavy sigh.

Who the hell am I kidding? That son of a bitch is shooting a rifle with an effective range of at least five hundred yards. This lightweight Colt? What do I have? A hundred yards. Two hundred at the most. And I'm shooting uphill. With the wind. And I'm fifty damned years old.

More white smoke drifted above the rocks. The bullet ricocheted again.

And he remembered the stories about Billy Dixon.

Legend had it the fabled buffalo hunter down in Texas had killed an Indian with one shot from a Sharps rifle from a mile or more away. Someone who heard about McMasters's Civil War experience asked him how anyone could see that far to even make a shot.

"You don't have to see," he answered. "The bullet sees." He said nothing else and left the saloon.

"McMasters!" Bloody Zeke The Younger was yelling. "Do something, damn it!"

"McMasters!" Mary Lovelace screamed from the other side of the twin tall rocks. "Please!"

He uttered a blasphemy. He also remembered.

Do something.

He swallowed down the bile. Most Colt rifles were furnished with a semi-buckhorn rear sight, but this one had a special tang sight. He thumbed it up, and adjusted it for distance. The front sight was an ivory bead combination, and he could see it clearly. His question was *Even with my spectacles, can I spot that guy up there?*

He watched the creosote bush ahead of him, thinking about the wind. He leaned closer, drew a deep breath, slowly exhaled. And he waited.

Smoke appeared suddenly. Then came the roar.

"Damn!" coincided with the whine of ricochet down near Mary Lovelace.

"Let the bullet see," McMasters prayed softly. He aimed high, and slowly squeezed the trigger.

Jacking a fresh .44-40 shell into the chamber while lowering the Burgess, he stared through the gun smoke before him and studied the rocks. He caught the movement, saw a thin outline weave, and then he saw it plummet, falling head over heels in silence, crashing off one rock, and then dropping silently and landing with a distant crunch beyond the rocks.

Lowering the Burgess, McMasters thought he heard

another shout. *McMasters! In the name of God . . . do something . . . Please!*

And he remembered.

March 1864. Somewhere in northern Virginia, he leaned against the pecan tree, the one tree that had not been blown apart by cannon balls or grapeshot. Down below, he saw the men of a Michigan infantry unit . . . being cut to ribbons by the Rebels up on the hill.

What struck him was the bravery of those Union soldiers. They did not scream. They did not panic. They did not fall or beg or cry. They kept right on running. Running but unable to touch the ground because dead soldiers carpeted the ground.

And here he sat under a pecan tree, about to have his breakfast before the sudden attack had begun. Watching the war . . . the real war . . . going on off in the distance, up the hill and across the still smoking clearing, six hundred and sixty-seven yards away.

The Rebs sat atop the far hill. He could see the puffs from the muskets as they fired. They were damned fine shots, but then again, they were Southerners. They were used to hunting. And this late in the war, they were used to killing Union soldiers.

An infantry soldier staggered, the impact of an Enfield rifled-musket ball spinning him around and dropping him to his knees. He appeared to be staring right at McMasters. No, not at him. Right through him. McMasters could have sworn he heard the boy say, "McMasters! In the name of God . . . do something . . . Please!"

But that couldn't have been. No one, except Lieutenant McDonald, knew he was here . . . and McMasters wasn't even certain the lieutenant knew he was here. McMasters didn't know anybody from Michigan except the sharpshooters with Berdan's men in green uniforms. And no one in that unit of brave young men knew him by name.

Another Enfield shot snapped the boy's spine. He collapsed and became just another piece of the hallowed blue-coated carpet.

McMasters brought the Sharps up, pulled back the heavy hammer, and looked through the brass telescopic sight. He found a man about to fire, kneeling in front of an overturned canister. He did not remember touching the trigger, but felt the stock of the heavy rifle slam against his shoulder. He did not look to see if his shot had been true. He knew it had. He just busied himself reloading.

The rifle came up, and he fired again. He saw the man in gray or butternut or maybe just in his long-handle underwear . . . at better than six hundred yards, across a field and up a hill in the early hours of morning.

His shoulder throbbed. He did not care. He felt no pain. His ears rang from the roar of the Sharps. Yet he still heard that boy screaming, looking at him as death coated those young, innocent eyes.

"McMasters! In the name of God . . . do something . . . Please!"

The Sharps roared. A man flew backwards, knocked a good six feet by the impact of the heavy lead slug.

He reloaded. Fired again. Saw another man stagger, sink, and topple to his left.

By then, the Rebs had spotted him. He saw a flash of flame and smoke, and heard the massive volley. He saw the ground torn up all around him. All in front of him, maybe a hundred yards ahead in the dirt. The rifles those Rebs fired did not have the range of the Sharps. Or maybe they just weren't as good as John McMasters was at killing men from a great distance.

Two Rebs in tan hats charged down the hill toward him. Trying to close in on the distance. McMasters heard the screams and that blood-curdling Rebel yell. He did not care. He had another round in the Sharps, and he aimed—not at the two men in butternut who ran toward him, but at another Rebel still shooting at the Michigan boys. He didn't care about those two men, even if they were trying to kill him. What he cared about was saving those men, those brave soldiers . . . those boys who saw Death every day . . . who charged into fortified positions through musket balls and grapeshot and brave Southern marksmen.

Those boys were not snakes in the grass.

The Sharps roared. Another Confederate soldier died.

About halfway down the hill, the two Rebs charging toward McMasters turned around and fled.

Southerners were not the only men who could scream out a Rebel yell. After years of war, some Union boys could do a damned fine imitation. The Michigan boys and platoons from Ohio and Wisconsin followed, waving their colors. Sabers glistened in the morning light.

And the Rebs retreated.

Chapter 33

The memories continued in spite of the circumstances.

They gave Private John McMasters the Medal of Honor for that skirmish.

"He killed a hundred men," the general bragged.

"Actually," Colonel Berdan said, "it had been fifteen. But from what a distance!"

And they said he had turned the battle—a skirmish, actually, *McMasters thought—and saved the day for the entire Corps, if not the entire United States. They had driven off the Rebs, and Grant could march on toward Richmond.*

And all John McMasters thought was that those who really deserved that medal the general had pinned onto his tunic were those lying on that field, hundreds of yards away from a pecan tree. Those who had died. Those who had faced death practically every single day of the war. Those who had not been blessed with a keen eye, a calm nerve, and the ability to shoot and kill with a big Sharps rifle that had a brass telescopic sight.

Shaking off the memory, McMasters stepped up, looked off at the rocks where the man had fallen, and dropped the Burgess in the dirt. He stared at the two dead men before him, the young punk who had ridden with the Butcher Gang, and the one-eyed Reb who had died in the cactus.

I killed because I had to kill, he told himself. *I killed to save those lives. And now I kill because I must kill.* He picked up the Burgess, moved back into the entrance in the rocks, picked up the Remington, and stepped back away from the twin rocks.

"It's over!" he yelled then heard his echoes. He saw the figures of Bloody Zeke The Younger and Marcus Patton climbing out of a ditch, bringing their horses behind them, and swinging into the saddle. He walked back, leaving the dead in the desert, and headed toward Mary Lovelace and his own horse.

She swung into her saddle and loped up the hill. He watched her ride past him, and stop, turning as the mustang carried her beyond the twin rocks.

"Where's she off to?" yelled Marcus Patton as he and Bloody Zeke The Younger rode up.

McMasters swore and gestured with the shotgun. "Catch up to Carter. Keep after Butcher. We'll be along directly."

Zeke kicked his horse into a trot, and Marcus Patton, shaking his head, followed. Once they cleared the incline, they spurred their mounts into gallops. Mc-

Masters watched them, but only for a minute. Then he took the reins to his horse and walked back to the bloody scene.

The redhead had carelessly ground-reined the mustang. McMasters cursed and grabbed the reins of her horse, which was backing away, snorting, about to run off from the blood and gore from the two dead men lying on the ground. He did not see Mary Lovelace anywhere, but heard the cabin door open.

"Hey," he shouted. When no response came, he tried again. "Mary?"

Silence. "Damn it," he said to himself, and pulled his chestnut and Mary's mustang behind the towering rocks. He tied them to a brush tight and short, drew the Remington from the scabbard and slid the Burgess into the empty scabbard on Mary's saddle. He moved back up the hill, around the rocks, and headed for the opening in the rocks. He did not look at the corpses on the ground.

He stopped when he saw her, suddenly feeling awkward, as if he had stepped into some private matter, seen something he was not supposed to see. She just stood, leaning against the door frame, looking inside at the Spartan quarters of the hideout.

The cabin smelled of dust, as it had been those years before. She saw the bottle of forty-rod whiskey, half empty, on the floor. She did not look through the porthole, did not turn to see McMasters waiting for her, annoyed, impatient, but silent. Her eyes kept returning to the bed.

She had been on the westbound stagecoach bound for Florence when the Butcher Gang had held up the stage about twelve miles east of her destination. *Twelve miles. Only twelve measly miles.* How her life might have turned out. She could have been in Florence, teaching at the subscription school, and not just making her students learn by memorizing the *Readers* and such. She thought she could actually teach. Make them think for themselves.

That had been the plan, anyway. Suddenly, she was lost in the memory.

She was going to teach school, save up what money she could, and then marry Chandler Taylor. He had left Monroe, Michigan, two years earlier but kept writing her. He had been a clerk but dreamed of becoming a farmer. It struck her odd that a clerk from Michigan would go to the Arizona desert to farm. But he had explained to her that a canal had been built from the Gila River, so farming would become profitable in Florence and Pinal County.

The stagecoach was suddenly surrounded by outlaws. They killed the messenger and wounded the driver. They ripped off an elderly woman's broach and stole the wallet, watch, and pocket pistol of the lone male passenger. The thin bandit with the wheat sack over his face took her billfold and her watch. He dropped them in the flour sack, and stepped back, staring at her. She looked down.

"What do you think?" the thin one asked.

"Take her," the big man on the dun horse said.

"Now just a danged minute—"

A rifle blast splintered the brake lever and silenced the driver.

And they took Mary Elizabeth Carmen. To the hut hidden in the Superstition Mountains.

* * *

Lost in the memory, she could hear their laughs. She stared at the bed.

She was there two weeks.

"The longest," Ben Butcher told her, "my brother has ever stayed put in this Superstition camp."

Then Chandler Taylor drifted in. He was no farmer. He had not been farming all those years. Not from the cut of his clothes, not from the Schofield revolver on his hip. Not from his slick, smooth hands.

He smiled when he saw her, but she did not smile. She wanted to die.

"How much?" Taylor asked Moses Butcher. "For the redhead?"

"You want her . . . after . . . ?" Young Ben Butcher laughed.

She hung her head in shame, and cried again.

"A hundred dollars," Moses Butcher said.

"We could play cards for her," Chandler Taylor suggested.

"I know how you play cards," Moses Butcher said. "A hundred dollars."

"She's not worth a hundred," Taylor said. "Not anymore."

For a brief moment, she thought he had ridden to her rescue. To buy her freedom, the way she had read—back home in the safety of the two-story home she shared with her parents and younger siblings—about Texas men buying white captives taken by savage Indians. Her beau had come to buy her freedom from savage white men.

But, no, Moses Butcher and Chandler Taylor knew each other. They were . . . she turned and gagged . . . bartering. Like they were trading horses or selling a cow. She wanted to die. But she hadn't died. She hadn't killed herself. She had let

Chandler Taylor buy her from Moses Butcher for forty-two dollars, and that came over Ben Butcher's protests that she could not leave, not alive. That had always been the rule.

"She won't remember nothing," Moses Butcher said. "Hell, Chandler here'll kill her when he tires of her."

And maybe he would have. Often, she prayed that he would. She wished to God Almighty that Moses Butcher had listened to his kid brother, and that one of them had put a bullet in the back of her head. That's what Ben said they did, after the fun wasn't fun anymore.

Instead, Chandler Taylor took her to Casa Grande, checked into a hotel, let her bathe and then . . . and then—

She shook her head, found herself shivering, and made herself stop the memories, yet she continued to stare at the room.

He'd taught her—forced her to learn—how to help him win at cards. He wasn't a good card player, and when the cards did not fall, he was an even worse cheat. But when he had a woman who looked like Mary Elizabeth Carmen to distract the gamblers at the table with him, he played a lot better poker.

Tucson . . . Tombstone . . . Phoenix . . . Wickenburg . . . Prescott . . . Fort Verde . . . Williams . . . until his luck finally ran out so much that even Mary could not help him. They had taken the last name Lovelace by then, and he said they were married, although no minister had blessed them while it felt like everyone had kissed the bride, especially when the cards did not fall his way. In Flagstaff, his luck had gone so cold, he'd made her help him hold up a stage.

More memories assailed her.

All those horrors, all that shame, from the Superstition Mountains to what had happened in Flagstaff. By then, she knew what he had done. Maybe he wasn't to blame. Hell, how could she blame the man for being a coward?

She knew.

In one of the rare drunken benders in which he did not hit her, he cried. "I didn't know what would happen. I mentioned to Moses Butcher and his kid brother over a poker game that my fiancé was coming to Florence. I didn't know they robbed the stagecoach and took you until the driver limped the Concord wagon into town with the news. I came after you, though. You have to know that."

As the posse closed in, Taylor's horse went lame. He hurried to her, lifted her from the saddle, and threw her into the rocks where she struck her head.

She knew something else about the man who called himself Taylor Lovelace. He had wanted Butcher to take her from that stage, to rape her, to shame her, to reduce her to some puppet that the cheating gambler and coward could use for his own personal gain. How had she not been able to see through his mask back in Monroe, Michigan, and in all those letters of lies he had written her?

"I'm sorry, Mary," Taylor Lovelace cried as he climbed onto her horse. "I'm sorry. They might go easy on you, baby. They won't on me. I'm sorry."

Before he could spur her horse, she told him, "I'm sorry, too."

He turned to see her holding the Schofield .45 . . . the last thing Taylor Lovelace ever saw.

Mary Lovelace straightened, turned away from the bed, and looked directly at John McMasters.

"Do you believe in God?"

The tough man with the sad eyes looked up. His Adam's apple bobbed.

"I did," he finally answered. "Maybe I still do."

"Fate?" she asked.

He shrugged. "What do you mean?"

"I mean you and me and Bloody Zeke . . . and Moses Butcher."

"I'm not good at thinking anymore, Mary Lovelace."

"It's Carmen. Mary Elizabeth Carmen. At least, that's who I used to be. Who I wish I could be. But she's dead. So Mary Lovelace will do."

His head tilted, and he drew in a deep breath. He had no clue what she was talking about.

"We best get going. Or you can stay. Wait here. Posse'll be along directly."

She let out a humorless laugh. "I'm not waiting. I'm going with you."

He turned, but she stopped him. "You got a match?"

As he came back toward her, she bent and picked up the whiskey bottle and splashed most of it on the blanket on the awful bed. The rest she tossed into the ceiling of dry brush and what she hoped would prove to be tinder.

"This is adobe," he told her. "It won't burn."

"Enough of it will." She took the match he held out in his hard fingers, struck its tip against the door, and the flame erupted. Raising it toward the ceiling, she watched the blaze erupt, and ducked down, astonished by the intensity. The match still burned, and she flipped it onto the bedding. The fierce whoosh drove her back, into the arms of John McMasters, who dropped his shotgun and pulled her back.

Her face felt flushed from the blaze.

He stopped, and she spun around, close to him. Too close. Their eyes met, and she could smell him. He could smell her. She saw something different in those eyes, then, not the hardness, the coldness, the ruthlessness that matched her own hatred. Somewhere beneath all that, there was human decency. Like she had once thought might be locked down somewhere, out of reach, in her own soul.

He released her, and she backed away from him, turned, picked up the twelve-gauge and held it out for him. He took it, but he did not look away from her. Maybe John McMasters had seen the same thing in her eyes that she had found in his.

"Let's go," he said.

She followed.

Behind them, black smoke and orange flames roared as the wind moaned through the open doorway and the porthole. Or was it the wind? It could have been, Mary thought, the souls of all those tortured in that awful place. But no more. No one else would have to endure what the late Mary Elizabeth Carmen, God rest her soul, had gone through in a nightmare that had begun two years, four months, and seven days ago.

They put their horses into a trot, riding side by side.

"You want to talk about it?" McMasters asked.

Mary Lovelace grinned to herself. She wondered how much strength that had taken the old man to ask.

"Do you?" she called out over the clopping of hooves.

He did not need to answer.

They rode on in silence. They did not look back at the belching black smoke.

That would, Mary figured, at least draw the attention of any of those idiot townsmen who came after them, which would occupy the posse long enough. Maybe by the time the good citizens of Goldfield resumed their chase, it would all be over. Moses Butcher could not be that far ahead of them. And the big black scout, Alamo Carter, would be following them.

She hoped she would find her peace—or as much of it as she could hope for—within the next few hours.

When the desert flattened, they pushed their horses into a lope. The mountains were soon behind them, and they slowed down, saving their horses. The trail was easy enough to follow.

She brought up her canteen, drank, and returned it to the horn. After wiping her lips with her shirtsleeve, and still looking across the desert in front of her, she asked, "Tonight?" One word was all she needed.

John McMasters knew what she meant.

"Tomorrow. Unless they ride through the night. We'll—" He stopped in midsentence and raised the shotgun slightly.

She saw them, as well. Two men on foot, holding their horses. One of them waved his hands in a signal, telling them to slow down, keep their horses quiet, and walk.

Even though he was a good two hundred yards away, that man was easy enough to recognize. Bloody Zeke The Younger still wore the prison duds he had been issued at Yuma Territorial Prison.

McMasters reined up, easily dismounted, and waited on Mary Lovelace to do the same. They covered half the distance together before he stopped and handed his reins to her.

"Wait here"

He took off at a jog toward Bloody Zeke The Younger, who was crouching as he sprinted to meet him. They met amid catclaw and the bleached, scattered bones of a coyote.

"We got us a bit of a problem," Bloody Zeke said, motioning to a wash that dropped off another hundred yards past where the gambler, holding his and Bloody Zeke's horses, waited.

McMasters waited.

"It's the darky."

McMasters frowned. "Butcher?"

"No. Six or seven white men. Miners. Likely fools out chasing after the Dutchman's mine. Southerners. Too bad Logan got himself kilt. At least he could understand their damned language."

McMasters cursed.

"Wait here with the girl." He moved ahead, straightening as he walked, and shifted the shotgun to his other hand. When he reached the gambler, Marcus Patton opened his mouth but quickly closed it. Something told him that John McMasters was not in a talkative mood . . . as if he ever felt like having a conversation. He moved on, slowing down until he could hear the laughter. He dropped to his belly and crawled to the edge of the wash.

He lifted his head and looked at the scene ten feet below. He looked for only five seconds then he rose and brought the shotgun to his shoulder.

Chapter 34

Six men in ragged clothes and filthy beards had somehow stopped Alamo Carter. His horse lay dead about forty yards down the wash. He must have been stunned from the fall after they had shot the horse out from under him. That's the only way they could have stripped him naked and lashed him to the arms of a saguaro. They had whipped him with a bullwhip, and one of them held a massive bowie knife in his right hand, taunting the black man with it, laughing as another of those worthless scum threw water in Alamo Carter's face to keep him conscious.

"Bastards!" McMasters fired the shotgun's first barrel, sending buckshot slamming into two men close together—but not the two nearest Alamo Carter. McMasters turned, triggered the second barrel, and leaped down the embankment, landing before the third of the fiends fell crashing against the picketed horses and mules, which freed themselves from the tethers and thundered off to the southeast.

McMasters pitched the smoking empty shotgun to the ground and clawed for his .45.

He saw the man with the knife drop his bowie and paw for a belted pistol. He saw the man with the gourd of water drop it and rip his shirt as he pulled the revolver he had stolen from Alamo Carter. Drawing the .45 from his holster, McMasters thumbed back the hammer. He knew he could not kill the remaining three . . . but he would do his damnedest to keep Alamo Carter alive as long as possible.

Blood spurted from the forehead of the man who had been wielding the knife, and he spun around and dropped behind the cactus. The other one stumbled back, turning his attention and his aim away from McMasters and looking up. He went down with a bullet in his throat and began rolling over and over, clutching at the blood that pulsated from the ghastly wound. But not for long. Within seconds, he lay facedown in the lake of blood that quickly soaked into the sand.

The only shot McMasters heard came from the one after that, and that slug buzzed past his nose. He turned and saw the last of the men working the lever on a Henry rifle. McMasters swung his right arm out. No time to aim because the man's finger was tightening on his trigger.

Four shots sounded as one—from McMasters's Colt and three guns above him. All three struck the last man in the chest, and he squeezed the trigger of the .44-caliber rifle as he fell . . . but the Henry had been pointing at the clear sky when it discharged. The rifle landed beside his quivering corpse.

McMasters stepped away from the sandy embankment. He saw Marcus Patton and Bloody Zeke The

Younger flanking Mary Lovelace. The gambler was on his knee, the dark-skinned killer still held his left hand over the revolver in his right as though he had fanned back the hammer, and Mary Lovelace gripped the Remington pistol with both hands. All of them kept their eyes on the last man and then looked down at McMasters.

He waited. They had their guns drawn. Killing him, and thus freeing themselves, would be easy. Lovelace looked at him first, swallowed, and shoved the nickel-plated revolver in the holster. Bloody Zeke leaped down alongside McMasters, and did not even send a glance his way as he headed quickly toward Alamo Carter. The gambler appeared to be the only one who even considered the other option, the one that would leave John McMasters dead . . . but he shook his head and sighed.

"I'll catch our horses," he said, and walked out of McMasters's view.

"Who pulled on my britches?" Alamo Carter asked through the pain.

"I did," McMasters said. He held the giant man up, letting Marcus Patton give him some water from a canteen.

"Hell," the black scout said, "I was hopin' it was the white woman."

McMasters shook his head as Patton guffawed, splashing out a healthy dose of water on the Negro's bare chest.

"We can leave you here," McMasters said. "Posse will find you soon enough, take you back—"

"You ain't leavin' me nowhere, McMasters." The man turned his head, freeing himself. "Leave me here? With six dead white men? They'll finish what them other cutthroats started. You've wasted enough time already. I'm goin' with you."

"You can't even stand up, let alone ride."

"Watch me."

McMasters watched the big man rise to his feet, falling once to his knees, but that man had a stubborn streak in him wider than the Sonoran Desert. He held his head down as though bowed in silent prayer for a long while, and then rose slowly. Managing to turn around without falling, he drew a deep breath and glared at McMasters and the gambler.

"Where's the girl? Where's Zeke?"

"Trying to pick up Butcher's trail." McMasters looked back toward Goldfield, searching the sky for dust, but seeing none . . . yet. "Can you put on your boots?"

"I'll do that later. Sons of bitches killed my horse. Shot it dead before I even saw them. Where'd their hosses take off to?"

McMasters pointed.

The black man nodded. "We'll find one in a jiffy, I expect. Patton, grab me that big fella's vest. That's all I need to protect my back. And that dude won't need no vest in Hell."

He walked into the desert.

Patton looked at McMasters, shrugged, and walked to one of the corpses. McMasters gathered a few extra canteens and went to his chestnut and the gambler's bay.

* * *

For days, they moved slowly . . . hiding when the sun turned the bleak desert into a dust- and cactus-covered inferno and moving at dark. Posses scoured the area for the Butcher gang and for those strange men who had shot up Goldfield and then murdered six prospectors around one of the trickling branches of Queen Creek. They had to move slowly until Alamo Carter gained strength.

They skirted a wide path around the town of Florence and followed a series of dry arroyos and empty washes, keeping the Tortilla Mountains over their left shoulders. When they saw Mount Lemon they knew Tucson would be close, so they turned east, disappearing into Cherry Valley Wash and climbing through rougher country until they neared the Rio San Pedro.

"I should have left you sons of bitches back in the Superstitions," Bloody Zeke said. "Butcher's in Mexico by now."

"No," Mary Lovelace told him, "he's not. He's avoiding the same posses we are. And he doesn't have enough money to go into Mexico. He'll need to rob something first."

Zeke laughed. "I know him from a few weeks with him. How long did you know him?" He said it with a sinister grin.

"Shut up," McMasters told him.

They kept along the western bank of the San Pedro, more ditch than river, even after the monsoons. Moving south, between Wild Horse Mountain and Lime Peak, they crossed the Southern Pacific Railroad tracks east of Benson.

Long ago, they had lost the trail of Moses Butcher. They found it between Benson and Tombstone.

The ambulance—with U.S. ARMY stenciled in green letters—sat on a turnoff in a dry wash, two mules dead in their traces, the rest of the team cut loose. The driver lay dead in his seat, but the buzzards had not finished with him when the arrival of McMasters, Carter, Lovelace, Patton, and Bloody Zeke frightened them away. There had been no soldier riding for protection, but, well, it was 1896 and Arizona Territory was supposed to be civilized.

"I guess Butcher has money to spend in Mexico now," Bloody Zeke said bitterly.

"Not much," Marcus Patton said. "If this was an Army payroll, it's coming away from Fort Huachuca. And if it was hauling soldiers, soldiers don't have much money to begin with."

"It might not have been Butcher," McMasters said, but he knew better.

Sighing, Bloody Zeke slipped off his horse, handed the reins to McMasters, and walked toward the coach. He kicked over the empty tin box, sending letters, some unopened, others ripped apart on the off chance someone might have been mailing a check or money. The wind scattered the papers, and Zeke stepped around a depression, stopped, knelt, and fingered the dirt.

"Driver winged one of them." He turned his hand and showed darkened sand on his fingers.

A noise startled him, and he spun, the revolver appearing instantly, cocked and ready, in his right hand. He crouched, moved toward the nearest dead mule, looked up at the mutilated body of the driver, and then slid along the coach. He came to the door, reached for the handle, jerked it open, and stepped around, leveling his gun toward the inside.

The pop that came from within the coach sounded faintly. McMasters leaped from the saddle, as Bloody Zeke The Younger stumbled away from the stagecoach and fell onto his knees. His revolver landed, unfired, in the dirt.

McMasters brought up the Remington and charged. He heard Mary Lovelace running behind him. Another pop came from inside the stagecoach, and smoke drifted through the open window and door. He did not run toward that open door, but cut around the dead mules, moving to the opposite side. He gripped the lever to the door in his left hand, held the Remington close and hard with his right, and jerked open the door.

He swore, lowered the shotgun, and tried to catch the girl as she tumbled out.

She was young—probably still in her teens—naked, face bruised, lip busted, and a few teeth had been knocked out. She stared at him with unblinking hazel eyes. Blood trickled down her head into her sweat-matted hair. McMasters saw the Remington derringer clutched in her right hand, and his chest heaved. He did not see the dead stranger but Bea . . . and Rosalee . . . and Eugénia.

Mary Lovelace came alongside him and let out a gasp. It wasn't in horror or pity or shame but something different. She saw no stranger, either. She saw herself.

He lowered the young woman onto the ground and stood, finding an Army blouse on the floor of the coach, which he dragged out and draped over her body. He moved past Mary, not wanting to be near the dead girl any longer, and fought his way through the brush behind the coach, and moved back to the other side.

Marcus Patton and Alamo Carter had come closer. McMasters lowered the shotgun and walked to Bloody Zeke The Younger, who slipped onto his buttocks and let out a slight laugh.

Blood seeped from one corner of his mouth. Both hands clutched his blood-stained shirt. "Hard to figure, ain't it, McMasters?"

McMasters caught him before he fell.

The killer's dark eyes opened as McMasters lifted his head against his chest. Alamo Carter stood, positioning himself to keep the sun out of the dying killer's eyes.

"What happened?" Marcus Patton asked.

"A girl." Bloody Zeke coughed out more blood and shook his head. "Butcher's bunch had their way with her. Guess she thought I was one of them coming back for more pleasures. Is the girl all right?"

"Yeah," McMasters lied.

"You ain't got enough without me to kill those bastards," Bloody Zeke said. "Best give it up."

McMasters said nothing.

"You're one stubborn son of a bitch." Zeke coughed again and gasped in pain. "Listen," he spoke in a whisper, knowing death would take him soon. "Mule Pass. Before Bisbee. Right before you get there. A crack in the mountains. Go east. Through it. Till it widens out. Creep along to the north, before there's a split. Little cut you can't hardly see. Push through it. That's where you'll find Butcher."

McMasters waited.

"I told him it ain't no fit hideout. But it's damned

hard to find. You catch him there, you might be able to kill him before he kills you. Box canyon. He'll have to come through you to get out."

McMasters waited, and then realized Bloody Zeke would be saying nothing else in this world. He lowered the outlaw's head onto the dirt, and rose.

"He wouldn't hold up in a box canyon," Marcus Patton said. "That close to Bisbee. When Mexico's just a hop and a skip away."

"He wouldn't hold up in the Superstition Mountains, either," Alamo Carter said. "But he did."

"What about the girl?" Patton asked.

She must have been an officer's daughter, being escorted to Tucson or someplace. The Butcher bunch would have thought it was carrying money. The Butchers were stupid. But, seeing the dead girl's body, he knew they were worse than stupid. They were evil.

McMasters shook his head. He was already walking toward the chestnut. Alamo Carter, Mary Lovelace, and the gambler in the yellow vest followed him in silence.

Chapter 35

The Army must have sent a patrol out from Fort Huachuca, way off to the east. McMasters' dwindling posse watched from the rocks as the raw young soldiers rode past. It was the second bunch they had avoided that day. Word of the robbery had also reached Bisbee. A dead army soldier and a dead, ravished young girl had raised the ire of not just the U.S. Army—but every man between Douglas and San Miguel.

Following the main roads, Payson lay around two hundred and seventy miles north. A man could learn a lot in that distance, and John McMasters had learned a few things. He had set out with six hardened killers to take revenge. He had watched three of them die.

One of those he had killed himself. One had died, "in the line of duty," or something along those lines. And the last had died needlessly, senselessly. Or maybe they all had been needless, senseless.

He was so close to Moses Butcher he could almost feel the killer's eyes on his back.

They had left the desert and climbed high into the Mule Mountains, where it was cooler, even if miners had chopped down and wiped out most of the forests that once grew in those rugged hills. They weaved through manzanita and juniper, climbed through the canyon, and saw it widen out into a meadow, more or less, where a family of javelinas scurried about. McMasters caught their musky odor, and reined in the chestnut.

He smelled something other than javelinas.

"Smoke," Alamo Carter said.

McMaster knew that. He also knew something else, and he turned around in the saddle.

"Carter, take Mary out of here."

"Like hell," she snapped in a whisper. "I'm—"

"This is my fight, and I'll go it alone. You got no part in this." He glanced at the gambler. "You don't, either."

Marcus Patton grinned. "You don't have to tell me that twice, McMasters."

The girl was reaching for her Remington, but Carter reached across his saddle and grabbed her right hand. She swerved, brought up her other hand to slap him, but by then the gambler had slid out of his saddle and grabbed the .44-40. He backed away quickly before she kicked him with her boot.

"You sons of bitches." Blood reddened her face. "You can't take me away. I got more right—"

"Take her," McMasters said. "Get to Mexico. You skirt through these hills, the law won't catch you. Good luck."

"Good luck to you, too," Patton said.

"There's seven of them, McMasters," Carter told him.

"Maybe the one that caught a bullet back south of Tombstone is dead by now." McMasters took Mary Lovelace's Remington revolver and shoved it into his waistband.

"Maybe," Alamo Carter said. "But them ain't good odds."

"That's why he is letting us fold our hand," Marcus Patton pleaded.

"I'm going nowhere," Mary said.

McMasters smiled at her. "Do this, Mary, for me. Please."

He saw her expression change and her muscles relax.

And he left them in the shadows and pushed through the clearing.

"I can't believe that little hussy shot me," Ben Butcher whined. "Can you get me to a doc, Mose?"

Moses Butcher pulled away the wrapping, which caused his kid brother to squirm, so he pulled it even harder and stared at the little hole the .41-caliber slug had put in his brother's belly. The smell sickened him, and he quickly shoved the bandage back over the bloody, swollen, rotting hole.

"Did Milt get the bullet out?"

"No." Ben rolled over and vomited. "No. He just dug around in there. I think he done more damage than that little bitch. I shoulda kilt her." He tried to push himself up, but couldn't, and collapsed back onto his bedroll.

"That's what you say about all the women you rape," Moses said sharply. "I go to Bisbee, try to get the lay of the land, see where we might sneak over the border. I have to dodge posse after posse, bounty hunters, hell the United States damned cavalry to get back here. You damned near got us killed in Goldfield. And now this."

Ben tried again to smile, but the look in his brother's eyes killed that weak attempt.

"Goldfield wasn't my fault. I done told you that."

"It's never your fault, Ben."

Already pale from the wound, he knew his face turned even whiter. "You just . . . get me to a . . . sawbones. That's all I need."

"Getting you to a doctor's out of the question, Ben. Getting our asses into Mexico is going to be hard. Before Mannagan and I left for Bisbee, I told you to head straight here. I didn't tell you to hold up an *army* wagon and rape and kill a *major's* daughter."

"I didn't kill her. I swear."

"She's dead now."

"Well, if you'd done like I told you a couple years back, and let me kill that redheaded bitch, none of this would've happened. But you thought it was funny, selling the slut to a gambler. Hell, that gambler told you all about her to begin with. I said, 'Kill her.' But you didn't do it."

Staring off into the brush, Moses Butcher made no comment.

Ben Butcher wet his lips and groaned. "Then just leave me here. I'll tend myself."

"I can't leave you here, kid."

What his brother was telling him registered. Ben

Butcher tried to push himself up once more, but again he fell. "You can't shoot me, Mose!" he wailed.

"You're right." Moses Butcher let out a heavy sigh. "I can't shoot you, Ben."

He saw the pepperbox pistol Ben was bringing up in his right hand. The kid was game. Always game. And stupid. Moses clamped his left hand on Ben's weak right wrist, pushing the arm down. The kid still managed to squeeze the trigger, and the little pistol barked, sending a bullet into the bushes. Meanwhile, Moses had the razor-sharp knife in his right hand. He smiled a grim smile.

Ben Butcher caught the reflection of sunlight as it came to his throat, and he felt a sudden fire across his throat. And then he was drowning, gurgling on the blood that sprayed the bushes as he rolled to his side and tried to gag. But couldn't. He thought he heard Moses's spurs as his brother walked away. Then Ben Butcher heard nothing but the demons of hell welcoming him.

Hearing the gunshot, Dirk Mannagan and Milt Hanks came running. They stopped as Moses Butcher stepped around the bushes, wiping the blood on his knife blade off on his britches.

"I'm sorry, Moses," Hanks said.

"You should be, you damned fool." Butcher sheathed the knife, and went straight to his horse where he began tightening the cinch.

The others—Miami, Bitter Page, and Greaser Gomez—gathered around.

"Maybe nobody heard that shot," Miami said.

Moses Butcher jerked the saddle cinch so tight the horse jumped. "Stay here then," he snapped. "I'm going to Mexico." He spit. "Hell, Dirk and I should've just ridden across the border whilst we was in Bisbee. We're the damned fools."

He took the reins, put his left foot in the stirrup, and climbed into the saddle. "Mount up. Let's ride," he barked.

His men quickly obeyed.

John McMasters pulled hard on the chestnut's reins. The muffled shot died in the rocks. No echo. He wet his lips and chuckled to himself. *What's that they say? When one sense goes south on you, the others pick up the slack. My hearing's making up for my failing eyes.* He drew a breath and slowly wiped the glasses on his bandanna, reset the spectacles, and leaned underneath a limb as he urged the buckskin into the clearing.

A box canyon, Bloody Zeke The Younger had told him. But it widened after you passed through the defile. A man with a Winchester might be able to hold off an army there for a while. McMasters had no Winchester, just a double-barreled shotgun and two six-shooters. As for picking off men from ambush, hidden in the rocks, well, he was done with that. The man he had shot dead in the Superstitions was the last. He had killed too many men like that during the Civil War. Butcher and his men, the last he knew he would ever kill, he would face man-to-man, face-to-face, and to the death.

He didn't expect it to happen so quickly, so unexpectedly.

He was easing the chestnut to his left and away from the entrance, when several men loped around the corner. McMasters took in the scene quickly, although some details would not register until later. He counted six men. It wasn't until later, he remembered that there should have been seven of them.

At the moment, however, the only thing that mattered was staying alive.

He brought the Remington twelve-gauge up, and squeezed one barrel as the men pulled hard on their reins and reached for their own hardware. Someone answered the shotgun with a pistol report, and he heard his horse snort, cry out, and felt it beginning to collapse. Kicking free of the stirrups, he leaped to his left, triggering the second barrel of the Remington without aiming as he fell, landing on his elbows and knees, and coming up, leaving the Remington on the ground, reaching and pulling and cocking—all in practically one motion—the nickel-plated .44-40 revolver he had given to, and taken away from, Mary Lovelace.

His vision was blurred—his glasses had fallen off when he left the chestnut's saddle—yet he could see enough.

One of their horses was bucking. Another wheeled, sending its rider crashing into the rocks, then turned around and raised dust toward the bend. McMasters touched the trigger on the Remington revolver without aiming. He tried to seek out the man who had to be Moses Butcher, or perhaps the outlaw's younger brother, but couldn't recognize either. Indeed, he could barely make out anyone's features.

A bullet clipped a rock hear him. He touched off another round. Coming to his knees, he saw one of the men running, fanning his pistol as he charged ahead.

Someone screamed before he leaped off his bucking horse, but McMasters didn't hear him because the .44-40 kicked in his right hand.

"Miami! You damned idiot!"

McMasters heard that. The men were scattering, leaving their horses, heading for the bushes. One man managed to grab the reins to two of the horses, and he hurried toward a massive reddish brown rock. McMasters snapped a shot at him, saw the bullet scar a tree well to the right of his target. He swore, and felt a bullet slam into his thigh.

Down he went. *Son of a bitch,* he thought. *I haven't killed any of those killers.*

He would not die empty-handed. He raised the Remington, thumbed back the hammer, fired.

And he kept firing, not caring, not even aiming, but the man who charged—the one called Miami—kept running, then spun around in a wild circle, dropping the rifle he had been levering and shooting as he sprinted toward McMasters. The Remington bucked again, and the man fell onto his face. He pushed himself up and staggered toward McMasters, who lifted the shiny six-shooter again. He cocked, did not have time to aim, and fired. The pistol did not kick. He thought he heard the hammer snap on an empty chamber.

He shifted the heavy, hot weapon, and threw it. Butt over barrel, he watched it sail. The man brought up his left hand, trying to deflect the tomahawking gun. He missed, and the Remington smashed into his chest. That staggered him, sent him reeling, and he could not recover. The man landed beside McMasters's dead chestnut. He kicked once, and McMasters saw the man quiver, and lay still.

So . . . I've killed one of them.

He sat up, and saw his leg. The bullet had torn into his thigh, and he was bleeding badly. Another bullet split a rock to his left.

Get up. That he told himself, and kept telling himself. Another bullet ripped off the heel of his left boot. He staggered, almost fell to the ground, but came up with the shotgun. He looked ahead, saw a hill covered by rocks and brush.

Make that, he thought, *and I might stand half a chance.* The only way to the passage would be right past him. They would have to race right by him. And he had an equalizer—the 1894 shotgun.

A bullet burned his collar.

But first, he had to make it across those fifteen yards to that piece of cover.

Keeping the Remington shotgun in his left hand, he moved, staggering as each step sent a tremendous bolt of pain up his blood-soaked leg. His right held the Colt .45, With each step, he thumbed back the hammer and squeezed the trigger as he moved closer and closer to cover that could, perhaps, keep him alive until he bled to death. Or until they managed to gun him down.

Step. Cock. Fire.

Step. Cock. Fire.

Step. Cock. Fire.

Step. Cock. Fire.

Step. Cock. Fire.

Clump. Groan. *Click.*

Clump. Groan. *Click.*

He dived, feeling the brambles scratch his forehead and cheek, and knock his hat off. A bullet splintered a branch. He dragged himself up, found his hat, tossed it up the three feet. He saw his Colt, knew it was empty, as was his shell belt, and almost threw the revolver away.

No, a voice told him. *You'll need it.*

He threw it up with his hat.

McMasters rolled over and opened the breech of the shotgun.

"Get him!" a voice shouted. "Kill that son of a bitch before he gets out of view! Kill him! Kill him!"

One of the men ran, working a repeating rifle.

McMasters shoved a shell into one hole, then filled the remaining void. The shotgun snapped closed, and the Remington came up. He pulled one trigger.

The man cried out, spinning around and dropping his rifle in the rocks. McMasters touched the second trigger and felt the explosion, heard the roar, and saw the white smoke. The man shouted something, and then he was gone, diving behind a fallen tree.

McMasters tossed the empty shotgun up and pulled himself up. He rolled over, caught his breath, and sat up.

First, he reloaded the Remington. He wasn't certain how many shells he had left. Then he saw his thigh and frowned. He removed his bandanna and took the empty Colt, somehow fashioning a tourniquet above the blood hole in his leg.

His throat and mouth begged for water, but he knew he had none. The canteen was on his saddle on his horse, and his horse lay dead thirty feet away.

All right, he told himself. *This is what you wanted.*

They have to come through you to get out of here, the damned fools. And all that gunfire. That was no little puff of a pistol. As many folks who've been on the roads and trails and washes in this country . . . someone must have heard this little set-to.

"Hold on," he said to himself. "Hold on."

Before he knew it, he was asleep.

He remained asleep until a voice called out, "Hola . . . hombre?"

Jerking awake, John McMasters opened his eyes.

Chapter 36

After he killed the Mexican bandit who had flashed the scarf McMasters had bought his oldest daughter, McMasters fell forward, covering his head with his arms as though they might protect him from the deadly hail of bullets.

Almost as quickly as the cannonade had started, it stopped, and the echoes finally faded. McMasters reached out for the shotgun in front of him. He reloaded it and snapped the breech shut. He did his best to wet his cracked lips. He tried even harder to block out the agony in his wounded leg. He looked through the thick brush.

The silence stretched on for several seconds, although it felt like a lifetime.

At last, a voice broke the stillness. "Mister . . . listen to me . . . the kid that killed your daughter in that wagon. He's dead. I shot him myself. You got no quarrel with me, mister. Hell, I was in Bisbee when my brother robbed that coach."

That's Moses Butcher talking, McMasters thought, realizing Butcher thought McMasters was the father of the girl who had killed herself after . . . after . . . He did not want to think about that. But if what Butcher said were true, and he had killed his kid brother, then that meant all he had to face was—he let out a silent laugh—four men.

"Mister?" The shout was louder, and it echoed. "That's who you are, right? Pa . . . or kin . . . or what?"

McMasters peered through the openings in the brush. Butcher was trying to get him to answer, so they'd know where to concentrate their shots.

"Mister?"

He swallowed and finally answered. "Wrong girl, Butcher. I didn't know that girl." He wanted Moses Butcher to know who he was fighting . . . and why. He thought of something else. *If Butcher had killed his brother* . . . "And Ben didn't kill her, though he sure as hell drove her to killing herself!" McMasters rolled over and dropped down into a small sinkhole.

Sure enough, bullets riddled the timber and leaves and whined off rocks. Butcher had to be thinking, wondering if his target was dead.

McMasters rolled onto his back, pulled the empty Colt, and laid it on the rocks. He tightened the bandanna as best he could.

"Mister?"

McMasters waited.

"Mister?"

Another voice. "Maybe we kilt that bastard."

"Mister?"

"Yeah?" McMasters shouted. He felt safe in the depression surrounded by granite.

"Who the hell are you then? Some damned bounty hunter? Scout for the Army? We can pay you a hell of a lot more that they're paying you. Mister?"

Pay me? McMasters shook his head. *In bullets.*

He raised his voice as loud as he could. "The name's . . . McMasters." He heard the echo, eerily bouncing across the canyon.

Another voice reached him. "McMasters . . . Who? . . . Oh . . . hell."

A longer silence passed. Sweat dripped down McMasters's forehead as he listened, watched, and waited.

Finally, the voice that had to be Moses Butcher yelled again. "McMasters. There's only three of us left."

He was lying, McMasters knew. There had to be four, possibly five.

"You want revenge for what we did to your family, well, why don't we do it like men, not from cover, not like damned snipers? What do you say, you lousy bastard?"

Butcher had no choice. All that gunfire? Even the canyon couldn't keep that noise from reaching all those posses scouring the country. If he wanted to get out of there, he had to make his play before the army came.

And McMasters knew, if he wanted to kill Moses Butcher, he'd have to move quickly, too.

"Wouldn't that little redhead you married want that?" Butcher shouted. "Or that fine little catamount of a daughter?"

McMasters felt blood rush to his head, but he managed to force back the anger.

"Let's do it like men, you craven coward! Meet in the open. Let's one of us die like it was in the good days, not like it is in 1896."

McMasters swallowed, knowing it would be some sort of trap. Yet he could not wait out those killers forever—even if the army never found this canyon. Stay up there, and he'd bleed to death eventually. Besides, he was getting what he had wanted, wasn't he? To fight man-to-man, face-to-face, to put all those Civil War years behind him.

"Here, you yellow bastard. We're stepping out. You want us. Come and get us!"

To his surprise, he saw three men come out from behind the rocks, and spread out. Slowly, they began walking.

It's still a trap, he told himself. *They know I have a shotgun and a pistol.*

He watched. They carried rifles in their arms. They figured they would have the advantage against a man with a scattergun. He sat up, groaning from the pain, and opened the shotgun's breech to withdraw the two shells of double-ought buckshot. He had bought something else in that store in Goldfield, and he reached inside his vest pocket and withdrew two rifled slugs. They were heavy, and he figured they would kick like a son of a bitch, but they'd also give him extra distance. Buckshot was effective at fifty yards at the most. The clerk at the store had said the slugs would go perhaps a hundred yards. The problem was they weren't anywhere near as accurate as a rifle.

McMasters knew he had another problem. He had only two slugs. He had three, four, or five men he'd have to kill. But the slugs gave him a chance, an advantage, and he loaded the Remington, snapped it shut, and pushed himself forward until he slid down the embankment. He weaved through brush and cactus, and around another rock. Panting, he reached overhead, latched onto a stout limb, and pulled himself up.

They had stopped, likely surprised to find him willing to accept their offer.

He was surprised, too . . . that he could actually walk. He took a painful step toward the three men. He stepped again, grimacing each time, watching the three killers as they came toward him.

The bullet came from the rocks to his left, tugging on his collar . . . but also giving away where the fourth man was hiding.

Bitter Page missed, the worthless bastard. But it doesn't matter, Moses Butcher thought. That old dude was already shot to hell. He had only a shotgun and they were eighty yards away.

The other three raised their rifles, and McMasters dived, hit the ground and cried out in pain, but tilted the shotgun and touched the trigger.

Butcher saw the puff of white smoke from McMasters's shotgun, and he heard Milt Hanks scream. That spoiled Butcher's shot, and he spun around as he levered another round into his rifle. Milt Hanks had dropped his buffalo gun and catapulted ten feet, landing in a sickening splat against the rocks behind him. He did not move.

Turning back to the man with the shotgun, Butcher dropped to a knee. McMasters shot the second round, and Butcher felt a roar of fiery air singe his right ear. He felt relief. That shot had missed. Butcher drew a bead on McMasters who pushed himself up and began reloading. Dirk Mannagan was sprinting toward the wounded man, shucking his rifle—he always said he was better with a short gun—and fanning the hammer as he fired.

We'll get that son of a bitch now, Butcher said to himself. Suddenly, he heard a roar behind him. He turned to see Bitter Page tumbling out of the rocks and landing on his head. It was a sickening sight. A moment later, a big black man stepped into the clearing, aiming a rifle straight at Dirk Mannagan. Then two horses burst through the opening, and Mannagan slid to a stop.

Butcher snapped a shot at the black man, who ducked, and fired. Butcher turned back. A guy in a yellow vest had leaped out of the saddle and was running . . . and shooting . . . right at Mannagan. A tiny man had dismounted, too, only he was coming straight at Butcher. Rather quickly, Butcher understood it wasn't a man. But a woman. A woman with red hair.

Mannagan fell. A bullet clipped Butcher's earlobe. Shotgun pellets suddenly staggered him, and he turned, tripped, and felt blood pouring down his face. McMasters had somehow coaxed more distance from his shotgun than was possible. Buckshot had hit him, but at that range, had more of an effect of birdshot. Butcher rose, spit out blood, tried to see, and knew he had to run. *Run. Run.*

Something punched his back, and he fell to his knees. He tried to stand, but another bullet knocked him onto his face. His rifle? He couldn't find it. He reached and drew the revolver, when another bullet hit him in the back.

Moses Butcher cried. He coughed, and rolled over. He tried to sit up, to fight, but couldn't. He had three bullets in his back.

"Oh, God. How am I gonna explain this to Auntie Faye?"

The redhead stood over him. He lifted the gun, but her right foot came down on his wrist.

He felt the bone snap, and he sank back into the dirt.

"You?"

Brother Ben had been right. He should have killed that bitch back in the Superstition Mountains two years ago.

"Kill me," he said. "Go ahead."

She kicked his Colt away, turned, and left him there, bleeding to death with bullets in his back.

McMasters had the Remington loaded, but the echoes of gunshots started to drift into the canyon. Mary Lovelace walked to him and dropped the rifle. McMasters stood and almost fell, but she caught him.

They turned, and he saw Marcus Patton leaning against a boulder, blood staining that yellow vest in two breast pockets. They saw the other killer, lying spread-eagle a few feet away from the gambler.

When they reached Patton, they knew it was hopeless. He must have known it, too, yet he smiled. "I told you"—blood trickled down his bottom lip—"I never lose."

"Patton—" That's all McMasters could say. He turned away, looking at the bandit who stared at the blue sky with vacant, dead eyes. McMasters sighed and looked back at Patton.

"Didn't lose," Patton said, his voice just audible. "That's what . . . us gamblers call . . . a push." His eyes closed, and he slumped over on his side.

"Can you walk?" Mary asked McMasters.

"Yeah," he said, although he wasn't sure.

They met Alamo Carter standing over Moses Butcher, who coughed, and groaned.

"Another one's in the trees back yonder," Carter said. "Had a bullet in his belly . . . and his throat cut from here to here." He brought his finger from one ear to the other.

So Butcher had not lied. He had killed his own brother.

"You got that . . . shotgun," Moses Butcher begged. "Use it."

McMasters brought the twelve-gauge up. Butcher smiled and seemed to relax . . . until McMasters opened the breech and withdrew the two shells. Those he let fall to the ground then snapped the breech shut.

"I've used it enough . . . and you ought to suffer." The Remington dropped to the ground, too.

Butcher pushed himself up. "I can't die . . ." He groaned. "I'm back-shot. Don't you understand? I can't die . . . like this."

But he did.

Alamo Carter picked up the twelve-gauge. "We best hurry. Army's comin' right behind us. But I think I can get you to Mexico." The black man grinned. "I know this country better 'n most Apaches."

"You go, Alamo," McMasters said. "Take the Remington. Take Mary with you. And this time"—he somehow managed to smile—"don't come back."

The scout tucked the twelve-gauge under his left arm and held out his right. McMasters managed to move away from Mary Lovelace. Still standing on his own feet, he shook the big man's hand.

"Army's bound to have a sawbones with 'm," Carter said. "They'll be able to patch you up. And likely haul your arse to jail. You might be lookin' at prison time. Best you change your mind. Come with me."

McMasters shook his head. "Get moving. Both of you."

He did not look at Mary. He turned around and slowly, taking one agonizing step after another, he started for the opening. He walked to the army he knew was approaching. He might go to prison, but he was a Medal of Honor winner, and he had wiped out Moses Butcher's gang. If some judge did send him to Yuma Territorial Prison, it likely wouldn't be forever. And maybe, once he was out, he could rebuild his life. Again.

One step. Another.

He stopped. A handful of soldiers pushed through the opening, stopping when they saw him. They raised their rifles, but did not fire. An officer came behind them, and then a buckskin-clad scout. The officer said something, but McMasters could not hear. The soldiers and Indian just stared . . . at McMasters and at the dead that littered the ground. He raised one hand over his head. His other pulled on the ends of the bandanna, to keep the blood from pouring out of that hole in his leg.

Another step, and something sounded behind him. He stopped, but before he could turn around, he felt Mary Lovelace slip to his side. She put her arm around his waist, and McMasters could not help himself. He leaned against her for support.

"Come on, John," she said softly. "Let me help you."

Together, they slowly walked toward the soldiers.

KEEP READING FOR A SPECIAL EXCERPT!

From the bestselling masters of frontier fiction come two tough frontier detectives who solve the bloodiest crimes with bravado, brains, and bullets blazing . . .

THE RANGE DETECTIVES

A killer is on the loose in the Arizona Territory. One by one, Tonto Basin ranchers are being murdered for their livestock—and the Cattle Raisers Association has hired two range detectives to catch the culprit. From the looks of them, Stovepipe Stewart and Wilbur Coleman are just another pair of high plains drifters. But with their razor-sharp detective skills and rare talent for trouble, they're the last remaining hope for one young cowboy who's been arrested for the murders. Stovepipe and Wilbur believe the boy is innocent. In short order the trail of clues leads to a secret canyon hideout, and the duo find themselves in the middle of an all-out range war—with the dirtiest gang of cutthroats, thieves, and outlaws the West has ever known . . .

There's just one mystery left to solve: *How will they get out of this alive?*

Coming Soon from Pinnacle Books!

JOHNSTONE JUSTICE. WHAT AMERICA NEEDS NOW.

Chapter 1

The rider who brought his horse to a stop at the edge of a pine-covered bluff so he could look out over the verdant Tonto Basin country was young, with clean-cut features and dark hair under a thumbed-back Stetson. He sat his saddle with the easy grace of a born horseman, but a certain tenseness gripped him as well, a readiness for trouble.

Lord knew he had ridden into plenty of it here in this corner of Arizona Territory.

The basin rolled away to the northeast. On the far side of it was a dark line marking the Mogollon Rim. The country below the rim was good rangeland for the most part, although in some areas the grass was a little sparse. There were a number of successful ranches in the basin, including the Box D, the spread Dan Hartford rode for.

He was on Box D range now and was supposed to be looking for some cattle that might have strayed in this direction. The herd was bunched in the higher pastures, but for some reason a few cows always got it into their heads to drift back down to the lower reaches of the basin where they had spent the winter. Dan's eyes searched the landscape below him but didn't spot any of the stock he was looking for. He stiffened in his saddle and turned his horse as he heard hoofbeats approaching from behind him.

A rider emerged from the pines and headed for the edge of the rocky bluff. Dan recognized her instantly. She sat a saddle with the ease and grace of a Western gal, born and bred. Her long brown hair was pulled into a ponytail that hung down her back. She wore a soft flannel shirt, a split riding skirt, and a flat-crowned black hat with a cord pulled snug under her chin.

A sheath strapped to the young woman's saddle carried a short-barreled Winchester carbine. It had been a good while since there had been any Indian trouble around here, but there were always four-legged varmints to think about—and plenty of two-legged ones as well.

The young woman rode up to Dan and reined in. He gave her a curt nod and said, "Mrs. Dempsey."

"Hello, Mr. Hartford," the wife of his employer said, her voice cool but not unfriendly. "What are you doing up here this morning?"

"Looking for stray stock, as usual."

"Have you found any?"

"Not yet. The day's young, though."

Dan heard other horses moving through the trees. Three men rode into view and came straight toward Dan and Mrs. Dempsey.

The rider in the lead had a crisp, military bearing,

an impression that his neatly trimmed gray mustache reinforced. His clothes weren't fancy, but they were functional and of high quality, from the boots to the gray Stetson that matched his hair and mustache.

The other two men were clearly ranch hands, one of them lean and middle-aged, the other younger and burlier, with a thatch of blond hair under his sweat-stained hat. His face was either flushed or had a permanent sunburn.

The leader of the group said to the young woman in an annoyed voice, "You shouldn't have galloped off from us like that, Laura. You know there's no telling what you might run into out here."

"I didn't run into anything except Mr. Hartford," Laura Dempsey said. "I don't think he represents any sort of threat, Abel."

Dempsey grunted and seemed unconvinced of that. He said, "What are you doing over here, Hartford?"

Dan was getting a little tired of people asking him that question, but he said, "Just looking for some cows that might have strayed down from the higher pastures."

"I told Dan to do that, Mr. Dempsey," the older of the two cowhands said. "Figured I could spare him from any other chores this mornin'."

Dempsey nodded and said, "All right, then, that's fine. You know I trust your judgment, Lew. That's why you're my foreman." The rancher looked at Dan and made a brusque motion with his head. "Get on with your work, Hartford."

"Sure, boss," Dan said, even though the words

tasted a little bitter in his mouth. He lifted his reins and nudged his horse into motion toward the head of the trail that led down into the basin.

He heard Dempsey say behind him, "Come along, Laura, and don't run off like that again. I know you're young and impulsive, but you're too reckless. You're going to ride right into trouble one of these days."

"I'm sure I won't as long as I have you around to look after me, Abel," Laura said.

Dan looked back to see her turning her horse and falling in alongside her husband as Dempsey rode away. Lew Martin, who ramrodded the Box D for Dempsey, and the stocky cowboy, Jube Connolly, followed them back into the trees.

They had been quick to ask him what he was doing, thought Dan, but none of them had offered any explanations for their presence here. Of course, that wasn't surprising. This was Dempsey's range, and he had a right to go wherever he wanted. And as a rich man, he wasn't in the habit of explaining himself to any of the hombres who worked for him.

As a rich man's wife, Laura was the same way, Dan supposed. Martin and Connolly were employees, and it wasn't their place to speak up.

Dan told himself to concentrate on the chore that had brought him to this part of the ranch and not waste time brooding over situations he couldn't do anything about.

He had been riding through the basin for another fifteen minutes or so, still without spotting any strays, when he heard hoofbeats drumming rapidly behind him. He reined in and turned his horse, moving his hand to the well-worn butt of the gun on his hip as he did so.

Even though this was a basin, the elevation was still high enough that the air didn't get as hot as it did farther south, closer to the border, but the day was still warm enough that no Westerner worth his salt would run a horse that hard unless there was a good reason.

Dan spotted the rider and recognized him, but that didn't make him relax. If anything, the tension inside him increased. He didn't particularly like Jube Connolly, and since Jube had been with Dempsey, Laura, and Lew Martin just a short time earlier, his presence here made Dan think something might have happened to one of those three.

"Something wrong, Jube?" Dan called to the florid-faced puncher as Connolly reined in.

"The boss sent me to talk to you," Connolly replied. He swung down from the saddle and added, "Light down from that horse."

A puzzled frown creased Dan's face, but he did as Connolly said. As he stood there holding his mount's reins, he asked, "When you say the boss, do you mean Lew or Mr. Dempsey?"

"Mr. Dempsey," Connolly replied. He moved closer. "He's got a message he wants me to give you."

Dan was more confused than ever. He said, "What sort of message?"

"This," Connolly said.

He uncorked a sudden punch that took Dan by surprise. Connolly's blocky fist crashed into Dan's jaw and sent him reeling back as his hat flew off his head. He lost his balance and sat down hard, thankfully not landing on any of the cactus plants that were scattered around here.

He was stunned, and pain from the blow filled his head, but he was able to exclaim, "What the hell!"

Instinctively, his hand went to his gun again. Connolly rushed him, and just as Dan cleared leather, the toe of Connolly's boot smacked into the wrist of his gun hand. The revolver went flying from Dan's fingers and landed in the dirt several yards away.

"Damn it! Jube, what—"

Connolly reached down, grabbed hold of Dan's shirt, and hauled him to his feet. Connolly's fist sunk into his gut. Dan doubled over as sickness filled his belly.

"Mr. Dempsey don't like you hangin' around his wife," Connolly said. "It ain't fittin' for the two of you to be out here alone together, talkin'."

Dan was able to straighten up some as he pressed his hands to his aching belly. He said angrily, "It wasn't my idea! I was just doing my job when she rode up. And talking is *all* we were doing. Not much of that, either. She'd been there less than a minute when the rest of you rode up."

That much talking exhausted him, as bad as he felt at the moment. He stood there gasping for breath while Connolly leered at him.

"Mr. Dempsey saw the way you was lookin' at her. You can't blame him for gettin' a mite hot under the collar. Fella his age, married to a gal as young and easy on the eyes as Mrs. Dempsey, he's gotta be worried all the time about no-account saddle tramps sniffin' around her, makin' eyes at her—"

"I wasn't doing any of that!" Dan protested. "And I'm not a damned saddle tramp, either."

"No? You was ridin' the grub line, that's for sure, when you drifted in and talked Lew into hirin' you. I thought it was a bad idea then, and I still do. I don't trust you, Hartford. Might be a good idea for you to just draw your time and ride on. Then you wouldn't be tempted to bother Mrs. Dempsey again."

"I wasn't—" Dan stopped short and glared at Connolly. He said through clenched teeth, "You can go back to Mr. Dempsey and tell him I'm not going anywhere, Jube. Or you can just go to hell. I don't care."

That leering grin spread even wider across Connolly's beefy face. He balled his hands into fists and stepped closer as he said, "I was hopin' you'd take more convincin'—"

Dan didn't let him get any farther than that. The young cowboy lowered his head and launched himself into a diving tackle.

CHAPTER 2

The counterattack seemed to surprise Connolly as much as Dan had been surprised by that sucker punch. Dan rammed a shoulder into the bigger man's solar plexus and pushed hard with his legs, forcing Connolly backward. Even though Connolly outweighed him, Dan was muscular and possessed plenty of wiry strength. He drove Connolly off his feet.

Dan landed on top of him and hooked a right and a left into Connolly's midsection. Connolly might look a little soft, but he wasn't. Hitting him in the belly was like punching a side of beef. He didn't even grunt in pain.

Instead he grabbed Dan's bib-front shirt and slung him off. Dan rolled over a couple of times before he came to a stop on his stomach. He looked up to see Connolly scrambling to his feet.

"This ain't just a chore for the boss anymore," Connolly said. "I'm gonna stomp the guts outta you and enjoy it!"

He charged like a maddened bull. Desperately, Dan flung himself out of the way as Connolly's boots pounded the ground where he had been a heartbeat earlier. Dan rolled again, came up and wrapped both arms around one of Connolly's legs, and heaved. Once again the big man came crashing to earth.

This time when Dan went after him, he swung his fists at Connolly's face. He connected with the cowboy's squarish jaw and rocked Connolly's head to the side. That seemed to have a little more effect than punching him in the belly, but not much. Connolly roared and lashed out with an arm. It slammed into Dan's chest and knocked him away.

Both men made it to their feet at the same time. Connolly fumbled at the holster on his hip, but it was empty, the gun he normally carried there having fallen out during the fracas. Dan thought about making a diving leap for his gun, but Connolly didn't give him time. The big man charged again, windmilling punches.

Dan was quick enough to block most of the blows, but a few of them got through and jolted him to his core. At the same time, Connolly was attacking, not trying to defend himself, so Dan was able to land some punches of his own, mostly jabs that landed cleanly on his opponent's face. Connolly's head rocked back with each punch. Blood began trailing from his nostrils as his nose swelled.

More blood spurted when Dan smashed a hard left to Connolly's mouth. Connolly bellowed in pain and rage and renewed his attack, flailing even more wildly than before. He was big and strong and could take a lot of punishment, but he was stupid, thought Dan. Connolly was out of control now, and he proved it with another ill-advised charge.

Dan ducked out of the way, thrust out his leg, and swept Connolly's legs from under him. Connolly pitched forward and yelled as he realized he was about to land face-first in a clump of cactus. He got his hands down enough to partially catch himself, but dozens of the wicked spines lanced into his palms and some stuck in his face despite his best efforts.

Connolly bucked and twisted away from the cactus. His bellows turned into screams as he writhed on the ground. Dan almost felt sorry for the brute—almost.

"Stop squirming around, Jube," he said. "I'll help you. Lord knows, you don't deserve it after the way you sucker-punched me like that, but—"

Connolly interrupted by spewing curses at him. As the profanity became even more vile, Dan turned away and scooped up his fallen gun. A quick glance down the barrel told him it wasn't fouled. He swung back toward Connolly, raised the gun, and eared back the hammer.

The metallic ratcheting of a gun being cocked was enough to shut up most men, no matter how they were carrying on. It worked on Connolly, who fell silent and lay there glaring up at Dan. His face and hands were already swelling from the cactus needles embedded in them.

"Just settle down," Dan told him. "I'll get those needles out of you, but you've got to give me your word this fight is over."

"I'll kill you," Connolly grated. "You don't know how bad an enemy you made today, Hartford."

"This is ridiculous," Dan snapped. "You attacked me for no reason. I didn't do a damned thing to act improperly toward Mrs. Dempsey. She's the boss's wife, for God's sake! You think I'd risk my job that way?"

Connolly didn't answer. Instead he started cursing again. Dan blew out his breath in an exasperated sigh and shook his head.

"All right, I'll just ride away and leave you like this," he said. "How about that?"

"No! . . . Damn it, all right. I won't try anything else."

"Do I need to bend a gun barrel over your head to make sure of that?"

Connolly shook his head, grimacing because evidently that made his face hurt even more.

"No. Just get the blasted things outta me."

Dan holstered his gun and said, "Sit up where I can reach you."

He hunkered on his heels in front of Connolly, off to the side a little so it would be more difficult for the man to attack him if Connolly changed his mind. Dan was alert for trouble, but Connolly didn't do anything except cuss a blue streak as Dan plucked the cactus needles from his cheeks, chin, and forehead. Connolly couldn't very well throw any punches when his hands looked like pincushions.

"You look a little like a porcupine," Dan said with a wry smile.

"Shut up and get on with it," Connolly growled.

When Dan had all the spines out of the burly puncher's face, he straightened to his feet and backed off.

"You can pull the ones out of your hands yourself,"

he said. "Use your teeth if you have to. Just be careful you don't get any stuck in your tongue."

"That'll take a long time," Connolly protested.

"Yeah, I know, and I plan to be a long way from here by the time you finish. Don't try and jump me when we're both back in the bunkhouse tonight, either."

"You're gonna be sorry you ever met me, mister."

"I already am," Dan said.

He picked up his hat, slapped it against his thigh to knock some of the dust off it, and swung up into the saddle. He turned his horse and rode off, leaving Jube Connolly sitting there carefully picking cactus needles out of his palms.

Anger and disgust filled Dan, and a good chunk of those emotions was directed at himself. He was mad at Abel Dempsey for sending Connolly to give him a thrashing, and he was mad at Connolly for following that order so eagerly. But a lot of the trouble was his own fault because he should have known better than to come here to the Tonto Basin, to the Box D, where Abel Dempsey lived with his beautiful young wife.

Dan shoved those thoughts out of his head. Despite everything that had happened, he still had work to do, so he set about scouring the rangeland for those strays.

He found the wandering cattle, but working alone, it took him most of the day to do it. It was late afternoon before he was satisfied he had located all the missing stock and started driving the jag back toward the higher pastures.

His muscles were stiff and sore from the fight with Connolly, and his belly growled. He'd had a couple of biscuits left over from breakfast wrapped up in a cloth in one of his saddlebags, along with some jerky, so he'd made a midday meal out of that and washed it down with water from his canteen. He was looking forward to getting back to the bunkhouse and putting himself on the outside of some real grub as well as a few cups of coffee.

When Dan reached the higher pastures, he turned the cattle over to Hamp Jones and Charley Bartlett, the cowboys who were staying in the line shack up here.

"Don't lose 'em this time," Dan told them with a smile that took any sting out of the words.

"We'll try not to, but you know how damn muleheaded these critters can be," Hamp said.

"They're cows," Charley pointed out. "I don't see how they can be muleheaded."

"Yeah, well, *cowheaded* ain't a word, as far as I know," Hamp responded.

Dan left them to their good-hearted wrangling and headed for the ranch headquarters.

Night had fallen by the time he got there. By now supper was over, but he knew the stove-up old cowboy turned cook Willie Hill would have saved him some. He rode into the barn and started to unsaddle his horse in the dark, not needing a light to carry out a task he had performed thousands of times.

He wondered as he did so how Jube Connolly had explained the scores of little puncture wounds on his hands and face. Any seasoned range rider could guess that Connolly had landed in some cactus, but he wouldn't know the reason why.

Dan had just slung his saddle on one of the stands

when he heard a soft step behind him. He turned quickly, his hand going to his gun, in case Connolly was about to try settling that score.

Instead he heard a gasp in the darkness of the barn and knew it wasn't Connolly sneaking up on him.

"Dan, don't . . . It's me . . ."

A lantern was burning on the front porch of the main house. Dan saw her silhouetted against the glow from it as she moved deeper into the barn.

"Hello, Mrs. Dempsey," he said stiffly.

"You don't have to be like that," Laura said. "Not now."

As if he hadn't heard her, he said, "You probably shouldn't be wandering around out here in the dark. There might be a rattler—"

"You're not worried about snakes. You're worried that somebody might see us." She was close enough now that he could smell the faint scent of lilac water that clung to her. "But it's all right. No one's around. I made sure of that. Abel is in his office, going over the books. He won't come out for hours. Lew has gone to his cabin, Willie is in the cook shack, and all the other hands are in the bunkhouse. There's nothing to worry about."

"Damn it, Laura . . ." The name came out of his mouth before he could stop it. "It was a mistake me ever coming here. We both know that. If I had a lick of sense, I'd put that saddle back on my horse, ride out, and never look back."

She reached out with her right hand, rested the fingertips on his chest, and whispered, "Is that what you're going to do, Dan?"

"You know good and well it's not," he rasped, then he closed his hands around her upper arms, pulled her tight against him, and brought his mouth down on hers in a kiss with enough hunger in it to jolt him more than Jube Connolly's fists ever could.